DEAD HEAT

Also by Arthur F. Nehrbass

DEAD EASY

DEAD HEAT

ARTHUR F. NEHRBASS

A DUTTON BOOK

DUTTON
Published by the Penguin Group
Penguin Books USA Inc., 375 Hudson Street,
New York, New York 10014, U.S.A.
Penguin Books Ltd, 27 Wrights Lane,
London W8 5TZ, England
Penguin Books Australia Ltd, Ringwood,
Victoria, Australia
Penguin Books Canada Ltd, 10 Alcorn Avenue,
Toronto, Ontario, Canada M4V 3B2
Penguin Books (N.Z.) Ltd, 182–190 Wairau Road,
Auckland 10, New Zealand

Penguin Books Ltd, Registered Offices:
Harmondsworth, Middlesex, England

First published by Dutton, an imprint of New American Library,
a division of Penguin Books USA Inc.
Distributed in Canada by McClelland & Stewart Inc.

First Printing, April, 1994
10 9 8 7 6 5 4 3 2 1

 REGISTERED TRADEMARK—MARCA REGISTRADA

Nehrbass, Arthur F.
    Dead heat / Arthur F. Nehrbass.
        p. cm.
    ISBN 0-525-93664-5
    1. Government investigators--Florida--Fiction. 2. Organized crime--Florida--Fiction.
3. Mafia--Florida--Fiction. I. Title.
PS3564.E2642D42 1994
813'.54--dc20   93-39637
                                                                                     CIP

Printed in the United States of America
Set in Janson
Designed by Leonard Telesca

PUBLISHER'S NOTE
This is a work of fiction. Names, characters, places, and incidents either are the products of
the author's imagination or are used fictitiously, and any resemblance to actual persons,
living or dead, events, or locales is entirely coincidental.

For Brian, Gary, and Alan
who shared the precious gift of childhood with us
and now let us share that gift again, in their children.

• P A R T •
ONE

"Ambition drove men to become false;
To have one thought locked in the breast
Another ready on the tongue."

—Gaius Sallustius Cripus,
The War With Catiline

• C H A P T E R •
ONE

The farmhouse had not been decorated for Christmas, so there was nothing to take down and pack away. Even if it had been decorated, Paul Volpe's thoughts would not have been on the holiday season. He was just glad to be home. It had been a rough month, he thought as he looked out his living-room window.

The farm was a mess. The feds' backhoe and frontloader had left deep ruts across the driveway, and the concrete front porch had been jackhammered apart. A wooden plank now served to connect the front door to the ground. The digging had destroyed all the vegetation, and the earth had been unevenly replaced. The snow had, for a time, hidden the destruction, but now it had melted into a morass of mud. A Jersey winter evening, penetrating cold and damp, had settled in.

The federal detention center had not been a country-club experience. Being held as a material witness was softer than being a regular inmate, but he had still been "in." He had not talked, and finally the feds had been forced to release him. The pressure on him had been enormous, but he had held out. He had gotten good words from the outfit. He knew that stand-up guys were respected and taken care of. And he had been a stand-up guy. He wasn't made—that is, he wasn't a soldier or button in the Mafia, but he had every reason to expect that his display of *omerta*, silence, would earn him the reward of being made.

The front doorbell shook him out of his reverie. He would have to answer it. It was bingo night and his wife was at church. He shook his head in puzzlement at how she could spend so many hours playing that senseless game.

He shrugged and hesitatingly moved toward the door, hoping it wasn't the FBI again. When he looked through the peephole, though, he recognized an old friend from Bensonhurst, Jimmy Amari.

Jimmy teetered uncertainly on the narrow plank that rested on the doorsill while balancing a beautifully wrapped Christmas present in his arms.

Volpe, pleased to see his old friend, eagerly grasped the door latch, turned the deadbolt, threw back the door, and extended his arms for an embrace. "Jimmy! Jimmy! My friend! What a great surprise!"

Amari, encumbered by his present, could not respond to Volpe's offered embrace. Instead he placed the package between the outstretched arms. Amari's face was wreathed in a Christmas smile and the joy of Christmas was in his voice. "Merry Christmas, Paul."

A warm answering smile on his face, Volpe exuded genuine pleasure at Amari's visit.

"Jimmy, thank you, come in, come in."

As Volpe's hands closed on the package, both barrels of the twelve-gauge sawed-off shotgun concealed in it let go. The Magnum double-ought buckshot, twenty-four pellets, each the size of a .32-caliber bullet, caught Volpe square in the chest and tore open a giant, ragged hole, disintegrating his heart and lungs.

The hands that had just grasped the package now leaped from it and clawed the air, trying to grasp something to hold him upright, to hold on to life itself. Then he tumbled back into the house. His face was an expression of surprise and disbelief. His eyes were wide, first in surprise and then in the terror of death. His last conscious perception was of Amari moving toward him as he struggled for a breath that would not come.

Amari stepped inside the house, removed the shotgun from what was left of the package, ejected the empty casings, and put them in his coat pocket. He slipped two more rounds into the barrels and snapped the shotgun closed. The remains of the Christmas package he put in a plastic shopping bag he carried in his overcoat pocket. Then he sat down to wait.

Within a half hour he saw the headlights of a car bouncing down the rutted driveway. He rose and walked into the kitchen, which adjoined the garage. He heard the garage door open and the car pulling in. When he heard the electric motor on the garage door whine again, closing the door, he focused on the doorknob on the kitchen door. When it turned, Amari was poised behind the door, so that someone coming in could not see him.

Amelia, Volpe's wife, came through the door calling out, "Hi, honey, I'm home. Who's our company?"

Her answer was both barrels of the twelve-gauge from a foot away. Her head literally disappeared.

Amari stepped carefully out of the kitchen, making sure not to pick up any traces of Amelia's head on his boots. He extracted the spent casings and reloaded the shotgun. He put it under his overcoat, holding the pistol grip through the slash in the pocket of the coat. He stepped around Volpe, again careful not to pick up traces of the body, and hurried through the front door to his waiting rental car.

At seven, on a bitter cold Sunday morning in January, the Lower East Side of New York City was deserted, except for a black Cadillac parked in front of the Eagle Social Club. Its driver remained in the car, running the engine to stay warm. The bland, windowless, former warehouse had a small sign over its narrow front entrance: *Members Only.*

Another black Cadillac pulled in behind the first car. A passenger quickly exited from the front seat and opened the back door. The man who emerged was about seventy-five, of medium height, and lately given to paunchiness. His hair was still dark though graying. He was immaculately dressed in a navy pinstripe business suit and black double-breasted overcoat. This was Carlo Magliocco, boss, capo, of the largest Mafia family in the United States.

Magliocco had been born in Agira, Sicily, to hardworking peasants. He was three when his father died in the pyrite mines, and his mother, tired of living, followed soon after. He and his seven brothers and sisters were scattered among relatives. His mother's cousin, Guissepe, eventually came to the United States with his wife, three children and stepson, Carlo.

He grew up on the Lower East Side, and by the time he was twelve, he was running errands for mafioso. His initiation as a soldier was preordained, and he rose through the ranks by dint of ruthlessness and brains to head the most powerful of all the New York families. He was recognized as the boss of all bosses, *capo de tutti capi*, chairman of the Commission, which was made up of the bosses of the leading Families and settled disputes and kept peace among them.

Today Magliocco was visiting the Eagle Social Club on his family's business. The club was the meeting place for mafioso. That was its only purpose. Guards prevented nonmembers from entering and maintained security against police scrutiny. Carlo Magliocco almost never visited the club. In fact, he had not been there in the last five years. But today it presented a secure place to hold a long conversation with Vincent Strollo.

The small door opened as Magliocco approached, and a dark-suited man bowed as he entered; the front seat passenger followed.

Vincent Strollo was a *caporegime* in Magliocco's family, the boss of a group of soldiers or buttons. He was fifty-two, tall, six foot, and a solid 190 pounds. His hair was thick and black with just a hint of gray at his temples. His voice was low and deep, so that when he spoke one had to listen carefully to pick out the words from the flow of bass. He was born in the United States of a Sicilian father and Calabrian mother.

His father had been a button, and Strollo had naturally gravitated that way. His rise in the hierarchy of the Mafia was the result of his ability to make money for the family. He had successfully combined the ruthlessness of a killer with the modern business skills of an entrepreneur.

Strollo was now facing mounting problems from the FBI and the New York Crime Commission. The purpose of the meeting was to decide his future with the Family.

The problem had become acute six months ago when Henry Colletti, vice-president of the longshoremen's local, had agreed to cooperate with the FBI in return for consideration of a lighter sentence on his recent conviction. He had guided the FBI to a chicken farm in New Jersey that had once been the site of a bootleg still. It was here, he told the FBI, that the bodies of Frank Bioff and several others had been disposed of. The Bureau obtained a search warrant for the farm and moved in backhoes and frontloaders to excavate an old mash pit and most of the untreed land. Parts of twenty-six individual bodies were found in the pit. Colletti had given the FBI a Mafia cemetery.

Bioff, whose body the FBI was seeking, had been trying to clean up the Mafia-controlled longshoremen's local. The affidavit, on which the search warrant for the farm was based, carried Colletti's description of how he had walked into the union hall one night:

"It was close to ten o'clock at night. I went back for a folder I forgot. I heard some noise in one of the offices. I saw Jim Bioff in the center of the room. He was standing, but kind of sagging. He had two nooses around his neck, one end of rope was held by a guy I never seen before and the other by Willie Bazzano. By keeping tension on each end of the rope Bioff couldn't get to either guy. They'd choke him for awhile and then let up some so he could get his breath back. Then they'd strangle him some more. They was laughing and hollering. They saw me and asked if I wanted a turn. I said no and moved back. They finally killed him. Bazzano told the other guy I was okay."

Bazzano was currently a fugitive, but safely out of the way in Sicily. He was known to have been a button in Strollo's regime.

The resident on the chicken farm, Paul Volpe, had refused to talk to the FBI and had for a time been held as a material witness. His continued silence had now been assured by Amari's visit. Bazzano's partner on the Bioff killing had been similarly disposed of by Amari.

Another problem for Strollo's *regime* stemmed from a colossal banking scam. They had corrupted a teletype clerk in the Bank of International Industry, first by threats of blackmail and then by threats of harm to his wife and children. From another corrupted employee they obtained the bank codes for international money transfers.

They had fed coded wire transfers of huge amounts of money to the teletype clerk. His teletypes to banks in Europe and the Middle and Far East had caused almost twenty million dollars to be transferred from the banks to waiting numbered accounts in Geneva. From there the money went to numbered accounts in Liechtenstein and then on to the Netherlands Antilles where it was split between Nassau banks and banks in the Caymans.

It was the arrests of some of the *regime*'s associates, not made men, that had Magliocco worried. They were nearing trial, and as the jail door began to swing shut, they were considering making deals to talk.

While there was not sufficient information to arrest Strollo, the FBI and the New York State Police knew who was behind the action. The New York Crime Commission was scheduling hearings, and sources available to the Family said Strollo would be subpoenaed. All things considered, Strollo was getting much too much attention from everyone.

The man Strollo had chosen as security for the meeting was a stone killer, Jimmy "Blue Eyes" Amari. They had grown up together in Brooklyn and had been initiated into the Mafia in the same ceremony. When Strollo had been a button, on his way up, they had often worked together on a hit. Strollo and Amari were very close. Strollo was godfather to one of Amari's sons. Amari was totally committed to Strollo and intensely loyal to the Mafia.

Amari was well known to Magliocco, who had used him on over twenty occasions to kill people who interfered with business. Most recently he had insured Volpe's silence. The majority of the bodies that had resulted from these hits were at the New Jersey farm.

As Magliocco entered, Blue Eyes bowed and was rewarded with a warm smile and a pat on the cheek.

Magliocco's own bodyguard went to the bar and drew an espresso. Strollo rose from his chair as Magliocco approached, and they embraced. He positioned the boss's chair for him and helped him off with his overcoat. When they were seated, Blue Eyes brought two cups of espresso, a small pot for refills, spoons, lemon peel, and a bottle of anisette. He placed them on the table and withdrew to the bar, well out of earshot.

The conversation, in Italian, but with the dialect so peculiar to the island of Sicily, opened with pleasantries. Each asked about wives, sons, daughters, grandchildren. The lack of respect that young people exhibited toward their elders was duly covered; then Magliocco, on his second espresso with anisette, approached the business at hand.

"Besides being my dearest friend," Magliocco said, "you are my most valued business associate. Today you face serious attacks from our enemies, which could endanger the Family. While I know you will preserve *omerta*, your peril is our peril.

"Jimmy's talents are of no use against these people. We learned a long time ago those tactics only make things worse. We must protect you and at the same time preserve your talents for the good of the Family."

Strollo was concerned about this remark. Magliocco was telling him he was a threat to the Family. Strollo knew what happened to people who endangered the Family.

"Don Carlo, you know my purpose in life is to serve you, the Family and Cosa Nostra," Strollo said warily. "I will do whatever you suggest."

Magliocco smiled and, reaching across the table, placed his hand warmly on Strollo's forearm. This increased Strollo's concern. A friendly embrace was often the "kiss of death."

Magliocco continued, "Once again you have proved my faith in you is well placed. I have carefully studied the matter, and I suggest you move to Miami. Don Santo Tramunti is a dear friend of mine. His family has much influence in Florida, but he has only slight interests in the Miami area. Your business would not compete with his. South Florida is open to the business interests of other Families. You would, of course, pay your respects to Don Santo, and share with him a portion of any good fortune that our business produces. You would remain with me. As far as our enemies are concerned, you have gone to Miami to retire."

Strollo stiffened ever so slightly in his chair. While he sensed a possible reprieve, he recognized he was being stripped of his rank and sent into exile.

"What would you have me do in Miami?"

Magliocco looked Strollo square in the eye. He had looked in eyes like that before. They were the eyes of death. Strollo thought, "Perhaps, this time, my death."

Magliocco, his elbows on the table, hands forming a steeple, continued. "You would not take with you anyone from your regime. I want everyone to think you have retired."

Strollo's eyes blinked, Magliocco's remained fixed. Strollo recognized his physical responses were exhibiting weakness, but this could be his end. Without his regime he had no power.

Magliocco continued, "Tony Iannello is in Miami now; he belongs to Carmine Licata. He will be with you when you move. After a period of study, you will report to me what areas of business would be most receptive to our operations. During that period I will send what people you request, either from your *regime* or another's. As you know, I visit Fort Lauderdale regularly. I would be there now if it were not for this problem of yours."

Strollo took this as a rebuke, and so he interrupted.

"Don Carlo, I am sorry that these problems of mine have interrupted your stay in Fort Lauderdale. I appreciate your confidence in me, and I promise that this chance you have given me will benefit the Family a hundred fold."

Magliocco dismissed his remarks with an imperious wave and went on.

"The economy in South Florida is growing rapidly. The business climate is made for our operations. You have done well with our recent banking business. It is only unfortunate that your planning failed to take into account these developments."

The mixed praise and criticism caused a slight tick to appear in the corner of Strollo's left eye.

If Magliocco noticed, it did not interrupt the flow of his speech.

"Perhaps it is time to move to other fields that may be as promising. One such possibility involves my dear friend in Cleveland, Don Sebastian Maranzano. He has told me of a very talented printer who can produce paper of great commercial value. This resource, coupled with your talents at business, should prove very valuable."

Strollo refilled Magliocco's espresso cup and moved the anisette bottle closer to him. Magliocco nodded in acknowledgment. "Growth also demands housing. Housing requires construction. You know how well situated we are in the trades. I could go on and mention our garbage industry. Growth increases waste. American society throws away."

Strollo began to breathe a little easier but remained cautious. Magliocco was giving him an ultimatum: leave and remove the heat, or . . .

Strollo's expression was a study in gravity and dedication.

"Don Carlo, I will not disappoint you. You have given me an unparalleled opportunity to serve you and the Family. I promise, you will not regret this. There will be no problems in Miami such as we are facing here, and my earnings for the Family will double."

Strollo reached across the table, took Magliocco's right hand in his, and kissed it. Magliocco responded with a light touch on Strollo's cheek.

The two stood, embraced, and Magliocco turned and left the social club preceded by his bodyguard. He was again bowed to by Amari. As the door closed behind the boss a deep frown crossed Strollo's face. He had been stripped of his *regime* and sent into exile.

Strollo, standing by the table that Magliocco had just left, saw the marked respect that Amari reserved for Magliocco. Strollo's eyes locked on Amari. They had been friends since childhood. They had killed together. Strollo knew that Amari considered him closer than a brother. Strollo also knew that Amari was almost fanatical in his devotion to Cosa Nostra and the family.

The questions that forced themselves into Strollo's mind were:

"Would Magliocco use Amari to hit me?

"What would Amari do if he was ordered to hit me?"

· C H A P T E R ·
TWO

The clock radio came on at six o'clock with the sound of WLYF, Helen Lawrence's favorite FM station. Her husband, Al, was as usual awake before the radio came on. He was up and shaving within seconds. He dressed quietly and walked to the kitchen for a quick coffee and cereal. Helen would rise at six forty-five for her morning walk and the beginning of her day.

This was the beginning of Al's second month in Miami. An FBI agent for twenty-three years, he had transferred in from Detroit. He was a lawyer and had come up through the ranks. This was his third office as SAC—special agent in charge—and his experience was varied. During part of eight years in New York he had supervised a squad targeting one of the La Cosa Nostra families. LCN remained a strong interest but one that he knew would be eclipsed by the drug scene in Miami.

This morning he headed north, driving the new FBI blue Chevrolet along Old Cutler Road. He knew it was shorter to follow Dixie Highway and I-95 to the office, but the Old Cutler route was peaceful, not like the hectic traffic on the expressway. It was, for the most part, a quiet untroubled drive through stately oaks and banyans that dropped roots down from their branches into the earth, supporting a broad canopy of foliage. The road meandered about, and he eventually found his way through Coconut Grove, a laid-back community of upscale homes, condominiums, shops, and fine restaurants, the Greenwich Village of Miami. From there he picked up I-95 for the last few miles to the office.

He arrived just before seven and, as always, used this quiet time, before the rush of business, to review the teletypes that had been sent or received during the night. He would have been called at home on anything marked Immediate. The other priorities, Urgent and Routine, were twenty-four- or forty-eight-hour handling.

Reading all of the teletype traffic kept him abreast of most of the cases in the office. He had two ASACs—assistant special agents in charge—and eight supervisors to handle the day-to-day operations, but that did not relieve the SAC from responsibility for what happened in his office. And Al preferred a hands-on style of leadership.

The Miami FBI office occupied a four-story building with a gray coral facade and dark reflective windows that prevented a view of the interior. The building was unpretentious, its identity betrayed only by the American flag, several antennas on its roof, and the modest bronze plaque by its entrance door that read, "Federal Bureau of Investigation, United States Department of Justice."

The first floor was occupied by the receptionist, behind bullet-proof glass, an elevator, garage, auto maintenance, and radio repair. The second floor housed the stenos and the chief clerk's office, which maintained the investigative files, evidence vaults, weapons vault, communications, and general administration of the office.

The third and fourth floors were office space for the agents and supervisory personnel. Al's office was on the fourth floor in the southeast corner from which he had a view of Biscayne Bay over the tops of some houses and palm trees. It was a large rectangular room.

A burgundy leather sofa faced a coffee table and two leather armchairs with two small tables supporting lamps at each end of the sofa. To his right was an American flag in a floor stand and on the left the Florida flag. On the wall, over the center of a credenza, hung a heavy replica of the FBI seal.

The desk was government-issue mahogany. A family picture and lamp was on the left corner, a black marble desk set in the center. Facing the desk were three wooden armchairs with brown leather seats and backs. The walls were painted beige and decorated with photographs of the FBI training facility at the Marine Corps base at Quantico, Virginia, and some scenery photographs taken by Al.

This morning, Al's principal secretary, Dolores Spencer, was in by seven-thirty and gave him her usual cheery good morning. "I'm sure you and Mrs. Lawrence are happy you're not in Detroit now. Last night's weather showed them at fifteen degrees and two feet of snow."

Al looked up from his teletypes and chuckled. "You know, I remember when I arrived in Detroit. It was in January, and I looked out of my office at ice-covered roads and all this snow. My sole thought was, 'What the hell am I doing here?'"

Laughing, she said, "Now you've only got one beautiful day of sunshine after the other. Boring, huh?"

Al replied with a smile, then said, "Dolores, when Bill Baskin gets in, tell him I'm ready for him. Then I need to see Steve Donnelly."

Heading back into her office, she said, "Sure thing, and the coffee's ready."

Al had no doubts about the role of south Florida in the narcotics trade and the need for the bulk of the office resources to be targeted there. But one of his early concerns, as the new SAC, was that the office, in its almost total preoccupation with the drug problem, was unbalancing itself. In fact, one of his supervisors, Steve Donnelly, had urged an even greater commitment of manpower to narcotics enforcement. That issue Al planned to address this morning.

His days in New York had sensitized him to the Mafia, and one of his first requests had been for a current assessment of mob activity in south Florida. That had been two weeks ago. The presentation had ended with Al imparting more information about who was in south Florida than the office had in its brief. Al had instructed the organized crime supervisor, Bill Baskin, to come up with an up-to-date comprehensive briefing.

Bill Baskin was fairly new to the world of organized crime. His education had been in accounting, and he had worked in white-collar crime for eight years before being given the Miami OC desk three months ago. He was thirty-four, tall and slender, with receding brown hair and steel-rimmed glasses that made him look more like a teacher than an FBI agent. One thing Al liked about him was that when Bill took a position, Al didn't feel he was being "sold" on it.

Bill was in Al's office twenty minutes later, accompanied by Terry Washington, the ASAC who oversaw Bill's area of responsibility. The briefing was much improved over the last one and ended with a report on a person Al remembered very well.

Bill, occasionally glancing at notes on a legal pad on his lap, continued:

"Vincent Strollo, *caporegime*, Magliocco family, is apparently moving to Miami. Two confidential informants in the family say he's been retired by Magliocco. Based on the CI's information and their investigation, New York considers him responsible for setting up a major bank scam, and for many of the bodies they found in a mob 'cemetery.' He probably also ordered the hit on the guy and his wife who lived on the farm where the bodies were found."

Bill removed his glasses and for a moment studied them as though they held some vital information. Then he looked at Al.

"We'll give him what coverage we can, but if he's retired—and it seems he is, since he's got no people down here—we'll probably move on to more promising targets."

Al complimented Bill on his progress in the past two weeks. "Well done—a good comprehensive report. I sense you've got a good handle on who's here, and we're beginning to learn what they're doing. I'd like another update in thirty days."

Al drew a concentric doodle on the pad in front of him, thinking over what he'd been told, and finally looked up. "Vincent Strollo and I are old 'friends'; we sparred in New York, you know. We were never able to put him away. We got several of his soldiers and associates, but not him. Any idea why he picked Miami?"

Bill responded, "No, except south Florida is a favored spot. It equates to New York but with sunshine. The word the New York office gets is that the heat was too much and Magliocco allowed his big moneymaker an early retirement. Strollo's *regime* is still in New York. As far as we can tell, nobody has followed him here. It looks like the move is permanent and not a ploy."

Al shook his head in mild disagreement. "Bill, I hate to say 'never' because whenever I do, I'm wrong on some overlooked factor, but nobody retires from the mob. The only way you retire is by dying—or getting murdered. He's here for a reason, Bill. It may be the heat in New York sent him south for his health, but he's working. Tell me on what." He was struck by a new idea, and added, "Put SPIT on him for a few days, whatever can be spared."

SPIT, Special Investigative Team, had been a tough battle with Bureau headquarters, but approval had given Miami three five-man teams of professional, full-time surveillance people. Along with the street surveillance group came four pilots and two high-wing Cessna aircraft, slow-flying, quiet surveillance machines. They were unshakable eyes in the sky. Coupling these assets with radio tracking devices that could be attached to vehicles under surveillance, night vision equipment, special body-pack radios, infrared strobe markers, and other specialty gear made for a powerful investigative tool.

Bill rose to leave, but Al waved him back to his seat and turned to the ASAC, Terry Washington. "So what's your feeling about organized crime in Miami? Is it a problem we ought to address, and if so to what extent?"

Terry shrugged. "Sure, it's a problem, but we need to keep it in perspective. Bill is handling it just right. He's monitoring it and will move when he sees a good target. Al, the mob's a New York problem. Our problem's dope. That's why the Bureau gave Miami another ASAC and why people are being transferred here. Listen to Steve when he talks dope—he knows what he's doing."

At that moment, Steve Donnelly stuck his head in the door, remarking, "Did I hear someone using my name in vain?"

Steve was an immaculate dresser who would have been at home on the cover of *Gentlemen's Quarterly*. He was young, robust, and a real comer in the Bureau. His good looks, affability, and backslapping good humor were definite assets. He was also considered by Bureau headquarters to be the oracle of all truth in narcotics matters.

Al waved him in and jokingly said, "Terry was just setting me up to buy your program when I had about decided to abolish your job." Steve did not smile, and there was not the usual flippant retort. Somewhat puzzled by Steve's lack of response, Al went on. "Okay, Steve, what was it you wanted to brief Terry and me on this morning?"

Steve glanced questioningly at Bill Baskin and settled into one of the leather armchairs, folding back the top sheet from a yellow legal pad that he consulted.

"Two Miami PD Narcotics detectives have come up with a top-level informant who supervises the receipt and distribution of Medellín coke shipments in south Florida and ensures the money is collected and shipped to Colombia via an intricate laundering route. He's their number one man here, Enrique Zamorano. We've had some intelligence about him from our legal attaché in Bogotá, and his name's come up a couple of times in some cases here. It checks out."

Al was impressed. "How'd they come up with someone of that stature?"

Steve tried to control the boast in his voice, but flashed a smile that said, I'm glad you asked me that question. "We helped. He's concerned about having to leave the country and return to Colombia. He's much like those old Russian defectors. He's Americanized. Got his money, wants to stay. He's worried about his family. They don't want to go back, and two of his kids are in trouble. These two detectives got an airtight case on the kids. Seems they branched out on their own. Stole some of Dad's coke and sold it to the cops who were undercover. We need to grease Immigration so they can stay. They're here illegally."

Al asked, "Why us and not the Drug Enforcement Administration?"

"Cops said DEA can't handle the money-laundering part as well as we can, and we got more clout with INS. They want to work only with us and don't even want their department to know what they've got. They're afraid of leaks."

Steve's impatience began to show. He was not used to explaining himself. He wondered why this new SAC couldn't just accept the importance of what he was being told. Would he have to draw pictures for this guy?

"This is a real chance at crippling their operation here. I figure we can seize maybe three tons of coke and over forty million in cash plus a lot of property, including some banks. There's no telling how many arrests will be involved. We're talking everything from off-loaders to dealers to bankers."

As Al reached to the corner of his desk for his ever present coffee cup, Donnelly looked him over. He saw a forty-eight-year-old, six-foot, mostly gray-haired man, still in good shape. Donnelly had been part of the usual office dissecting of an about-to-arrive new boss. A few of the agents had known him as a street agent, others later.

As he looked at Al, he recalled a disturbing story: When Al was SAC in Tampa, a squad was attempting to locate a top-ten fugitive while Al was supervising a bank robbery stake-out elsewhere. A pretext call to the house produced an answering voice believed to be the fugitive. The inhabitants refused to come out, and the supervisor gassed the house. The occupants were forced out, but a search of the house found nothing.

Al, having been advised by radio of the use of gas, arrived as they finished searching. The agent was positive in his voice-recognition. The supervisor was gathering up his men to leave.

Al assumed command of the scene, donned a gas mask he habitually carried in his car trunk, and went in with three agents. Within minutes Al found a loaded Thompson submachine gun hidden under a bed. Next he found a thin, false wooden panel in the side wall of the bedroom closet that he tore down with one hand as he trained his .357 Magnum on the widening aperture. The badly gassed fugitive's eyes focused with difficulty at the leveled gun, and then he wheezed in surrender.

Steve's disquiet was occasioned by his vision of Al taking command away from one of his supervisors and succeeding where the supervisor had failed.

He knew Al had a reputation for action, but so far all he had seen was a typical untalented bureaucrat, perhaps occasionally lucky but too careful, not willing to take the chances necessary to make the big cases.

Steve had a way of overcoming problems with bureaucrats. Al would know only what he chose to tell him.

After some thought, Al responded. "Terry, if you disagree with this, say so. You too, Steve." Addressing him directly, Al continued, "I'd like you to interview this CI personally and evaluate him. Do some quiet background checks on him. Also, how much do you know about the detectives?"

Steve felt he was being challenged, and his voice carried a defensive edge. "I've known the detectives for three years. We've worked with them before. They're good. Trustworthy. No problem in me contacting the CI."

The last part of that statement was a lie. Steve had asked to have one of his men interview the CI—the confidential informant—and had been told that was impossible. The officers had stated that the CI would meet with no one except them.

Al continued, "After you've talked to the CI, put together an operational memo and we'll talk about what you need."

"I'll have a memo for you in two days. Meanwhile I need SPIT full-time and six more agents to start some background investigation before this case starts getting away from us."

Al removed his reading glasses and pointed with one end of them. "No, Steve, you haven't given me enough on which to base a decision. You may utilize SPIT within existing office priorities." He glanced over at the other supervisor. "Bill has some use for them too on an OC matter."

Steve came out of his chair.

"OC! A bunch of old mustaches out of New York that make better comedy than crime! Al, that's yesterday's problem. New York works OC when it has nothing better to do. Get with today's problem. Headquarters knows where the priorities are: narcotics. Give me what I need, and this office'll lead the whole Bureau."

Al's voice and expression registered surprise at the heat of Steve's retort. He leaned forward, smiling, trying to reassure his supervisor. "Steve, I'm not disagreeing with you. I just want to make my judgments on the best information I can get."

Still not satisfied, Steve sensed weakness in this response. He began advancing toward Al's desk, his whole manner exhibiting challenge. "I just gave you that information. Are you saying you don't have confidence in me?"

Al firmly pushed back his chair and stood up. "Steve, I have every confidence in you. But the Bureau doesn't pay me to be a rubber stamp. Now please comply with my request."

Steve's color mounted. The veins on his neck stood out. His voice was strong, accusatory. "The last SAC gave me the same bullshit until headquarters straightened him out! When he stopped being an obstacle, we started making progress."

Al's hands became fists that were knuckle down on the desktop. His face showed no emotion, but his voice cut the air like steel. "This discussion is over. I expect your memo in two days. We'll evaluate your recommendations then."

Steve was about to respond when Bill Baskin came up behind him, grasped him by the arm, and gently urged him away. Bill's voice was low. "Time for everyone to cool off."

Steve spun on him and shouted, "Mind your own fucking business," and stormed out of the office.

Terry Washington shrugged. "He's hotheaded. He believes in what he's doing. A fighter."

Al stood for a moment looking at the open doorway. "Terry, you'd better have a talk with that boy before our next meeting. He either settles down or he starts looking for a new home. I don't need prima donnas in my office."

Vincent Strollo and his wife, Rosa, arrived in Florida two weeks after his conversation with Magliocco. He stopped first in Tampa, where he met with Santo Tramunti, the head of the small family there. The meeting was perfunctory, and Strollo was feeling rather bored as the old man gave his blessing. His blood rose, however, when he left the private room of Tramunti's club and saw his wife seated at the bar, drinking a Coke and talking to an attentive bartender. Strollo abruptly walked up to her, grabbed her by the arm, and, ignoring the bartender, brought her roughly to her feet. "Let's go."

Rosa was upset. "I haven't finished my Coke."

"I told you to wait in the car."

"I'm sorry, I got thirsty. I saw no harm."

"I don't want bar bums slobbering all over you. You shouldn't either. You're my wife. The wife of Vincent Strollo. Show me respect."

Submissively, she allowed herself to be led out of the bar.

Rosa and Vincent had been married when she was seventeen, and she had been a good Mafia wife. She never inquired about her husband's business. Yes, she knew what he did, but she had trouble admitting she knew, even to herself. This ambivalence of knowing, being proud of his stature, and denying it because of his crimes, was one of the great contradictions she lived with. Her life centered on their three children and Vincent. She knew he had girlfriends, but she would never even hint at that. She was Vincent's wife, and that's what counted.

A year ago, at forty-five, she had looked seventy. Her hair had been graying and she wore it in a severe bun. She usually dressed in black, and had become heavier after each child. At seventeen she had been one of the most beautiful girls in Bensonhurst. Even overweight, and poorly groomed and dressed, she revealed traces of her former beauty in her face and hands.

Then one of her daughters had taken her in hand and convinced her to become "Americanized." Strollo wasn't sure yet whether he liked this new Italian wife that settled into the car beside him. She had lost forty pounds, and her hair was rich and black and styled. She wore an expensive, beautifully tailored suit and just the right amount of jewelry. Much of her seventeen-year-old beauty had been recovered.

Her changeover hadn't stopped with the physical, however. Yesterday she asked him a question about business. He had been so shocked he answered her. This new Rosa was becoming too independent, he thought, grousing, as he roared out of the club's parking lot.

Strollo followed I-75 south from Tampa to Alligator Alley and in four hours was on the Broad Causeway coming into Bal Harbour. They drove through an area of fashionable and exclusive shops and found the elegant ten-story building on the beach that Tony Iannello had described.

The furnished condominium he had obtained for Strollo was a luxuriously appointed penthouse with an ocean view in one of Bal Harbour's newest buildings. The owner was happy to have Don Vincent as his guest.

Iannello was waiting for him in the condo, and after he'd given Strollo a quick tour without earning a word of thanks, he was concerned. Strollo gruffly took him by the arm and walked him to the elevator, downstairs, and out into the warm February afternoon.

Tony Iannello was short and heavy with wiry black hair and a perpetual five o'clock shadow. His voice was a continual growl, in keeping with his bearlike appearance. He had come to south Florida about ten years before, and he was one of about twenty-five buttons from various families that had been allowed to work in the area. His strength was in his organization of the local bookies, the shylocked loans that went with that action, and some influence at the horse tracks. He could also handle dog action and jai-alai. In all three sports he had the ability to arrange for a winner, or loser, every so often.

Once they were on the street, in the open, Strollo snapped off a question. "Do we have a friend who can check the condo for bugs?"

"Yes, I have someone from the phone company. Tell me when."

Strollo didn't answer but abruptly moved on to other topics. "I'm to be in the financial and perhaps construction area. I need a list of all those associated with those businesses who owe you. Better yet, give me a rundown on the people you own and what you think they can do. I'd like this tomorrow." The slick, fast-talking New Yorker hardly glanced at Iannello as he went on. "Also, I need to know any other friends of ours who are here, who they're with and what business they're in, and whether we can work with them. I need to know what politicians you control—or that our friends control. And give me a list of good public phone numbers and their location, preferably around here."

Iannello, surprised by these rapid-fire demands, forced his expression to go blank as Strollo settled his gaze on him. "I'll have all that tomorrow," he found himself replying. "Let's meet at the Leisure Hotel coffee shop. I have a small operation there, and I know who comes in. Ten o'clock?"

"Okay."

They separated, and Iannello walked slowly to his car, pulling at his right earlobe. He was worried about this sudden change in his affairs. "I don't need this take-charge guy," he muttered. "I got good things going here. This guy's going to bring nothing but trouble."

• C H A P T E R •
THREE

Still feeling uneasy, Tony Iannello was fifteen minutes early for the morning meeting with Strollo. He was a good soldier, and the system had been good to him, he kept telling himself. Plus, he knew Strollo was a real moneymaker, so he stood to gain if he could deliver. He also knew that Strollo's *regime* had made more bones than any other. He didn't like this, but it magnified his fear and respect for the man.

The Leisure Hotel, where Iannello was waiting, was a center for one of his bookmaking rings. He used several of the rooms, equipped with multiple phones, to receive the action. No one stayed in any of the rooms. The phones were call-forwarded to other numbers where they were answered. Any cops who picked up on the operation would raid empty hotel rooms. The hotel got a piece, and Iannello was immediately informed of any strangers in the area.

Strollo arrived ten minutes late, while Iannello was on his third cup of coffee. The caffeine and the stress of the meeting had him on edge. He rose as Strollo approached the table.

"Mr. Strollo . . ."

"Call me Vincent. We'll be doing a lot of business together and Mister is too long."

Iannello relaxed. "Okay, thank you. You like some coffee, a danish?"

"No, I've had breakfast. Do you have what I asked for?"

This instant switch to business caught Tony by surprise. "Ah, yeah. Where you want to start?"

"Outside."

Iannello blinked. "What? What outside?"

Strollo fixed Iannello with a stare and in his low, deep bass voice said, "Tony, you want to stay with me, you start being careful. You're not careful and you fuck up a score, you don't get no second chance with me. You understand?"

Iannello blanched. He understood all too well. The first-name basis wouldn't stop Strollo from killing him. He was beginning to like this relationship less and less. The threat from Strollo, and the coffee, made him reach for an antacid tablet from his pocket.

"Yeah, boss," he gulped. "I understand. We'll go outside and take a walk. I should tell you, though, I own this place and I know who comes and goes. I really think we'd be all right here, but whatever you want, boss."

Strollo smiled inwardly. "Vincent" had become "boss" after that short exchange. He had handled that very well.

Tony got up from the table on Strollo's nod, and they walked out into the warm winter day.

"If it's okay, I'll have a phone guy, Stan Flemming, come by at noon tomorrow to check the condo. I own him. He tips us on wiretaps when he picks up on them. He cleans the phones and checks for bugs. He sometimes gets to the phone company computer, and then he can really check. I slip him three hundred for a quick check, just to keep him happy. He'd get canned if the company found out."

Strollo shrugged. "Okay, noon is fine, but I want a good job. There's a fucking wire in that condo he misses, you and him's meat."

There it was again, an ice-cold threat. Iannello grimaced as he reached for another antacid tablet. "You'll get a complete job. He's a supervisor. He's the best."

Strollo stopped walking and faced Iannello. "What about your people?"

Iannello tugged at his ear, stalling for time as he tried to figure out what Strollo wanted from him. "I got some that deal with me direct and know I'm made. I got others that don't know they're dealing with me, but I own the people they're dealing with. Mostly the politicians deal with people I own and don't know it's me controlling them. I can talk to almost all the county commissioners, not direct, but through somebody I own."

Iannello searched Strollo's expressionless face for some clue as to where this was going.

"The cities are mixed, you see. Hialeah is mostly Spanish, and it ain't as easy for me to get in as some of the others, but they're mostly all stealing with both hands there, and they can be dealt with. Miami's a piece of cake. Their commission's a fucking circus. We can get most anything there, and they won't even notice. I got hooks in others. You tell me what you need, and I probably can find it."

Strollo nodded and asked, "What about our friends?"

Iannello was hopeful. Could this be his out? Maybe Strollo would start working with other buttons and take some of the pressure off him.

"They got more hooks than me in the politicos," he responded. "There's more of them. I know a few they own, but not many. They're all available with a piece and a good move. There's maybe twenty-five made guys down here from five families. I can get you a list if you need one, but off the top of my head I can name most of them and you'll probably know them."

Iannello started rattling off the names of members in the area and what family they were with, but Strollo interrupted, as usual one step ahead.

"Could we get zoning passed, and could we get exceptions to zoning?"

"If they saw a piece coming to them in cash or favors, you got it."

Strollo paused, and his face became hard. "Who do you have by the balls that can't do nothing but what we say?"

Iannello's quandary about where this was going was clear in his puzzled expression. "About six guys I'm shylocking. I'm ready to bust legs."

"Anybody in business?"

"Yeah, really all. What kind of business you want?"

"A reasonably good-size business that with the right collateral could walk into a bank and get a loan of half a million with no sweat."

Iannello paused in thought, scratching his head. "Let me think on that. I got a guy, name's Knight, might be able to do that. He's got a good company on paper. I own most of it, because he's into horses. He's also chasing broads."

This was what Strollo was looking for. "I assume he'd like to find a way out?"

"Yeah, he'd fucking kill to get out from under."

Strollo smiled for the first time that morning. "So tell me something else. Who you got that's smart, professional, a good front, but we can control?"

Iannello's head was swimming from all these changes in direction. He thought long on this one but didn't come up with an answer.

"Nobody I own. But if you're talking a scam, there might be a few takers around that I know of."

"Okay. How about my list of public phones?"

Pleased to be back on solid ground, Iannello handed him a list. "The best are the phone booths here at the Leisure. You're off the street, and they're real booths, not just two-sided enclosures. You'll also know who comes and goes." Suddenly a light went off in his head, and he returned to Strollo's previous question. "There's this guy, young lawyer, accountant, who hangs at the Paddock. That's a condo and swinging spot in North Miami. I've talked to him. I think he knows I'm made. He comes on like he'd go. I really think he'd play."

"Okay, check him out good and come back to me. I'll call you."

With that, Strollo turned on his heel and left.

Striding toward his car, he felt good about this first real meeting with Iannello. He had instilled just the right amount of fear and respect and greed. The potential appeared promising. Promising enough that he thought he would communicate with Cleveland and get some "paper."

Before he could really move, though, he had to get Magliocco's approval. He'd been here a week, and he could smell money. The old man would say okay. He knew it. Perhaps these new ventures so soon after his arrival would put him back in favor.

Strollo went to a pay phone and called a number in New York. The party answered, "Funny Valentine."

"Let me talk to Mr. Sciandra."

"Who's calling, please?"

"Mr. Vincent."

"Thank you."

"Hello, this is Mr. Sciandra. May I help you?"

"Yes, thank you. This is Mr. Vincent from Miami. I need some merchandise from Cleveland that Mr. Carlo mentioned, and wonder if some samples could be arranged, perhaps through you."

"Let me check with him and see if the merchandise he had in mind is still available, and what the terms of delivery might be."

Strollo responded, "Okay, be in touch if we can do business."

It was a perfect winter day on Miami Beach. The sky was a deep Miami blue and cloudless, the sun warm and friendly. A slight breeze from the west carried with it a fragrance of the Everglades and gently stroked the palm fronds. Strollo had nothing else planned for the day, and he was in no hurry to get back to the condo. Rosa was busy trying to understand all the gadgets they had, and was going to go out with a real estate agent looking for a house. He had given her the house-hunting chore just to keep her occupied. When the time came, he would select the house, no matter what new-woman ideas she had.

He decided on a slow drive around Miami Beach, and walked to his black Cadillac near the hotel entrance. His New York plates were appropriate on the beach this time of year. But, he thought, I need a Miami car . . . a nice bright color.

As he started out into traffic, he considered some of the

things threatening him. He was concerned about the investigation in New York and New Jersey. Once he had left New York, the Crime Commission threat had disappeared. But would the FBI ease up?

Out of habit his eyes moved from the street ahead to his rearview mirror and back. Several of the people they had corrupted and used to front the bank scam were looking to cooperate with the FBI to lessen jail time. So far "Blue Eyes" had kept them in line.

In one case, Amari had walked a grocery cart down the aisle of a Food Fair and met the teletype clerk from the bank coming the other way. He recognized him immediately. The store's occupants were paralyzed for a second by his scream, and perplexed as he fled from the store. Jimmy hadn't said a word. He had just stopped and looked straight into his eyes.

Another associate about to agree to testify was located staying with his in-laws in South Jersey. The grandmother took his children to a park to play. Jimmy was there, and after chatting with the grandmother, he gave the three-year-old girl a ride on a swing.

The potential witness stopped at the park to pick up the kids and grandma. The rescue squad came next and took him to the hospital for observation of a suspected heart attack. The little girl chattered away about the nice man who was swinging her when her daddy got sick.

The last potential witness was dissuaded when his wife had a flat tire in a shopping center and, after calling her husband to come help, found a good Samaritan.

When the husband came on the scene, Jimmy was changing the tire.

Strollo could not help but smirk at how they had kept everybody in line.

The FBI tried to sell the witness-protection program. The lawyers, paid by the family, told their clients that as first-time offenders, for a white-collar crime, they'd do a couple of years at most, in a country-club prison, as opposed to a lifetime of prison in the witness-protection program. So far all had agreed not to cooperate.

Strollo positively beamed as he thought about the bank score. The family had split up almost twenty million. Well, maybe more like fifteen after expenses and payoffs. The gross had been almost twenty, and that was the figure he liked.

The bodies the FBI had found at the farm he did not see as a threat to him. Except for the shooters, there were no witnesses.

The smile of pleasure gave way to a frown as Strollo considered that the greatest threat was from Magliocco. If he was arrested, the boss would be nervous. Strollo could convict Magliocco. His left eye developed a tic.

Strollo rolled down his windows, and the clean, clear salt air seemed to embrace him in its welcome. As he eased into the right turn lane, he grinned at the thought of what he could do down here. He had several ideas in mind. The first, and simplest, was obtaining some good-quality bearer bonds that a bank would take as collateral for a loan. The second would take some work, but it would be the one that could really pay off. In booming Miami, what was a better scam than a bust-out of a major construction project?

· C H A P T E R ·
FOUR

Miami Narcotics detectives Cesar Morales and Jorge Fonseca were engaged in a quiet conversation in a restaurant located on Calle Ocho in Miami's Cuban section. Morales was tall and lifted weights regularly. So did his partner, Fonseca, who was shorter but much broader in the shoulders. They both were impeccably dressed and loaded with gold neck chains, bracelets, and rings, which they considered part of their undercover costume.

"You really think Donnelly's going to buy into this?" Fonseca said, speaking in Spanish. "And even if he does, can he sell it to the Bureau?"

Morales gave a knowing smile. "He's in. We fed him so much shit it was oozing out his ears. The more we shoveled, the more he bought in. People believe you when you tell them what they want to hear. He'll buy—he has to. Shit, we're gonna make him a fucking hero, right?"

With that remark they both burst out laughing.

Al was reading a New York teletype when Steve walked into his office carrying a two-page memo.

"You asked for an operational memo. Here it is."

Al put down the teletype without comment and began on the

memo outlining the narcotics case. When he had finished, he initialed it to show he had read it and laid it aside. He studied Steve for a few seconds, deciding how best to handle him.

"I'm as enthusiastic about a good dope case as you are. I just want as much control in a case like this as we can possibly have. The bad guys will give us enough surprises. We don't need any of our own."

Steve moved restlessly in one of the leather chairs facing Al's desk. "No surprises. The CI, Zamorano, is solid. I talked to him," he lied. "He's got no place to go now; he's committed himself. He stays with us or Ochoa has him whacked. Medellín doesn't like it when their boys talk to us."

Al still wasn't comfortable. "Who's going to be in day-to-day contact with him? Who's controlling him?"

"We are. The cops'll probably have most of the contact. We just can't walk in and take him away."

Al picked up the memo, tendering it back to Steve. "Okay, let's start off slow. Test what he can do. Do an in-depth debriefing. Get all the intelligence you can. For now, use your squad. As an operation is going down or a specific need arises, we'll give you more people."

Steve did not try to hide his disagreement as he stood up. He did not bother retrieving the memo. "This half-assed shit isn't going to work. We either go in with both feet or these cops are going to take the CI to DEA or Customs and we'll lose the case."

Al was forced to look up to the standing Donnelly, but he refused to rise for a confrontation. "We'll do it my way for now. Keep me posted on your progress."

As Al picked up the New York teletype again, Steve dug his fingers into his palm in frustration. There was only so far he could push this guy. He wanted a confrontation but did not want to appear the initiator. He paused for a moment, snatched up the memo, then turned and walked out.

As soon as Steve had left, Al laid the teletype back down and leaned back in thought. While he didn't want to undercut a supervisor, he felt he might need to do a little work on his own to satisfy that nagging in the back of his head. He flipped his card file and punched up Carlos Mendoza.

Carlos was a major in the Miami PD, a graduate of the FBI National Academy, a leadership school for local command officers. Al had met him several times at NA functions. Mendoza was now executive officer in Internal Affairs, the unit that investigated allegations of misconduct against Miami police officers.

"Mendosa," a gruff voice answered.

Al responded, "Carlos, this is Al Lawrence. How are you?"

"Good, thanks," Carlos said. "To what do I owe the honor of this call?"

"Carlos, I need a little advice. Could we have lunch today?"

"Sure, got no plans. When and where?"

"La Hacienda, in half an hour?"

"Good choice. You must be *cubano.*"

Al laughed, "No, just an aficionado."

La Hacienda, a small, brightly decorated restaurant on Calle Ocho, was frequented by both police and narcotics traffickers. Carlos and Al arrived within minutes of each other and chose a table in a far corner where they could observe customers entering and where their backs were to a wall.

After they had ordered the special of the day, paella, Al began. "I'd like this to be a conversation that never happened."

Carlos grinned. "For that you get to pick up the check."

Al hesitated a moment before starting. He was not going to be able to level with Carlos, as much as he liked and trusted him. If he told him the whole story, Carlos would be obligated to inform his superiors, and, as Steve had pointed out, there were leaks in the Miami PD.

"Carlos, two narcotics officers, Jorge Fonseca and Cesar Morales, have been working with one of my squads on narcotics, and we may be entrusting them with some really sensitive information. Do you know these two? In effect, the tough question, can we trust them? Are they all right?"

"I've met Morales. He's a flashy weight-lifter type. Very into himself, considers himself a gift to the ladies." He tapped his fork idly on the table as he considered. "I believe there've been some Use of Force reports which indicate he might be heavy-handed. But other than that, I don't know anything bad about him.

"The other guy, I only recognize the name. There might be some Use of Force reports on him also. I'll have to check our files."

"Thanks, Carlos, I'd appreciate that."

Jorge Ochoa rested easily in a soft cowhide recliner, his eyes half open, about to surrender to sleep. The hacienda he was visiting today was one of his smaller properties, about 150 kilometers east of Medellín, situated in a verdant valley at the foot of the towering Cordillera Central. The Magdalena River bisected its two thousand hectares and watered his pampered horses.

The noise from the single-side-band radio, or its operator trying to raise a station, occasionally roused him from his lethargy.

Finally, through the voice scrambler, Ochoa heard the voice he had been waiting for and came awake. The operator had made contact with Enrique.

Enrique Zamorano was Ochoa's number one man in Miami. He had the final say for how, and when, coke shipments came into south Florida from the Medellín cartel. He controlled the wholesale distribution of the cocaine and coordinated the collection and transfer of money back to Colombia.

At the moment, Zamorano was ten miles off Key Largo on his fifty-four-foot Bertram sport fisherman, and had been delayed in his broadcast by a poorly tuned antenna. The multitude of channels available to single-side-band and the heavy use by marine interests and ham operators, coupled with the scrambler, gave maximum security. The scrambler converted the Spanish they spoke into unintelligible bursts of static that were decoded at the other end. Ochoa's equipment was always state-of-the-art and often better than American law enforcement's.

Zamorano's message, voiced by his operator, was apologetic.

"My regrets. We had an antenna problem that is now fixed. We are ready to receive the next consignment."

Ochoa heaved himself out of the recliner and stood over the seated operator, who was reading from a sheet of paper.

"If you concur we will follow plan three, and the date you can expect us will be advanced by one and ten."

Plan three called for delivery of two metric tons of cocaine concealed in the false forward section of four truck trailers loaded with a varied assortment of Venezuelan products being shipped from Caracas. The "advanced by one and ten" gave the digits to be added to a preset month number and day number.

The trailers had been leased from a company controlled by Ochoa. The lessees shipping the goods did not know their trailers also contained cocaine. After the Venezuelan goods were removed, Zamorano would arrange to pick up the leased trailers and unload the cocaine.

Zamorano was seated next to his captain, who doubled as his radio operator, in the spacious salon of the yacht. Dom Pérignon was at hand, and Zamorano dipped beluga from a silver dish as he sipped from his tulip glass. He looked up as the captain repeated back what he had heard to ensure he had understood. Then the captain continued.

"That's satisfactory. Our payment for the last consignment has been verified and will be delivered in three sections at plus five. We will use C, F, and I. Repeat C, F, and I. Acknowledge, please."

Zamorano was telling Ochoa that five days from now the money would be transferred to Medellín by three predetermined methods. "C" was a courier flight to Grand Cayman to deposit the money in an offshore account. "F" was a series of deposits in four banks for cashier's checks that would be mailed to Medellín and sold for Colombian pesos on the black market. "I" was a deposit in Netherlands Antilles banks for the purchase of additional Florida real estate.

Ochoa's operator acknowledged and then asked, "Are we still on schedule for the current activity?"

Zamorano's captain replied, "All arrangements are complete. Everything should be safely home as scheduled."

This concerned a current cocaine shipment that was to be air-dropped.

Ochoa's operator acknowledged, and Ochoa picked up the mike. "When can we review the books?"

Startled at his boss's voice, Zamorano grabbed the mike, spilling his champagne on his pants. Trying not to show any concern, he said, "They will be sent by pouch at plus five."

Ochoa understood that the records of payments for the last cocaine delivery would be sent to Bogotá in the Colombian diplomatic pouch through a second secretary in the embassy and delivered to Ochoa's group by one of their people in the Colombian state department. "Okay, that's good."

The business ended, Zamorano exhaled with relief. Gazing down at his grossly obese body, he snapped, "Now, get me a goddam towel for this mess."

The telephone call later that afternoon added little to Al's assessment of the Miami detectives. Carlos told him that Morales had three allegations of use of excessive force and Fonseca one. Investigation had failed to substantiate them.

"Narcotics work always entails use of force, and complaints are to be expected. The department puts aggressive officers in narcotics, as you'd expect. As far as the trustworthy issue is concerned, there's nothing here that would indicate a problem."

"Okay, thanks a lot, Carlos."

As Al hung up, he was still troubled. He wanted Steve to run his own show, but he still couldn't trust Steve's salesman approach. And his memo of that morning was too vague to instill any confidence. Reluctantly, Al made a decision, got up, and started toward Steve's squad area.

Steve was in his small glass-fronted cubicle, reviewing a lengthy informant report prepared by one of his top agents, Claude Williams, from information he had received from MM 152-C.

About three years ago, Claude, then recently transferred from Chicago to Miami, had been looking for one Jimmy Lee Jones, a fugitive from Alabama charged with unlawful flight to avoid prosecution—robbery. He had robbed a series of convenience stores and shot a clerk. Williams picked up his trail in Miami and located his girlfriend, Ruby.

Ruby was pregnant with Jimmy Lee's child, as it turned out. He had deserted her, and she didn't know where he was. She was literally destitute, and Claude felt sorry for her. He gave her twenty dollars out of his own pocket for food. Three days later, Ruby called Claude and gave him Jimmy Lee's address. Claude paid her three hundred dollars in FBI money, and she had become confidential informant MM 152-C, file number 137-765. The "MM" designated the informant as a Miami office CI. "152" was her assigned number, in sequence with other CIs, and "C" designated her as a criminal informant.

Ruby was a very attractive redhead, and she could draw a lot of men, particularly narcotics traffickers.

Claude had called Ruby that morning for a routine debriefing on her assigned target, Manolo "Sonny" Arango, one of the biggest narcotics off-loaders in Miami.

"I was with Sonny and his friends last night at the Mutiny bar. Sonny was hitting the sauce pretty good, celebrating closing the deal on the coke I told you was coming. He's got his off-loaders lined up. It's to be an airdrop. An old C-47 flew from Colombia, I don't know where yet, to Haiti. They're going to change tail numbers and then fly to Miami. They've got loran coordinates worked out for a spot off Elliott Key. The coke'll be in sealed plastic pipe that the plane will drop on the coordinates.

"They're going to do it at night or at daybreak, like five A.M. The boats will have infrared strobes so the plane can spot them at the coordinates. Each of the pipes will have a firefly on it, sealed. Two go-fast boats will do the pickup. They're going to run into a house, probably in Cocoplum. Haven't got that yet."

Steve glanced up at Al's approach, thinking that he couldn't have planned this better if he'd tried. As Al entered the office, Steve, a smug expression on his face, handed him the report.

"Here's the kind of work we do. This is a major cartel shipment, and it's going to be ours, along with an assortment of major traffickers, an airplane, boats, and a Cocoplum mansion."

Al accepted the report, put on his glasses, and began reading as he settled into a chair. As he read through it, he realized that this was just the opportunity he was looking for.

"This is great work, Steve. I'll tell you what. I'm going to be personally involved in this at every step, including being on the scene when we take these guys down."

Steve was dumbfounded. His SAC looking over his shoulder? This was not what he wanted at all.

FIVE

Dominic Sciandra, a soldier with Carmine Licata's *regime*, owned My Funny Valentine, a front company that actually did sell novelties and party favors. As soon as he disconnected from Strollo, he locked his office and walked a block west on 14th Street, where there were several public phones. He dialed Licata's home number, and it was picked up on the third ring.

"Hello. If you're the man of the house I have a message of great importance for you."

Licata replied, "I ain't got time for this shit today," and hung up.

Licata walked to the hall closet, pulled on his coat, and walked two blocks down Bayview Avenue to a convenience store. He bought a newspaper, looked around, and, seeing no interest in him, walked to a bank of pay phones and called Sciandra back.

"What you got?"

"Call from our partner who just went south. He says he needs some sample merchandise from Cleveland. He's going to call me tomorrow. You want it should go direct or through me?"

"Direct. I'll handle it. Call you at three, use number five."

Dominic understood he would receive a call from Licata with

instructions at three o'clock at a pay phone; number five was in a sandwich shop just down the street.

Licata had been briefed by Magliocco on Strollo. He also knew that Cleveland had just produced some "paper" that was available to New York. He fished a book of matches out of his pocket. On the flap was a carelessly scrawled number. He did some mental arithmetic, subtracting from the first digit and adding to the next until he had decoded the number. He dumped a handful of change on the telephone counter and punched up a number in Cleveland. The phone was answered, "Melody Restaurant."

"This is a friend of Sam's from out of town." He emphasized the word *friend*. "I need to talk with him in fifteen minutes. Can it be arranged?"

"Yeah, I think so. He know where to call ya?"

"Yeah, tell him New York, number three. Got it?"

"Number three, got it."

Sam Lonardo was the *sotto capo*—underboss—of the Cleveland family. A big man, six foot and 250 pounds, he had been the one to recognize the potential for good commercial paper, and the family had just gone into production with an excellent printer who was located just over the line in Wheeling, West Virginia. That town was wide open. Nobody bothered them in Wheeling.

They had first bought some clean, unwrinkled bonds, in itself something of a job. A person buying bearer bonds usually does not care if they are folded, since most are. But folds show up in a photograph as broken letters, and photography is the first step to offset printing. The bonds they had finally bought had some light folds that ironed out. The camera and lens that took the photos had been a major investment, but the negatives were excellent. Sensitized aluminum plates were printed from the negatives for the colors in the bonds, and the press carefully indexed to register all lines and colors accurately.

The first test run was beautiful. The printer rented a numbering wheel to give each bond its own serial number and each coupon the same serial number. Four bonds were printed: Indiana Toll Road, New York Housing Authority, General Motors

Acceptance Corporation, and Philadelphia School District. Each had a face value of one thousand dollars, but traded at various prices depending on interest and rating of the bond.

The initial run was at three thousand of each bond, giving them a total face value of twelve million dollars. Lonardo was offering them at twenty cents on the dollar, but was taking as low as ten when the sale was to another family.

Lonardo left the restaurant and walked to a pay phone down the block. Licata was seated in a phone booth in a small hotel about ten minutes from his house, and he picked up on the first ring.

"Hey, my old friend, this is a voice from New York. If you remember, we last had a glass of wine together when you visited here."

"How can I help you, my friend?"

"As I think you were told, we might use the new material you've been manufacturing. We're told that they come at one thousand and you have a good supply. We'd like a sample of two of each."

Lonardo responded, "Of course. How can I get them to you?"

"Send them registered mail to Steven C. Smith, room 203, Leisure Hotel, Miami Beach."

"They'll be in the mail today," Lonardo said. "Call me after you've had a chance to look at them. I hope we can do business."

Licata headed to another pay phone, called Sciandra, and relayed the delivery information to him. Sciandra would advise Strollo when he called the following day.

Tony Iannello was at the Paddock bar with a very dry Beefeater martini, hoping that Nathan Hersch would drop by as he usually did. Iannello's patience was rewarded within a half hour. As he was just beginning a second martini, he saw the unmistakable fashion-plate figure of Nathan Hersch coming through the dim hallway. Iannello nodded, and Hersch acknowledged the greeting as he moved toward Iannello, who ordered a dry Rob Roy with a twist of lemon, straight up, for Hersch.

Hersch was twenty-nine, five feet eight in elevator shoes, with brown hair and dark horn-rim glasses. He spoke deliberately, in a voice unmistakably from the Bronx. He was headed to a bright future with a degree in accounting, a CPA license, and a degree in law, admitted to practice in New York and Florida. Law and accounting are an unbeatable business combination. Hersch was single, liked the fast track, was impatient to make money and not particular where the money came from. He was convinced that with the expertise of his twin degrees, nobody could ever lay a glove on him.

After they shook hands and the drink was served, Iannello took Hersch by the elbow and steered him to a small table in a far corner of the bar where they could talk in private. Hersch was perplexed. Iannello had never done this before, and Hersch was not sure he wanted to hear what Iannello had to say.

"Nate, you look good. That's a nice set of threads, good quality, looks at least a grand." Iannello ran his hand down the sleeve of Hersch's jacket. "You ever need suits, I got a contact. Suit like this, cost you a hundred. They come out of New York. Some friends of mine on the docks. Ever so many boxes fall off the ships and break open; my friends, they get the breakage. Sometimes boxes fall off the tailgates of trucks; my friends pick 'em up. You know, you come with us and there's a lot we can do for you. You know money ain't needed when friends deal. You do me a favor, I do you a favor."

Hersch was on guard. He knew Iannello was made, and while he got a thrill from being around wise guys, he also knew that he could get hurt if he wasn't careful.

"Hey, thanks, Tony. You get some good stuff, let me know. I can always use some quality."

Iannello, satisfied with the response he had elicited so far, decided he could progress to the next stage. "Say, what are you doing these days? Any money coming in?"

"Yeah, doing all right. With a firm downtown, Peters Jepson Solomon and Enright. Not bad, but I ain't cut out for sixty- to eighty-hour weeks, and that's what these guys expect."

Iannello waved his hand, a look of disdain on his face. "Fuck, that's for shitheads. Anybody connected don't work like that. Use your fucking brains and make it big. Do some playing. Hey, there's a million dickheads out there just waiting to donate their dough to someone smart enough to take it."

Hersch was intrigued by the way this conversation was heading. Was Iannello about to put a proposition to him? He was at once frightened and curious to hear it.

Hersch took the plunge. "That might be true for you, Tony, but so far nobody's put anything in my collection plate."

Chuckling, Iannello leaned across the table, cupping his hand to his mouth. "That's because you ain't never been shown how to take up a collection. You want a lesson with guaranteed results, I'm ready to make you a million."

Hersch used a sip of his drink as an excuse to cover his excitement. A million bucks? That was a tempting amount, and then some. "Come on, Tony, what are you talking about? You want me to kill the pope?"

Iannello grinned, shaking his head. "Right now, just some information. Later maybe we'll talk about your piece. I got an investor. He's looking for a building. Plans all done, ground there. Construction maybe a short time away. Either financed or needs financing to go ahead. It's gotta be bucks. Not less than thirty mil."

Hersch sucked in his breath. Iannello was for real on this deal. And if information was all he wanted, there was no risk. It would merely put his foot in the door. If he liked what came up, he'd walk in; if not, he'd step away.

"Yeah, there's maybe a couple I'm aware of that are close to what your friend's looking for. Give me a day, and I'll put a rough package together for you."

"Okay." Iannello snapped his fingers and winked. "You know, my friend knows how to show appreciation. Let's meet here tomorrow night and see where we are. In the meantime, if you're looking for something tonight, there's a game in suite 2324; you're welcome to join. Just say I sent you up. Your credit's good. The bar and dinner tonight's on my tab. If you come with us, you may not have much need for money."

Iannello gave him a friendly, knowing glance. "Enjoy. I got a date and she's a hell of a lot better-looking than you. See you tomorrow."

About the time Strollo arrived in Miami, an old man in Millbourne, Pennsylvania, had suddenly developed a massive pain in his chest. The national news had just ended and his favorite game show was about to begin. This didn't feel like indigestion. Thomas Siragusa had lived alone since his wife died two years ago. He knew he had to get to his telephone in the kitchen. The pain was getting worse. It was running down his arm. He had to call his son. His son would get help.

The last thing Siragusa would ever see was the weave and color of his living room rug.

After the funeral, his son, Peter, and his wife had been faced with the task of cleaning out thirty years of accumulation from the old house in Millbourne. For two days they had labored, filling plastic garbage bags full of what had once been a couple's life. The mess had to be cleaned up if they wanted to sell the place.

Early on the third day, Peter was almost finished in the basement when he bent over to pick up an old wooden box, like an army foot locker, with a padlock on it. He was surprised to find he could hardly budge it.

"What did the old man put in here? It's like lead."

He had no idea where the key was, so he took a crowbar to the hasp. He just wanted to empty the box so he could move it. The hasp popped easily, revealing old newspapers spread on top.

Peter was pulling them off carelessly when suddenly he froze. He abruptly sat on the cement floor and gazed at his find. After a minute he got up, put the newspapers back on top, and closed the lid. He walked up the stairs and called, "Mildred, stop what you're doing. Got something in the cellar you need to see right now. Then we've got to figure out what to do with it."

Mildred, disturbed at being interrupted in her packing of china, asked, "What is it that I've got to see right now?"

Peter shook his head. "I can't really describe it. You've got to see it. It wouldn't come out right my just telling it."

He took Mildred by the arm and led her down the stairs. When he had positioned her, he opened the lid of the box and removed the newspaper. He looked too, half expecting it not to be there. Mildred stifled a scream.

"Where—where did it come from? Is it real?"

"Yeah, I expect it's real, all right. Where it came from? Has to have come from the old man's job. The big question is, what are we going to do with it? We can't sell it. And I'm not giving it back. It's gotta weigh almost two hundred pounds. Over a million dollars' worth."

Mildred just stared at the gold. "Your dad worked for Philadelphia Refining for forty years. You figure he snuck this out of their gold-refining area?"

"Had to. No other place he could have put this together. Each bar is the same size, about a pound, and was done in a mold. Probably took out scrap or dust and cooked it down and molded it someplace. We'll never know how he did it, but he sure as shit did. Come on, help me drag it up the stairs and over to the car. We'll get it home and then decide what to do with it."

Later that day, Iannello was having an unaccustomed beer. The meeting with Hersch could be critical, and he needed to be clear-headed. He'd go a martini later.

He was at one end of the long bar, from which point he could look down the long entrance hallway. That way he would be able to observe Hersch before he entered the bar.

The Paddock was a luxury condominium development in North Miami on the Intracoastal Waterway. The bar, restaurant, and other facilities were restricted to condo owners, their guests, and members of the Paddock Club—an exclusive club, and something of a status symbol. Most of the local politicians frequented it.

Tony was a member, though he never paid any dues. He was "comp," a sign of respect by the owners. There were other members, who did pay, and occasionally found themselves lodged in the federal correctional center or at one of the white-collar-crime country-club prisons. It was a swinging club, full of bored wives and roving husbands.

When Iannello spotted Hersch, he immediately got the bartender's attention.

"Dry Rob Roy, straight up, and make sure that glass is never empty." He dropped a bill on the bar.

As the lawyer approached, Tony extended a hand, which Hersch took in a rather weak grip. Iannello indicated a table off to the side, and as they sat down, a barmaid brought over the Rob Roy.

Seeing Hersch slump into his chair, Iannello asked, "You look tired, Nate. Tough day?"

Hersch took a long pull on the drink. "That and your damn crap game last night. I'm out three thousand, which is on markers, and I didn't get home till four."

Iannello pursed his lips in sympathy, but inside he was cheered. Nothing like a little debt to push a man in the right direction. "Well, you can relax now. No work pressure here, and there's another game tonight if you want to get even."

Hersch shook his head and shrugged absently. "I don't know, I'll see. I feel better already, though. I guess I needed a drink to smooth off the edges."

Iannello did not hesitate. "Hell, let's smooth out the whole thing, not just the edges." He signaled, and another Rob Roy, straight up, appeared.

"So, tell me, were you able to do anything on the construction project?"

Hersch sipped at the second drink as he removed a large manila envelope from inside his jacket. "I pulled several, or had them pulled by zoning, and looked some over. I got a clerk down there, and for a twenty I can get most anything." He grinned at Iannello: slick talking to slick.

"There's two that are good," he went on. "One might be especially good. A group put together a condo and office building combination. The land is bought and zoned; it's about half a mile from here. They cleared the land and were about ready to build when their financing dried up. It just needs somebody with capital to invest. The estimate is maybe twenty-five million to build it. New contracts for material and labor would have to be negotiated. The drawings could be bought or the architect retained. You could use the contractor that was going to do it, or buy him out. Here's a summary on them both." He handed over the envelope, noting, "The one I like is called Towers of Light. Let me know if you need anything else."

Iannello was pleased and he tapped the envelope smartly. "If my investor decides to go with one of these, we'd need a sharp attorney full-time. Maybe someone to actually take charge of the whole project. It could be that he'd want the project in that person's name. He's not given to much publicity."

Hersch had been half expecting something like this, but now that it had been offered he really wasn't sure what to do. Another Rob Roy arrived as Iannello continued.

"I'll tell you this. If you're lucky enough to hook up with this guy, your money worries are over. I guarantee you'll have a million the first year. This guy invented making money."

Hersch's mind was whirling. A million bucks in the first year was beyond anything he'd ever dreamed of. Yes, he knew the mob would kill him if they felt threatened, but he sure as hell wasn't going to run to the cops.

Hersch heard himself saying, "Yeah, I'd be interested in talking to him."

After the fourth Rob Roy, Iannello pointed Hersch toward the game of the evening and left the club to meet Harold Knight. This would be a different sort of encounter.

Harold Knight was forty, given to paunchiness, and spoke in a slightly high-pitched, rapid manner. He was married and the father of a fifteen-year-old girl and ten-year-old boy. He had developed a profitable office maintenance business, but two recently developed vices, slow horses and fast women, were affecting the black of his balance sheets. To keep his family in the style to which they had become accustomed, and to maintain his own interests, he was running a sizable tab with his bookie and skimming from the company income. He was also fully extended on his line of credit at his bank.

Iannello had loaned him twenty thousand dollars at 5 percent interest per week. That debt had now tripled. Knight was convinced he only needed a couple of good races to make him whole. He was doing what every gambler does, doubling his losing bets to get even.

Knight was worrying over a cup of coffee in the Broadway Deli, a restaurant at Biscayne Boulevard and 125th Street, when he saw Iannello drive up. He got out of his car, but did not enter. Instead he waved through the glass door for Knight to come outside. He went out and extended his hand; it was ignored.

Iannello growled, "You got the money this time?"

Knight reached into his pocket. "I got five hundred."

As he handed it over, Iannello's left hand knocked the money out of Knight's hand and his right landed a stinging open-handed slap to the face. Knight, frightened and confused, bent to pick up the money. Iannello grabbed him by the hair and held him in a bent-over position. Knight saw sidewalk and Iannello's shoes.

"Okay, fuck, pick up your money. You and me are gonna take a ride and discuss this."

Knight was terrified, sure Iannello was going to kill him. With most of the five hundred in one hand he began to protest. Iannello brought him up to full height with a quick lift of Knight's hair.

"Don't say another fucking word. Get in your fucking car. You drive, asshole. I'll tell you where."

Iannello threw him up against his car, and Knight hurriedly opened the door and got in. Iannello directed him to drive to 165th Street, where there was an open, deserted area of construction shacks for a new building going up. During the drive, Iannello did not say a word. Knight tried to open conversation and was told to shut up and drive.

When they arrived, he ordered Knight out, and they walked over to an excavation site. Along the way, Iannello picked up a long two-by-four. Knight tried to move away from him, but Iannello had him by his shirt collar, half dragging him along.

Iannello moved his hand to the back of Knight's neck, directing his gaze.

"Look down there. See that fucking hole? After I break your fucking legs, I'm gonna dump you in there. With busted legs, you don't crawl. Then I'm gonna dump dirt on ya, and you're planted."

Knight started shaking, and perspiration rolled off his face.

Iannello increased the pressure on Knight's neck, his fingers digging deep.

"You got thirty seconds to pay me ten thousand dollars, and I want five thousand every week with no more shit. You owe me sixty thousand. There's people on my ass for this money. You think I'm gonna take your fucking heat? I deliver money to them, or I deliver a body. Which you want?"

Knight was shivering uncontrollably as he pleaded, "Tony, I don't have it. I've tried to get it. There's nothing left. There's no more in the business. Killing me won't get it for you. Let me work. Give me a break on the vigorish and I'll pay. I only borrowed twenty thousand—the rest is vig, interest. It's the vig that's eating me up."

Iannello was unmoved. "Don't cry that shit to me. You knew up front it was five percent a week. It was you that missed payments, asshole."

Knight moaned, "Tony, what do you want from me? I don't have it."

Iannello suddenly relaxed his hold. "Listen, asshole, tell you what. You got one way besides the pit." Like a beaten dog, Knight looked up at him. "And you owe me for this. I stood up and took a lot of heat. You screw this chance I got for you, and your wife gets an acid bath."

Iannello, again increasing the pressure of his hold on Knight's neck, pulled him back to his car. He reached in his jacket pocket and pulled the stopper from a bottle and poured the contents onto the hood of Knight's car. The acid boiled and vaporized, destroying the paint and eating into the metal.

Iannello pushed Knight's face close to the acid. "You fuck this up and your wife's in a bathtub. I'll be pouring this out of a gallon jug on her, and you'll be watching. When she's a lump of tar you go in. Is that what you want? Or do you do what you're told?"

Knight was terrified. "Whatever you say, Tony."

Iannello finally let go, and Knight straightened up. "Okay, we got a clean deal going," Iannello said softly. "You do what you're told, you work your way outa this, and I'll get you something to put in your pocket. You fuck up and you're dead meat. No more screwing around."

Iannello punctuated his threat by lashing out and hitting him with his fist, full force, in the stomach. Knight balled over, retching. He got into Knight's car and drove off, leaving Knight gasping for breath.

• C H A P T E R •
SIX

The planning for the cocaine drop had been fairly straightfor-
ward. Al could find no real fault except perhaps that Steve was
a trifle superficial in his general briefing and instructions, but
then he had to balance this with the fact that the men in this
operation had worked together. And, as commonly happened
among law enforcement officers, they could read one another's
mind.

The following morning at five o'clock, Al was in a U.S. Customs Blackhawk helicopter, painted jet black, running silent, or
as silent as one of these got with full mufflers. With him were
five heavily armed SWAT trained agents and Steve, together
with a Customs agent and the two pilots.

The smugglers' World War II C-47 was first tracked by the
radar balloon on Cudjoe Key and the station at MacDill Air
Force Base. It was then acquired by the Miami Intelligence
Center. It had entered Florida between Fort Myers and
Sarasota, trying to look like a flight from New Orleans. The
Blackhawk then picked up the C-47 on its radar and also had
the two go-fast boats in the ocean below on its low-light tele-
vision monitor.

Two miles from the go-fasts was an FBI-manned ocean racer,
code-named Dolphin, blacked out, its hull low and invisible

against the Elliott Key shoreline. The go-fasts couldn't pick out the boat on their radar from the Elliott Key ground clutter, but Dolphin had a radar lock on them. On shore the FBI had tailed some of the off-load crew to a three-million-dollar house in Cocoplum. With this FBI group were Morales and Fonseca.

Al frowned as he remembered the presence of the two detectives. The case did not seem to involve them or the Miami PD, so why had Steve brought them along? Al planned to ask him after the operation.

The C-47, virtually identical to the DC-3s used by Dade County for aerial mosquito spraying, streaked over the Everglades, about to enter south Dade County at five thousand feet and begin a descent. The pilots were combing the skies with their radar.

The Blackhawk, though, hovered at two hundred feet, too low for the C-47's radar and too high for the go-fasts'.

The C-47 dropped rapidly, and by the time it passed north of Turkey Point, over Cutler Ridge, it was at three hundred feet, seemingly on a spraying mission. It did not turn back for another mosquito run as it passed over the bay but continued east. At this dangerous altitude both pilots were intent on flying the plane. When the copilot picked up the helicopter on his screen and yelled, "Bogey, two o'clock," the pilot gave it a quick glance and dropped another hundred feet. He shrugged, committed now to the drop. His loran showed him four miles from the designated point, and he shouted in the intercom, "We're almost there!"

He pulled back the throttles and said to the copilot, "Get ready to give me flaps. I'm taking her to stall speed."

The plane slowed, and then the copilot saw two strobes, dead ahead, through his infrared goggles. "There they are!"

The pilot answered, "I got them."

The crewman had already pulled the firefly switches and opened the cargo door. A hundred-mile-an-hour blast rushed into the plane and jolted the crewman, who was tethered in place. The plane dropped to fifty feet and took full flaps as it slowed dangerously.

Just as the nose seemed to touch the boats, the copilot screamed, "Now!"

The crewman kicked a third of the plastic pipes free. The plane banked for a return run. A quarter of the load was dropped on the second pass and the rest on the third.

The sea was dotted with infrared fireflies marking the location of the pipes. All but one. That one was being cursed by one of the go-fast boat crews as they pulled it from the shattered windshield.

The boats swiftly maneuvered to pick up the other thirty-nine pipes. Each was partially loaded, to ensure buoyancy, with twenty-five kilograms of pure cocaine. That translated to $225 million street value, $20 million wholesale.

The pilot advanced his throttles as the copilot began raising the flaps. The crewman had secured the door, and the plane began an ascent as it gathered speed. They were to fly up the coast to the north of Fort Lauderdale, cut inland, fly south, and land at Tamiami Airport. They had a light load of Haitian paintings, wood carvings, and straw hats in case Customs came snooping. Since they had not been intercepted, they felt reasonably secure. The radar blip they had seen was forgotten in the relief of having ditched the coke.

Thanks to Ruby, FBI and U.S. Customs agents were waiting to greet them on their arrival.

The Blackhawk stayed with the go-fast boats and followed them to the Cocoplum mansion. Once the off-loading to Cocoplum commenced, the helicopter put down at Matheson Hammock Park and Marina, where cars were waiting to take the group north to Cocoplum. They would wait for the buyers to show.

Cocoplum is a growing development of million-dollar-plus homes. The only land access is one road through the center of a manmade peninsula. The homes front on the road and back onto deep-water canals.

Al had asked for a car for himself and Steve, so they could talk privately and issue instructions in a unified command. As they drove north, leading the other cars, to take up predetermined positions, Al asked, "Steve, why are Fonseca and Morales with us tonight?"

Steve was his usual condescending self. "Al, when someone does you a favor by giving you a CI like Zamorano, you show your gratitude by including them in major action so they look good to their bosses."

Al shook his head. "You mean they're just along for the ride?"

"If you want to put it that way, yes. Look, we owe these guys."

Al looked askance across the darkened front seat. "In a sense we do, Steve, but both they and we are doing our job. They'll get the recognition due them when the Zamorano operation comes down. From now on, let's not hand out phony assignments to make people look good, okay?"

Steve was about to make a sharp retort when a panicked voice on the radio shouted, "Agent down! We're under fire!"

Al flipped a panel switch that activated blue lights just behind his grille and placed a magnetic blue light on his roof. Then he hit the siren button.

Another radio voice came on. "They got a countersurveillance, automatic weapons! They made us! Cars leaving the house! Boats are taking off!"

Al could hear bursts of machine-gun fire in the background of the transmission. Steve was frozen with disbelief as Al reached for the microphone.

"Dolphin, from One, did you copy the two sharks are loose?"

The FBI boat, lying in the bay off Cocoplum, responded. "We read it. We're calling Coast Guard for backup. We can take one for sure, and we'll try for two."

Al clicked off and instantly called the outer perimeter at Cocoplum. "S-Two, One. Can you block the exit road?"

"Ten-four, we're moving there now."

In another moment he contacted the inner perimeter around the stash house. "S-One, from One. Status?"

"They winged Terry, but he's okay. Only one boat got off—we hit the other one. One car was able to head out.

There's at least one subject in the house and maybe one or two on foot."

Al answered, "Ten-four. Just try to contain them. We're almost there."

He turned to Steve. "The dopers may not know we're FBI. They may think it's a rip-off. Use the Customs radio next to you. Get the Blackhawk back here and tell him to light the place up and loudspeaker 'Police.' "

Steve picked up the hand-held Customs radio and made the contact.

As they turned onto the road that was the only way in or out of Cocoplum, they saw three FBI cars blocking the road. The agents had someone in custody. Al stopped, and an agent approached him.

"We got the car and one guy, boss. Want us to go in?"

Al responded, "No. Keep your position as backup. SWAT's with me. Interview the hell out of that guy. Let us know what we've got here."

"You got it, boss."

As they drove into Cocoplum, the office called. "One, Station."

"One, go."

"Police just dispatched a car to answer a panic alarm at the house two doors down from the target."

Al transmitted, "Contact police, advise our situation. Try to determine nature of panic."

"We did. Police advise that alarm company said there was no answer to their call to the house."

Al banged the steering wheel with his fist. "Shit! They've got hostages!"

He instructed the inner perimeter to continue containing the target house and instructed SWAT to deploy around the house that had triggered the panic alarm.

The helicopter appeared overhead as they were deploying. Its ground lights were turned on, and night became day. An amplified voice boomed out, "This is the FBI. Come out of the house backward, hands on head."

Within minutes there was movement in the target house, and two men appeared at the front door backing out in surrender.

So that part of the operation had gone smoothly, Al thought. Soon after that, when SWAT was positioned, he faced his car into the house where the alarm system had been triggered. Switching on his bright lights to flood the front, he turned his electronic siren to loudspeaker:

"This is the FBI," he stated firmly. "We have the house surrounded. All occupants, back out hands on head."

After a delay a male voice from the house called out, "We can't. They won't let us. They'll kill us if you don't let them go!"

Al said, "I want to talk to them."

A harsh voice screamed, "Get away or they die!"

Al flicked off the loudspeaker and turned to Steve. "Tell the station to get the phone number for the house. I'll call it on the cellular phone. Then see if S-Two can learn from their prisoner who's in the house."

Over the car PA, Al said, "Everybody relax, nobody's going to get hurt. We can work this out."

After some hurried transmissions, Steve finally reported, "S-Two says there's probably only one in there, and his name's Hector. Don't have a last name."

Al turned on the loudspeaker and announced, "Listen, I'm going to call the house on the phone. We have the number. Let's discuss how we can work this out."

The homeowner answered the phone on the third ring, totally panic-stricken. Al instructed the man to try to get the doper on the phone. After considerable frenzied discussion, he agreed to talk to Al.

Hector picked up the phone and began screaming in a heavy Spanish accent, "Get away. Leave a car. I'll kill them."

Al interrupted, talking over him. "Easy, there. Relax, everything will be all right. Hector, I'm Al. Are you okay?"

There was silence on the other end, the dope runner stunned both from the inquiry as to his well-being and the use of his name. Calmer, he answered, "How'd you know who I was?"

"Hector, we know all about this operation. We're FBI, and

you know we're not going to hurt anyone unless they start something. Why did you-all shoot at us?"

"Hey, man, we didn't know, we thought you were ripping us."

Al nodded as this guess of his from before was confirmed. Now he knew how to proceed. "If you had known it was us from the beginning, you would have given up and let the lawyers work it out, right?"

"Man, you got that right."

"Okay," Al continued, easy as pie, "let's turn the clock back. We just arrived. We told you who we were, no shooting, and you guys all surrendered. Nobody gets hurt."

"You want me to give up? I got these people. I can trade."

"No, Hector, it doesn't work that way. I'm giving you a break. I'm going to let you do what you would have done fifteen minutes ago."

Confused, Hector had to think that over for a while. He was tired. He'd been partying all night waiting for the shipment. As the adrenaline rush from taking hostages stopped flowing and he calmed down, surrender started to seem a good deal. "Okay, I'm coming out."

On the outer perimeter around the house, Morales and Fonseca were both chuckling.

"The Fee Bees really fucked this one up," Morales said. "Say, that's their boss over there with Donnelly. What say we go over and say hello?"

When he was still a good distance away, Morales called out, "Hey, Steve, that was a good job." Donnelly looked up and smiled when he saw who it was. "Eleven collars, a ton of coke, the house, two go-fasts . . . good night's work."

Donnelly puffed up and glanced at Al. He hoped this SAC realized Morales was right. Problems were to be expected when you had a big operation, and it had ended well. Donnelly dismissed the loss of the buyers and the gunfight as minor incidents in the big picture.

Introductions were made, and Morales and Fonseca stroked Donnelly, building him up for his boss. In turn, Donnelly mentioned what great Narcotics detectives they were.

After a few minutes, Al said to the two, "My congratulations on your turning Zamorano. That had to take real doing. Are we on track?"

The detectives shared a knowing glance. "Man, this is going to be the biggest score this town has ever seen."

Al came away with the feeling that the two detectives played a very loose game, just as Steve did. He also had a gnawing feeling that he was being conned.

After all the subjects and the boats, cars, and house as well as the ton of cocaine had been secured, Al took Steve aside. "Steve, we need to have a constructive discussion." He saw his supervisor's face tighten, and he rushed to add, "The operation was not unsuccessful, but there were some major flaws that we can learn from for next time. A prime objective was to roll up not only the smugglers and off-loaders but also the dealers and buyers. We lost the dealers and buyers—plus got one of our people hurt—primarily because we failed to plan adequately for a countersurveillance."

Steve was prepared for this. "The planning was there, Al. The guys just didn't handle it right. They failed to make the countersurveillance."

Al sadly shook his head, disappointed at this response. "We'll get nothing from this if we try to lay the responsibility on someone else. I'll share the blame. I was at the briefing. But you did the planning and issued the instructions. You've got to take your share of the blame."

Steve heatedly gestured with both hands. "You don't lay this on me. You were so hot to take over command. It was you and the agents at the house who screwed up my plan."

Al was about to fire back when he stopped. If he lost his temper he'd be on Steve's ground. "This is getting us nowhere. I was hoping we could critique the operation and profit from it. Let's let it cool down. You debrief the agents, because we're going to need written memos for headquarters on the shooting in any event. We'll revisit this in a few days, after you've put together the reports."

Steve smiled inwardly, feeling he had won this round.

"There's no doubt the reports will bear me out. Now, give me some room on Zamorano and you'll have a real coup."

The coming Zamorano operation would make his reputation with headquarters unassailable. The Zamorano case would show he was top man in Miami, not this new SAC clown.

Iannello had been waiting only five minutes when Strollo walked into the coffee shop of the Leisure Hotel. He noticed Strollo's impeccably tailored and pressed gray wool suit, white shirt with French cuffs, and gold horseshoe-shaped studs. The blue-and-red-striped tie and blue breast-pocket handkerchief were perfect. Iannello smiled inwardly, wondering how long that suit would last in Miami's summer heat.

Iannello rose as Strollo approached the table. He extended the folder from Nathan Hersch, and Strollo glanced at it.

"We got some papers to look at?"

"Yeah, got some things for you to examine."

Strollo hesitated a second. "Tell you what. Get a room for us. You pick it out, not the clerk. Not one where your phones are working. While you're doing that, I gotta make a call."

Strollo entered one of the two phone booths in the hotel lobby and called Sciandra in New York. He gave the phone number of the pay phone he was using and told him to call right back.

Sciandra left the office and stopped at the first pay phone he encountered, calling back within five minutes.

"My friend, I got the samples you wanted. They're coming registered mail to Steven Smith, room 203, at the place where your associate has his business. I'm sure you'll be able to pick it up at your leisure."

Strollo was satisfied. "Thank you. I'll be in touch."

Iannello was waiting in the lobby, key in hand. Strollo waved him over, out of sight of the desk clerk.

"Tell your clerk you're getting a package by registered mail, Steven Smith, room 203. He's to sign for it and then give it to you. Give me the key. Meet me in the room."

The key was to room 607, the top floor. The room was high-ceilinged, with a fan. The furniture was old, but not in bad shape. The bathroom had an old-fashioned toilet, basin, and tub with an added shower head.

Strollo had just finished his inspection when Iannello entered. As he was about to speak, Strollo stopped him with an upraised hand. He walked over to the television set and turned it up loud. Pulling a table and chairs in front of the set, they both sat down. Strollo began in his low bass that Iannello had to strain to hear.

"What ya got?"

"First, I had a talk with Knight last night. He's ours. He'll do what you want. Here's a brochure on his business and an accountant's statement that's a year old."

Strollo took the documents and started scanning them as Iannello continued.

"Nathan Hersch came up with two good prospects, and I think he's in, if you want him. Here they are. He likes Towers of Light; it's got the most room to move. We can switch contractor and architect or keep them. Financing is to be negotiated, and all contracts got to be let. He figgers it's twenty-five mil."

Strollo put the documents down. "Okay, I'll study these later. When that package arrives, call me. Don't open it yourself, you hear me?" Tony flinched at the growl in his voice, and Strollo fixed him with a cold gaze.

"Tony, your guy Hersch, let's test him. I want him to do a new statement for Knight's company. I want him with lots of assets, company in the black. Then I want a personal net worth statement for Knight." He paused as Iannello whipped out a notepad and started writing. "His money is all in bearer bonds. He's worth two mil. Sign that old accountant's name to it or make up a bullshit one. I want this stuff to look right. We may go to the bank with it. I want the name of the company blank, and the name on the personal balance sheet blank. No point in telling Hersch anything at this point. When you give him the old ones, just cut out the names."

Iannello jotted a note and then reminded Strollo, "Don't forget, Flemming from the telephone company will be at your place this afternoon."

"Yeah, okay," Strollo said absently. "Now, look, we've talked about this Knight and Hersch. If we do business with them, how do we know they'll stay with us?"

Iannello had no doubts. "Knight's scared shitless. I played a version of looking down the elevator shaft with him. That little fuck ain't got noplace to go."

Strollo seemed impressed, and Iannello warmed to his pitch. "Hersch is a lawyer and accountant. I've known him about two, three years. Knew him when he was an accountant and going to law school. He always was fast buck, big splash. Wants money and wants to spend money. He knows I'm made, likes the excitement. He's okay. No way he's a snitch."

Strollo was satisfied for now.

"Okay, get Hersch going on those statements. Ask him how long it'd take to locate about eight or ten dormant companies, corporations that are over three years old that are just shells, and what it'd take to get them. When you got time, I need eight or ten offices, as small as possible. Just a place to receive mail. We'll use call forwarding on the phones there to one of the eight, where we'll probably have a girl. Let's put the real office in a warehouse. We might need a warehouse as we get going."

Iannello looked up from his notepad, overwhelmed. He couldn't believe the orders this *caporegime* could spit out.

Then Strollo switched gears. "Now, I've heard from the guys in New York about the cops and the FBI down here. How do you see it?"

Iannello was at ease on this subject. "Piece of cake. Metro just told their cops there's no organized crime here, so they ain't looking for any. Judges don't sentence gamblers, so Metro shut down its bookie squad. The state cops and FBI are so involved in dope that they got no time for anything else. About all else they do is some cases against doper cops and some stuff against politicians. Shit, I'm home free."

Strollo raised a hand, abruptly deflating him. "That's enough for now. Get that stuff together as soon as you can, and call me about the package. Now, wait here for a few minutes before you follow me out."

They shook hands, and Strollo left.

There was no doubt in Iannello's mind Strollo was a mover. His initial fears were being overtaken by a flood of greed. He was going to make serious money with this guy.

In a few hours, Strollo, seated at the dining-room table of his condo, had finished studying the papers that had been provided on the construction projects. He had come to the same conclusion as Hersch. Towers of Light was just what he was looking for. This Hersch was smart. He could be used . . . and then thrown away.

Strollo decided it was time for a visit to New York. In no time he had found all kinds of ways to make money down here. He'd fly up day after tomorrow. He needed to see Magliocco.

Rosa entered the dining room and interrupted his thoughts. He noticed that she no longer wore the apron that had once been her habitual dress. She wore a light print silk that clung to the curves of her body. Her diamond pendant forced the eye to the beginning of her cleavage. He was surprised and almost embarrassed by the stirring he felt. This was, after all, his wife, not a girlfriend.

Rosa said, "I forgot to mention, I got a call from Petey. He was asking how we were doing and said when you get a chance to call. He needs some advice. Something about his father leaving something."

Rosa saw him shake his head, and she began to scold him. "Vincent, you should have gone to the funeral. He was your cousin. They're nice, honest people, not looking for anything from you, not like some you work with."

The reference to work brought his head up. "Rosa, that's enough," he said sternly. "You got no say in my work or my people. If I'm with somebody, that's enough for you. You like who I like."

A retort formed in her throat, but she held back.

Pete Siragusa worked for a Buick dealership as an auto mechanic. His wife, Mildred, was a part-time receptionist for a dentist. They had two children, ages four and two. They looked to their cousin Vincent as a remarkably successful businessman. They knew he probably was "connected" somehow, but chose not to recognize it.

Seeing her fall submissively silent, Strollo reached out and put his hand on her hip. The fabric was cool and smooth. Her hip trembled slightly under his touch, and he felt slightly aroused.

"Rosa, I know you like the Siragusas. I'm sorry I let you talk me into inviting them for the christening last year. They're not with it. But I'll call."

Rosa liked his hand on her hip, so out of character for him. It made her feel sensuous, and with that came a small feeling of power. She volunteered, "I'll get them for you."

Strollo's hand dropped away, and he was about to say no, but she picked up the phone and rapidly punched in their home number. Strollo sat, wondering how far he could let Rosa's new attitude go before he had to put a stop to it. He had to admit he liked some of it.

She connected with them and talked for a moment before putting Strollo on the phone. The call put the Siragusas in a totally different light.

"Vincent, I'm sorry to disturb you, but Mildred and I need help, and we thought with your business connections you could guide us. In going through Dad's place we found a box. It must weigh near two hundred pounds. You know where Dad worked, of course. The stuff probably came from there, and it ain't lead."

Strollo was silent. What was the value of two hundred pounds of gold? Had to be over a million. . . .

"Who knows about this?"

"Nobody but Mildred and me."

Strollo did all he could not to sound harsh. "Keep it that way. If I'm going to help, it's got to be just the three of us. I assume you need someone to move it for you?"

"That's exactly it. We don't know where to go, and we're afraid if somebody finds out they'll take it from us."

"Okay. I got to be in New York day after tomorrow. Tell you

what, I'll see you then." He assured them, "Don't worry, I can handle this easy."

"Vincent, I can't tell you how much we appreciate this. We just didn't know where to turn."

Strollo brimmed with almost genuine feeling. "You did just right. Hell, that's what family's for, to help each other."

He knew precisely where he could sell the gold, and at a good price. Who could have believed it? A million dollars had just fallen into his lap. And there'd be no split with the family. This would be all his. Stiffing the Siragusas, of course, would be no problem. People like that asked to be taken.

After he hung up, he said to Rosa, "No problem, they just need some help in moving some junk the old man left. I'll do them this favor only because you've been on my back about them."

Rosa smiled in thanks and moved close to the table again, inviting his touch. This time, though, he was too preoccupied to notice. He was liking Miami more and more. It was bringing him all kinds of luck.

• C H A P T E R •
SEVEN

Strollo watched Flemming doing his electronic tricks to detect a tap on the phone or a microphone bug. First Flemming measured the line voltage for any drop, mistakenly believing that FBI taps still registered a voltage drop. He then located the junction boxes and found no bridging of pairs. There were no other lines into the condo from the box to carry out a microphone signal.

He used an RF detector to determine if any radio signals were emanating from Strollo's condo, which would indicate that a mike was using radio transmission rather than hard wire to transmit signals. Plus, he made a "just in case" visual check of places that a mike would ordinarily be hidden.

After three hours he told Strollo, "You're clean. All your voltage measurements check. There's no RF in any of the rooms. The junction box is clean, and I've made a visual check. I guarantee no tap, no bugs."

Strollo thanked him and asked that he come back each month to sweep, and Flemming agreed.

The moment the door closed behind him, Rosa rushed into the room announcing she had found the perfect house on Star Island in Biscayne Bay.

"Vinny, it's two-story, three bedrooms, three baths. Two-story is unusual for Miami, apparently. It's got a nice office for you. And the agent said the main living area is perfect Miami, no separate living room, dining room, family room, just what they call a great room. There's a pool and huge wooden-decked patio, and it's all screen-enclosed. The house is on deep water with a new dock. The realtor says it's a steal at six hundred and fifty thousand, and if we like it we'd better move, 'cause it won't last."

Strollo was less than enthusiastic, since he had not been the one to find it. "Sounds like a strange arrangement to me. What kind of furniture do you put in a room like that? What do you do if you have people for dinner?" He stopped short, seeing the wounded look on her face. "Okay, okay," he said, annoyed, "we'll go out tomorrow."

Strollo was saved from further discussion of the house by the phone ringing. There was no greeting. Iannello said, "It's here."

Strollo turned to Rosa. "I gotta go out."

Iannello was waiting outside the hotel when Strollo drove up. The package was dropped through his open car window, and he roared off.

When he arrived back at the condo, he put the package aside and prepared a very dry Sapphire gin martini, straight up. A sign of the joy of anticipation. He placed the long-stemmed glass of crystal-clear liquid off to his right, on the dining-room table, and pulled out the chair. He sat at the head of the table. With both hands he slowly tore open the flap of the brown envelope, removed the contents, and placed the envelope aside. He would burn it tomorrow.

Only after he had sipped his drink did he begin to examine the contents. There were eight certificates, two examples of each bearer bond. Strollo was familiar with securities, and these were excellent. If he hadn't known they were counterfeit, he would never have suspected them. Each had its own serial number, and each coupon had a corresponding number. The vignette was sharp and clear. All the colors were excellent. The whole bond was sharp, no fuzziness that he could see. Even knowing they were counterfeit, he could not detect a problem.

He needed to divulge the plan to Iannello so he in turn could inform Knight. It was time to discuss some of this with Magliocco. He might need some more people, since the rules had to be observed: he could have no personal involvement. There had to be a button between him and the scam.

He had just finished his martini and examination of the bonds when Rosa burst into the room and pounced on him.

"I want you to see the house, Vincent. The agent's free this afternoon and waiting for a call. We'll meet her there. I got directions."

He had to scramble to cover the bonds with the envelope, but she was so intent on delivering the news that she never glanced at what he had.

"Rosa! That's enough," he barked, still unsettled by her sudden appearance. "I got things to do. You don't come in here and just say we're going somewhere. We'll go when I tell you we go."

Rosa's excitement died, as if he had blown out the flame of a candle. Immediately she seemed like the old, fat, dumpy woman he had known for so many years. He paused, rubbing his fingertips irritably against his temple. He had to face it: he liked her better when she was exuberant. "Okay, Rosa," he said, "you win this time. I'll go see your house. But go a little slower, huh?"

Rosa couldn't have been more pleased. She leaned over and kissed him on the cheek. When he touched her hand on his shoulder, she gushed with enthusiasm. "Vinnie, thank you. You'll like it, you'll see."

The agent was at the house when they arrived, and Rosa introduced her as Pam Sumpter. Strollo devoured her in one glance. She was in her thirties, perhaps five foot five, blond, stylishly dressed with an excellent figure. Her eyes were an off shade of green and seemed to draw Strollo into them.

He held her extended hand overlong, and from that point on remained more interested in Pam than in the house. During the tour he stayed right with her, appreciating her, the way she walked, the way she stopped, almost posing on her heels. She was assured yet all woman. And he did like the house. Grudgingly he had to admit that it would suit him well. A security system was already installed. There was a suitable office. All he had to do was check out the neighbors. And it would be interesting to buy the house through Pam.

She interrupted his train of thought. "If you decided to make an offer, Mr. Strollo, how much would you be putting down?"

He knew that Pam was aware he'd been watching her through every room in the house. "There'd be no financing. I'd pay cash."

He saw her eyes light up. She was now becoming interested. Wealth talks.

Of course, she didn't know that he had no choice but to pay cash. He was a millionaire several times over, but he could never have filled out a loan application and withstood even the most rudimentary inquiry into his finances.

"Can you get me a list of neighbors, two houses on either side and across the street, with some background on them, like business and how long they've been here?"

Pam nodded, certain she had a sale. She had already calculated the commission, nearly $13,000. "Certainly, Mr. Strollo. I could have that for you tomorrow."

She would do whatever was necessary to keep this client happy. At the same time, though, she had to be careful not to alienate his wife. She moved closer to Rosa and put her hand on her arm, giving it a little conspiratorial squeeze. "Mrs. Strollo, you've made a wonderful find in this house. I'm sure you'll love it."

She turned to Strollo again, flashing an inviting look that she hid from Rosa. "May I ask what business you're in?"

He peered into her eyes again. "Investments."

"I see," she said, dropping her gaze. "I'll call tomorrow and drop off the list of neighbors, if you like."

Rosa had become silent. She sensed an undercurrent between her husband and Pam that made her uneasy. She had been hoping that now they had moved, he would settle down.

"No," he said, ignoring his wife entirely, "I'm going to be out most of the day. If you think it'd be ready about twelve or one, I'll stop by your office and pick it up."

He was looking for an excuse for a spur-of-the-moment lunch, Pam realized, and smiled. "It'll be ready by noon."

Rosa was quiet on the drive back, and Strollo knew why. He was not overly concerned. Rosa had always accepted his extra-marital activities, but part of this acceptance was conditioned on their unspoken agreement that he not flaunt them, and that she not know whom he was screwing. He felt he needed to smooth over any pique that she might have.

"Rosa, you did good."

Praise from her husband was rare indeed, and Rosa looked up in delight.

He continued, "The house is just right. If the neighbors check out okay, we'll sign a contract. I think I'll put you in charge of real estate from now on."

Rosa stammered her appreciation. "Vinnie, I'm so glad you liked it. I hoped you would. I looked at a lot of houses before I found that one."

Strollo saw his praise had had its desired effect. Now he just had to work on the moves that would get Pam in the sack.

Iannello was waiting at a side table in the Paddock bar when Hersch made his entrance at about five-thirty. He was wearing a new white silk sport coat, custom-tailored pink shirt, and burgundy tie. Not seeing Iannello at the bar, he was almost relieved. Then he noticed him at the table and headed toward him.

"Hey, Tony, did better last night. I'm only down a thousand."

Iannello made a mental note to talk to the guy running the game. He needed to keep Hersch a loser. Maybe about ten in the hole would keep him in line better.

"Told you, you're a natural with dice. Stay with it, you're on your way back. Now's the time to get ahead."

Iannello raised his hand, and the waitress brought over a dry Rob Roy. He saw Hersch was feeling good and decided to hit him with Strollo's proposition.

"I gave the stuff you dug up to my investor. He likes it. Even better, he likes what I told him about you. You could have a spot in this, and I kid you not when I say this project is shitting money. You get lucky enough to get asked in, you're gonna need the biggest shovel you can find to pick up the money that's gonna be dumped on you."

Hersch's index finger drew a circle on his icy glass. Was Iannello for real? he was wondering. Was there a possibility of this kind of money? Nobody put out that kind of money for nothing. What would he have to do?

All the while, Iannello was sizing him up. "He likes you 'cause he can see you're smart, a lawyer and an accountant. He also knows you can keep your mouth shut, and you know how to move."

Hersch was unsure what Iannello had in mind, and he replied, "You know me, Tony. If I can turn a buck, I'm interested."

Iannello nodded. The pitch was going just fine. "He's got something going on the side and needs some accounting work done quick. Here's an old balance sheet. Ain't no name on it, don't matter. He needs it redone so's the company's in the black, looks good, and could go to a bank. He needs an individual net worth statement of the guy who owns the company showing him worth maybe two mil."

Funny how these number-cruncher types could get hooked on a balance sheet, he thought. Hersch was looking the thing over like it was a centerfold.

"The company and investments in bearer bonds'll be his assets," Iannello continued, "together with house, car, furniture, all that good shit. It'll be certified by the guy who did this one, or a bullshit name, or maybe somebody you suggest. If it looks good, we'll let you put it in final form so's it can pass a bank."

He saw the flicker of alarm pass over Hersch's face, and he rushed to reassure him. "All we need is your know-how. You ain't never being connected with the reports."

Hersch hesitated, but only for a moment. He sipped his Rob Roy and nodded. "Yeah, okay, I can put something together that'll pass. I could have it for you tomorrow."

Hersch knew once he did this, he'd be in. Could he get out? But this was clean, no association to him.

He paused again over his drink, thinking, and then decided

to take the next step. "If he likes what I put together and we do a final, I assume it will be used to someone's financial advantage. Will I get to share in what it produces?"

Iannello smiled, both inwardly and outwardly. Hersch was his. "You bet. The man knows how to show appreciation. You come in for a piece."

The two Miami detectives, Morales and Fonseca, had just finished meeting with Donnelly. They got in an unmarked light tan Ford and pulled into traffic. Fonseca was driving, and he looked over, concerned.

"You don't think we gave him too much, do you?"

"No, it was just right. We've got to keep him interested, and our info's got to jibe with what they might get from their snitches."

"Yeah, but we don't want them grabbing any coke and screwing up the money."

"Hey, don't worry," Morales said, waving a hand breezily. "We gave him shit. Only said a couple tons was coming in and our guy wanted guarantees what was going to be done with his info before he took the step and gave us everything. Besides, they agreed to try for a simultaneous grab for cash from a previous load and the shit coming in. If they stay with that, we should be okay."

Fonseca was not satisfied. The deeper they got into this, the more he was sweating bricks. He looked straight at his partner and was about to speak when Morales shouted:

"Watch it!"

Fonseca looked back to the road and braked sharply, just avoiding the car slowing in front of them.

Morales swore. "Jesus Christ, what's the matter? You can't talk and drive?"

Fonseca ignored the remark. "Suppose the Fee Bees make a move on Zamorano on their own? Like they just step into him and say: 'Hey, we're with Morales and Fonseca, and we need to talk to you.'"

Morales laughed out loud and had trouble stopping.

"I'd like to be there to see that. Zamorano's going to say:

'Who? Who the fuck's Morales and Fonseca?' We already told them he wouldn't talk to no one but us. And he won't. He won't even talk to us."

With that he burst out laughing again.

"Besides, he don't even know us, so they'd get the right answer."

· C H A P T E R ·
EIGHT

The morning meeting with Iannello at the Leisure Hotel, which developed into a walk, went well. Hersch had been hooked, and the phony reports should be ready for inspection that evening. Strollo said just to sit on them, that he'd be away for a day or two, but they'd meet as soon as he got back.

Then he guided Iannello to a bench. He wanted to show him how they were going to use Knight, so he could begin preparing Knight for the scam and assessing whether he could carry it off. After an hour, Strollo was satisfied that Iannello knew enough to at least start the process. Now for the day's pleasure, Pam.

Strollo was pleased with himself. Things could not be going better. He was developing excellent business opportunities, a million in gold had fallen in his lap, and now Pam for lunch. "Perhaps two lunches." He laughed to himself. "Who knows, I might score right out of the box."

He parked at her office, went in, and said to the receptionist, "Mr. Strollo to see Ms. Sumpter." He realized he didn't know yet if she was married.

The receptionist smiled brightly. "Oh, yes, sir."

Strollo made a mental note that even the receptionist was pretty. Rosa had picked the right agency.

The girl continued, "Pam was expecting you, but was called to show a house. She left this envelope for you, with her apologies for not being here."

Strollo's mood suddenly turned sour. He took the envelope handed to him and walked out without a word. Was this real estate bitch rejecting him?

He tore open the envelope. There were two typewritten pages. One was the report on neighbors. The other began: "Dear Vincent."

He paused on the use of his first name. "I'm sorry I couldn't be here to say hello when you came by, but a man in investments would surely agree that business must come before pleasure. I hope we will soon be celebrating our closing. Pam."

He noted the "*our* closing."

Vincent was satisfied, and smiled. This one would be worth a small chase. A chase, he felt certain, he would win.

His next stop was a pay phone. He dialed the number for My Funny Valentine and was soon talking to Dominic Sciandra.

"Dom, this is Vincent. Can I call you in about ten on four?"

"Yeah."

The pay phone he had stopped at was in a convenience store, and Strollo bought a can of beer and some chips. He sat in his car waiting for the ten minutes to pass.

His watch finally signaled the time, and he glanced at the typewritten list of coded addresses and coded phone numbers he had in his wallet. He walked to the phone and punched up pay phone four in Manhattan. At the end of the second ring, Dominic answered.

"Dom, I got something good here, and I need the okay for two big projects and some more people. Part involves an order to the people we talked about before. I got reservations to come up if he wants to see me. I figure same time and place as before."

Sciandra replied, "I'll work on it now and be back to you on your number one at six, okay?"

"Got it."

At six o'clock, Strollo was at a phone in the Leisure Hotel.

When it rang he picked up instantly. Sciandra came right to the point.

"The weather in New York is good. Have a nice trip."

"Thanks, Dom."

Iannello drove to the Broadway Deli and found Knight seated at the counter. This time Iannello, with a broad smile, walked up and laid a friendly hand on his back. Knight involuntarily cringed as the hand moved toward him.

Iannello said, "I think I got us both off the hook. Let's talk."

Knight followed him to a table, and after the waitress got an order for coffee and a Reuben sandwich for Iannello, he began, "Something you got to understand when you're into my people for the kind of bread you are. Those people put pressure on me. They don't play games."

His bearish growl put heavy emphasis on the word *games*, and his eyes bored into Knight. The scene at the construction site flashed across Knight's mind, and he shuddered.

Iannello judged he was having the desired effect.

"I finally had a sit-down with the man, and I explained how you ain't trying to stiff nobody, that you just need a way to get even. So he says okay, that they got something coming that'll pay off the debt and give you some bread to get your business back on its feet. It's absolutely foolproof and legit. You couldn't get hurt."

Watching his prey, Iannello could see suspicion growing there. He could handle that. Knight had no place to go, and Iannello had the answers.

"I got to be honest with you, this is different. It involves a guy trying to get away from his wife, so we got to keep it quiet. We only got this chance because he stands to lose half or more in a divorce. We're going to be helping him hide his assets. You got no problem with that, do you?"

Iannello saw relief cross Knight's face; he had him. Strollo had been right. His respect for this take-charge New York *caporegime* was climbing.

Knight spooned sugar in the coffee the waitress had just

brought. "No, I got no problem with helping a guy in a divorce."

Iannello continued, "Okay. Here's how it's going to work. He's going to give you his assets, no strings. He's going to walk in and hand you about two million."

Iannello now saw a hint of greed flicker in Knight's eyes. He had his total attention. "With that kind of money, banking's going to be needed. You and your company are in lousy shape on paper, so there's no way you could walk into a bank with that kind of dough and not raise eyebrows."

Knight looked as though he was about to protest, but he quickly subsided. Iannello had him pegged, and he knew it.

"We got an accountant going to make you and your company look good based on the two mil you're getting. All you do is deposit the dough in a couple banks, and then draw it out slow and pay it when we tell you. You get your sixty thousand debt wiped out, and if all goes well, the man says you get fifty thou in your pocket."

There were a lot of questions anyone except a desperate Harold Knight would have asked. At the moment he was grateful to be alive, let alone have the chance to make a dollar. Iannello accepted his professions of gratitude, his promises to do whatever he said. Iannello had seen this before, get a guy down far enough and he'd lick crumbs out of your hand.

It was cold in New York, and Strollo was beginning to appreciate Miami for weather as well as economic opportunity. Rosa had driven him to the airport. There was no need for Iannello to know he was in New York. Jimmy Amari picked him up at La Guardia and informed him that the meeting would not take place at the social club, but at a restaurant on the Island where he was to join Don Carlo for lunch.

When they arrived, Strollo recognized the restaurant right off. Pappagallo was a favorite of Magliocco's. The restaurant was closed, but he and Amari were nonetheless admitted, and Amari sat at the bar, where some food had been laid out. Joey "Socks" Boccia, Magliocco's bodyguard, was already there, chowing down. Strollo followed the owner to a private room, where he found Magliocco eating calamari.

Magliocco did not rise for the usual embrace. He waved Strollo to a seat opposite him and gestured at the wine.

Strollo sat down cautiously. As he poured himself some wine and replenished Magliocco's glass, he was wondering if he had been smart to make this trip. A tic began at the outer corner of his left eye. A cool greeting—and this was decidedly cool—could portend real trouble.

Magliocco's full attention was on the calamari and a side dish of pasta. Starting to perspire, Strollo decided to take the initiative, without the usual preliminary pleasantries. "Don Carlo, I very much appreciate your consenting to see me, and I apologize for this inconvenience."

Magliocco continued eating as he spoke. "Don't trouble yourself. I am confident the business you bring me, so soon after leaving, is most important, and will justify this unexpected meeting."

That remark, and no offer of food as yet, told Strollo he was in deep trouble. The tic became more pronounced.

Without looking up from his plate, Magliocco continued, "It was my understanding you were going to remain quiet in Miami, look around, study the area, and at some future time we would consider business opportunities. The purpose in your move to Florida was to convince our enemies you had retired, and perhaps divert some attention from you and from the family."

Strollo realized he had not fully appreciated Magliocco's concerns. The move to Florida had not been just for his benefit. Strollo heat might become Magliocco heat. Strollo now understood Magliocco's frame of mind. He had got rid of his heat producer by sending him into exile in Miami, and now here he was back again, with some schemes that could produce more heat.

Strollo's mind raced. Magliocco's concept of the problem had to be altered, but subtly. "Don Carlo, the reason I traveled back here so quickly is that the opportunities for business are just as you had predicted. To delay would sacrifice considerable profit for the family. Also, things are arranged so that I will not appear anywhere near the business that I propose to you. There will be no reason for our enemies not to accept my retirement. If for some reason someone should become curious about my trip here, I am visiting my cousins, the Siragusas."

Strollo shifted in his chair, fighting off the tic and pulling at his French cuffs.

"My concern, above all, is not to bring trouble on our family. This trip was carefully planned to avoid any possible problem, and was undertaken only to further the business of the family. Your consideration for my welfare, in arranging my relocation to Florida, has bound me even closer to you, and I would do nothing to jeopardize the arrangements you have made for me."

At last Magliocco looked up from his plate and called out loudly, "Joey, where are your manners? Get Vincenzo a plate, some pasta, some calamari."

Boccia, in the adjacent room, muttered an apology, and a plate, silverware, napkin, and more food appeared with a waiter, who left as soon as he deposited it on the table.

Strollo breathed more freely. He had temporarily extracted himself from a difficult position. Now he had to prove the worth of his trip.

"Your grasp of the economy in Miami told me exactly where to look for opportunities. Iannello has at least two people we can use right now. One is a businessman and the other a lawyer-accountant. The paper that Cleveland has is fresh. Those that use it first will reap the greatest benefits and will have the least risk. To delay will be to invite trouble, for such a commodity will soon become known to our enemies."

Magliocco had to agree. "That is true. We intend to avail ourselves of this material here, in New York, but ..." He smiled. "You have moved faster than our people here."

Encouraged by this tacit approval, Strollo decided to lay out the rest of the plans. "We have located a construction project that we can take over and operate to our advantage. It's a condominium with provision for some offices on the lower floors. The location is excellent. It's called Towers of Light."

Strollo took a bite of calamari and warmed to his proposal.

"The original builders were ready to go when their financing dried up. We can pick up from where they left off. It's a ready-made opportunity. We should be able to skim millions. I'm confident we can get financing. We can use some of the money from the Cleveland paper to start this off, although I see very little money up front. I'm convinced we can get one hundred percent bank financing. The bank won't know it's a hundred percent, though. The accountant guy can arrange some balance sheets and investors that will impress the bank. I need only your blessing to go forward with this."

Strollo had not mentioned the gold. He had decided that was his, alone. In so doing he had broken one of the commandments of La Cosa Nostra. No member has private business. All business belongs to the family. The hierarchy always shares in every operation.

Magliocco's silence was nerve-racking. Only the sounds of eating and drinking filled the room. As Strollo waited for an answer, he chafed at the other man's slowness to respond. It was the conservatism of the old dons that was causing problems in the ranks. Bosses like Magliocco had made their money and didn't want to do anything that might rock the boat, Strollo thought. The younger buttons wanted theirs and were impatient just like him. A few of the old men had even been hit because they were holding down the Young Turks who wanted to make money. In fact, Strollo saw himself someday as capo of the family. As always, he was careful to mask this ambition.

Magliocco finally pushed his plate away. "Vincenzo, I understand your eagerness to create new opportunities for the family, but it must also be protected. My greatest responsibility is its protection and preservation. What you are proposing is feasible, but the timing is very bad. I cannot give my blessing to what you propose, but I will not forbid it. If you so choose, you may go forward on your responsibility. If any harm comes to the family as a result of these operations, I will look to you."

Strollo was surprised that Magliocco would openly give him this ultimatum.

The old man continued, "You may utilize some of our people, and the family will guarantee compensation to Cleveland. I trust it will not again be necessary for us to meet about this until you have successfully concluded it."

Strollo knew he was dismissed. He kissed the old man's hand and, rising, said, "Don Carlo, I will consider what you have said. If I do undertake this business, it will not be done lightly. You may be sure it will only be if I am totally confident of success, and absolutely assured that neither you nor the family will suffer, but will only profit from it."

Strollo turned and left, followed by Amari. He was shaken. He had never experienced an audience like that. If these deals blew up, he would be a dead man.

Hurriedly he shook off these thoughts. He had more pressing matters at hand: handling the Siragusas and their gold. For what was to come next that day he needed his friend Jimmy Amari. As they left the restaurant, Strollo said, "Say, Jimmy, I got a move that I need your help with. But nobody else in the *regime* can know about it. It's off the record."

Amari focused cold, expressionless eyes on Strollo. Their long friendship was such that he ordinarily would obey orders instantly, but this was an unusual request.

Strollo hastened to answer his friend's unasked question.

"My cousins, the Siragusas, want me to help them move some gold. That's right, these losers got about two hundred pounds. We're going to pick it up, and then we'll move it through our friend on 47th Street. I'll make the arrangements myself, Jimmy. I just need you to help me carry it and get it into Herman's place. Also, if any problem comes up, you'll be in a position to take care of it from this end."

They were walking to the car, and Amari stopped and turned to Strollo, who continued on a pace before he realized Amari was no longer in step with him. Strollo halted and turned, examining his old friend.

Amari was short and heavy, and he looked as if he perpetually needed a shave. His heavy eyebrows weighted his forehead and continued over the bridge of his nose. But it was his deep-set eyes that were his most distinctive feature. They were blue but a peculiar shade of blue. They were as cold as an iceberg.

Amari's voice was low, and Strollo had to strain to hear. "Vincent, I'll do what you ask, because your family and mine are like one. You are my son's godfather. But I ask you to think on this. This is business and belongs to *la famiglia.*"

Strollo put his hand on Amari's arm. "Thanks, Jimmy, I accept what you say. I'll consider it. I believe, however, the gold came to me outside of our business. I'm only using business contacts to move it."

Amari did not respond. He did not agree with Strollo, but for now he would keep his peace.

They got into the car in silence, and remained that way as Amari drove south to the Shore Parkway and Verrazano Bridge, crossed Staten Island, and got on the New Jersey Turnpike. The day was bleak and cold. The snow, piled along the roadways, was now more black than white.

Amari tried several times to engage Strollo in conversation, hoping to find a way to open a discussion about the gold being off the record. But after three short, disinterested answers, he fiddled with the car radio to fill the time. Strollo was examining and reexamining his position with Magliocco, and deciding and undeciding the direction he should take. And so the ride to Pennsylvania was a long one. They arrived toward nightfall and checked into a motel. Strollo called Peter Siragusa and went to dinner at their home, alone.

The dinner was obligatory, and Strollo did not enjoy it. He saw his cousins as common, unsophisticated hicks. Two plain, hardworking people who loved each other and their two children.

Strollo concentrated on explaining what would happen. "The gold has to be sold quietly and slowly, you see. I know people who can handle it. If it goes too fast, or not quiet, it attracts attention. People would ask questions, like where'd it come from? Your old man pay taxes on it? You going to pay taxes on it? Things like that. And pretty soon you won't have it."

They watched Strollo intently, absorbing every word.

"The way I do it, you'll have no worries. Just be patient. It can't go fast, and after a while I'll be able to slip the money to you through some business connections. Just leave it all to me."

Peter reached across the table toward Strollo. "Vinnie, I can't tell you how much Millie and I appreciate your taking the time to help us. We had no idea what to do with this, or which way to go. If you hadn't been there, I know we'd have gotten in all kinds of trouble over this."

Mildred nodded in agreement. "Petey's right. We didn't know which way to turn, and then we thought of you. You sure saved us. We want to do something real nice for your new grandson, and for you and Rosa."

Strollo wanted to laugh in their faces. "Thanks, but that ain't necessary. As I said on the phone, this is exactly what family's for."

He got away as soon as he could, and the next morning he and Amari were at the Siragusa house and loaded the trunk of gold into the car. Peter and Mildred had met Amari at the christening of Strollo's grandson, and greeted him warmly. Once the two had driven away, they shared broad smiles.

The ride back to New York did not seem anywhere near as long as the ride down. Having all that gold made a difference.

Herman Littman was not made. He couldn't be. He was not Sicilian, or even Italian. But he was as close to being made as anyone could be. He was one of the most trusted associates the Mafia had, and had been with the family for forty years. Herman owned a reasonably large jewelry-manufacturing outfit, Herman's Fashions, on 47th Street.

That afternoon Littman greeted Strollo and Amari warmly. A handcart eased the trunk into his office-workshop and then into his vault. After some conversation and an espresso, Strollo told Amari to drop off the rental car they had been using. Littman would take him to the airport when he was finished.

When they were alone, both went back to the vault and roughly weighed the gold and sampled it. Littman put the weight at 212 pounds and determined that the three bars they had tested were about twenty-four karats. With a radio playing loudly in the office, they put their heads together.

"Herman, I'm not asking your business, I know you can

move this, but we need to settle a couple matters. How much do I get, and where and when is payday?"

Littman rocked back in his chair. "Well, a troy ounce is at three eighty-five right now. I don't know whether all the bars are of the quality of the three we tested. I assume they are. This much gold will take some spreading around, and I can't get market, plus we have to figure my usual commission."

Leaning forward, his face close to Strollo's, he said, "I am gathering this is off the record, private business? I don't need an answer. You're a big boy. You take care of your end. I volunteer nothing. If I'm asked, I moved it for you. What you did with the money is your problem and whoever you owe."

Strollo swallowed hard but replied, "Fair enough."

Littman punched the keys of his calculator, and after a moment he said, "I expect you would realize between eight hundred and eight hundred and fifty thousand, perhaps a little more if I can make some good trades."

Strollo responded, "That's fine. We've done business before, and you know I trust you."

Of course, he did not trust anyone in money matters, but he had little choice in this instance. He continued, "I want the money deposited out of the country. How you move it out is your business. You've done that often enough. I want it in the Caymans. The account number's written on here. Use our phone code to get the right numbers. The name of the account you'll have to remember—don't write it down. Same with the bank. It's Cayman Bank of Commerce and Trust, the account is Epic Investments."

Littman smiled. "No problem. I'll use a wire transfer to Montreal from here and then from Montreal to Liechtenstein and then to the Caymans. I may move a part through the Bahamas, but don't worry, there's no way anybody will ever trace it."

The next morning, before meeting Iannello, Strollo went to a pay phone and called Sam Lonardo in Cleveland. Lonardo called him back on the pay phone about ten minutes later. Strollo picked up on the first ring.

"Hello, Sam?"

"Yeah, Vinnie. How you doing? Like what I sent you?"

Strollo answered, "Looks good. We might be able to move it. I hear you're looking for ten."

Lonardo said, "It's twenty, except to friends. Yeah, a volume deal, cash up front, to friends it's ten."

Strollo countered, "The people I'm with will guarantee payment. That's same as cash."

Lonardo hesitated. "How long before payment?"

"It'll take about a month to move it."

Lonardo agreed. "Okay. I'll front it for a month."

Strollo, ever seeking an edge, decided to try to negotiate the price as well. "We want a good load, five hundred of each. How about eight points?"

Lonardo was adamant. "No way, this stuff's fresh. You got a bargain at ten, and I wait a month."

Strollo pushed. "If it's ten, it's ten of market. Most are selling at discount."

Lonardo, an edge in his voice, replied, "Shit, you're in the wrong business. You need a table to sell crap at a flea market. This ain't no fucking flea market. This is top-line merchandise, and you're getting a hell of a break in price and terms as it is. Tell you what, you move this and I'll give you future orders at nine points."

Strollo grinned into the phone mouthpiece. He hadn't expected any better than ten points. That was rock bottom on quality, fresh merchandise.

"Done."

"How you want it?" Lonardo questioned. "Come up here and pick it up?"

Strollo wasn't sure. "I'll come back to you on that. Anybody coming down that could carry it?"

"Possible. I'll check. Call me tomorrow."

"Okay."

Now Strollo had to make sure that Iannello was doing his job. Knight had to be coached and primed. The banks had to be identified and specific officers targeted for treatment. Hersch had to have the documentation ready. He also had to be persuaded to front the construction project. He probably was going to have to work for Tony full-time.

Iannello arrived a little early, and Strollo nodded to him. He headed toward the small park near the hotel with Iannello following. It was another bright, warm day, and the snowbirds were out and about. Strollo saw two people on separate benches with aluminum sun reflectors around their necks, and for a moment he thought he was back in New York.

He selected an empty bench, and Iannello joined him. After some small talk, Iannello handed him a manila envelope. Strollo opened it and glanced at the contents. It was Hersch's audit material.

"I need to study these. I'll get back to you with any changes."

Iannello shrugged. "Yeah, okay, that ain't my specialty. I was impressed, but then I ain't never really studied anything like that before. Hersch says it's good, and with the right bullshit he could bank it."

"What about Knight?"

"He absolutely buys in. He bought that bit about the divorce. I think he actually believes it. He'll do whatever we want."

Strollo nodded, then set the envelope aside, as if that business was finished. Placing a hand on Iannello's arm, he turned him so they were looking each other full in the face. "Now, listen up. This is important. We need to select three banks, and Knight has to get to know somebody in loan approval, at least a vice-president. What's on the street about banks that are easy to deal with? You know anybody in a bank we can reach?"

Iannello thought for a moment. "I don't have a hook in any banks. I got two that I use for my book, but that's on the level of a couple tellers I take care of. I'd have to ask around for any friends with hooks." He looked away, ashamed to sound so small-time. Suddenly he straightened his back and his arm came up.

"Hey, I know. I got a couple guys in the car business! They've been telling me about two banks they deal with for dough to buy cars. Let me talk to them. There might be somebody a little bent in them banks."

Strollo began to raise himself off the bench. "Work on that and get back to me by tomorrow. The merchandise'll be here soon, and we don't want it to get stale. Also, feel Hersch out about full-time with us. We need to get started on the construction project."

"Okay, boss, you got it."

Parked a block away was a panel truck with signs identifying it as Pest Away, Inc. Through the roof vent a camera equipped with a long lens recorded the scene. Bill Baskin was about to make his first steps.

· C H A P T E R ·
NINE

Al was wandering about the office. He tried to devote at least an hour each day to this. It was a good break from the paperwork, but more important, it was what he called "management by walking around." He stopped and chatted with supervisors, agents, secretaries, and clerks. He asked questions and gathered opinions. Sometimes he gave suggestions.

The Miami FBI field office was staffed with 192 agents, and the case load was approaching 2,500. Although Al could not be conversant with all of those cases, he could keep tabs on the major investigations, and did so during his walks, speaking with both case agents and supervisors.

When he spotted Bill Baskin and Ken Stacy, the agents assigned the Strollo case, he said, "Hello, Ken, Bill. What's new on my favorite mafioso?"

Ken was the one to respond. "Nothing earth-shattering. SPIT is on him whenever they're free from more urgent matters. The New York CIs in the Magliocco family are saying now that Strollo may not be retired. They claim he was in New York meeting with Magliocco. We're trying to locate any airline travel for him. Also, we've subpoenaed his home-phone toll calls, but I wouldn't expect much there."

Al lowered himself into a chair in Bill's office. "Did they tell us the reason for this maybe meeting?"

Ken answered, "No, but they say Strollo asked for it, and Magliocco is a little pissed at him."

Al was intrigued. "Any reason for Magliocco being pissed?"

Ken shook his head. "That's all New York's told us. We've gone back and asked your questions, plus a few more. We requested that the CIs be instructed to find out more about Strollo."

Satisfied, Al stood up and was about to move to another office when Bill handed him an envelope, accompanying it with a wry grin. The photos had just been printed and were still warm from the dryer.

Laying a finger on the person next to Strollo, he said, "That's Tony Iannello. He is Magliocco family, but he belongs to Licata's *regime*. He's here alone, runs some books, shylocks, and is in at the tracks."

Al's curiosity was aroused. "Any educated guess as to what he might be doing with or for Strollo?"

"No. From what I know of them they have different action."

Al nodded. "That makes it all the more interesting. Tell me about the envelope."

Bill reached into the photo pile. "Here's a photo of Iannello passing it. It was a large legal-size manila envelope. Here you see him pulling some papers partway out. Looks like maybe a dozen or so sheets."

Al rubbed his chin, thought for a moment. "Okay, I know SPIT has got a number of assignments, and this is not top-priority. But whenever they have time, cover Iannello and Strollo. Since Iannello is probably doing the work, concentrate on him. Look for a violation we can hang a T-3 on if we need one. With Tony, gambling looks the easiest."

Al knew that without an informant inside Strollo's operation, a telephone tap or microphone installation under Title III of the Omnibus Crime Bill, would undoubtedly be necessary.

Bill handed over some other photos. "You might want to have a look at these. When Tony split, Strollo drove over to a real estate agency. He was only inside for a minute. SPIT made a pretext inquiry and found out he was asking for a Pam Sumpter, an agent for the company. He's probably buying a house. SPIT figured a real estate agent could be a good source, if that was the relationship."

Al examined the five photographs, of an attractive woman leaving the real estate office and walking toward a car, as Bill continued, "Not a bad looker, huh? Strollo like the ladies?"

Al thumped the top photo. "Let me know what you find out about her. Some of the Bureau wives are in real estate. See if any know her, and maybe they can even find out what Strollo's buying, if he is."

Al's interest in Strollo had to be taken in context with the 2,500 cases in the office that also had to be pursued.

The Strollo investigation was not a breaking case or, at this point, a major investigation. It was primarily an intelligence matter, to determine if Strollo was involved in criminal activity. Al was certain of the outcome. He had to be dirty.

Harold Knight had just finished the sports section of the *Herald* when his wife called, "Dinner's ready!" Brian and Celeste had been doing their homework and appeared from their rooms. Harold and the children sat at the round kitchen table as Connie brought over the last dish and joined them.

Dinner conversation started with schoolwork, extracurricular activities, and then Connie's day with her church group. Connie was on the Church Council and headed a women's club at the church.

As she talked, Knight watched her appreciatively. He was still in love with her. She was an attractive and, until one night a few months ago, a warm and responsive wife. They had been married eighteen years. And for the hundredth time he asked himself how the hell he had got into gambling and fooling around with other women. How come he had turned a good business into almost total financial ruin?

He swallowed hard as he recalled the night three months ago when Connie confronted him. He had just settled into bed when she sat on her side, facing away from him.

"Harold, I can't sleep in the same bed with you anymore. I've tried to ignore it, not believe it, but I just can't anymore."

He had stiffened, unsure how to answer. "What do you mean, baby? What's wrong?"

He could only see Connie's slumped back, looking defeated. Her head was down, and he could picture her hands loose in her lap. Her voice was low, holding back tears.

"The women, Harold. How many affairs have you had? Are they all one-night stands? Or do you stay with the same slut for more than one lay?"

He stuttered, "You're imagining things. There's no other woman. Where did you get this from? Some crazy gossip?"

Connie half turned and looked him in the eye.

"Don't lie to me, Harold. What you've done is enough. You've touched me with the same hands you've used to touch those whores. The same mouth that kissed them has been kissing me, and now you want to lay me just like you lay them. The dirt you've brought to my bed's enough! I want a divorce, and I want the children. I have the names of some of your whores and where and when you screwed them."

His eyes dropped, his defense collapsed. "Connie, don't," he said quietly, trembling. "I've got myself into a jam. The business is in bad shape. Yes, there have been some women. It's all part of this unbelievable mess I've made. But I love you, and I love the kids. Help me straighten this out. Don't leave. I'll stop. I'll do whatever you want."

Connie was softly crying. "No, Harold, don't try your sales pitch on me. You screwed up, not me. Don't ask me for help to clean up your dirt. You clean it up. If you can straighten yourself out, we'll talk about what, if anything, is left of our marriage. As of now I'm finished."

They had kept up appearances for the sake of the children until the final decision on divorce was made. The children had sensed strain between them, but so far normalcy had been maintained. He had not touched Connie since that night and had been sleeping on the day bed in their room. He had not immediately changed his ways, though. "Tomorrow" was always the day he would turn around.

He had finally learned. Iannello's assault had done it. The lesson had almost cost him his life and his family. He had stopped gambling. He stayed away from the Paddock, and had not had a date since.

He had made up his mind. He wanted his family back the way it was. He was going through with the deal. He could feel the love around the dinner table. This was what he wanted. He wanted Connie back. He wanted his children to respect their father.

Iannello was seated in the coffee shop at the usual time and spotted Strollo pulling up. He remained in his car, so Iannello walked out. As he drew close, he was motioned in by Strollo.

"We'll drive down to the beach and take a walk. Do you have what I asked for?"

"Yeah."

Within two minutes they were walking along a sidewalk with a hundred yards of beach to the east.

Iannello began, "I got your three banks. In two I got something of a rundown on a couple VPs. The other, I got a name, but don't know anything about him. None of these guys is bent, but the two I got a line on like to booze it up and party. They've been known to do favors for 'wine buyers.' Their names are Herman Frank at National Bank of the South and Lester Billings at Builders and Traders." He looked over to see how Strollo was taking this news, but the stony face betrayed nothing.

"A bank that's got a reputation for being loose is Cooperative National, and a VP there is John Meacham. I did get a name of a customer to use as an intro to him."

To their right a few bathers had ventured into the moderate surf. Strollo had his eye on a particularly fine young blonde as he said, "We won't know until we try. Get to Knight this morning. I want him in all three banks today, by tomorrow for sure. Give him copies of the new balance sheet for his company and explain that we're just fudging a little to make it easier to put the paper in the banks. Then point him toward the VPs with the program I laid out."

Iannello had never been involved in a scheme like this, and he was beginning to enjoy it. Scamming banks was a whole new level of operation. "You got it, boss."

They went back to the car, and after he was dropped at the hotel, Iannello went to the phone and called Knight.

"Harold, we're in business. It's what you been waiting for. Talked to the man, he says go. You're about to get even with us and make a buck. Now, listen, I'm going to drop off your new balance sheets. Don't worry about them. The bank is lending on the securities you bring in. The sheets just make you look good so you got a good up-front explanation for where the securities come from."

Iannello glanced through the glass panel of the closed phone booth door, a habitual check of the lobby for strangers, and then bent his head to the paper he had placed on the shelf under the phone.

"I'm going to give you the names and banks over the phone. I want you to call each of them now. Introduce yourself as a prospective new account and invite each to lunch until you get an acceptance for today. Set up lunch with the others for following days. But meet each one sometime today. Get personal with each. Follow what I told you before. Talk about family."

Whatever his faults, Knight was a smooth salesman. It was why his business had succeeded. He was able to talk to each banker on the phone, and made appointments for that day.

His lunch would be with John Meacham. He stopped by the bank at twelve forty-five for their one o'clock luncheon date, asked for Meacham, and after a few minutes was ushered into his office. Meacham was about fifty-five, a short, florid, overweight banker.

After introductions, Harold said, "I called you because of your good reputation with our mutual friend Lonny Watkins, and the esteem in which I find you are held by the banking community. I need a man like you to protect some of my investments, and I think after we get to know each other we can do some business."

He drew an envelope from his jacket pocket. "When you get a chance, you might want to have a look at this recent audit of my company. There's also some stuff in there on my personal position. I'd appreciate it if you'd sort of keep that information to yourself. Don't want curious folks knowing my business. I'm sure you understand."

Meacham took the proffered envelope. "Certainly do, Mr. Knight. It'll stay here in my personal file."

Knight rose. "Good. Call me Hal, by the way. Ready for some lunch?"

The Paddock Club was the destination. Meacham was impressed by the surroundings, and by the fact that everyone greeted Knight by name. The lunch was convivial, expensive, and convincing. By the end of the meal, Meacham, with two martinis and three glasses of wine, felt Knight was a solid guy, and he was anticipating congratulations for landing this wealthy client.

When he arrived home that evening, Meacham's greeting was most unusual. His wife was waiting at the door, which she never did. Even more unusual, she was smiling broadly.

He hadn't even said hello when she asked, "Who's Hal Knight?"

Meacham was perplexed. "A new client I met today. Why? Where'd you get his name from?"

His wife led him into the living room. "He sent me these—two dozen long-stemmed roses, with this card."

Meacham read: "For a lady I am most anxious to meet. In appreciation for John's concern and willing assistance in the problems I bring to him. Hal Knight."

His wife said, "John, that's just the most thoughtful thing anybody's ever done for us. He must be a real gentleman."

Over the next few days, Knight lunched with both of the other bankers, and each lunch went as well as the first. Within three days, Knight had opened an account at each bank. The accounts, as he put it, were not large, since he was in the process of transferring some of his assets. Iannello had given him three cashier's checks for ten thousand dollars each.

Strollo had instructed Iannello to park his car in garage number four on the top level at the Miami Airport. He was then to go to the passenger paging desk and page Peter Finch. When "Finch" appeared, Iannello swore he'd have recognized him without an introduction.

Finch introduced himself as Joe Lonardo, Sam's nephew. Both walked over to garage number four, and Lonardo parked his car by Iannello's, so the trunks were at right angles to each other. Five cardboard boxes moved from Lonardo's trunk to Iannello's, filling it to the point he had to force the lid closed.

Once Iannello got home, he followed Strollo's instructions and, wearing surgical gloves, clipped the next year's coupons from the bonds. As he did this, he divided each issue into three batches. The bonds were, for the most part, in sequential serial number order, and so the listing was fairly easy.

The job nevertheless took two days. Next he bought three of the largest suitcases he could find and packed the bonds in each case along with a copy of the typed bond list for that case. The suitcases were delivered to Knight's business, and he typed the lists Iannello gave him and returned the handwritten ones to him. Knight then called each of his banker friends, using virtually the same pitch, which had been scripted by Strollo.

"Lester, this is Hal Knight. Finally getting my act together. You may recall I mentioned moving some of my assets? Well, I made arrangements for some bonds to be taken out of a trust account, and I'd like to ship them to you by armored car."

The voice on the other end sounded impressed. "Sure, just let me know when they're coming in, and we'll set up a custodial account."

"I called Wells Fargo today, and they said they'd deliver them tomorrow."

"Okay, Hal, I'll be on the lookout for them. How many will be coming in?"

"I'll have a list delivered by messenger today. There's six hundred and seventy bonds, market value about six hundred and fifty thousand."

The psychology of this operation was a source of personal pride for Strollo. Cutting off a year's interest coupons would ensure that for the next year the bank could not submit them for payment and have the bonds detected as counterfeit. And he regarded the delivery of the bonds by armored car as a stroke of genius. There was no better way to emphasize value—much more authentic than lugging in a suitcase full of bonds. Now the bonds would just sit in the bank. No one was asking for anything . . . yet.

As other cases permitted, Bill continued his coverage of Strollo. Today, he was briefing Al on the riddle of Pam Sumpter, together with some of Iannello's activities.

"Pam Sumpter, age forty, lives alone, divorced, son age twenty, in the service, Marines. Real estate agent since her divorce ten years ago. Ex-husband in New York, editor for a publishing house. She has no contact with him. Does very well in real estate, in the President's Council each year for multimillion-dollar gross sales. She's popular with men, dates widely and often. No steady. The house she is selling to Strollo is on Star Island. He's paying almost asking price, six hundred and forty thousand. Cash." He glanced up and shared a knowing look with his boss.

"He's been by the real estate office trying to see Pam a couple of times. She apparently avoided him for a while, but our best information is she's at least had lunch with him. Closing on the house and move-in are set for next week. The impression we get is that he's interested in her."

Al asked, "Should we try an approach? Maybe we could use her for a shortcut and get some quick answers."

Bill advised caution. "I think we should wait a bit. See if Strollo's looking for something other than a night in the sack."

At that point, Ken picked up the briefing. "We've identified three of Iannello's books and know how he accepts wagers through call forwarding at the Leisure Hotel. The hotel coffee shop is a gathering place for every bad guy in the area. If it's stolen, you can buy it there. If it's not stolen, you can arrange for it to get stolen." He frowned and waved a hand, as if to say, Where are the locals on this?

"In addition, a main base of operation for Iannello is the Paddock Club. He's got a comp membership and has free run of the place. Tough for us to get in, but we did. Whenever we can, we cover him there. We're working on identifying people he spends time with, and they'll be checked out."

Ken flipped the pages of his notepad.

"We could go up on a tap on his three books with a little more work. The Bureau won't authorize a mere bookie tap anymore, but probably would if the target is Strollo. I think we'd spin off from bookies to Iannello in the first couple days and then probably pick up Strollo. Whether we could spin off on him, I can't say."

Bill took over from Ken. "In our limited coverage of Strollo we've noted he uses pay phones a lot, and receives calls at some. We're compiling a list. First impression is that he's got designated phones he communicates from. If this pans out, we may be looking at an intercept on some pay phones. That's about it for now."

Al smiled his appreciation, touching Bill on his arm.

"Good report. I think we're making progress. Let's consider an approach to Pam if you think it might succeed. And the payphone thought is interesting. We may have trouble with probable cause for an intercept of the pay phones unless we get a good informant who can tell us about the use of the phones, or we develop his use of them on a separate intercept. Any idea what he and Tony are up to?"

Bill answered, "No. So far we haven't developed anything that even comes close to answering that. As we come off Tony and start surveilling his associates, we may come up with answers."

A week later, Strollo closed on his house and moved in. That very day, Harold made an identical scripted call to each banker.

"Herm, buddy, this is Hal. Say, you remember those bonds Wells Fargo delivered and you're holding for me?"

"Yeah, sure do. They're nice and safe in the vault."

Knight continued, "Got an opportunity for a short-term investment, like about six months. A little venture capital, ought to pay real good. I hate to sell the bonds, because I only need the money for about six months, but my cash is committed right now. Guess I want my cake and want to eat it too. You figure you could lend me about five hundred thousand dollars for six months using the bonds as collateral?"

"Hell, yes. They're good as gold."

• C H A P T E R •
TEN

Morales had just pulled the completed report from the type-writer when the "hello" phone rang. It was listed to a fictitious person and address, and was used by informants to contact the officers. The Miami Narcotics squad room was empty, since everyone but Morales was staging a raid on a crack lab. He had begged off, saying he was anticipating an important contact from a CI, which was the truth.

He picked up on the first ring. "Hello?"

In Spanish, a low voice said, "Seven twenty-nine."

"Be there shortly."

He left the office and hurried out to the multilevel garage, where he quickly found his unmarked car and drove east to the Omni Hotel a few blocks away. It was a massive white stone mirror-windowed complex of hotel, upscale shops, and restaurants. He pulled into its garage and hurried to the elevator.

He first descended to the automobile entrance lobby, attempting to detect a surveillance. From there he took an escalator to the spacious main lobby, where he walked about pretending to admire the marble walls and floor, while really trying to detect any interest in him. Next he chose an elevator filled with people, entered, and stood off to the side near the door. As the door closed, he reached out a hand, triggering the electronic eye, and stepped out. He walked across the hall to another elevator, got in, and waited until the elevator was moving before he punched number nine.

Finding himself the only one getting off on the ninth floor, he quickly walked to the stairwell, went down to the seventh floor, and knocked at room 729.

The knock was answered in Spanish. "Yes?"

"It's me."

The door opened on an attractive room with a king-size bed, the covers of which had been partially drawn back for a nap. Two windows looked out on the glass-smooth waters of Biscayne Bay. The occupant of the room was a small man, thin and wiry, balding but sporting a huge black mustache. He was dressed in a light blue long-sleeved guayabera and tan pants. In his right hand he held a MAC-10 with a silencer. Morales took no notice of the gun as he entered. The man shifted the gun to his left hand, and they silently shook hands. The occupant closed the door and bolted it.

Morales advanced to the dresser, where there was a bottle of Chivas Regal with ice and glasses. As he began to pour himself a tumbler of whiskey, he glanced up, and with a crooked smile he said in Spanish, "Well, Pablo, is this it?"

Gilberto Fernandez, nicknamed Pablo, was a member of the Ochoa group in Miami and worked several rungs under Enrique Zamorano. He laid the MAC-10 on the table by the window and sat next to his gun sipping a whiskey, regarding Morales for a few seconds before he answered.

"Yes, I am told the merchandise is here, two tons, and the money from the last shipment should have been gathered together to move."

Morales asked, "Do you know where the money and the dope are?"

"No. Zamorano is very close-mouthed. The person I talk to has not been told. I am sure it is here, however. The coke is hidden in four trailers loaded with goods from Venezuela. They should be unloaded within a day or two and then moved to a location where the coke can be removed."

Morales sat in the second chair at the table and took a long pull on his scotch. He looked closely at Pablo. "Then we have to do it the hard way?"

"Yes."

He sighed, "Okay, you have to let us know when and where."

"Tonight, after one. He will be with his girlfriend, Teresa."

"Can you get us in?"

"I have a key. Her sister is one of my girlfriends. I borrowed Teresa's key from her and made a copy." He handed it to Morales.

The policeman gulped his scotch and rose to leave. "Be careful, my friend. Be with people tonight. In a few days all will be well."

Pablo put down his glass and reached for the MAC-10 as he rose to escort Morales to the door and see it locked again.

Morales hurried back to the Narcotics office and called Steve Donnelly at the FBI. After a long conversation he paged his partner, Jorge Fonseca; they needed to get together at once.

Steve, after receiving Morales's call, rushed to the ASAC, and with him went into Al's office. Al was engrossed in paperwork and looked up at their entrance.

"This is it!" Steve said excitedly. "Zamorano just told the cops there's two tons of coke here. We'll have the location within days, if not sooner. He'll also be able to tell us where the money due Medellín is located. We need to gear up. I suggest a couple standby crews, since we may not have a lot of lead time, and active surveillance on some of our known players as backup."

Al pushed aside the report he'd been reading and took off his glasses. "Sounds good. Tell me exactly what you've got."

"Morales called just a few minutes ago. Zamorano told him there's two tons of coke concealed in four over-the-road trailers. They also are carrying goods from Venezuela. When the goods are unloaded, some of Zamorano's people will pick up the trailers and take them to a warehouse, where they'll remove the coke. Zamorano will tell us when and where, and we'll grab the coke and everybody in sight."

Steve glanced to his superior for approval, but Al merely asked, "Anything else?"

"Yeah. Not only do we get the coke, but Zamorano will feed us the location of the books for the Ochoa group and locate their money cache for us."

"When do you anticipate this happening?"

"At about the same time as we hit the dope."

"Okay. Keep in close touch with Zamorano. Try to meet with him if you can so you can get straight unfiltered info from him." Turning to his ASAC, Terry Washington, he said, "Anything to add?"

"No. Looks like a great shot at the Ochoa group."

Al replied, "I agree. Let's give Steve everything he needs."

The night showed only the sliver of a moon. Morales and Fonseca were parked in the street, watching the third-floor windows of Teresa Fuentes. They had seen Zamorano enter with her earlier in the evening. The building was an old Art Deco hotel just off Collins Avenue on South Beach, recently refurbished into condominiums.

At one-thirty the lights went out. Still they waited, sometimes conversing quietly about trivial things, avoiding discussion of what was to come. They knew what had to be done. They had planned it for weeks. Discussing it now, just before they were about to do it, might somehow affect them, even make them lose their nerve.

At four, both quietly left the car and, wearing rubber-soled shoes, walked across the deserted street to the silent building. Fuentes carried a black nylon overnight bag in his left hand. His right was inside his blue nylon windbreaker, holding a 9mm semiautomatic with a silencer. Both wore latex surgical gloves.

Morales approached the brightly lit main entrance to the salmon-and-white stucco building and, using the key Pablo had given him, opened the door. The foyer was a deep pink imitation marble with planters along the walls leading to the elevator bank. They took the elevator to the third floor and quietly opened Teresa's door.

Once inside, they relocked the door and began looking for the bedroom. Only a narrow beam of light escaped the four pieces of tape that masked most of the flashlight lens. The foyer opened onto a living-dining room, a tiny kitchen off to the left. The bedrooms appeared to be off the living room. The first was empty. As they approached the second, they heard the wheezing of the corpulent Zamorano.

The bedroom door was open and the room was dimly illuminated by a night light in the adjoining bathroom. They could make out a king-size bed with two figures, one very large on the right and a small one on the other side. There was a large dresser against one wall and a door next to it which was probably a closet. Nightstands flanked the bed.

Fonseca put his bag on the floor just inside the bedroom door. His pistol was now out and ready. Both slipped into the room. Morales's hand swept the wall by the door, looking for a light switch. When he found it, he motioned to Fonseca, who approached the bed. In the dim light his free hand swept the nightstand next to the sleeping Zamorano and found a gun, which he pushed into his waistband. He now took his badge, which had been clipped to his belt, in his left hand and waved to Morales. The lights burst on.

A pink satin sheet covered them both. Neither stirred at the glare of the lights, and Morales quickly moved toward Teresa as Fonseca prodded Zamorano with the muzzle of his gun.

In a low voice Fonseca announced in Spanish, "Zamorano! Police! You're under arrest."

Both came awake instantly. Teresa's scream was stopped by Morales's hand.

"Quiet, little one. No need to be afraid. We're the police. Just stay where you are. Be quiet and you have no problem."

Teresa was a very small girl, only about nineteen or twenty years old. She could not have weighed more than a hundred pounds. Her large luminescent eyes were wide with fright, and she trembled under Morales's hand. He slowly removed it and she seemed to relax a bit.

Zamorano said nothing. He stared at Fonseca, waiting to be shot. Finally he said, "What do you want?"

Fonseca smiled. "Nothing, my friend. Just you. We have a warrant for your arrest. We get your clothes; we get you dressed; you go downtown; you get booked and your lawyer gets you out on bond. Just do what you're told and it's that easy."

Zamorano swallowed hard, not sure. But he had no choice. "My clothes are on the chair."

Morales looked down at Teresa. "Little bird, there is no problem, but we must be sure there are no weapons. Stay still."

He swept off the sheet, admiring the slender naked figure revealed beneath. He pulled her pillow to the floor. Fonseca did the same with Zamorano's pillow. Zamorano lay on his back. The fat seemed to be rolling off his body in waves with each wheezing breath of air. Fonseca stopped himself from asking how Zamorano could get close enough to a girl to screw her. Instead he reached over to the chair and threw Zamorano his clothes.

The drug captain struggled into his clothes and then stood with great effort. Fonseca tried to cuff him from behind, but his wrists would not meet at his back, so he cuffed him in front. The bracelets of the handcuffs were fully extended, and even then cut into the fat on his wrists. Both officers led him out of the bedroom and into the dining area, where they seated him at the table.

Morales said, "Just sit and be quiet. My partner's going to search the bedroom and talk to Teresa for a minute."

Zamorano was recovering some of his courage, and he snapped, "She doesn't know anything, and she won't talk to you anyway."

"I'm sure you're right, but the book says we've got to try."

Fonseca went back in the bedroom. Teresa had pulled up the satin sheet and lay there looking at him. When he closed the door, she became apprehensive, but he smiled at her disarmingly.

"Sorry, honey, but I've got to look around and talk to you. Cover yourself with the sheet if you want, but get out of bed so I can check it carefully."

She grimaced with displeasure but pulled the sheet up to her neck. Swinging her legs over the edge of the bed, she stood up, bringing the sheet around her, her back to Fonseca. In a blur of motion he looped his right arm around her neck and pulled

with his other hand to block the blood flowing through the carotid arteries. Her hands went up to grasp his arms in a futile
attempt to pull them away. The sheet fell to the floor. She was
unconscious in seconds.

He relaxed his hold and lifted her onto the bed, thinking
how much he would enjoy that young body under different circumstances. Regret at what was to come next flooded over him,
and he sighed deeply.

Retrieving his bag, he opened it and took out an oversize
plastic raincoat and plastic boots, which he put on. He drew a
hunting knife with a razor-sharp blade from its sheath. He
looked down at her. She looked like she was asleep. She was so
tiny, almost childlike. He shuddered, then, turning his head so
he was not looking directly at her, he slit her throat.

He paused and breathed deeply several times, trying to
steady himself. Then, grimacing, forcing himself, he looked at
her. The cut had almost severed her head from her body. The
wound was wide and deep, and blood was flowing onto the bed.
His hands and arms and the side of his raincoat were splattered
in blood from the initial spurting of the carotid arteries.

Again averting his eyes as much as possible, he steeled himself and proceeded to carve her body until the thing on the bed
took on the appearance of a butchered animal.

When he finished, he took a kilogram of cocaine from the
bag and broke it open, throwing the powder about the room.
Then he walked to an uncontaminated corner of the room and
removed his coat and boots, placing them in a plastic bag. His
hunting knife was wiped clean with a towel, and both knife and
towel went into the plastic bag. He stripped off the bloody
gloves, disposing of them as well, and then the plastic bag went
into the nylon case. He put on a fresh pair of surgical gloves.

Fonseca surveyed the scene of his butchery and winced. He
had killed twice before in "rips" of druggers, but never like this.
He should have insisted that Morales do this. Now that it was
over, the scene would be forever seared in his memory. He
picked up the bag, closed his eyes, and rushed out of the room,
slamming the door shut.

His face was white and drawn, and there was a tremor in his hand as he entered the dining area.

Zamorano saw his distraught appearance and began to struggle to get up. Frightened and excited, he squealed, "What happened?"

Morales restrained him, saying quietly to Fonseca, "You okay, pal?"

Fonseca stopped and got hold of himself, taking a deep breath. His brutal side finally returned. "Your little bitch kicked me in the nuts. All I wanted was what you get. Fuck her. Let's go, partner."

They hoisted Zamorano out of his chair and walked out of the building to their car. Morales drove west but did not stop at the Miami Police Department or the county jail. He continued on to a warehouse district on 107th Avenue.

Zamorano started getting nervous.

"Hey, where you guys taking me?"

Morales grinned into the rearview mirror. "FBI's got a special office out here. They want to talk to you before we book you."

Within minutes they arrived at a warehouse that had a small office in front with a street door and a garage door next to it that opened electronically. Morales activated it and pulled the car in. The door closed behind them.

The warehouse had a high ceiling and cinder-block walls painted white. There was a small boxlike room in a corner in the rear of the open area. It was to this room they now dragged a resisting Zamorano.

He screamed, "You guys ain't cops! What're you doing? I can pay! Let me go, I'll set things right for you."

They shoved him into a corner, and he collapsed on a stool there. Morales shut the door. There were no windows.

Then he said, "Scream your head off. No sound can escape here." Smiling evilly, he poked a finger into Zamorano's fleshy chest. "We want to know where the coke is and where the money is. We want both."

The doper was outraged. "Who the hell are you guys?

Ochoa'll feed you your balls when he finds out what you're doing. Now let me go and we'll forget this."

Morales's smile turned ugly. "Fat man, you tell us now or we're going to skin you just like a fat rabbit."

He reached into Fonseca's bag and took out the hunting knife. Eyes widening in horror, Zamorano squeezed himself into the corner, turning to show them only his back. Morales sliced down with the knife, cutting clothes and fat. Zamorano screamed.

"Okay! Okay! Whatever you want!"

Morales moved back a step and said quietly, "The coke?"

"It's in four trailers, false front. Tomorrow"—he caught himself—"no, today, the trailers'll be at Southern Forwarding on Tamiami Trail."

"What happens there?"

Zamorano was panting; his eyes scrunched against the pain. "Half a dozen guys are there to unload the shit."

"And the money?"

Zamorano looked up fiercely at this, but Morales raised the knife in warning.

"It's being counted now and checked. I'm supposed to be there tonight to give a final check on the figures."

"Where is 'there'?"

"A stash house."

"Where?"

The fat man looked up in pleading. "Ocha'll kill me if I lose that money."

"I'll kill you right now if you don't tell me."

Morales stepped forward, and the knife came up this time, slicing Zamorano's shirt front and the rolls of fat under his chin.

Clutching his neck, feeling blood running freely, he screamed in fright and pain. "Okay! It's in the Redlands! It's a nursery that raises fruit and palm trees, Avocado Acres."

"How many people are there?"

"Four."

"Shooters?"

Zamorano was beyond calculating odds, and he blubbered, "One. The other three are counters."

"The counters armed?"

"Yeah, everybody's got a MAC-10."

"How much is there?"

"Probably ten million."

Fonseca exhaled loudly.

A crooked grin spread across Morales's face. "Okay, Enrique, you're doing good. You take us there and you're finished with us. All we want is the money. I can't help you with Ochoa, but that's for another day." He regarded the trembling doper and snorted. Squealed like pigs every time.

"Now, one more question. Give me the address of another stash house you've used for counting. Any one."

"6010 South West 168th Street, a private house."

"Anybody there?"

"Yeah, two guys."

"House dirty now?"

"No."

Morales nodded in satisfaction as he turned to Fonseca. "We got it made, pal."

Zamorano was bandaged, securely tied, and left in the corner of the locked room. While Fonseca stood guard in the warehouse, Morales left to secure clean clothes for Zamorano for the night's work. First, though, he would head for the FBI office.

Any remorse about Teresa disappeared as Fonseca thought about the millions that were just within his grasp. Everything was going just as Morales had said it would. They'd walk away with the money right under the feds' nose. Nobody would even know it had happened. Sure, there'd be a bunch of dead dopers, but that was par for the course in Miami.

Donnelly, Washington, and Morales gathered in Al's office. As Morales slumped into one of the chairs facing the coffee table and sofa, Al remarked, "You look tired. Tough night?"

"Long night." Morales smiled as the work of that night vividly came back to him. Al read the smile as one of pleasure at a job well done. And so it was.

"My partner and I have been up all night trying to chase down Zamorano. The guy's paranoid. Afraid of shadows. We had half a dozen meets set up, and he kept breaking them because he was so scared. We finally got with him an hour ago. My partner is seeing him out of the area—from a distance."

Morales accepted the *café cubano* with double sugar handed him by Donnelly.

The three FBI agents, all standing, looked at Morales eagerly, expectantly. He smiled expansively and waved a hand.

"I guess you guys want to know what happened. We got the location of the load and the counting house."

Steve's face lit up, and he slammed a fist into his palm. "Goddam!" he shouted.

Al put his hand on Morales's shoulder. "Good work. This could really hurt them. What do you have?"

"Two tons of coke at a place called Southern Forwarding off the Trail. It's being broken out of false compartments in four trailers and will be distributed from there tonight. I can swear to the search warrant for the place." Al's eyes were gleaming at the thought of that large a bust, just as Morales had figured.

"Also there's about ten mil at 6010 South West 168th Street. Again, I can do the search warrant, and we can hit them when we hit the coke."

Steve interrupted excitedly, "Al, surveillance of those spots so they don't move anything before we're ready?"

Morales said, "According to Zamorano, they're supposed to stay put."

Al concurred. "Okay, Steve, do it. If we see anything being moved, take them away from the spot and take them down. Let's get all the detail we can from Cesar and then put together two groups for simultaneous raids."

Morales sipped his *café cubano* and offered, "Jorge and I would like to go with you to the counting house. We've seen dope before, but never this much money."

Al replied, "You got it. Let's do the warrants. While they're being typed and the troops are being briefed and deployed, you get some rest."

The raids were set for eight o'clock and went off without a hitch. Al led the group at Southern Forwarding, and the bust yielded the two tons of coke and six arrests. The raid on the house came up dry, but both occupants were DEA fugitives.

Morales and Fonseca, at 168th Street, stood with grave expressions afterward.

Morales said, "Steve, I don't know what happened. We need to get back with Zamorano and try to figure this out."

He hesitated and then with an accusing stare he asked, "You're sure they didn't make the surveillance like the time at Cocoplum and manage to clean out the money? It's obvious the place is a counting house. There's three money-counting machines in there."

Donnelly shook his head. "I agree it's the counting house, but nothing left here and they didn't make the surveillance."

Fonseca shook his head, as if mystified. "No question the info was on the money. After all, we got the dope just like he said. And we got the counting house just like he said, but we're missing the cash and records."

"I agree," Steve said. "You need to contact Zamorano."

"Okay. We'll be in touch." As they left a mournful Donnelly behind, the two had all they could do not to burst out laughing. "What a fucking clown."

Both officers headed back to their warehouse. Zamorano, who was stiff and hurting, was given a hurried run to a toilet. After he was cleaned up and dressed, Morales forcefully instructed him in his role for the evening.

By ten o'clock, they were pulling up to the electric gate in front of Avocado Acres. Morales was driving and Fonseca was on the floor of the backseat. Each officer had a department twelve-gauge Remington 870 pump shotgun and their side arms. Fonseca also had the gun he had taken from Zamorano.

Zamorano reached through the open car window for the phone at the gate and lifted the handset from its cradle. A metallic voice came through the earpiece. "What do you want?"

"This is Zamorano. Open the gate."

The tone of the voice became instantly respectful.

"Yes, sir, boss. I'll put up the dogs and open the gate in a minute."

Zamorano was on edge, trying to decide what to do. Should he warn the people inside? Could they take down these two? But even if they did, it was a sure bet the cops would unload on him first. For now he had to do as he was told. He'd look for an opportunity to surprise them and kill them.

The gate buzzed open, and the car entered. A hundred yards ahead they could see the lights of a low house. When they arrived, the guard, a MAC-10 slung on his shoulder, came over to open the car door for Zamorano. When he had the door open, the door handle in his hand, Fonseca leaned out of the open rear door window and put the barrel of the shotgun in his face.

"Freeze. Not a sound or I'll blow your head off."

The guard's eyes focused on the huge hole that was the barrel of the shotgun. Morales quickly took his MAC-10 and bound his hands behind him with plastic cuffs.

The four of them, the two in back nudging the two in front, walked up to the front door of the house. Entering, they found themselves in a living room. It was large and furnished with a sofa, some overstuffed chairs, a big-screen television, and three long tables. Seated at each table was a man stuffing currency into the holder on the top of the money-counting machines. The machines whirred and spat out the currency in a pile as wheels in the face of the machine totaled the number of bills counted. Scattered about the room were cardboard packing boxes full of money.

Morales yelled, "Police! Freeze!"

The men stopped. Turning their heads only, they saw the two shotguns, the guard, and Zamorano.

While Morales held them with the shotgun, Fonseca bound their wrists with plastic cuffs. They gathered up the guns and threw them into the car trunk.

The guard and the three counters were forced to kneel in a bedroom facing a wall. Their ankles were bound and the rope attached to their wrists so they could not stand.

The steel handcuffs were taken off Zamorano and he was bound with plastic cuffs, but he was shoved into the backseat of the car. He protested, "Why am I in the car? Leave me with—" before Fonseca taped his mouth.

The boxes of cash filled the trunk of the car, and two of them had to be put in the backseat. After the car was loaded, Fonseca handed his partner Zamorano's gun and said, "Your turn."

Morales took the gun and walked into the house. In the bedroom he shot each man in the back of the head.

When Zamorano heard the shots, he began bucking wildly against his bonds. Now he knew what was coming.

Morales returned to the car, and they roared down the driveway. Fonseca opened the gate with the remote switch taken from the guard, and it closed automatically as the car tripped the exit switch. After about twenty minutes of driving on dirt roads, they stopped at the edge of a large tract of the Everglades. Before them was the shallow embankment of a large pond. It took both of them to heave the struggling, kicking Zamorano out of the car.

They laid him on the edge of the embankment, and Morales began making rapid incisions with the knife. Zamorano's eyes bulged in pain and terror. He screamed through the tape. After three or four deep gashes they rolled him down into the black water and walked away.

Within seconds they heard the water boil with the thrashing of alligators. A fourteen-foot bull pulled Zamorano under the water and held him until he stopped moving. Then it wedged Zamorano's body in the roots of some trees where it could find him later. It liked its meat well aged.

• C H A P T E R •
ELEVEN

She slid in under the steering wheel of the Cadillac, closed the door, and adjusted her body to a comfortable position as she attached the lap and shoulder belts. A turn of the ignition key brought the engine to life, and a glance at the electronic controls told her the air conditioner was set at seventy-eight degrees. She put both hands on the steering wheel, but she made no effort to put the car in gear. She just sat, looking vacantly through the windshield, deep in thought.

Pam was assessing what, if any, relationship she should develop with Strollo. She quickly dismissed any "friendship" ideas. A man like Strollo didn't have female friends. The contract on the house was signed, she had her commission, she could limit the relationship to business.

She frowned. She was interested in him. He was wealthy, yes, but what drew her was the mystery, the intrigue, and the power. He seemed to exude power, authority. It was obvious he was accustomed to controlling others. She had tried, but had been unable to learn what he did all day, yet he always seemed busy. Then too, there was a dark side to him. She could not put it into words, but there seemed to be a lurking, attractive, stimulating evil about him.

Timing and circumstance were important considerations in any business venture, and she would carry this over to her relationship with Strollo. Her first acceptance of a date with him must be just right. If she accepted a relationship with him, it would not be casual. It would be carefully crafted to give her as much control as possible. Yes, she would explore this attractive man.

Strollo saw a challenge in Pam. Her physical beauty and sexual suggestiveness, his failure to even get a lunch date with her, all made him determined to have her. His planning was not long-term. He just wanted a quick lay or two and then he'd see what developed.

He put some effort into devising a situation where she would be hard pressed to refuse him. He parked across the street from the real estate agency, and when he saw her pull into the parking lot, he crossed over and met her at the door to the agency. His greeting was terse. "You've been avoiding me."

Pam was inwardly pleased that he had made this move, but she feigned being flustered. "No, not at all. Fortunately for me there are buyers and sellers, and a poor girl has to hustle to keep bread on the table."

"Well, today the bread on the table comes from me. Lunch at one?"

Her green eyes met his. "I really have appointments all day."

He felt her heat and decided he would not be put off. "You have to eat."

"Okay, but it'll have to be a short lunch, not the kind I'd like to have."

The suggestion in that remark was not lost on him. "Cancel your appointments."

"That's not possible. These people are in your price range and ready to buy. That commission will keep me going for months."

Strollo compromised. "All right, a short lunch will do for starters. I'll pick you up here at one."

She smiled because she saw herself in control; he took it as an expression of pleasure. "No, let me meet you. I really have a full day, and that way I won't have to come back here. I can just continue on to my appointments."

Pam's real purpose was to eliminate having to fight off Strollo. For now she needed an escape route, and separate cars would give her that.

They met at Black Caesar's in Coconut Grove. The maître d' was expecting them. Strollo had reserved a small room off the main dining area overlooking Dinner Key Marina. As she was seated, Pam looked at the tall man opposite her, wondering how far he would go to please her when he had gone to this trouble just for lunch.

Strollo asked, "Wine?"

"That would be nice."

Strollo's hand halted the maître d' as he said to Pam, "I'm going to suggest fish—is that all right?"

"Wonderful."

Then to the maître d', "My usual bottle."

The maître d' made a shallow bow and left.

There was silence for a moment as both searched for the right opening.

Pam found a source of conversation in the menu. "Have you had stone crabs yet?"

"No. What are they?"

"Large succulent claws, cracked, ready to eat, served cold with mayonnaise-mustard sauce. They're a Florida specialty."

"Sounds good. I like to try new things."

Pam did not miss the "try new things," and she rejoined, "I hope I shall be able to introduce you to other Florida delights."

Strollo reached across the table and touched her hand. She did not withdraw it. His eyes found hers.

"I think as we get to know each other, we will find that each of us has a delightful surprise for the other."

"I'm sure. Pleasurable surprises keep up one's interest."

The waiter entered with the wine, and Strollo told him to just pour. As he handed them menus, Strollo declined and ordered stone crabs, wanting to get rid of this intrusion quickly.

Alone once again, he said, "This lunch is like an apéritif. It increases the appetite."

"Good," she replied. "Then when the main course comes you will enjoy it that much more."

Strollo laughed, taking delight in this double entendre. "And what will my main course be?"

"Perhaps a more leisurely lunch?"

Strollo's disappointment was evident. "But that will be another apéritif."

"Good," she said, smiling suggestively. "After two apéritifs, we can expect dinner."

"Will there be a special dessert?"

"I would not be surprised to find something delightful on the menu."

The stone crabs arrived. Strollo pronounced them excellent. The wine was just right. The conversation continued to flow until Pam announced she must leave for her appointments.

Strollo displayed his displeasure with a rather long face. "I was hoping you would cancel, and we could continue this very pleasant conversation."

"I can't, but I would like to meet next week for lunch. Say Tuesday?"

"With no place to run to afterward?"

She laughed, enjoying his pressing her. "I can't promise that, but we will have the better part of the afternoon. Do you think I should have a place to 'run to'?"

"Yes, but with me."

She laughed again and took his hand. He moved to kiss her, and she gave him her cheek. With a wave she was gone.

All things considered, she thought, the lunch was a success. They had explored each other. She had not committed herself to anything. She had kept him wanting more.

She had to admit that she was more than a little interested in Vincent Strollo. He definitely had an aura of power about him, but as a practical girl she knew that much of his pleasure would be in the anticipation. The chase was important. To really hook him she had to lengthen and intensify that anticipation until it was just at the breaking point. If she could manage that, he'd be back for more.

Iannello, at Strollo's direction, met Hersch for dinner at the Paddock. Iannello had a Rob Roy waiting and then ordered a bottle of Fetzer zinfandel and some breaded fried mozzarella. As they exchanged small talk over the wine and cheese, Hersch toyed with his wineglass, enjoying the deep ruby color. He sensed that Iannello was going to approach him for more help in that shadowy somebody's dealings. He wasn't disappointed.

"Nate, the Man really liked what you did on that audit report, and next time we meet I may have a piece of something for you."

Hersch displayed his pleasure with a smile and nod.

Iannello continued, "It gets better. He wants to do the construction project and wants you to handle the whole thing. President of the corporation. He'll give you a draw every week and a piece of the project."

Hersch stiffened, not expecting this at all. "That means I'd have to quit the firm. This job would only be for a year or so."

Iannello dismissed these concerns with a wave of his hand. "Yeah, but we're talking serious bucks in that year. Plus, this one works out good, there's a lot more a smart guy like you can walk into." He grinned slyly and waggled a finger for Hersch to come closer. "He's offering fifteen hundred a week plus five percent of the gross—right off the top, what we sell her for. That means we sell for forty mil, you get two mil. Not bad for a year's work, hey? You checked the project out. You know it better than anyone. Will it sell? You want a piece?"

Hersch stumbled over himself in his hurry to say, "Count me in."

The day after the raids, Steve reported back to Al.

"We're not sure what happened to the money. And the cops are trying to locate Zamorano. His girl's body was found this morning. It looks like Ochoa found out that Zamorano was cooperating. His goons brutally chopped her up trying to get her to talk."

Al nodded. "Sounds like Ochoa. Any ideas on the money?"

Donnelly avoided mentioning the possibility that the surveillance had been made. He hoped the cops wouldn't bring it up again. "Lots of theories but no facts. Zamorano could have decided we weren't enough protection and taken the money into retirement. Ochoa could have got there before us and moved it. We've got an APB on Zamorano. He'll show up somewhere, if Ochoa hasn't gotten to him." Donnelly smiled. "He's too big to hide."

Al frowned at all these untidy pieces. "Who's handling the homicide?"

"Miami Beach."

"Offer our full cooperation—and give it. Work with them until we get complete answers. We'll keep the people we assigned to you for the narcotics case on this, and we'll continue to hold what investigations we can until we've exhausted all leads."

Al's secretary came in to announce an important call for Donnelly. He took it in Al's office. When he had finished, he looked a picture of confusion.

"Al, that was Metro Homicide. They just found four of Ochoa's people in a counting house in the Redlands. All shot in the back of the head last night."

Al was stunned for a moment. Then he got up and began pacing the room. "It's got to be part of our case. Get with Metro. Give them everything we've got."

"Zamorano too?"

Al hesitated. "Let's wait to the end of the day for him to come in. After that, give them the identity. For now, just say informant."

Steve voiced the question in both of their minds. "You think Zamorano grabbed the money and skipped?"

Al nodded. "It's possible he was using us to help him cross Ochoa. Let's find him."

Troubled, Donnelly walked slowly out of Al's office. He had a bad feeling about this case, and he wished now he had talked to Zamorano. He'd have to make doubly sure from now on that his ass was covered.

Morales and Fonseca were leaving Jimmy's Gym, having just completed their every-other-day weight training. They were en route to lunch at Café Colón, where two police groupies were waiting for them.

Morales chuckled. "Partner, we earned that money last night. Five dopers gone that won't take up court time and eat off the state for years. Plus Ochoa loses his dope and money. Suppose the feds or the state got the money? They'd just piss it away on useless equipment they can buy with other money."

Fonseca nodded. "The only regret I got is the little broad."

"Fuck, she took her chances when she became Zamorano's whore." Seeing Fonseca was not convinced, he slapped the top of the car seat. "Forget her, Jorge. We got only one loose end to worry about now, and that's Pablo. When we pay him off to-night, then we got no worries. There'll be nobody who can point a finger. We fuck around with this job for a year to make it look good and to keep an ear on the situation, and then"—he looked over and winked—"and then we take off."

The loan committees at each bank held a special meeting to approve Knight's loans, and he proceeded to draw a series of cashier checks for the loan amounts and all but about $2,500 of the initial deposits. Within a week he had delivered $1,520,000 to Iannello.

The checks went to New York by Federal Express. From there they were transported to Canada and deposited to two corporate accounts. Then the money was transferred to four corporate accounts in a bank in Liechtenstein. The money was then moved to two accounts in Geneva, from where it found its way to the Netherlands Antilles. There two companies invested it in Florida real estate.

Each account, save the Canadian, was a confidential account that the U.S. government could not access. Even the Canadian account would be difficult, for there was no branch of that bank in the United States. La Cosa Nostra had the best legal, ac-counting, and banking advice that money could buy, and this money route was well traveled.

Harold Knight met Iannello at the Paddock to turn over the last of the checks.

"Harold, you done great. The Man is pleased as shit. Your loan is paid off. You made sixty gees, plus the Man wants you to have the fifty he promised. As soon as the checks clear, and the Man gets the money transferred, it's payday."

"Tony, that's fantastic. I can't tell you how relieved I am. But what happens in six months when the loan is due?"

"Oh, not to worry. You get a six-month extension."

"Then what?"

"By then the guy's free of his old lady and we sell the bonds outright, pay off the loan, take another piece, and give some back to the happy ex-husband."

He watched Knight consider this. A year was a long way off. But the fact was, Knight was the only one out front.

Harold went home a happier man than his family had seen in the past year. He burst in the door calling for Connie.

She came from the kitchen, wiping her hands on a paper towel. "What's the matter?"

He responded by sweeping her up in his arms. She resisted but only slightly, curious about the cause of this outburst.

"I'm back in the black, honey. I did it—I saved the business."

In his exuberance he started to tell her about the bonds and the fifty thousand dollars that was coming but checked himself. "I worked out a deal to get us out of debt," he said simply. "Just a little careful management for a few weeks and we're home free."

Connie gently extracted herself from his grasp and pushed herself a little away so she could see his face. There was a glimmer of hope for a return to the way their life had been before his gambling and womanizing.

"That's wonderful, Harold. I pray things continue to work out for you."

Knight's mood deflated as he realized his news had not broken the barrier between them. "I thought that this might make a difference between us," he said hesitatingly. "That we might be able to try again."

"Please, Harold. I am happy for you. I just don't know. I need more time. You need more time."

"Okay. I'm going to keep working and trying. I want you just like we used to be. I'll make it happen."

Connie looked up at him and smiled. "Deep down that's all I really want too."

Strollo made the decision to go forward on Towers of Light. This necessitated a call to Licata via the pay-phone ritual.

"Carmine, I filled the Man in on what we have here. I'm now ready to go. I'm gonna need two people from my crew, Blacky and Phil. They've handled deals like this before. Clear it with the Man, and get them down here by next week if you can."

"No problem. They'll be calling you direct within a day or two to get together."

Within three days, both were in Miami, glad to escape the cold of a New York winter. Iannello arranged for a room at the Leisure Hotel, which Flemming swept for bugs. Just to make sure, the radio and television were turned on during the meeting.

Augie "Blacky" Plumeri and Philip Milano had worked with Strollo on his bank scam, and it did not take long before they grasped the essentials of this con.

Strollo opened the meeting. "We own a condo-office project, Towers of Light; no work has been done. Blacky, you work with Tony—he knows all of our friends down here. You select a contractor we can work with; use friendly unions for labor. We need a payroll with plenty of ghosts. Make arrangements where you can for cash pay. Where we pay ghosts by check, we cash them at the hotel. The guy out front is an accountant, Nathan Hersch. He'll give you the ghost cash and checks. Any problems with him, let Tony know. Your job is to make sure labor is in our pocket, no problems, and we skim as much as we can."

Plumeri nodded. "I got the picture. We'll be ready to move when you give the word."

Strollo next turned his attention to Milano.

"Phil, we got some shell companies. Get addresses and phones for them. Tony's got some already. Rent a warehouse, get a broad to answer the phone and do invoices. You're purchasing all the building materials. The contractor'll deal with Hersch, and he'll come to you. Buy from friends of ours where you can. Deal close with others."

The two recently arrived mafiosi were intently leaning forward in their chairs. Tony, while attentive, sat back, assuming the air of the initiated, the insider.

Strollo continued, "When Hersch buys for the project, he'll buy from one of our shells. The shell will have bought it, on paper, from a supplier. Like the contractor needs five hundred toilets. Good Friends, Inc., one of our shells, buys them at a hundred dollars each. Towers then buys them from Good Friends, Inc., at one seventy-five each."

Milano was enthusiastic. "It's good to be working with you again, boss."

Plumeri said, "Yeah, the banks will pay our jackup on the supplies and the ghosts on our payrolls, and stay fat, dumb, and happy."

The anticipation of the score was shining on all their faces.

Milano continued, "The day the banks wake up and find we're gone, that's the part I like. Gonna be champagne and broads again, boss?"

Strollo put his hand on Milano's shoulder. "There'll be a bigger celebration this time. When you can fuck the banks twice, it's cause for one hell of a party." Reminded of the next step he needed to take, he turned to Iannello. "How's financing coming?"

"Hersch has got the construction loans from both banks approved. He used the real estate, plans, and zoning variance as our equity, so we got nothing of ours invested."

Iannello was enjoying the attention. He sounded like Strollo's right-hand man outlining the scam to these newcomers. "The guys that went bust signed over the land and everything to us in return for a piece of the finished project, so that came to us free." He looked around with his hands spread wide. "They'll get a piece of nothing."

This brought a hearty burst of laughter all around.

Zamorano had not been found, and the narcotics case seemed to be at a dead end. Al had decided it was time for a long-delayed courtesy call to Captain Juan Marín, head of Metro Homicide. He had to admit he was using the protocol

required of a new SAC as an excuse to dig for firsthand information on the Zamorano case. He couldn't shake the feeling
that Donnelly wasn't leveling with him.

Juan Marín had been commander of the overworked Homicide detail for five years. Bodies of all shapes, ages, nationalities,
and races were regularly discovered in all sorts of odd places
and circumstances. Nowhere in the country did homicide work
present a greater challenge and variety than in Dade County.
Juan was forty-five, slender, with dark wavy hair, a quiet, retir-
ing man who shunned and mistrusted the press.

His office consisted of a desk and conference table and half
a dozen chairs. The walls were an antiseptic white. After a *café
cubano* and polite conversation, Al steered the talk to the homicides.

"Any developments in the counting-house homicides?"

Juan shrugged. "Not really. As you know, we believed they
were connected with Zamorano's girlfriend and that Ochoa's
people had tortured her, possibly looking for Zamorano. What
we get now confuses us. The medical examiner says Teresa
wasn't a torture victim. He says all those knife wounds were in-
flicted at about the same time, not individually, slow, like you
would expect in torture. And some, at least, were done after she
was dead."

Al's brow creased in thought. "What does that tell us?"

"That's not all. The forensic boys say there was somebody in
bed with her—hairs, fibers, body fluids, et cetera on the sheet.
They match hairs from Zamorano's place. Plus in Zamorano's
house they found two nine-millimeter bullets that had once
been in a gun and cranked through the action. The ejector
marks match the ejector marks on the casings found at the
scene where the four dopers were killed."

Al emitted a low whistle.

Juan looked quizzical. "Is this the first you're hearing this?"

Al was puzzled. "Yes."

"Steve got this a couple days ago," Juan said, unsure whether
to proceed further.

Al feigned a lightness he did not feel. "I guess the boss is always the last to know what's going on."

Both men fell silent for a second. Al sensed Juan was turning something over in his mind, and he asked, "What else is bothering you?"

"Not bothering me. Just trying to make some sense of Teresa's homicide."

Juan paused for a moment, then continued, "The other item you might be interested in is the homicide of a guy named Gilberto Fernandez, a.k.a. Pablo. He's a low-to-medium dealer in the Ochoa group."

"Ochoa seems to be having problems keeping his people alive."

"Yeah, well, this guy was found in a room in the Voyager's Retreat motel at the junction of I-95 and the Palmetto. Somebody put five .45s in his head from a MAC-10 with a silencer that had the deceased's prints all over it. Looks like whoever did it used Pablo's gun."

Al said, "Five rounds? They wanted him dead."

"Yeah, the head was about gone."

"Anything else?"

Juan looked to one side, avoiding Al's eyes. "We talked to his girlfriend. She's Teresa's sister."

Al suddenly sat up straight at this connection. All these links were forming a circle.

"Pablo asked her for, and got, a key to Teresa's apartment about a week before she was killed. He told her he had to drop something off. He returned the key the next day." He saw he had Al's complete attention. "There were no pick marks or other signs of forced entry on Teresa's door, so whoever killed her either came in with a key or she let him in. Pablo was with the sister and some other people that night."

Al was still for a moment, thinking, and then said, "If Pablo was whacked because of the Teresa killing, it was probably because he supplied a copy of the key to her apartment to whoever did it. Zamorano didn't need a key. And Ochoa and his crew wouldn't need to kill Pablo if he gave them a key. He's part of their outfit. Maybe we've been looking in the wrong places for this killer. Maybe it's not Ochoa or Zamorano."

Juan nodded. "That's the way we're thinking."

"Has that thinking fixed on any direction?"

"Possible rip."

Again silence fell between them. Al rose to leave.

"Thanks, Juan. I need to review our case based on this additional information you've given me. I think I'll be back . . . with Steve."

• P A R T •
TWO

"Looks like the innocent flower,
But be the serpent under 't."

—William Shakespeare,
Macbeth

• C H A P T E R •
TWELVE

Most of the air conditioning in Miami was not in use. Rather, area houses were open to the cooling breezes of November. Nine months ago, Al had first heard of Strollo's arrival. Today, he was conducting a periodic file review with Bill Baskin.

Bill dropped into one of the deep leather chairs and set out files and papers on the coffee table. He had shed his suit coat, and the cuffs of his pale blue shirt were rolled up. He tugged at his maroon-and-blue-striped tie, loosening its hold around his neck.

During the meeting he discussed a number of OC cases with Al. They were mostly out-of-state mafiosi who were expected to arrive in Florida for the winter season. Coverage of their activities and contacts had been requested of Miami by the various offices. As the last item on the file review, Bill picked up the Strollo file.

"Al, we've got some interesting photos and background on a Harold Knight, who's been in Iannello's company. We've seen some real heads-together conversations. Knight's got a medium-sized business, office maintenance mostly. From what we can find out, he was doing great until about eighteen months ago."

As Bill talked about Strollo, Al got up from his desk and

came over to the sofa. He also was in shirt sleeves, an empty holster on his belt. He had a rule about not displaying weapons: if you removed your coat, you removed your gun.

"He apparently met Iannello and got into gambling and playing around, fast-track shit. His business went to hell, heavily in debt, almost bankrupt. The word is, Tony shylocked him."

Bill leaned forward, his elbows on his knees, glancing at the yellow legal pad of notes.

"But now Knight's business seems to be recovering. About nine months ago he moved into three banks where he never did business before. It's the three banks that's got us curious. Why does he need three?"

Al looked up from the notepad on which he had been doodling. "You figure some kind of scam?"

"Possible. We're considering stepping into them."

"If we do, and there's nothing there yet, do we tip our hand to Strollo?"

"Maybe, but we feel the case has developed the intelligence base we were striving for, and we need to start making some moves."

Bill had carefully planned this briefing to reach certain objectives. He was consciously building to the point where these objectives would seem logical and appropriate.

"There's another guy named Hersch, a lawyer-accountant, that's thick with Iannello. He's president of a company building a big office-condo. It looks like he got financing through two bank loans, but without subpoenas we're having problems understanding the mechanics of how he's set up and who his partners are. In other words, to go forward from here we've got to begin going open."

Al nodded in agreement. "Okay, get a grand jury subpoena duces tecum, but let's just do one bank that Knight's in. That way if it's clean, we don't give away everything we know. Hold on Hersch until we see the results of the bank subpoena."

This was the direction Bill wanted to go. "We'll do it tomorrow." He would have preferred going against Hersch at the same time, but he knew that would follow shortly.

With a crooked grin on his face, he handed Al a surveillance photo of Strollo and Pam Sumpter. "Now for Pam, our interesting girlfriend. From all indications it took Strollo about three weeks after that first lunch to get her in bed."

"So she wasn't that hard to get," Al threw in, and they chuckled.

"We've seen him in her condo frequently, in the evening, until about two months ago. He's still there, but not as often at night, mostly afternoons when she's not there. He may be working on another chippie, although we haven't seen one, and possibly cooling Pam off."

Bill quickly raised a finger, anticipating Al's next question. "We've been trying to get to her for a week, casually, sort of let it seem almost accidental. I hope we'll click today. We'll do an assessment and then decide whether to step into her."

Pam had just finished lunch with a client. As she was entering her office, a young couple, also entering, asked, "Miss, do you work here? We just got transferred in, and we're looking to buy a house."

Pam smiled, sensing a new client. "Yes, I do. Perhaps I can help you. Come in." As they followed her into the office, Pam was solicitous. "What kind of a house are you looking for?"

"We'd like three bedrooms, two baths. We have two children," the woman responded. "Even four bedrooms would be all right."

They moved into the small cubicle that was Pam's office.

"How much can you spend?"

The man held a chair for the woman Pam supposed was his wife. "We need to stay well under two hundred thousand. One fifty'd be comfortable. I'm with the FBI, and subject to transfer again, so we don't like to tie too much up. Plus we don't make all that much."

Her eyebrows rose slightly at the mention of the FBI. That was unusual.

"I understand. By the way, I'm Pam Sumpter."

"Nice to meet you. I'm Jerry Collins, and this's my wife, Shirley."

That first afternoon was spent examining sales books and computer printouts and lining up potential houses.

Jerry and Shirley, in addition to being husband and wife, were both agents, and were putting together an assessment for a possible pitch to Pam within the next few days.

The subpoena was served on the National Bank of the South at ten in the morning. It carried instructions that the customer to whose account the subpoena was directed was not to be informed of the subpoena under penalty of contempt of court.

Strollo was comfortably seated at his desk in his office, examining some documents Iannello had delivered, showing material purchases and draws on the bank loans for Towers of Light.

The ringing phone brought his head up, and he unconsciously reached to answer it, which he seldom did. The voice on the other end was someone he had been avoiding—in fact, one reason he seldom answered the phone.

It was Pete Siragusa. "Vinnie, good to hear your voice. Mildred and I have been trying to reach you. We know how busy you are."

Tapping a finger in irritation, Strollo said, "Yeah, it's been a hectic season, and hasn't let up yet. You caught me just as I was leaving for a meeting."

"I understand. We won't hold you up. I'll get right to the point. Vinnie, Mildred and me don't want to seem unappreciative, but we think after all these months we ought to get what you sold the gold for."

Almost bored, Strollo spun his line. "I told you, these things take time."

"How about us going to a lawyer? He has to keep our secret, he ain't allowed to tell. And you could send him a report or something on where the gold has gone and when payment is coming."

Strollo was shocked. He had to stop this idea now!

"No, a lawyer'll bleed you, and you're risking him turning you in to the IRS without you even knowing it. Let me call some people in Europe and see where we are. Maybe I can get a partial for you."

"Okay, Vinnie, that'd be great. We'll wait to hear from you."

Strollo put down the phone slowly. This idea of a lawyer did not bode well. The Siragusas could cause serious trouble. He might even have to call Jimmy to handle them.

Bill Baskin stuck his head in Al's office door and saw he was just hanging up the phone. Al waved him in.

"The guys who served the subpoena at National Bank of the South are back. They talked to a VP who opened the account for Knight, Herman Frank. There's a custodial account for Knight with six hundred and fifty thousand dollars in bearer bonds, and guess what? Knight borrowed five hundred thousand against them. His checking account is almost empty, been paying interest on the loan. The guys have Knight's financial statement. From what we know about him, it's a phony. But the VP says he's a personal friend of Knight's, and we're wasting our time."

"Are the bonds hot?"

"No, we ran some in NCIC and no hits. We even called the paying agent on each issue, and they have no report of thefts. As far as we can tell, the bonds are right, but with the phony statement something's wrong. We're working on our next move now, and as soon as we have a recommendation we'll be back."

Bill began to walk away, then stopped, thought for a moment. "You know, something's bothering me. For some reason Knight clipped a year's worth of interest coupons before the bonds went into the account. He hasn't redeemed them through this bank, but could have in another. The reason why it's weird is because ordinarily a custodial account would take care of clipping and redeeming the coupons."

Al was instantly all action. "Where are the bonds?"

"In the squad room," Bill said, taken aback at the determination in Al's voice. "They're being green-sheeted for entry in the exhibit vault."

"I want to see them."

Striding purposefully, he followed Bill to the squad room.

George Preston and his partner, Betty Leland, were at their desks making entries on property forms, or green sheets, preparatory to turning the items over to the clerk in charge of bulky exhibits.

"Betty, George." Al nodded to them as he eyed the piles on their desktops. "Quite a pile of bonds. Any feeling for what was going on?"

"Not really," Betty responded. "It's got to be a scam—obvious Federal Reserve Act violation with the phony balance sheet—but the bonds are apparently legit and cover the loan. So, at this point we can't articulate where the rip is."

Al donned a pair of latex gloves and picked up an Indiana Toll Road bond. It had been folded in four but otherwise showed no usage. He picked up several more. Each had its own serial number, and all the coupons were properly numbered.

"I assume the bank listed each serial number, just as you're doing on the property forms, so there are no duplicates, which would show them as counterfeit."

"Right." George was holding a bond and gestured at it. "They're also nice and sharp. Look at the vignette, the printing on the body. They look good to us."

Al agreed. "They do look good." He ran his hand over the face of the bond, particularly the vignette. Then he asked, "Do you have a pin?"

Bill's eyebrows came together. Betty and George were also puzzled. "Why, sure." Betty reached in her purse and found a safety pin.

Al took three Indiana Toll Road bonds and placed them, open, exactly square, on top of each other. The three agents looked on, mystified by what he was doing.

Al pushed the pin through the center of one of the colored dots scattered about on the face of the bond, and continued pushing the pin through all three bonds. Then he lifted the top bond, observed the second, lifted it, and observed the third.

"They're counterfeit."

All three spoke as one: "How did the pin tell you?"

Al was amused at their reaction of surprise and smiled. "Actually, the pin only confirmed what my eyes and hands told me.

A real bond would probably have been done on a letterpress, and the vignette would definitely have been engraved. There would be a three-dimensional appearance. When you run your fingers over the design, you should be able to feel the raised engraving." Al handed the three bonds, one to each of the agents, for their examination of the areas he was talking about.

"Counterfeits are usually printed offset, from photographic plates, not engraved. They're flat-looking and have no raised printing. They feel flat."

Then, pointing to specific spots on the bonds, he continued, "These colored dots you see scattered about on the bonds are planchettes. In manufacturing the paper they are scattered about in the paper mash at random and are at random in the finished paper stock."

Each of the three agents was absorbed in his inspection of the bond in his hands, and Al said, "Look here." He pointed to the colored dot he had pierced with the pin. "The planchettes on these bonds are all in the same position on the paper. They were printed on the paper. The pin pierced the same planchette in each bond."

Bill was surprised. "Where'd you pick up all this counterfeit background?"

Al laughed. "By accident, really. Had a friend of mine in Secret Service who worked counterfeit money cases. He gave me a crash course one time."

Bill sat down at the bond-strewn desk and leaned back in his chair, his hands thrust deep in his pants pockets. His accountant's mind was running a balance sheet of debits and credits to assess where this case was and where it ought to go.

"No question who's behind this. Now we've got to figure how to tie Iannello and Strollo in. This kind of printing and know-how took some doing. We've got a real shot at them. They don't know we know."

Al walked around the two desks, intent on the pile of bonds. "You're right. The question now is, will that banker keep quiet? Could someone else in the bank alert Knight?"

Betty shrugged. "We sat on him good, but you know there are no guarantees."

Al felt it was time for him to get personally involved. Strollo had become a major target. Baskin's patient investigation had produced. They had their violation. This time Al would get him. There was no question what he wanted done.

"Bill, get me the name and phone number of the bank president."

Then it was Betty's turn. "Call the VP you talked to, caution him again, and tell him I'm setting up a meeting with his president and him to discuss this."

To the group he said, "It's too much to hope that we can keep this quiet for more than a couple days, but I'd like some preparation time before we step into Knight. And we are going to step into Knight—hard!"

Bill came forward in his chair, excited by the prospect of finally taking action. "What about the other banks?"

"Not yet," Al said decisively. "We've got enough to proceed. Chances are we'd find a similar scam, and that would just compound our problem of keeping things quiet."

Bill rose to his feet, caught up in the spirit. "Okay. We've got a good idea of the Knight scam, and the banks have already been ripped, so we can sit on it for a while. But, Al, if Hersch is pulling a scam for Strollo with Towers of Light, we'd better move fast, because it's still going on and people are probably losing money."

"You're right, Bill, but we've got to take time to set up properly. Move fast on a wiretap on Iannello. Start with the bookies, unless the U.S. attorney thinks the surveillances have given you enough to go right up on him. I'll call Bureau headquarters to tell them where we are, and get them to call the Department of Justice, so they're ready and know this is not a bookie case. Have a teletype, confirming that call, summarizing where we are, ready for my signature tonight."

Al picked up a pad from one of the desks and handed it to Bill to write all this down.

"Start compiling the Strollo surveillance of pay-phone use so we'll be in a position to apply for a T-3 on them if we can spin off on Strollo. I don't want to touch Towers of Light until we're up on our wires. Then we'll hit them and listen to the chatter as they try to cover it up."

With a wry smile, he looked at Bill. "Looks like your squad's going to be busy for a while."

Within the hour, Al had met with the VP, Herman Frank, and the president of the bank. Al explained the gravity of the case, and the VP understood from his president that if Knight was informed of the subpoena, he would not only have a contempt citation from the court but be looking for another job.

Shirley and Jerry Collins had arranged lunch at Cocoplum in Coconut Grove with Pam. As they sampled each other's tapas, they read brochures on houses that were for sale. In reality, though, Shirley was critically observing Pam. She grudgingly admired Pam's taste in clothes and the way she wore them. Today's dress, for example, while businesslike, accented her excellent figure and blond hair.

The waiter came by to clear the table of the remnants of their tapas and served *café cubano* and flan. They were all relaxed, making small talk, and putting aside houses for the moment. The time was right, Jerry decided, to spring on her.

"Yesterday," he said casually, "when we stopped by to pick up the printout on some houses, Shirley and I sat in the car for a while studying them, and we noticed you leave with a man I know, Vincent Strollo. Is he a client or a friend?"

As he spoke, Jerry was looking at some papers he had just picked up, but Shirley was looking at Pam. She first saw annoyance, and then a flicker of concern, in her face.

Pam answered the question with a question. "Where do you know him from?"

Without a moment's hesitation, in a matter-of-fact tone, he responded, "He's a high-ranking mafioso. He came down here from New York trying to evade the authorities up there."

The news was far more serious than Pam had expected. Jerry was now looking right at her, as was Shirley.

His blunt answer and their penetrating attention unnerved her. The color drained from her face, and for a full ten seconds there was total silence.

Then Jerry asked again, "Is he a friend?"

Pam, her voice flat, responded, "Yes. He came to me as a client. I sold him his house. I've had lunch with him a few times since then."

Meanwhile, her mind was working furiously. She had known he was in something not quite legitimate, had suspected—yes, deep inside, had known—he was Mafia. It was partly that aura of danger about him that had attracted her. For the first time she allowed herself to accept that he really was a mafioso. But even if he was, why should that affect her?

Pam said defensively, "I don't know anything about the Mafia. I only know him as an interesting, entertaining person."

In a neutral, quiet voice, Jerry said, "Pam, I never intended to suggest otherwise. But since we are working closely, I thought it best to ask about him, and let you know a little about my professional interest in him."

Feeling slightly threatened, she decided to head this off altogether. Ignoring Shirley, she fixed her luminous green eyes on Jerry and inclined her body slightly toward him, touching his forearm with her hand. "My relationship with him is no different from the pleasure I find in your company."

Shirley was stunned at this come-on to her husband with her seated next to him. She maintained her professional cool, though.

The suggestion was not lost on Jerry, who continued as though she had not spoken, but this time in a somewhat lighter vein. "If you don't mind, I'd like to pursue this conversation later. Perhaps share with you some of our concerns about Strollo."

Pam didn't know how to handle this, but at least this topic was finished for now, so she merely nodded.

Jerry added, deadly serious, "Until we have our second talk, I suggest you not tell Strollo about this conversation. It could have a decidedly adverse effect on your relationship."

Pam suddenly realized from the way this was said that Jerry was aware she was having an affair with Strollo.

"I won't be seeing him until Thursday."

"Good. May I come by your home tomorrow night?"

"All right, about seven."

As soon as she said this she was sorry. She should have just broken off the whole subject here, refused to pursue it further. But then she thought, why not play with it a little? This turn of events was sort of intriguing. All along she had been screwing a Mafia type, and now she'd been contacted by the FBI. It was almost as if a new game had started.

• CHAPTER •
THIRTEEN

Hersch's ostentatious gold cufflinks clattered on the desktop as he pulled the ledger to him. It had taken him less than a week on the job to figure out the scam. Now, eight months later, he was trying to calculate how much Iannello and his shadowy boss had stolen.

He was fairly certain of at least four million, and construction was only about half finished. For the hundredth time, Hersch shook his head, smiling at the simplicity, and audacity, of the scheme.

There were a half-dozen material suppliers for the project, and all were shells. A name on an invoice. They were all indirectly owned by Iannello's boss. The material was initially purchased by the shell companies from legitimate suppliers. Hersch was certain hard bargains had been made, and the prices paid were as low as one could get. The shell company jacked up the cost by 50 to 100 percent and then "sold" the material to the Towers of Light contractor, who bought what he was told to buy.

Construction costs were further inflated by an untold number of ghosts on various payrolls. Someone was collecting thousands every week for people who didn't exist.

All of these inflated costs were paid by the lending banks as certificates of completion of the various stages of construction were presented, and additional funds from the borrowed capital were advanced.

What was beginning to concern him was what would happen when Towers of Light was finished. If the scam went the way he was beginning to think, he would be very far out front and could catch a lot of shit. Still, he was afraid to broach his concerns to Iannello. He suspected that's why he was getting the big payoff at the end.

Except . . . there might be no big payoff. He had been promised a percentage on the sale of the project. But Hersch could smell a bust-out coming, planned bankruptcy, and then he'd be a fall guy.

Steve Donnelly was just beginning to update Al on the Zamorano-Ochoa case when Bill Baskin burst into the room and interrupted. The normally mild-mannered supervisor was red in the face with anger.

"I was just told that our illustrious U.S. attorney, Neil Miller, has refused to request authority from the Department of Justice to apply to the court for the wiretap."

Al was furious. "We spend more of our damn time fighting with that goddam moron of a U.S. attorney than we do the bad guys. He just doesn't understand, or doesn't want to understand."

Al seldom allowed his anger to show, and Bill backed off a little. When he continued, he managed a more reasonable tone.

"This refusal came to us through the assistant U.S. attorney assigned to the case, who told us that Miller sent her memo, requesting authority to pursue the tap, back to her with the notation 'Premature, needs more work by FBI. This is bookie tap, against Department policy.' "

Al slammed his fist down on his desk in exasperation. "He's got the imagination of a pin. If it's not in his damn rule book, that's all she done wrote. We're paying this shithead ninety thousand a year because he can read a damn rule book."

Steve Donnelly saw the sparks flying, and took this opportunity to escape. The last thing he wanted to discuss was the problems in the Zamorano case. "I'll be back later. This can wait. It looks like you guys have a more immediate problem."

Al waved him out, intent on the matter at hand.

Bill moved uneasily in the chair facing Al's desk, concerned that Al might think the presentation to the assistant U.S. attorney reflected poorly on him or his squad. "The AUSA says she can't discuss it with Miller. He's got a policy of no verbal discussions. Everything's got to be in writing."

Al got up from behind his desk, needing movement to lessen the anger and frustration building inside him.

"Well, I'll discuss it with him!" he said as he started pacing. "If the sonofabitch refuses to discuss it, I'll ask the Department for a special prosecutor. My basis is obvious: the USA won't talk to the SAC about a case."

Al paused to pick up his coffee cup, but he didn't drink from it. "No," he said, looking at Bill. "It's so easy to say no. That's the safe way. People don't get in trouble for not doing things. So the bureaucrats who play it safe say no. If this guy ever said yes to a project, I'd be suspicious of it. All he wants are the street crooks—the bank robbers, the dopers. Anything above that spells problems."

Determined, Al leveled a finger at Bill and said, "We don't need Department authority for a pen register. Get a court order for one on Iannello, Strollo, and Knight."

Al began pacing again as Bill made a note.

"Your surveillances have identified four public phones that Strollo and Iannello seem to favor for both receiving and placing calls. Let's pick the two that they use the most and put pen registers on those as well. We'll know what telephone numbers they're calling. It'll certainly add to our probable cause for the tap."

Al stopped pacing, his forehead creased in concentration. "We'll consider Hersch as the investigation develops. Once we're up on the pens, we can switch to full intercept with a flick of a switch."

The Siragusas now became more than an irritant to Strollo. Rosa answered the phone one evening when he was out, and

Mildred, out of frustration, unloaded the news on her. They were pretty sure Strollo had been evading their calls.

"Rosa, we don't know what to do. Daddy left us about two hundred pounds of gold. We gave it to Vincent to sell for us, and now we don't hear nothing. We talked to him about going to a lawyer to help, since he seems to be having trouble getting our money."

Rosa inhaled sharply, for she knew, even though she wasn't supposed to know, that the gold was gone, in her husband's pocket, for she knew Vincent. She was in a quandary. She knew that she was forbidden to meddle in her husband's business. But this was family, this couldn't be business.

"I'm sorry, Mildred. Vincent never told me. This is the first I've heard about this. There must be some problem with selling, and that's why he hasn't given you the money." She made her decision. "I'll ask him."

But what could she do? Rosa went to the bedroom and undressed. She would shower. Showers always helped her think. She lathered and then stood overlong under the hot pulsating jets of water that turned her skin a prickly pink. Her course of action decided, she dried off with a soft fluffy towel and put on a sheer nightgown and cover. She walked barefoot into the living room to wait for her husband.

When he arrived, he found Rosa sitting on the sofa, her legs folded underneath her. He could see she was fresh from the shower, her hair still moist. Her position, her sheer gown that showed her every contour, stirred him, and he bent down and kissed her damp forehead.

Rosa had been waiting for a moment like this—but then she turned her attention to the decision she had made. "Mildred and Pete called while you were out."

She had decided to just let it hang, hoping to draw a response.

Strollo showed no interest in her comment, but whatever ardor he had felt drained away. He tried to change the subject. "You're up kind of late, aren't you?"

He headed over to the wet bar and poured himself a double scotch and soda.

His unresponsive answer forced her to go further than she wanted to. "They were very upset. They said they gave you some gold to sell for them after their father died and that you haven't given them the money for it. They said they're thinking about getting a lawyer to help you get the money."

He spun around to face Rosa, upsetting his glass and spilling his drink over the bar.

"Goddammit, Rosa, you know better than to talk about my business! All these years you learned nothing? What kind of stupid remarks did you make to those damn people?"

A string of profanities was about to follow, but he stopped himself, struggling to regain control. Thoroughly frightened by his explosion, Rosa immediately sat up straight. Her timing in bringing up the gold had been bad. She had made Vincent angry. But if he was stealing from the Siragusas . . .

Strollo softened a bit. "Rosa, you let me handle this. It isn't all it seems. There's lots of problems here. I do what the Siragusas want, they'll get in trouble with Uncle Sam and get me in trouble too."

Rosa was unsure what to do. She wanted to believe her husband. At the same time she felt an obligation to the Siragusas. She really hadn't done anything wrong. There was no reason for him to be upset with her—unless he had really stolen the gold.

"Vincent, this isn't business. This is family. Our family, I mean. These are our cousins. I can talk about family, can't I? You'll tell me what's happening, won't you?"

Strollo was beginning to lose control again, and the tic in his left eye started twitching. Rosa talking back to him? Rosa never talked back.

"Look, that's enough! You keep out of this! When and if you need to know any more, I'll tell you. I say this is business. Now clean up this mess."

Rosa dutifully retrieved a sponge and began to clean off the bar.

The next morning, using a pay phone at the Leisure Hotel, Strollo called Jimmy Amari in New Jersey. Amari went to a pay phone, and fifteen minutes later called Strollo back.

Strollo began, "You remember that heavy box you helped me carry last time?"

"Yeah?" Jimmy said uncertainly, not wanting to be reminded of it.

"Well, the two people who gave it to me are definitely sick, and their sickness could be contagious. They need a visit from a doctor. Probably two doctors, so that each one can be treated for their sickness at the same time. Can you arrange that?"

"It's possible," Amari said cautiously. "How serious is the sickness? What kind of medicine do you think the doctor will give them?"

"From what I know," Vincent said harshly, "the illness is terminal, and all the doctor may be able to do is ease their suffering."

There was silence for a moment, and then Amari asked, "Is somebody authorizing the doctor to treat them?"

He got the answer he was expecting, but didn't want.

"I am."

Amari again had to consider this, and then in a low tone he said, "Do you remember our conversation when we left Littman, concerning business?"

"Yes, but this is not business," Strollo said. "This is you and me. This is over thirty years of being together."

Amari let a long sigh escape and finally replied, "Let me look into it, find a second doctor, and I'll get back to you. Since there may be a problem with the doctor getting his medical instruments from up here, we may have to get them down there."

Strollo was satisfied. "We can get what you need."

Amari hung up the phone deeply troubled. Strollo had just ordered an unauthorized hit. Magliocco was not aware of the gold deal, so Strollo could not get his permission to hit the Siragusas. This was off the record, not family business. Amari would have to find somebody to help with the hit who wouldn't talk to other family members. He'd also have to get any special equipment from Florida, since the family, out of the loop, couldn't be asked to supply it. Amari didn't like it.

He would have liked it even less had he known that a court order had earlier been obtained for the installation of pen registers on the targets, and the telephone company had tagged the telephone pairs for the "sound agents" to tie into.

The installation had been up for the last day, and all the numbers being called were being recorded in a computer. They were checked, each phone against the others, for common numbers called, and those numbers were being checked for subscriber information.

The pen register picked up the number Strollo called in New Jersey, Amari's home. SPIT put Strollo in the hotel where the phone was located at the time the call was placed. SPIT was able to watch him on that phone when he received the call from Amari. Since only the pen register and not an oral intercept was in effect, the FBI was not aware of the content of the conversation.

Al certainly had enough probable cause for a telephone intercept on the bookie lines, and arguably directly on Iannello for bookmaking. If he went on the bookies, he would spin off to Iannello as he was picked up on the phones. The expectation was that Iannello would be picked up talking to Strollo, and they could then spin off on Strollo.

There was another route as well. Knight had used the phone in his office and home to discuss the counterfeit bond deal with the bank. That, with their surveillance and investigation of Knight, gave the FBI probable cause to go up on Knight's phones—another avenue to Iannello and Strollo.

Al had decided to hold off further subpoenas for fear of alerting Strollo. Towers of Light had not been approached. Surveillance, record checks, and public-source inquiries continued.

Efforts to turn Pam would continue. The only practical way to unravel Strollo's operations was from the inside. A good informant and/or a telephone tap.

Now as Al waited in the U.S. attorney's outer office for Neil Miller to get off the phone, he was promising himself he wouldn't lose his temper. He knew that the man who loses his temper loses the argument. Finally the light on the multibutton phone on the secretary's desk blinked off, and she rose and admitted Al to the office.

Miller was fifty, from a good-old-boy law firm, more given to handshaking and backslapping than litigation. In the year he had been United States attorney he had been truly undistinguished. His firm hoped this stint as USA would open doors for them when he came back to the firm. Miller might even get a U.S. district court judgeship, which would also enhance the market value of the firm.

He approached Al with his hand extended and led him to a chair facing his desk. "Good to see you, Al! It's been much too long since we had a quiet chat, just the two of us. Some coffee?"

Al took the proffered chair while Miller walked around the desk to seat himself. "Thank you, yes. Black, please."

As the secretary, who had remained at the door, went for the requested coffee, Miller continued, "There's a Dade County chiefs' meeting Friday evening, with golf in the morning. Are you planning on making it?"

Al hated small talk. He wanted to hammer Miller for his refusal to authorize the tap. He controlled his impatience, though.

"Don't think I'll make the golf, Neil. I do intend to make the dinner meeting, though."

Miller knew full well that Al had requested this meeting to discuss the tap, and he was in no hurry to start an unpleasant discussion.

"Well, good, look forward to having a quiet drink with you. We really need to get together socially on a regular basis. Helen is fine, I trust."

But Al was finished with the niceties. "Neil, I asked to see you today to discuss the wiretap we requested on Iannello's bookies and on Knight's office and home. Thought we could get the straight of it, just us two, without filtering it through assistants."

Miller winced at Al's directness. "Well, you know I don't think this is the way to do business. That's what we have those assistants for, to put problems in perspective, with all the pluses and minuses, so that we can make cool, reasoned judgments." Miller warmed to his argument, seeing a way out. "When we sit down like this, you and I, the bosses, we are apt to overlook things and make decisions that are ill-advised and unworkable, only because we didn't allow the staff to do their work."

Al was not about to be sidetracked. He intended to pin Miller down and not let go. "In this case I think the staff has done their work and we can talk about their findings, and the interpretation that has been placed on those findings, upon which this office has declined to request authority for an intercept."

"Al, if you disagree with the decision of the office, I think the appropriate avenue would be through your agent or supervisor to my assistant, or section chief, with a written request for reconsideration or clarification."

The color began to mount in Al's face as he struggled to hold his temper. "Neil, there's been no trial. We don't need posttrial motions for reconsideration or clarification. What we need is an understanding that decisions have to be made with some degree of dispatch. We've uncovered a huge banking swindle by LCN, with a likely second construction scam of some kind we haven't even touched."

Miller seized on Al's words. "You've just said my main objection, 'haven't even touched.' You're premature. Do some investigation. You probably don't need an intercept. Also, you know the Department has said there'll be no more bookie taps."

Al, exasperated, felt as if he were teaching a class of new agents, but he continued in a controlled tone.

"Neil, if we go open with an investigation, we'll get Knight and maybe Hersch. Iannello and Strollo will skate, as always. We need to be in the operation while it's still working. Only then will we have a chance at Strollo and company. This isn't a bookie tap. We're looking to spin off to some good people, targets of the Department."

The discussion continued for ten agonizing minutes with little progress. It ended with Miller agreeing to send a neutral memo to Washington, pointing out Department policy and asking whether the Department would authorize a tap under the existing circumstances. There would be no recommendation from him either pro or con. He would leave the decision totally to the Department.

Al did get an assurance it would be sent the next day. Perhaps within a week they would hear back.

As Al reached the basement of the U.S. attorney's office, where he had parked his car, he yanked loose his tie and opened his collar. "Goddam bureaucrats," he muttered. He started the engine and turned up the air conditioner full blast. He needed to sit for a few moments and let the frustration and anger subside before he drove off.

Strollo had begun using Pam's apartment for business some months ago. It was more comfortable than running to phone booths, and she was clean with the cops. Strollo had checked. Plus any call he made came back to her, not him. He had even had Flemming sweep her apartment and phone for bugs. He felt secure, but never discussed anything open. They always used a loose code they both understood. Just like the conversation with Jimmy. He hadn't said anything anybody couldn't hear.

He was also charging some of his public-phone long-distance calls to her number. It was easier than carrying pocketfuls of quarters.

Pam, of course, was aware he was doing some business from her place but had never objected. He explained that he needed a place away from home to do some business; he always was just on the verge of renting office space but never did. He gave her a few hundred a month to cover the bills, and she had been unconcerned.

Pam was thinking about those phone bills as she entered her office the next morning. She now realized she should not have agreed to the evening meeting. She was being rushed. She would rather not hear any more about Strollo. She called the FBI office and left a message canceling the meeting.

She was glad she did, for Strollo appeared at her apartment at ten that evening, unannounced. Her surprise was evident in the sudden intake of breath as he walked into the middle of her reverie. He noticed it and with a half-smile said, "You expecting someone else?"

The thought flashed through her mind, "He knows." She

quickly dismissed this idea, but still answered lamely, "You just startled me, that's all."

Strollo crossed the room to the recliner where Pam was seated, an unread fashion magazine on her lap. He leaned over for a kiss and was immediately aroused by the delicious body that waited under the light wrapper she was wearing. His hand strayed inside, up the inside of her thigh, and found no underwear to impede his exploration.

Strollo sensed her remoteness but brushed it aside. "It's been a tough day. I need some comforting that only a little love can provide. May I entice you to our playground?"

He took her hand and gently lifted her from the chair toward the bedroom. Again there was a slight resistance that had not been there on prior occasions, but Strollo ignored it.

The bedroom was large, with a king-size bed covered with satin sheets and four large pillows. An entertainment center with television, VCR, and CD player lined the wall at the foot of the bed. A headboard contained the controls for the entertainment center, switches for the indirect room lights, and a telephone. A large bath with shower and whirlpool tub adjoined a walk-in closet.

A half hour later, an unhappy, disappointed Strollo was standing by the bed pulling on his pants. As he moved to the chair to put on his shoes, he looked at Pam, half covered with the sheet, eyes closed.

"Where were you tonight? Certainly not with me."

"You caught me when I was overtired."

"I've always been able to wake you up before."

Pam just wanted him to leave. She hadn't asked to make love, he just did it. And all the while she was wondering what would happen if he found out about the FBI contact. Would he get her in trouble with the law?

Even before the FBI had contacted her, she had been thinking of breaking off the relationship. The novelty, the adventure, had gone out of it some time ago. Now there was no doubt, it had to end.

"Well, you didn't wake me up tonight," Pam said almost absently, not giving much thought to it.

Strollo came upright in the chair, dropping the shoelace he was tying. No bitch had ever said anything like that to him. Scowling with anger, he stood, walked over to the bed, and looked down on her.

"You were meat, dead meat. It was like fucking a corpse."

Pam's eyes widened in fear. It looked like he was going to hit her. She pulled the sheet up higher.

He continued, "You expect me to wake the dead? You put a little life back in that pussy, and I'll screw you till you scream. You've got to be a woman before I can be a man."

He picked up his jacket and stormed out.

The ugly scene stayed with her the next day and into the evening. Alone, musing over after-dinner coffee, she was going over in her mind, for the hundredth time, how she should handle Strollo. Jerry Collins had called her twice that day and left messages, but she had not returned his calls. She was trying to decide her best course of action. After last night's menacing performance, she had decided she had to break up with Strollo immediately. The decision could not be put off.

He'd given her some expensive jewelry, taken her to Las Vegas, Nassau, Atlantic City, and Santo Domingo. She understood now why he had spent time away from her when they were there. He obviously had gambling interests.

The sex had been good but not singular. She had been attracted and held by the power, the mystery, the intrigue, the evil that he exuded. The flame now threatened to consume the moth.

She had never really achieved her objective. There was no doubt she had a degree of control over him, yet she had never been able to use it. He had never opened up to her. Is that what happened after you had killed a few people?

She was startled by a knock on her door. Who could it be? Strollo had a key, and other visitors had to use the speaker at the main door to get access to the building. Puzzled, she walked over to the door and opened it. She saw Shirley and Jerry smiling a greeting.

"Sorry to show up uninvited," Shirley said, "but we do need

to talk to you, and we saw your car out front, so we thought this might be a good time."

Pam, taken by surprise, stood by the open door as both agents took advantage of her confusion and walked in.

"I hope we're not interrupting dinner," Shirley said.

Pam, beginning to regain her balance, responded, "I'm finished, but really, this is a poor idea. Vincent may stop over this evening."

Jerry shook his head. "We're on him. He's home with his wife. If he starts moving they'll let us know."

Checked, Pam started searching for another excuse to rid herself of the agents. "I'm sorry, but this is really inconvenient. I'd rather talk about this some other time."

Jerry took her elbow and turned her away from the door.

"We really need to talk. This could be very important to your future."

Pam relented some. There could be no harm, and perhaps some benefit, in listening to what they had to say. Perhaps it would help her find a way to end the relationship. Pam nodded, still uncertain, and led them into the living room. She chose an overstuffed chair and Shirley and Jerry sat on the sofa.

The conversation lasted over an hour. There was some show-and-tell as the agents displayed photos of Strollo with some of his soldiers, then with her. Overwhelmed with information, Pam finally called a halt.

"All right, you guys have sold me, Vinnie is Mafia. With some people, a not nice guy, even though with me he's always been a gentleman. I'll stop seeing him. Is that what you want?"

Shirley responded without answering her question. "Could you tell us something about him? What has he talked to you about? Do you know anything about his business?"

Pam hesitated, thinking this over, then decided that since she knew almost nothing, it was to her advantage to appear to cooperate. Perhaps she might even learn something more about this man that she could use to her benefit.

"I haven't met any of his business associates. He says he's in investments, which really covers a broad field. I think he may have an interest in Towers of Light. He's driven by there, with me, several times, looking at it in what appeared to be an admiring way. I once asked him about it. He denied an interest, said it might be the office site he was looking for."

Shirley and Jerry made no visible response to this bit of crucial information. This would be an area of exploration if they could bring Pam around to full cooperation.

Pam continued, "He does use my apartment as a kind of office. At least he's been using my phone to make long-distance calls."

Shirley picked up on this. "Do you have the toll records?"

"Sure, I have to keep all my toll records. In real estate, long-distance business calls are deductible."

"May we see them?"

Pam frowned at this, then shrugged. "I don't see why not. The IRS can, anytime they want to."

Pam produced the phone bills and agreed to let the agents borrow them to make Xerox copies.

After fifteen more minutes of interviewing the agents were satisfied that Pam knew little about Strollo's affairs but was in a perfect position to learn, with the proper coaching.

Jerry led off on this line. "Pam, I think you're satisfied that this guy's bad news. He's been using your phone to conduct business that has to be illegal. He's never done an honest day's work in his life. So he's involved you in criminal activity."

The skin on Pam's face tightened. This was what she was afraid of. She had unknowingly been dragged into something and she would be arrested.

Jerry saw her fear and nodded. "If we weren't having this conversation now, we would be having it a year from now when we'd fully developed his illegal ventures. We'd come looking for you as a subject based on these telephone calls that we would have subpoenaed from the phone company. The guy uses and throws away. He will throw you away when he's finished with you."

Shirley picked up, easily slipping in an alternative to this scenario. "We'd like you to help us develop his criminal activities here and stop him before he destroys more innocent people."

Disturbed, Pam looked Shirley square in the eye. "How do you propose I do that?"

Shirley unblinkingly responded, "Keep dating him."

"Keep dating—?"

Pam thought about this for several moments. After last night, she couldn't imagine taking him to bed again. Finally she said, "I can't do that."

Jerry quickly held up a hand. "If you feel some degree of loyalty or affection for him, remember he has none for you. In fact, quite the opposite. His use of your home and phone for his business would have put you in a real spot."

Pam felt a wave of cold fear creep up her back. She had never faced anything like this before. The thought of being arrested terrified her. Her hands involuntarily clenched and unclenched.

The agents could see the fear in her face, and Jerry bored in. "You know he'll never leave his wife. If he told you that, he was lying. You're one in a long list of girls he's played with. In fact, there's a honey at the Paddock Club he may be screwing already. Our surveillance just hasn't put them in bed yet."

So there is another girl, Pam thought. She had half suspected it. His visits had been less frequent. He wasn't as attentive to her desires. And he had had the gall to call her a corpse last night. That low-down sonofabitch. He wasn't going to treat her like dirt.

She was steely, composed, as she looked up and said, "If I do help you, what will I get out of it? I know all that duty and service stuff, and it matters to me, but I've been dating this guy for almost nine months with nothing to show for it. Now you're telling me I've been getting myself in trouble with the law."

Shirley stood up and crossed over to Pam. Pulling a chair up close, she placed her hand on Pam's, which was resting on an arm of her chair. "Your work with Strollo," she said softly, "will save us untold agent hours of investigation. What we would do is pay your expenses. You certainly shouldn't be out of pocket in helping us. Then at the end of the case we would compute, as closely as possible, the value of your services in helping to disrupt this part of La Cosa Nostra."

Pam was only mildly interested in Shirley's offer of payment for her assistance. What she was focusing on was bringing down Strollo. She would be flirting with danger. It would be a challenge. And in the end she'd destroy the powerful bastard.

A decision was forming in Pam's mind.

"Am I in any danger?"

Jerry, from across the room, responded, "No one can give you an absolute answer on that. Your identity as a helping source will be protected. No one will know you're working with us. That's your best protection. And that's largely in your hands. If you tell someone, then you put yourself at risk. We won't let you out in the cold. If something should happen, we'll help."

Pam was a shrewd businesswoman given to unemotional decisions. The mystery, the Mata Hari angle to it, nonetheless appealed to her. It would be exciting, if she could pull it off.

"Okay, tell me what you want me to do."

• CHAPTER •
FOURTEEN

It was early morning and Al was in his office in shirt sleeves, ready to grill an elusive Steve Donnelly. Al was becoming increasingly concerned with the lack of progress in the Zamorano investigation, especially since the meeting with Captain Juan Marín had convinced him that for some reason Steve wasn't telling him everything. He had confronted Steve and got the usual explanations that he had tried to get in to tell Al but that Al was busy with Baskin and the Strollo case and then things just slipped by. It appeared to Al that Donnelly seemed to be actually avoiding having to talk about the case.

Al opened the conversation. "Steve, we've been looking for Zamorano for months and haven't found a trace of him. If he had Ochoa's money, he'd have surfaced somewhere. If the informants are right, and Ochoa is looking for Zamorano too, and hasn't found him, he's got to be dead. You know Ochoa has as good a fugitive squad as we do."

Steve shifted uncomfortably. Zamorano was his Achilles' heel.

"He's got to be out there somewhere. He's the only one who could have stolen Ochoa's money. He's the only one missing. I told you the cops identified Zamorano's latents on some of the spent shell casings at the doper homicide scene. It had to be Zamorano who killed them and then stole the money."

Al wasn't satisfied. "Why did someone kill his girlfriend and make it look like Ochoa was torturing her to force her to locate Zamorano? Why was Pablo killed? Why do the CIs say Ochoa is looking for Zamorano or whoever stole his money? Even Ochoa's not sure that Zamorano did it."

Steve hoped Zamorano was dead. A live Zamorano could hurt him. "Al, let me handle this. We'll find Zamorano and the whole thing will fall into place."

Al got out of his chair and walked around the coffee table to where Steve was seated. Staring down at him, he said, "No. I want the focus of the investigation to change. I want you to assume Zamorano's dead. I want to know who stole Ochoa's money. When we learn that, we'll know who killed the girl and the dopers at the counting house. Zamorano's bullets may have, but that doesn't mean he pulled the trigger. If he did do it, he may not have done it alone. I want him or his body, any accomplices, and the money."

Angry, feeling cornered, Steve was about to remark that if Al didn't have confidence in him, he should give the case to another supervisor. He caught himself just in time. He couldn't let that happen. As long as he had the case, he could protect himself. He swallowed his pride. "Okay, we'll take a fresh look."

Al added, "And I want both of us to meet with Metro Homicide."

Steve knew he had to avoid this. He'd delay, and maybe Al would forget about it. "Let me see what I can do to arrange a mutually agreeable time."

He was grateful for the arrival of Assistant U.S. Attorney Karla Delisi, who was handling the Strollo case, and edged out of the office.

Al greeted Karla warmly. She had a well-deserved reputation as a conscientious prosecutor. The agents who worked with her admired her knowledge of the law, her willingness to work, and her combativeness. She had been the AUSA who first attempted to get Miller to request electronic surveillance authority. The Department of Justice had at last given the green light to the applications, though reluctantly, because of Neil Miller's refusal to make a positive recommendation.

As the supervising prosecutor assigned to the wiretap, she had come to address twenty-five FBI agents who had been delegated to monitor the taps on Iannello and Knight. These were being installed at that very moment on both their homes and businesses, as well as on the two public phones in the Leisure Hotel. There was sufficient probable cause to go up directly on Iannello without the bookie taps. The toll records from Pam, the pen registers, and the surveillance provided probable cause for the public phones.

The agents, together with Bill Baskin and Al, assembled in one of the open squad areas filled with the agents' individual desks. Everyone had a pad, and they all took notes as Karla instructed them on keeping proper logs of every call intercepted, with times of ring, answer, and disconnect together with a summary of the call.

A considerable time was spent on minimization—not listening to conversation that did not concern criminal activity. This would be especially critical on the public phones. Surveillance would play a part here, for the order provided that the agents could listen only when Iannello or Strollo was using the phone.

Proper recording on original and duplicate tape and sealing of original tapes was covered.

After the agents' conference, Karla and Bill agreed on the procedure for ten-day progress reports to the authorizing judge on the taps.

The first shift of monitoring agents proceeded to the office intercept rooms, where the monitoring equipment was set up. Other agents took to the street to be in place to surveil any activity the taps developed. The sound agents threw their switches, and the pen registers instantly became intercepts.

The first call was an outgoing from Knight's home to a number that the pen had identified before. It was Connie calling to arrange a lunch with a friend. As soon as the caller and recipient were identified and the first sentence spoken, the call was minimized. This would prove to be the pattern on the Knight home phone.

His business phones that first day also failed to produce any relevant calls. All were minimized.

Iannello was moving about the city, and no calls were placed or received until late evening.

Al, Bill, and Karla moved to Al's office to discuss the events of three days ago, when Pam had signed on.

Bill was tired and looked it. The strain of long hours of concentration showed in his face and rumpled shirt. He began by glancing over his notes. "Our subscriber checks on Strollo's toll calls from Pam's phone, the pen registers, and SPIT surveillance gave us probable cause for the public phones. He also made calls from Pam's which the timing indicates set up the pay-phone calls. It's a Who's Who of LCN. I think there's enough PC to go up on Pam's phone."

He turned to Karla. "The pen-register order you got for Pam's phone was carried to the phone company, and we were up last night."

Karla sat in one of the leather chairs by the coffee table as Al took the other, and Bill lowered himself onto the leather couch.

Karla picked up from there. "I think a few calls from the Pam phone to Iannello, or from Iannello, will give us enough to go up on the Pam phone. By the way, how did Shirley and Jerry convince Pam to cooperate? This guy's got to be jabbing her, and she's going to stay with him?"

Al shrugged his shoulders. "One of the great mysteries of human nature. What motivates people to become informants? Certainly part of that motivation has to be supplied by the agent who is recruiting the CI, and Shirley and Jerry did a great job."

Al's enigmatic smile was in keeping with his reply. "The best answer I have is a non-answer I picked up from an old history professor of mine who said, 'Men's motives are complex, seldom logical, and usually unknown even to themselves.' If I had a better answer I probably would break all records at being a salesman."

Bill continued in a tired voice. "So far, 728-C, as she will be referred to from this point on, has consented to a microphone in her apartment and a tap on her phone. We can use those, of course, only when she's present or a party to the conversation. We hope that these will develop quickly into full, court-approved T-3s."

At 18:02.10 a call was placed from Pam's phone to a number in New Jersey that had previously been identified as being used by James Amari. The call lasted thirteen seconds.

The agent who observed the outgoing call on the pen register radioed the surveillance team:

"S-One from Guide."

"Guide, go."

"Your package had short contact north. Probably leaving Beauty and heading to coin machine. If he's at one of our machines, advise."

The transmission was via scrambled radio signal but nevertheless used shorthand codes. It was understood, and S-One replied, "Ten-four."

Twenty-five minutes later, surveillance team one called the intercept room.

"Guide, S-One."

"Guide, go."

"Our package in the Leisure Hotel. No foot inside as yet. Countersurveillance in hotel tough. Unless advised to contrary will remain outside."

The intercept agent responded, "Ten-four," and prepared to listen to any calls on the public phones in the hotel.

At 18:33.25, a call was placed from one of the pay phones to a public phone in New Jersey. Amari answered at 18:33.31, and the call was duly logged and recorded.

"Hello?"

"Jimmy, how are ya?"

"Good, boss. Quiet day."

"I talked to Tony on this end. You know Tony? You got his number down here?"

"Yeah, I can reach him at the hotel, right?"

"Yeah. Tony's arranging to find a shoemaker who can make us some size twenty-two sneakers that are real quiet. Nobody will hear you walk in them. You understand? Will that size be okay?"

"I guess so. Size forty-five is usually better. Make sure the sneakers got socks attached to them. You understand?"

"Yeah, whatever size we get, they'll be ready to go. We thought about size forty-five, but Tony says the only ones available that are really quiet are big, more like boots, and are high, like twenty inches. You understand?"

There was a pause as Amari thought this over. "I think so. These size forty-five sneakers are made for real fast running, right?"

"You got it. That's why we thought the size twenty-two would be better."

"Okay. Don't forget I got to have a pair."

"You find somebody to help you with our medical problem?"

"Yeah, I think so."

"Good. You can call Tony direct if you want to work out details. We'll get them to you as quick as we can."

"Okay, boss, I'll stay in touch."

Disconnect was recorded at 18:34.51.

Bill, the intercepts in place and surveillance running smoothly, had left the office at five to get some rest. He was called at home, and the intercept was played for him. He had the agent call Al and Karla in turn. All three headed for the listening post.

While they were en route, another call was picked up.

Knight had been trying to reach Iannello for a week. All he had got was his answering machine, and the calls had not been returned. Knight needed two things. Most important was reassurance that everything was all right. That in three months' time they could sell the bonds and there would be no problems. The other item was the fifty thousand dollars he had been promised. He could certainly use the money and had been asking for it for months. Iannello had excuses, but now just wasn't returning calls. Knight was worried that something, besides the fifty thousand owed him, was making Iannello play hide-and-seek.

At 18:39.21 the monitoring agent on Knight's business phone

got a "receiver off hook" and then a dial-out. The agent on Iannello had an incoming ring at 18:39.35 and connection at 18:39.53.

"Hello?"

"Hey, Tony, Hal. How goes it these days? Been trying to get you for a couple weeks."

"Yeah, well, I been kinda under the weather, and then the business started having some problems, and I been up to my ears. You know how it is."

"Sure, Tony, we've all been there. The reason for my call is the fifty big ones. The ones that were coming to me after our deal. I really need them now. The business is hurting, and that would take off all the pressure."

"Yeah, I know. I told you the Man was arranging to move some stuff around. It all takes time. The way things are looking now, it might be that when we sell the whole works in about three months, you'll take it off the top, together with the rest that's coming to you."

"Tony, I really could use it now. Three months may be too late."

"Hal, I been trying, but the Man's at the mercy of the people overseas. Things are all bogged down. As soon as I can get it, you'll have it. For sure no later than sale time."

"Tony, with the money coming, could I borrow some against it, like an advance?"

"Hal, baby, you want that road again?"

"No, but since I'm owed, I thought I could borrow without the vig."

"Hey, baby, two different pockets. Don't work that way. Sorry, Hal, got to run. I'm late now. I'll talk to the Man, and get back to you next week."

Disconnect 18:41.50.

Pam came into her apartment just before seven and found Strollo there, about to mix some martinis. She had contacted him and made a conciliatory overture after the disappointment of the other night. This was their first meeting since then.

She dropped her briefcase and handbag at the door and

walked directly to Strollo, who took her in his arms and kissed her hard and long. She was warm and yielding, and Strollo's hand began moving from her back to her front.

She broke the embrace as she kicked her shoes off, removed her short jacket, and began unbuttoning her blouse.

"I really need a drink tonight. It's been a rough day. Make it a Gibson. I'm going to change out of these work clothes and get into something comfortable."

"It'll be ready. Straight up or on the rocks?"

"On the rocks."

With that she headed back to the bedroom, and Strollo continued his preparations. He took a bottle of Sapphire gin and vermouth out of the refrigerator and poured gin into the chilled cocktail mixer with a dash of vermouth, and then filled the mixer with ice. A couple of stirs and his drink was poured into a long-stemmed glass he had just removed from the freezer.

By the time he had tasted his, she was back in white shorts that accented her long legs and a pink cutoff T-shirt that was several inches shy of meeting the shorts.

He poured her martini over ice in an old-fashioned glass, adding two cocktail onions. After she took her first sip, she exhaled in relief. Some pâté and biscuits were found, and they moved to the living room to relax on the sofa.

The first martini went down very smoothly, and Pam rose to get the second. A fresh one for Strollo, a diluted one for her.

Each was feeling out the other, wanting to address their argument of the other night but not knowing quite how to get there. So they talked about a few of her real estate prospects. Soon she announced, "Time for another drink. Want one?"

Strollo demurred, but Pam insisted she needed another and didn't want to drink alone, and so he acquiesced. A fresh one came in for him, a diluted one for Pam.

Halfway through the third martini, Pam announced she would start dinner, and Strollo, feeling the buzz of the martinis, accompanied her to the kitchen.

Pam decided she would have Dolphin à la Popeye, and began mixing mayonnaise with mustard and defrosting some chopped spinach. As she worked, she felt Strollo undressing her with his eyes. She moved sensuously, slowly, bending several times, allowing her short T-shirt to fall away from her breasts and further straining the tight white shorts. She saw Strollo responding. Without comment, she freshened his drink.

As the dolphin layered with chopped spinach and mayonnaise-mustard went into the microwave to poach in lime juice and fumé blanc, Pam decided to test the waters.

"I'm putting together some tax information for my accountant next week, and I've got to give him the telephone toll records to deduct as expenses. I had no idea you were such a phone freak."

She saw a hint of concern in his face, so she laughed, making light of the issue. "Who are all those people you call from here? My Lord, you must know everyone in New York and New Jersey."

Strollo watched her T-shirt as she took the fish out of the microwave and placed it under the broiler to brown the mustard-mayonnaise topping. He was totally relaxed, mellow, his brief moment of concern gone.

"Got lots of business friends up there."

Stretching to reach some plates on the top shelf of the cupboard, she remarked casually, "You always say you're in investments, but I never see or hear anything about these investments. What are you investing in?"

Strollo, watching the T-shirt rise several inches, laughed, now eager to demonstrate his financial machismo. "Honey, I don't invest. I let other people invest their money with me, and then I take the whole pile in my pocket. I got no overhead, I only cut back to the boss, and a piece to my guy out front. Investors get shit." With that, he laughed gruffly.

Pam, sensing she was close, pushed him by subtly challenging his statement. "All that sounds good, but give me a for instance."

With a stern expression, not willing to surrender the image he was creating, he responded, "You like Towers of Light? Well, that's mine. I don't have a cent in it. The banks are investing in it and carrying me. I've already made mine before the building's even finished. You show me anybody can do that."

Pam hoped the mike was working and the FBI was happy with her work. She smiled in pleasure—men really could be led by the nose—as she said, "Dinner's ready."

Bill, Al, and Karla arrived at the FBI office within ten minutes of one another and proceeded to the basement, where the listening post was located in a large room.

Along one wall were cubicles which housed the pen register that recorded outgoing calls and the trap that deciphered the number calling the intercepted number. Earphones and a large dual-cassette tape head allowed the agent to listen and make two simultaneous recordings. Pads and log sheets were on the small desks in the cubicles. One cubicle served each installed wire.

A large library table was in the middle of the room, and on it had been placed a tape recorder. As the three entered it was the center of interest for all the agents on monitor duty.

The tape of the Strollo call was played, and the agent handling the recorder held up his hand to halt discussion, an impish smile on his face.

"Before you go off on discussing the implications of that call, we have a bonus for you, just so you won't think your trip has been wasted."

He punched the play button, and the three listened to the Knight call and to Strollo's comments to Pam about Towers of Light.

A silence followed after the tapes had finished, as each weighed what he had heard. Finally, Al addressed the agent who had played the tapes. "Good work, Rob. I think you've succeeded in getting our attention."

Then, addressing all the agents who were at their stations as well as Bill and Karla, he said, "Let's take the calls in order and analyze what we've heard. Bill, you want to start, or one of you guys on the intercept?"

Bill, realizing this moment belonged to the troops, asked Rob, "What do you guys make of the Amari-Strollo call?"

The agents in the room all broke into broad grins as Rob summed up what they had talked about earlier.

"Well, we've sure discussed it, and we all believe Strollo is discussing two silenced .22-caliber pistols for a hit."

Bill and Al nodded in agreement.

"The sneakers thing is pretty obviously not what they're really talking about. The socks attached is gun and silencer attached. The size forty-five is .45-caliber. When Strollo talks about big like boots and twenty inches high, we're not sure, but think he's probably referring to the MAC-10 machine guns that are down here, with silencers, and twenty-round clips."

The attention of everyone in the room was riveted on Rob. The agents occasionally glanced at Al to see his reaction.

"Amari wasn't sure what he meant—note the pause. Then Amari gets it and says something about real fast running. Got to be talking about a machine gun."

Proud of his guys, Al took Rob by the arm and addressed the monitoring agents. "I agree. We're listening to a double murder being planned by LCN. Now we need to know who they plan to hit and when and where. You see? The intercepts have already proved their worth."

Then, turning to include Bill in his remarks, he said, "A good surveillance of Iannello may provide some interesting contacts as he tries to locate the guns. Stay with it, and give us the benefit of any thoughts you may have as you continue to pick up conversation."

He could almost feel the determination in the room to solve this riddle. The agents valued the commitment of an SAC and worked the harder for it.

Al continued, "Rob, sit down. Join us in discussing the other two contacts and the best use we can make of them. Karla, I think we have several basic decisions to make. Do we approach Knight? Do we now do an open investigation of Towers of Light? How far can we let the homicide preparations go? What direction or directions can we take to identify the victims, and learn the when and where?"

Amari knew he'd have to whack both Siragusas at the same time. If he didn't, whoever was scheduled second was sure to run to the cops. He needed another man and two silenced guns.

He approached Salvatore Magaddino, who agreed, reluctantly, to take out one of them with Jimmy. He was a young mafioso, eager to make his mark, and therefore willing to make an unauthorized hit with someone of the stature of the legendary Blue Eyes Amari, and for someone of Strollo's status.

Amari decided the hit had to be fast and quiet, possibly in the Siragusa home. So all they needed now was the guns.

The comforts of his new black Jaguar did not ease Iannello's tension as he drove from bar to bar in Hialeah, attempting to set up a contact for "quiet sneakers."

He had made money with Strollo, to be sure. Always, however, in the back of his mind were nagging doubts about how Strollo operated. Several times he had considered ways to protect himself if Strollo's plans were to go wrong. Always he had put the thoughts aside, especially as money came in. So now Strollo had told him to get two silenced .22s. Two people were going to be whacked. Iannello didn't know who. Amari would do the work.

Iannello knew that if anything went wrong, he'd be standing right next to Amari when the judge sentenced them. There was no money in his pocket on this one, and he had no control over the action. His life was in the hands of Strollo and Amari.

Iannello made up his mind. He would take out some insurance, just in case. His plan involved some risk. He'd have to walk a very thin line, but it was the only out he could think of. Very carefully, he'd have to make a move toward the FBI. If Strollo found out, he'd be dead. But Iannello knew what he had to do.

Claude Williams had taken some time off, and he and his wife were on a one-week cruise in the Caribbean. He had instructed MM 152-C, Ruby, to contact in his absence either the alternate agent, Henry Cummings, assigned to her or his supervisor, Steve Donnelly, if she had anything requiring action.

When Ruby called, Henry Cummings was out of the office, so she asked for Donnelly. When Donnelly's secretary advised him that Ruby was on the phone, he absently picked up the instrument and greeted her. "Hi, Ruby, what you got?"

She was brimming over with excitement. "You know, Sonny's been catching a lot of shit from the Ochoa crew since you grabbed that coke I gave you. He talks to one of them almost every day, and they been dropping some stuff about how they're trying to find out who ripped some money from the place where those guys were killed. They don't seem too concerned about the two tons of coke you guys got at about the same time."

Donnelly stiffened in his chair, not knowing what was coming next, not sure he wanted to hear it.

Ruby continued, "At first they were looking at Zamorano, but they told Sonny Zamorano's dead and he didn't do it."

Donnelly glanced about the office to make sure no one was within earshot. His secretary's phone was in its cradle.

The excited voice in his ear seemed about to explode. "They said it was two Miami cops who probably killed Zamorano, and his girl, whacked Pablo and the guys at the house, and stole the money. They're going to tell Ochoa about it, and Ochoa will probably hit the cops."

With great effort, Donnelly controlled the sour fear that rose in his throat. He forced his voice to be calm as he said, "Good work, Ruby. Stay with this, it's important to us. I'm sure Ochoa's people are wrong, but we need to know what they're up to. I want you to talk only to me about this, okay?"

"Sure."

"I mean nobody else, not Claude, not Henry, nobody but me."

Ruby's voice showed her confusion. "What's the problem?"

Donnelly was immediately concerned that perhaps he had pushed her too far. As casually as he could, he said, "None, except this is very sensitive. You know, the guys have to work with the locals, and when they get this kind of stuff they have problems handling it. Let me take the burden for them."

Ruby was still puzzled, but she agreed to talk only to Donnelly about this.

There was no doubt in his mind that Ruby was talking about Morales and Fonseca. It all made sense. It had to be them.

He couldn't expose them without risk of exposing himself. He had falsified a report of an interview with Zamorano. The interview had never happened. It was an automatic firing offense. His career would be destroyed. The cops had only killed worthless dopers. Who really cared? It was not worth his future to expose them. Except for Teresa. Why had they killed her?

Donnelly's head dropped into the cradle of his hands.

• CHAPTER •
FIFTEEN

Karla, Bill, and Al dissected the three intercepts for an hour. Rob kept them supplied with coffee as they talked around the library table in the large intercept room. They finally decided there was no advantage at present to attempting to flip Knight. The taps were producing, and for now they would suffice.

Karla committed herself to getting a tap on the Sumpter phone. Strollo's use of it to call known mafiosi in the Northeast and the intercepted call setting up the Amari sneakers call were sufficient probable cause.

Based on Strollo's admitted interest in Towers of Light, every effort would be made to enlarge the intelligence base there. The intercept agents would be alert for any call to or from a Towers phone that might provide probable cause to go up on those lines.

Al commented, "Towers is obviously a scam. We've got a chance here to catch them dirty, before they can walk away and hand up some nobody to take their heat."

He thought that a week was enough time to wait, and if nothing developed by then the investigation should go open. That should generate chatter on the lines which were up.

The homicides were the real problem. The case would have to be followed very closely. At some point it might be necessary to tell Strollo that they knew. This would stop the plans from going further and remove the danger to the two unknown victims. Still, would the intercepts alert them in time?

The morning produced several nonevidentiary calls of a personal nature from Iannello's and Knight's phones. By afternoon they would be up on Pam's phone and the mike in her house, with a court order, so they could listen even when she was not there.

At 09:37.21, Knight answered his phone at his office.

"Hello, Knight Maintenance."

"Hal, Herm. Need to see you sometime today."

"Sure. Is there a problem?"

"Maybe, but I think it's more a misunderstanding. That's why I want to talk about it."

"I can come by and see you in half an hour."

"No, let's meet at Denny's, on Biscayne and 36th. We'll have a cup and relax more that way."

"All right, see you in twenty minutes."

"Right."

The intercept agent noted the number of the incoming phone but did not check his list. The voice and name did not strike a familiar chord. The conversation was innocuous. If it had gone longer he would have minimized it. Since Knight was about to leave his office, the agent walked over to the radio that had been installed at one end of the room and contacted the surveillance crew that was on Knight.

"S-Three from Guide."

"Guide, go."

"S-Three, package leaving to meet unsub 'Herm' at Denny's, 36th and Biscayne."

"Ten-four, we'll eye him and ident Herm."

Knight was mildly puzzled. He hadn't spoken to Herman Frank for about two weeks. The unusual part of the call was the morning meeting, away from the bank.

Knight called home and told Connie he had to meet someone and was putting his phone on call forwarding so she could

answer it. Knight hoped that by next month he'd be able to afford a secretary again. This call was not recorded, it was minimized.

Knight locked up, and as he got behind the wheel of his
white Lincoln Continental—two years old, but thank God
paid for—the specter of the bond loan repayment suddenly
struck him full-bore. Could that be what this odd meeting
was for?

One surveillance car followed Knight, two preceded him, and
four agents were scattered about the restaurant when Knight
entered.

He spotted Frank at a window booth, walked over, and
greeted him warmly. "Herm, good to see you. Wife and family
okay?"

Frank did not return Knight's smile or greeting. "Hal, this is
a conversation that never happened."

The blood drained from Knight's face, and his hands trembled as he sank into the booth opposite Frank. "Sure, Herm,
whatever you want. This smells like trouble."

Herman Frank had agonized over this meeting for days.
Now he spit out, "Anytime the president of my bank says I'm
fired if I talk to you, and some wise-assed FBI agent threatens
me with jail, I guess that's trouble."

Knight's world collapsed around him as he leaned back
against the high plastic booth cushions for support. Both his
hands were flat, pressed hard on the table.

A voice said, "Can I take your order?"

After a moment of silence, Frank responded, "Just two coffees for now." He looked at Knight, concerned. "Hal, you all
right? You look terrible."

Then Knight's reaction to his opening remarks began to
come home. He suddenly realized this meeting was a mistake.
He could be fired. He might even go to jail. Starting to panic,
he said, "Look, Hal, I shouldn't be here. I really mean it—this
meeting never happened."

With that, Frank dropped two dollars on the table and
walked out.

Knight saw him leave but did not react. He was still in shock.

The waitress arrived with the coffee. "If you want anything else, I'm Denise. Just give me a wave."

Her friendly voice somewhat revived him. "Thank you, no."

He rose and walked out unsteadily. His car was familiar, a refuge where he could hide. He opened the door and managed to get behind the wheel, where he sat, not thinking, just dazed. He was overpowered by what little Frank had said to him. His worst fears had been realized. The bonds were not only worthless, there was a crime involved. They must have been stolen.

Slowly his power of reasoning returned, and he began to analyze his situation. There had to be a solution, some way out of this. His first reaction was to talk to Iannello. After all, Iannello had given him the bonds. This was as much Iannello's problem as his. He needed to call and set up an appointment to see him. With this resolve he drove back to his office.

At the fifth ring, Iannello's answering machine kicked in with its message to leave a message. Knight responded, "Tony, this is Hal. It's imperative we get together today. I just got word there's a problem with the bonds at National Bank of the South."

The agents who had observed the meeting were perplexed. They knew something significant had happened. It was obvious this was no ordinary business meeting. One car stayed on Knight. The other two cars, now augmented by a third, followed Frank back to the National Bank of the South.

The tap on Iannello's phone picked up Knight's recorded message. The message and the aborted meeting told the agents that Frank had ignored his president's order and Al's stern warning.

They had a decision to make. This was a tactical problem that would probably affect the entire case. Bill Baskin told the monitoring agents to advise him immediately if Knight got in contact with Iannello.

The Iannello surveillance advised that he was in Shooters Empire, a gun store in Hialeah.

Upon hearing the news, Bill rushed upstairs and into Al's office, where he related what they had learned. Al called Karla on the speaker phone so both he and Bill could talk. As soon as she came on, Al began:

"Karla, this is Al. You're on the speaker phone. Bill is with me. We surveilled Knight to a meeting at a restaurant with Herman Frank, the VP from the bank we served the subpoena on. Knight was very upset, left the restaurant, and called Iannello for a meeting saying something was wrong with the bonds. Iannello wasn't in, so he left that message on his machine."

Bill's fingers drummed nervously on the arm of his chair. Al's hand was poised to write on the pad in front of him, but nothing came. The tension of the moment filled the room.

Al continued, "Karla, I think our hand's been forced. We really don't have a choice now. As I see it, we've got to step into Knight; see if we can turn him, and tape any meeting he has with Iannello."

"I agree, Al. I don't see any alternative."

Iannello had just finished his negotiations. The gunshop owner had three Hi-Standard .22-caliber semiautomatic pistols with silencers, and he had agreed to sell two of them for $2,500.

Before Iannello left the shop, he used the phone to access his answering machine. He received Knight's message and almost dropped the bag carrying the two guns. The listening post was aware the message had been picked up by Iannello.

As Iannello left the shop in his Jaguar, with both guns in the trunk, he began to consider what to do next. He had intended, at some point close to the day the loan was due, to tell Knight he had a problem. He could either redeem the bonds by paying off the loan or take his lumps and do two or three years in Eglin, a country-club prison in north Florida. He would have added that these were Knight's only choices. Any finger-pointing would result in his family being whacked.

This discussion would have occurred at Iannello's chosen time and place. A discussion like this with Knight, on his terms, was dangerous. A thought crossed his mind. There was a way: take him by surprise, now.

Iannello drove straight to Knight's office.

* * *

The decision to interview Knight made, Al and Bill turned to the details.

"Who do you want to send out?" Al asked. "Who's your best interviewer that's up on the case?"

"Ken Stacy is the case agent and is up on the case," Bill said, weighing the possibilities as he spoke. "But Brian Marion is my top interrogator, and most likely to succeed in flipping Knight. Ken could bring Brian up to speed in a half hour and be his partner during the interview."

"Fine, let's get moving. I assume you'll just walk in on him."

"Right. What about deals? If he sets up Iannello, he's going to ask what's in it for him."

Al knew that deals weakened the credibility of courtroom testimony. "Let's hope Brian is good enough that he can sell co-operation on Iannello's screwing of Knight in this whole deal. This is the only way to show a court that Iannello, and not Knight, is the real culprit. Brian can assure him that we'll be putting in a good word with the judge. Beyond that we'll need a conference call with Karla."

Bill was satisfied. "Okay, we're on the move."

Ken Stacy was a tall, slender, brown-haired man whose rimless glasses and authoritative demeanor reminded one of a high school math teacher. Brian was shorter, black-haired, and slightly paunchy. His eyes always seemed half closed, giving a deceptive air of languor. His unthreatening appearance was his most potent weapon.

As Ken began his briefing, the intercept office advised that Iannello had accessed his answering machine but so far had not returned Knight's call.

Ken took this as a good sign. "Based on the Knight-Iannello call we intercepted before, Iannello may not be in a hurry to talk to Knight, believing he's trying to collect fifty thousand dollars that apparently is due him."

Brian was less optimistic. "I think we'd better reach this guy as fast as we can. Can we talk as we drive to Knight's office?"

"Sure, I'll brief you in the car. Just give me a minute to grab some serials from the file that may be of use."

The surveillance team three was informed that Ken and Brian were going to Knight's office to attempt a flip. In turn, both agents monitored the surveillance channel S-Three was using as they drove.

Ten minutes from Knight's office they heard:

"S-Three from S-Two."

"S-Two, go."

"We're on our guy, and about a minute away from your guy's office. We think he's going to visit."

Brian aptly summed up the situation for all: "Shit."

The radio spoke. "Station, from S-Three."

"S-Three, go."

"Inform the boss, and tell him we're taking no action."

"Ten-four."

The next transmission was from S-Two. "S-Three, he just pulled into your guy's parking lot."

Armed with this knowledge, Ken and Brian proceeded to a restaurant parking lot about three blocks from Knight's office. At this point they could only sit and wait. Ken transmitted: "Station, twenty-four-ten."

The office dispatcher replied, "Twenty-four-ten, go."

"Advise the boss we'll interview as soon as number two leaves."

"Ten-four."

Iannello walked into the bare office of Harold Knight, who actually seemed relieved to see him. He started to say something but was stopped by Iannello's thrust-out palm. He put an index finger on his lips and shook his head, indicating silence.

Knight's face changed from relief to consternation as Iannello took him by the arm and led him to the bathroom. Iannello turned on the water, flushed the toilet, and in a barely audible whisper told Knight, "Okay, strip. I mean it, asshole, take off your clothes, all of them."

Frightened, Knight obediently did as he was told. Iannello returned to the office area and quickly searched it for cameras and bugs. On the way past, he turned on both the radio and the television.

When he returned to the bathroom, he was greeted by the sight of an overweight Harold Knight in his underwear. Iannello picked up the discarded clothes, quickly searching them for any recording device. He then again leaned close to Knight's ear.

"You don't say nothing, nothing! Not a peep! You chirp and I'll kill you right here."

Knight was terrified, and his nakedness seemed to compound his feeling of vulnerability. He trembled, his face contorted as if expecting a blow.

Iannello continued his rasping, whispered conversation.

"The bonds in those three banks are phony. You put them there. You got sixty grand for it. You either get them out or plead guilty when they come for you. You point any finger at me, and I'll cook you and your old lady in acid, you get me?"

Seeing Knight cowering so pathetically told Iannello all he needed to know. "You tell the cops the bonds were given to you by a guy named Smith. Use the divorce story. You gave him the checks, he gave you sixty thousand. That's all you know. Any problem? Just shake your head, yes or no."

Knight shook his head no.

Iannello smiled and patted him on the cheek. "That's a good boy," he said and quickly left the office.

S-Two broadcast, "Package number two just left the office. Proceeding toward his car. . . . He's in and leaving."

Ken and Brian looked at each other, wondering what had just occurred.

Brian commented, "Short interview. We may still be alive. They may not have covered our territory. I think we should go ahead, right now. You agree?"

Ken didn't hesitate. "Let's do it."

Knight stood for a moment after Iannello left and then methodically, without spirit, began to dress. He was devastated. There was only one route left for him. "The insurance will carry the family for a while," he mumbled. It would be better if the suicide looked like an accident. He had double indemnity.

Ken and Brian walked into the office without knocking. They saw a rumpled-looking Knight walking their way, about to leave.

"Sorry, I'm closed. Come back tomorrow."

Ken placed a hand on Knight's chest, stopping him short. With his other hand he flipped open his credential case. "FBI, Mr. Knight. I'm Ken Stacy and this is Brian Marion."

Brian also flipped open his credential case.

Knight stiffened, expecting the next words would announce his arrest. He had to get out. He had made his decision. Summoning his last reserves of strength, he decided to try the brazen way.

"Good. Come back tomorrow. I said I was leaving."

He attempted to walk by, but Ken gently held his arm.

Brian responded, "You mean you don't have time to talk to us when you made time to talk to Tony Iannello?"

Knight went white, and all the fight went out of him.

Brian continued mildly, "I think we're entitled to equal time. What we have to tell you will surely be more comforting than anything Iannello said."

Knight did not answer, but turned back into his office. He literally stumbled to his desk chair and fell into it. Ken and Brian took chairs opposite him, both astounded at his pale, almost deathlike appearance. With someone who was reacting so unpredictably, they had to be on their guard in case he tried anything.

Eyeing his man closely, Brian began, "Mr. Knight, would you like to tell us what you and Iannello discussed a few minutes ago?"

Knight did not respond. He sat like a lump, looking blankly at the two agents. Finally, after several seconds, he roused himself enough to say, "Why are you asking me this? What do you want? Are you going to arrest me? Aren't you supposed to advise me of my rights?"

The words seemed to exhaust him. Just the effort of speaking made him appear weaker.

Brian leaned forward slightly. "Mr. Knight, the reason for advising a person of his rights before questioning is to make what he tells you admissible in court. In your case we aren't interested in using anything you tell us against you. We have more than enough evidence to convict you of a wide assortment of charges. You're already gone."

Knight's hand went to his face and covered his eyes.

Brian continued, "We're here to help you avoid a long jail term, and to give you a chance to prevent the bastard who caused you all this trouble, who royally screwed you, from walking away with a pile of money. Are you going to let him screw you again, and do his time for him?"

Ken interjected in a sharp tone, "Come on, man, stop acting like a whipped dog. Fight the sonofabitch. Stand up to him. Be a man."

Knight placed both hands on the armrests of his chair, levering himself up with great effort. Slowly, uncertainly, he began walking toward the door.

Brian rose with him and turned, following Knight with his gaze. "We won't stop you from leaving. But you have to know you'll never get out of this on your own."

Knight managed five steps and then collapsed onto a sofa in the waiting room, gasping for breath. The two agents looked at each other with unspoken understanding.

Ken said, "Mr. Knight, are you all right? Do you need a doctor?"

There was silence as Knight took several long, deep breaths. Some color began to return to his face, and then he hunched over and began to cry.

The two agents shifted uneasily. Ken went to the bathroom and got a glass of water. "Here, Mr. Knight, drink this. Buck up, fella, we can help you."

Knight took the proffered glass and sipped it. Slowly he began to regain some of his composure. The agents found flanking chairs and sat, waiting for the pathetic figure to get a hold of himself.

Finally after long, uneasy minutes had passed, Knight asked, "What do you want? There's nothing left for you. I've got no business. I've got no wife. I've got no children. I've got no life. I'm either going to prison or going to hell, and it doesn't make much difference which. At least if I go to hell, my family might benefit."

Pity showed on Brian's face as he responded, "There might be other alternatives. I can't speak to your family status, but I can assure you that there is a future for you. That's why we're here. I said before, Tony Iannello's the one who destroyed your business."

Knight was having none of it. His course was ordained.

Brian saw he was not yet getting through to him. "I expect he also destroyed your relationship with your wife and children. It's Iannello who has brought you to the two roads you see, prison or hell."

Brian was slowly getting Knight's attention. In his low-key, reassuring manner he went on, "To avoid those roads and find an alternative, you've got to fight the cause of your destruction. And that's Iannello. If you surrender to him, you will go down one of those roads."

Knight's voice was barely audible. "What do you want?"

"The same thing you want. Iannello facing your alternatives, prison or hell, and you with hope for the future."

Knight smiled weakly, mockingly. "And how do you propose to accomplish that?"

"With your help in proving he was the source for the bonds and took all the money."

Still dispirited, Knight asked, "What do you want me to do?"

"We know most of what happened, the phony business record, the three banks, the counterfeit bonds . . ."

Knight straightened up. "Counterfeit! They were counterfeit?"

Brian was about to continue, but Knight stopped him with a gesture of his hand. "Look, it doesn't make any difference. Your help is too late. I don't know if either of you has family, but mine will take an acid bath if I go any further with you. My choice is my life or theirs, really, my life and theirs if I keep on talking to you."

Brian found himself fighting for a man's life as well as the case. "You disappoint me. I took you for a businessman who knew how to bargain, negotiate his way around problems, not a quitter."

Knight, without emotion, replied, "A smart businessman knows when to quit."

Brian, with a sleepy half-smile, said, "A smart businessman listens to all offers before he decides."

Looking up, Knight smiled as well. "You should be a salesman. You've got a good line."

"Will you listen to what I have to say?"

"Yeah, I'll listen. What do I have to lose? But I'm not making any promises."

Brian nodded his agreement, and almost apologetically laid out the facts. "As it stands now, we've got a cinch case against you. Three banks, counterfeit bonds, a million and a half, no restitution. You face big time, especially if you tell the judge you won't say where the money went or where the bonds came from."

Knight shrugged, unmoved. So the die was cast.

Brian, though, was painting black before he painted white. "Iannello walks with the money. We know he's the source, and we know he's got the money. Even if you testify, it may not be enough. We'd have to corroborate what you say."

Knight threw up his hands. "So what's new? I know all that. I'm holding shit."

Brian shook his head. "We can turn that picture around with your help. If you're willing to wear a wire, a hidden microphone, and follow our script in a conversation with Iannello, we'll have him and you'll get the biggest break of your life."

Both agents were astonished when Knight began to laugh uncontrollably.

When he finally recovered, he said, "When he came in here, he made me strip. He turned on the radio and television and whispered in my ear. You guys are amateurs. I couldn't figure out what he was doing at the time, but now I understand. Forget it. You don't stand a chance."

Brian quietly persisted, "If you follow our directions,

Iannello will come to you, and he'll talk. We have a scenario that he won't be able to resist."

"Suppose he does and it doesn't work. I'm left out in the cold."

"No, you give us your best effort, and we'll honor our commitment."

Knight, his strength returning, hoisted himself off the sofa and walked once around the office. "If it works or not, Iannello kills my family and me too."

Brian leaning back, seemingly relaxed, shook his head. "Iannello trades on fear. I'm sure he used it when he was shylocking you. He used it just now when he had you strip." Brian jabbed a finger into his palm, emphasizing his next point. "Fear only works if you let it. Iannello in jail has no teeth. Harming you after he's convicted earns him nothing. There's also the possibility of the witness protection plan."

Knight had heard of this. Maybe there was hope after all. "I'm not saying no, but I need to think about this. I want to talk to my wife, and maybe a lawyer."

Brian realized he had to counter this. "You obviously can talk to anyone you want to, but this won't work if Iannello gets wind of what you're doing. I strongly urge you to keep your own counsel. Think about it if you want, but I wouldn't discuss it, even with your wife."

"How much time do I have?" As Knight said this, an unspoken appendage to the sentence flashed through his mind: to live?

"We're in no rush to arrest you, but events in other areas are moving, so we need an answer tomorrow morning."

So they weren't going to pressure him then and there. Relieved, he said, "All right, I'll call you then. Do you have a card?"

Brian and Ken gave him their cards. They stood up, making as if to leave.

As Ken reached the door, he stopped. He knew they were close to flipping him. Knight was on the brink. He just needed a little shove.

"I should tell you, this train is leaving the station. You either get on it or find your own way. You said it—your way's prison or suicide."

Knight stood still for a moment. He sagged again, then looked up, and in a defeated voice said, "You've got a deal. What do you want me to do?"

• CHAPTER •
SIXTEEN

Iannello proceeded to the Leisure Hotel and was duly reported there by his surveillance. He called Amari and said, "Hey, Jimmy, good to hear your voice. This is Tony in Miami."

"Yeah, the Man said you might call."

"You freezing your balls off up there?"

"Nah, ain't too cold yet, but it'll get there. When it gets too bad, I'll come down your way for a while."

"Jimmy, can you come back to me? I'm at my place."

"Sure thing, give me ten minutes."

At the end of twelve minutes the intercept agent got a ring at one of the booths in the Leisure Hotel. Iannello answered, "Hello."

"Tony, it's me."

"Jimmy, I got the two pieces you need."

"What are they?"

"They're the small size, semis, with the quiet built in. You understand?"

"Yeah. Tony, you know what this is about?"

"Not all of it."

"I don't like it. It ain't business. It's personal. I never did one of these before."

Iannello was surprised to hear Amari talking this openly

about his misgivings. There was no doubt about it: from now on, Tony was going to watch his own back.

Amari continued, "How you gonna get them to me?"

"I got a guy that'll fly up with them, probably tomorrow. You don't know him, he's one of my books, but an all-right guy. I'll have him leave them in a locker at the airport and put the key somewhere, you tell me. Then you can pick them up when you see it's clear, and you and the guy don't never meet."

The stone killer was satisfied with this plan. "Good. When you call with the flight and stuff, I'll tell you what lockers and where to leave the key."

"Talk to you tomorrow."

The tape of this call went straight to Bill and Al.

To say the intercept agents were surprised when Iannello's phone was recorded as dialing the FBI office would be the understatement of the year. Iannello was heard to ask for Agent Lucania.

Nicolo Lucania was Bill Baskin's relief supervisor, but he was primarily a street agent and had been assigned to LCN investigations for the past seven years.

The following conversation was recorded when he answered his phone.

"Lucania."

"Hey, Nick, how's my FBI Sicilian token?"

"Who's this?"

"Nick, I'm wounded." At this point Iannello switched to Sicilian Italian. "You don't recognize the voice of your favorite mafioso . . . suspect, that is? This is Tony. Tony Iannello."

"Well, Tony. Sorry, but it's been two years since we talked."

"I know," Tony laughed, now speaking in English. "I've been neglecting you. But you haven't been by to see me either."

"The last time we talked I didn't feel too welcome."

Iannello laughed again. "Hey, where is your Sicilian ancestry? Mild rebuke sometimes means yes, later, or when the time is right."

"Is the time right now, Tony?"

"I think so."

"You want to talk to me, Tony?"

"Yeah, tomorrow."

"Okay, I'll book a room at the Intercontinental under the name Luca. Ten A.M. That all right?"

"Yeah, I'll be there. Just you and me, right, baby? Oh, and no wires, okay?"

"You want me to break all the rules for you? Okay, Tony, you got it. See you at ten."

"You won't be sorry, Nick. I'm gonna make you a fucking FBI hero. Your boss'll pin a medal on you when we're done."

"Tony, knowing you, I'm more likely to get fired."

Iannello laughed again and disconnected.

As he hung up, he smiled, pleased at the way the conversation had gone. Just the right amount of banter, just the right amount of bait. He was confident he could put himself in a win-win position. He just had to be very careful with Strollo.

Al was seated in one of the leather chairs in his office. On the coffee table a tape recorder had been placed. Bill Baskin sat on the sofa. They had just listened to the Iannello-Lucania tape.

Al paused in thought for a moment and then addressed Nick, who was seated in the leather chair next to him. "What do you make of it?"

Nick Lucania, a short, wiry man, had been born in Brooklyn forty-seven years before. His grandfather, a Sicilian immigrant, had insisted that Nick learn to speak the Sicilian dialect. After getting an accounting degree and working for a firm in New York, Nick had been recruited by the FBI. His language proficiency soon made him helpful in organized crime investigations.

Nick had his legs straight out in front of him, arms folded on his chest. "I don't know. About two years ago I gave Iannello the informant pitch. He was polite, as they always are—said he'd like to help me but didn't know anything about any Mafia. If anything ever came to his attention he'd call. I haven't heard from him since then."

Bill put in, "I can't see a down side. We listen to what he's got to say. If he's got heavy demands—and he will—you say you're just a grunt and you have to talk to the boss."

He glanced at Al for confirmation.

Al had long experience in these matters, and he didn't trust this offer one bit. "I don't feel strongly about this, but I'd prefer you not meet him alone. He's no public-spirited citizen. He wants something. I don't see how he can set you up for anything, but I'd rather err on the side of caution."

Nick smiled. "I agree. I was about to suggest we wire the room. The conversation can be monitored as it goes down, and we'll have a recording to amplify my poor memory."

Al hesitated and then added, "What Bill said about listening is good advice. As you know, we impart information when we ask questions. Let's play this one close. Keep the questions to what he offers. We can always go back if we feel we need to cover more ground. Okay, that's it."

Bill picked up the tape recorder and Nick got to his feet. Al walked out of his office with them. He had another matter to settle.

Steve Donnelly's office was small, with a desk and three chairs crammed into it. The walls were covered with photographs of narcotics searches or arrest scenes, all of which portrayed Donnelly as a central figure.

As usual well tailored, he was regaling several agents with an amusing, yet heroic, account of a case when he spotted Al coming his way. His demeanor changed from affability to concern.

The agents with him noted the change and in searching for its cause saw Al approaching. They didn't know what Steve's problem was, and they didn't want to be around to find out. They exchanged greetings with Al and rapidly melted away.

Al had come to find out why the Metro Homicide briefing hadn't been set up, but his greeting was friendly and kidding. "Caught you in your den where you can't escape."

Steve's guilt at withholding Ruby's information about the Miami cops was at the forefront of his mind. Defensively he retorted, "I'm not trying to escape anything. Why are you always accusing me of something?"

Al was taken by surprise. "I wasn't doing any such thing. I came by to see if you'd set up the date with Metro Homicide."

Irritably Steve muttered, "No. Haven't found a convenient time yet."

The guy's yanking me around again, Al thought. He was tired of asking and getting nowhere. Instantly he snatched up the phone, punched up the office operator, and told her, "Get me Captain Juan Marín in Metro Homicide."

Steve was both dumbfounded and panic-stricken. He began to protest, "Here, I'll handle it. Let me arrange this."

Al stopped him with an upraised palm. A minute of silence fell between them as he waited to be connected, then the captain was on the line.

"Juan, Al Lawrence. Sorry to disturb you, but I'd like to get with you and some of your men as soon as it's convenient for you."

The captain answered, "Sure. What about?"

"The Zamorano homicides."

"Oh, sure. How about tomorrow at about ten or eleven? I'll have my lead investigators here."

Al eyed Donnelly dubiously as he answered, "Thanks, Juan, that's fine. Let me check my calendar and we'll set an exact time."

"Anything special you want to go over?"

"No, just a general review."

"Okay, you got it."

They disconnected, and Al said, "There now, that wasn't so hard, was it?"

Unable to look Al in the eye, Steve was trying desperately to keep calm. His hands trembled as he picked up a file. Should he tell Al about Ruby's information? No, he couldn't, not yet. He had to find a way out. Once he opened that door, he'd never be able to close it. He'd be finished.

Steve's strange behavior was feeding Al's suspicions of him. "I want to review the entire Zamorano file. Have your clerk pull it and bring it to my office, now."

After Al had left, Steve sat for several minutes, his face ashen. There was no way he could send the whole file to Al. Part of it was in his bottom desk drawer. He called to his clerk and told her to pull the Zamorano files from her cabinet and take them to the SAC. Then he opened his bottom drawer and glanced in. Yes, the rest of it was still safe.

Nathan Hersch did not claim any expertise in the building industry, but he had to believe that the rapidity with which Towers of Light was reaching completion had to be some kind of record. He smiled as he thought that the swift progress had something to do with putting so much money in one's pocket quickly.

There had been no labor problems at all. One union steward had filed a grievance, and the next day he withdrew it. The laborers and craftsmen actually worked hard. There was very little goldbricking. Materials arrived on time, and they were actually the ones ordered.

With only a few more draws, the construction loans would be exhausted.

Hersch had thought many times that the Mafia was the most organized and efficient industry he had ever worked for.

He had decided that today he would contact Iannello and arrange a meeting. If bankruptcy was the intended end for the project, his five percent of the gross on the sale was hot air.

Disobeying instructions, he dialed Iannello's home from the Towers of Light office. The intercept agents picked up the incoming ring at 09:01.33. Iannello's answering machine came on at the end of the fourth ring. Hersch hesitated. He decided to leave a message, and to try his pager also. As he began speaking, Iannello picked up.

"Nate, baby, I was just about to go out and heard your voice. What's happening?"

"Tony, I got some bad vibes here. Some things about Towers are bothering me. I need some answers, from you or your boss. I need to see you today."

The genial voice turned harsh in an instant. "Say, aren't you at work? Where you calling from?"

Hersch was uneasy. He knew he shouldn't have used the office phone. "It's cool. Drugstore."

"Let me call you there in about five minutes."

Hersch was trapped. He didn't have a number. He had to cover himself. "No. Just let's get together."

"Well . . . okay. Lunch at the Paddock?"

"Done. Twelve-thirty?"

"I'll be there."

Bill Baskin was elated when he heard about the call. Ken Stacy was in his office, discussing the Knight interview, when Bill was given the recording. Bill leaned back in his chair after the tape finished, nodding with contentment.

"That's the PC we've been waiting for. We got Strollo saying Towers is his. Now we got Hersch using the Towers phone to set up a meeting with Iannello concerning Towers. The basic PC is there. What we're missing is a federal violation to tie Towers to. If we could establish what they're doing with Towers, we'd be able to go up on Hersch's Tower phone."

Ken stated what to him was obvious. "It's a bust-out."

"We all guess a bust-out, but so far we haven't developed any evidence to support that theory." He pondered how they could go about doing that, and finally said, "We need to subpoena some records. And that means we have to go open."

Iannello hung up the phone with an uneasy feeling. There was something in what Hersch said, and didn't say, that bothered him. He didn't need Towers problems now. He had enough to think about. When he finished with Nick this morning, he had to begin moving the guns north. Yet he couldn't get Hersch out of his mind as he headed west on the causeway to I-95 and then south for his exit onto Biscayne Boulevard.

Iannello pulled into the parking garage of the Hotel Intercontinental and drove up to the third level, where he parked the Jaguar and took the elevator to the lobby. He picked up the hotel phone and asked for Mr. Nick Luca. He soon was connected.

"Hey, Nick, I'm downstairs."

"Okay, I'm in 1211."

"Be right up."

The two sound agents assigned to plant bugs had just finished, and settled in the adjoining room to listen. Both bugs were radio transmitters. One was in the electrical outlet for a table lamp, and the other was in the outlet in the bathroom.

When Nick opened the door, Iannello ignored the proffered hand and swept Nick into an embrace. His hands roved Nick's body, obviously looking for a wire.

"Hey, Nick baby, you look good. Uncle Sam's treating you right?"

Nick returned a wry smile. "Yeah, things are going good. You finished feeling me up? Let's sit down and have some coffee."

"No offense, Nick, just an old habit. Like the gun on your hip. What you need a gun for, anyway? You know I don't fuck with that strong-arm shit. Hey, I'm a lover."

"You're right, Tony, habit. I feel undressed without it. But I would appreciate it if you'd keep your voice up so the wire don't miss what you're saying."

They both had a laugh, and Nick led Tony to a round table set with a carafe of espresso, two cups, a bottle of anisette, sugar, and lemon rinds.

"Not too early for you, is it, Tony?"

"Shit, you are Sicilian! No, never too early. You know, I'll never understand how a nice guy like you got involved with being a cop."

Nick genuinely chuckled at this twist and touched Iannello on the shoulder. "Tony, you're all right. Never mind that the wise guys I talk to say that your bookies all lose money."

Iannello pretended outrage. "Who the fuck says that? That's a fucking lie. I just keep a—what you guys say—yeah, a 'low profile.' Hey, I'm an honest merchant trying to make a living. I don't know about no wise guys."

Nick poured them each a cup of espresso and handed the anisette bottle to Iannello. He poured some in the cup and added a twist of lemon.

As Nick took a sip of his own espresso, he looked over his cup at Iannello. "Tony, if you don't know about wise guys, how are you going to keep your promise and make me a hero?"

Iannello had his spiel all laid out. He tugged at his ear, controlling any wisps of nervousness, and measured his words, which he had to assume were being recorded.

"Nick, seriously. I'm putting my life on the line coming to see you like this. This has got to be between you and me only. Nobody else in your office should know, and I rely on you that there ain't no wire of this talk."

Nick did not answer him directly. "Relax, Tony. I'm not out to hurt you."

Taking a deep breath, Iannello took the plunge.

"Nick, things sometimes come my way. I ain't looking for them, but they just kind of show up. You got to understand that what I get when these things show up is a partial picture. Pieces are usually missing. In other words, I don't get all the answers."

Nick eyed him coolly, not helping in any way. If Iannello wanted to talk, he'd talk.

"Nick, the other day something walks in my door. Like I said, I ain't lookin for it, and I don't ask questions. Questions can get a guy hurt sometimes. Anyway, it's this guy I know— right now I can't say his name, I may be the only one he approaches. Maybe as this thing goes on you'll get his name, but for now I got to go slow."

Nick remained attentive but expressionless.

"Anyway, we're talking, just like you and me are talking, and this guy says, 'Know where I can get some guns with silencers?' Well, I almost fell off my chair."

Here Iannello stopped and busied himself with taking another sip of espresso, trying to gauge the effect he was having. The FBI agent was impassive, showing only a hint of interest.

Nick blandly said, "And . . ."

Iannello was disappointed. He needed to draw Nick into this.

"Well, I didn't respond right away, and the guy says, 'I'd be willing to go a couple grand for them. If you got a connection, let me know.'

"I told him I didn't know of nothing, but I'd look around. That's when I remembered our talk of a couple years ago. I said if anything came my way, I'd let you know."

Iannello stopped and slumped back into the chair. He was obviously finished.

Nick sat for a moment, digesting what he had heard.

"Tony, what you've told me is interesting, but without names, dates, places, I got nothing. I got an unknown guy looking for two silenced guns. What am I supposed to do with that?"

Iannello shifted uneasily. This wasn't going right at all. He needed Nick to pick up the lead if his plan was going to work.

"I'm sorry if I'm wasting your time. I ain't no cop. I'm giving you what I can. You now know somebody's looking to hurt somebody. Everybody knows a silenced gun is only used for one thing. Now you gotta play cop and stop the thing."

"Okay, Tony," Nick said flatly, "tell me who this guy is that wants the guns."

Iannello saw that Nick wasn't going where he wanted him to, so he decided to point the way.

"Nick, I can't, yet. I gotta make sure it don't come back to me. I can see, though, you need more information. I really don't want to get involved in this thing, but if you want, I'll play the guy a little and see what else I can turn up. Maybe dig just a bit, and see if I can figure out who he's after."

Nick wished he could have a consultation with Bill and Al. What he was getting from Iannello was a bastardized version of what they had previously picked up on the wire. The big question was Iannello's motive here. What was he after? That would be a safe question. Nothing was given away by asking that.

"Tony, why are you telling me this? What do you want out of it?"

"Hey, believe me, my primary reason is keeping somebody from getting hurt. I could also use a buck if this turns out to be something really good."

Nick could not believe this conversation. Something was missing, and he couldn't point to it.

"All right, Tony. I'll take you at face value. Let's see what develops. If you can keep a string on this guy, go ahead. Let me know what happens. Can you call me every day?"

Iannello winced at the idea of calling the feds, but he said, "Sure, no problem. I'll work on it for you."

For some reason Nick felt as though he had just stepped in shit and was unknowingly tracking it all over the house.

"Call me tonight, Tony, even if you don't have anything, and every night till this is done."

Iannello finished off his espresso and rose to leave. Nick got up and moved to the door with him. "Remember, Tony, keep in touch."

"Talk to you tonight."

Once Iannello was gone, Nick said to his sound man, via the bug, "Let me have the tape. I need to see the boss."

Iannello was soon seating himself behind the wheel of his car, feeling very proud of himself. It had gone just the way he'd wanted.

Knight had arrived at the FBI office at seven that morning and by ten had finished an exhaustive session with Brian and Ken, the two agents who had flipped him, and Assistant U.S. Attorney Karla Delisi. They had left him to himself to try to relax and gather his thoughts before he called Iannello. The script they had given him seemed plausible. Iannello could bite.

A microphone and television camera had been installed in his office the night before, and a phone tap. This morning a microphone had been installed in his Lincoln. He had just been given a new pager. It still operated as a pager, but also had a transmitter built into it. Even if Iannello stripped him, the pager would be in the pile of clothes.

The two agents returned. It was time to make the call. Knight drove to a public phone and called Iannello's home. The machine answered.

Knight said, "This is Hal. I figured a way out, but I need more of the same. This time it'll be fifty-fifty."

He also activated Iannello's pager and left his office number.

Iannello's pager went off as he was driving to the Paddock to meet Hersch. When he saw Knight's number, he was surprised. "What the fuck does that turd want?" He decided that call could wait a long time.

Hersch was waiting for Iannello as he entered the bar, seated at the same corner table they had used when Iannello had first made the proposition on Towers of Light.

As Iannello approached the table a martini, straight up, appeared with a lovely young waitress, whose hand caressed Iannello's arm as she left the two men. Iannello saw his own moves being transparently imitated by this asshole. It was obvious as hell Hersch was setting him up for something.

"So, Nate, what's so burning you got to see me today?"

Hersch got straight to the point. "Tony, I'm concerned about what happens to me when Towers is finished."

So that's it, Iannello thought, he finally woke up. That wasn't any reason not to continue the fiction, though. "What happens? You get your piece. That's what happens."

Hersch reached across the table toward Iannello, the picture of concern. "Tony, no bullshit. I ain't one of your assholes. I'm a lawyer and a CPA. I'm with you because you know I can move. I can smell a bust-out a mile away. If it busts out, there isn't any sale, there isn't any five percent of gross, and I get shit."

Iannello would have liked to laugh in his face. To tell him that the big fucking CPA-lawyer had been screwed by a high school dropout and only now was beginning to realize it. And there wasn't a fucking thing he could do about it. He maintained his silence and let Hersch continue.

"Now, I've put a lot into this. I started with a draw of only fifteen hundred a week. I'm at two thousand now, but that doesn't pay for the shit that's coming my way when this goes bankrupt. It doesn't pay for what I lost by leaving the firm. I see what you guys are taking down with the shell companies and the ghosts on the payrolls. All I want is my piece. I deserve it—I'm out front."

Iannello was somewhat surprised. He hadn't expected him to have the guts to put his demands on the table this forcefully. It looked like all his assholes were after him today. Knight was paging him, and Hersch was crying. He'd have to cool Hersch until he could talk to Strollo. They still needed the swinging kid lawyer.

"Nate, baby, nobody's gonna screw you."

All of a sudden danger signals started going off in Iannello's head. He had to be careful what he said. Hersch had asked for this meeting. Could he be wired?

"Look, tell you what? I ain't really hungry, and I didn't need that martini. Let's you and me adjourn this discussion to the sauna room."

Hersch reared back with an incredulous look on his face. "Tony, what the hell's wrong with you? You crazy?"

Iannello didn't answer. He eased himself up and firmly took Hersch by the arm, leading him out of the bar and toward the men's locker room. Hersch held back for a moment and then followed him, as much out of curiosity as to hear what Iannello had to say.

When they entered the locker room, each proceeded to a locker and advised the attendant they were going to use the sauna. Iannello undressed hurriedly and was at Hersch's locker in time to see him strip out of his underwear. There was no sign of a wire. They moved into the sauna, which was unoccupied.

Hersch was still confused. Eyeing the hairy, bearlike figure wrapped in a towel, he asked, "Now, what the hell's going on? You've never taken a sauna before."

"Look, Nate, what you said up there don't get said when there's people around. Just sit here for five minutes. We'll get out, shower, and then take a walk. All your questions will get answered. Just humor me on this."

After the shower, Iannello made sure he watched Hersch getting dressed, and then they left for a walk in the small garden next to one of the condominiums.

They found a bench and sat down. Iannello began:

"Ain't nobody trying to screw you, Nate. We knew a bright guy like you would see which way things were going. When this started, we didn't know how to measure a piece for you other than a figure like five percent of gross. You're still entitled to a big piece—you've done a great job. The Man is pleased as hell."

Iannello was warming to his task. It was just another con. He derived satisfaction from successfully screwing a lawyer who knew he was being screwed but bought into it anyway.

"I can't tell you now, to the dollar, how much you're gonna carry away. It's gonna depend on how much we all end up with."

Hersch wanted to believe him. He had to. He was in. All he could hope for was to salvage something from the coming fall-out.

"Tell you what, Nate. I'll talk to the Man today and see what kind of arrangement he has in mind, so you'll have a good idea of what'll be coming to you. And you know what?" He took Hersch by the arm, looking him in the eye. "You ought to be thinking about how you want to move that money. It wouldn't look good for you to have a pile people can find. We can handle that for you too."

Hersch felt he had gone about as far as he could. His next move, if there was another move open to him, would depend on what Iannello came back with. He still had one more card to play.

"All right, Tony, I just wanted us to have a firm understanding. I can handle the heat. If I can't deal with the shit they throw at me, I've wasted my time studying law and accounting. But I expect an understanding within a couple days. Also, tell the Man I want some of what's coming to me now. You guys have been drawing all along."

"Hey, you've been drawing too, two grand a week. But, all right, I'll pass that along. Now, let's go have lunch."

Iannello's mind was working as they headed inside. Hersch was no Knight. He was looking for a big score. The chances of Strollo cutting him in, though, were zip. More likely, Strollo would ask Jimmy Blue Eyes to come south for a vacation.

That thought stayed with him through lunch. It was still with him as he left the club and headed south on I-95. All these pieces were getting away from him. He had to start thinking about how to bring them back in line. Like that piece of shit Knight. Maybe he should call him. He could see no harm in listening. He said aloud, "Sure, you can learn things when you listen."

· C H A P T E R ·
SEVENTEEN

Late that morning Al and Steve kept their appointment at Metro Homicide. In an antiseptic white office they sat at a round white Formica conference table. The captain's secretary served coffee as two of his detectives joined the group. Al was impressed by their bearing. Homicide was an elite assignment, and these officers had been handpicked and well trained.

Al asked for the briefing to be conducted as though he were being introduced to the case for the first time, and for the next hour the officers detailed the developments of Zamorano and the homicides.

During all of it, Donnelly continuously shifted about in his form-fitting plastic chair, uneasy, nervous about what was to come. Perhaps he should have excused himself, not come to the meeting at all. But that would have looked bad. Plus, that would lose him the opportunity of blunting the problems as they arose. For the tenth time he straightened his tie, adjusted his breast-pocket handkerchief, smoothed his perfectly tailored suit coat.

At the conclusion of the presentation, including the crime scenes, forensics, and backgrounds of the victims, Al nodded in congratulation. "Thank you, an excellent presentation. Even though I've read our reports, I now have a better feeling for what happened. I wish I could have had the advantage of reading your reports before."

Steve cringed as a puzzled expression came over Juan's face. "But, Al, you have all our reports."

Now it was Al's turn to be puzzled. He looked at Steve and said, "When I asked for the file and reviewed it, there were no Homicide reports."

Steve had prepared for this. "I have the reports in my safe. As you know, Homicide has a strict rule against dissemination of their reports until the case has gone through the courts. They made an exception for us because we were so deep in this matter, but out of respect for the rule, and the reason behind it, I chose not to put the reports in general files."

Al looked at him in disbelief. He didn't trust his own SAC. He was about to let Steve have it, but decided against an argument in the presence of these police officers. The tongue-lashing could wait until they were alone.

The briefing then turned to the police investigation in the days after the homicides. They laid out the many unproductive paths they had taken, and Al could not fault the thoroughness with which they had explored every logical avenue. In the end, though, they were no closer to a solution.

Steve began to breathe easier. The report thing might be the only problem he would have to face. He was getting off without any real damage. Then the two officers looked knowingly at Juan, and Steve had an uneasy feeling.

Juan picked up the briefing. "I'm bending a few rules in talking about this, but we're partners in this case and shouldn't hold back from each other. This information is very privileged. It comes to us from the Internal Affairs Unit of the Miami Police Department. Their chief authorized them to release it to us only for the purpose of this case."

Al leaned forward expectantly. Steve swore to himself, wondering what it was. Had they found out the cops might be the killers?

Juan saw that he had their attention. "Two City of Miami officers, Fonseca and Morales, were the ones who handled Zamorano as an informant and who funneled the information from him that led to the cocaine seizure and the missed money."

Steve was growing frightened. Would it come out?

Juan continued, "Their lavish spending habits have come to the attention of their department. They are living far beyond their salaries."

Al's thoughts immediately jumped to the millions stolen from the counting house. Could these two officers who had done such a masterful job of turning Zamorano be the perpetrators of the homicides? He began to see the possibilities.

Juan brushed back his unruly dark hair.

"The investigation began three days ago when a fellow officer mentioned to Internal Affairs that these two were coming to work in Porsches that they parked in a lot near headquarters. As you know, they can park free at headquarters. A visual check proved this to be true. A computer check disclosed they had each recently bought four-hundred-thousand-dollar homes with huge down payments. They both have expensive boats registered to them. We were advised yesterday afternoon."

This was news to Steve, but it confirmed what Ruby had told him. He straightened in his uncomfortable chair. Juan had his full attention. His problem might be more serious than he had thought. Should he tell the truth or stay with his story?

Juan was almost finished. "Since they're police officers, their lavish spending on meager salaries strongly presumes some bribery or other illegal activity. They were the only ones who were ever in contact with Zamorano, and all we know of the Zamorano information came through them. We must treat them as strong suspects. They are now the focus of our homicide investigation."

Steve flinched. This was it. If only Al didn't respond, he'd be all right.

Al shook his head, confused. "But that's not true. Steve met with Zamorano also."

All eyes turned to Steve Donnelly. He wished now he hadn't come. He had no choice: he had to bluff it out. His hands joined in front of him as he rested his forearms on the table.

"I did meet with him once. It was to assess his cooperation

and reliability and to ensure that we were all coordinated—on the same wavelength—for the coming operation."

Surprised, Juan said, "You never mentioned this before."

Al couldn't understand why Steve hadn't told the police.

Steve smiled weakly, shrugging. "No one ever asked me. I didn't see it as significant. There is a memo in the file, but it just never got incorporated in the final reports we sent you."

Juan was disappointed and showed it. "Is there anything else in your files you've held back?"

Steve defensively replied, "No."

Al was visibly upset. "Juan, I apologize for this. Have your people come over to the office today, review the raw file. I'll personally go over it again, including the police reports I haven't seen."

He placed heavy emphasis on the last three words, looking intently at Donnelly, who seemed to be trying to shrink into his seat.

Al continued, "I'll have a copy of the memo Steve prepared of the Zamorano contact hand-carried over to you today."

Al and Steve left the police and drove back to the FBI office. The first part of the ride passed in silence as Al went over in his mind what he had heard and its implications. Finally he turned to Steve, who was driving.

"Steve, I'm trying to understand this. You're a top-flight investigator. You know better than to withhold information."

Steve knew his story was weak, but he was stuck with it. Uncharacteristically he assumed a repentant attitude. "Al, I'm sorry as I can be about any embarrassment I may have caused. I guess I just have to plead a mental lapse. I really didn't see that interview of Zamorano as significant. It was sort of an administrative thing."

Al understood that mistakes were part of the territory. The only people who never made mistakes were those who didn't try. He was partially satisfied, but he still had a question about the police reports.

"When I asked for the Zamorano file, why didn't I get it all?"

Steve continued with his repentant line. "I didn't give it a thought. You asked for the file, and I just told my clerk to give you the file. I should have gone into my safe and got the reports. I was preoccupied and just didn't think."

Al looked out at the traffic, not satisfied. "That's two unthinking things you've done in this case. How many more will I discover?"

"That's it, Al. And while it's no excuse, I don't think either lapse has done any harm."

At the office, Al found Nick and Bill, with a tape recorder, waiting for him. Bill sat on the leather sofa and Al and Nick took the leather armchairs. After the tape of the Iannello meeting was played, all sat unmoving for long moments.

Finally Al pulled a yellow legal tablet toward him and began to make some notes, an outline of what he had heard, and, to one side of the notes, areas to be explored.

As he finished, Bill asked, "Nick, you were there. Did you get any sense of why Iannello was doing this?"

"Bill, I don't rely on intuition. But sometimes you have to respect your feelings. Yes, I did. Toward the end of the conversation, the thought came to me that I had stepped in shit, didn't know it, and had just tracked it all over the house."

Bill smiled broadly at this. "An apt description of any meeting with a lowlife like Iannello."

Nick was serious. "We all heard everything he said. I sure am glad we recorded this. He didn't really give us anything solid. Nothing we could work with, barring a surveillance of him for all his contacts."

Al was busy studying his notes, listening. Then Nick began to approach what was on Al's mind. "We have to ask what Iannello accomplished with this conversation. We agree, I think, that this was for his purpose, not ours. Somewhere in there is a hidden agenda. Iannello is not a good Samaritan."

Al leaned back in the leather chair, a pleased expression on his face. "Very good, Nick. I think you've hit squarely on our approach to analyzing this contact. It happens to be the first area to consider that I jotted down." He rephrased the question. "What did Iannello gain?"

Bill answered first. "A relationship with Nick. A call on a daily basis."

Al was not satisfied. "Yes, and that's at the core of it, but what else?"

Bill and Nick looked at each other in puzzlement.

Al drew a circle on the pad in front of him. "Let's play Nick's conversation with Iannello to a jury that's considering conspiracy-to-murder charges against Iannello. Is he our informant? Is he out seeking guns, delivering guns, to learn the identity of the victims so he can tell us and stop a killing?"

Bill and Nick both nodded in understanding.

Al continued, "The ploy won't work, because we can prove he was lying. The scheme was well advanced before he came to us, and he was a part of it then. He withheld crucial information from us, and continued in it for his own purposes."

Nick angrily rose to his feet. "That sonofabitch, he really used me. You know something else? All that talk about his life in jeopardy, and just between us, and don't record, was all for the recording he knew I was making. He was talking to a jury."

Al stood up and walked over to Nick, putting a friendly hand on his shoulder. "Don't let him get to you. You did great. We know what he's up to, and we can use him to screw himself."

Iannello accessed his answering machine from a public telephone on the beach. He found the message from Knight interesting. Did the asshole mean what Iannello thought he meant?

Iannello needed to talk to Strollo. He paged him twice, once using his home number, then immediately afterward using the number of the phone booth he was in.

Strollo was at Pam's, having just placed a call to Amari to arrange for a contact at the Leisure Hotel in a half hour. His pager went off, and he saw the number was Iannello's. When it went off again and displayed a second number, he assumed Iannello was at that number. He called the public phone where Iannello waited. The intercept caught it.

"Hello."

"You paged me?"

"Yeah. I need to see you on two matters."

"Okay. I'm gonna be at your hotel in half an hour. I'm calling our friend up north."

"I need to talk to him too, but later. I got his supplies and need to get them to him."

"I'll see you at the hotel."

Al recognized that this was the kind of contact that would build a case against Strollo. Iannello accesses his answering machine, gets the Knight message, scripted by the FBI, and immediately calls Strollo. This would be one element drawing Strollo into the counterfeit bond case. If Iannello rose to the FBI bait, Strollo would be close to indictment.

As Al pondered the complex series of events that were unraveling, Bill came in, teletype in hand.

"Have you had a chance to read your copies of the latest teletype traffic?"

Al looked up. "No, haven't reached that pile yet."

"Good news. We got Iannello. Unfortunately, it'll take a month to process all those bonds for latent fingerprints. The lab has been doing it as they get time. Nothing so far except Knight and some unidentified."

He paused, and Al asked the question he was hoping for. "How does that get us Iannello?"

Bill played his card with great relish. "They did process the phony audit report. Iannello's prints are all over it! Knight is there too, with the banker, and some unidentified."

Al got up and slapped the desk. "Damn, that's good news. You're right. With just a little finessing we've got him, and if we get him we're that much closer to Strollo."

Bill leaned over Al's desk. "Boss, there are no prints on file for Hersch, though. Think of it. He's a CPA; he's a good candidate for having prepared the reports. We need knowns on him."

"You're right. It's time to go open on Towers of Light."

Bill couldn't have been more pleased. "I was just going to push for that."

"Get grand jury subpoenas for the lending banks. Get a grand jury subpoena for Tower of Light records, and a grand jury subpoena for Hersch in the bond case to compel him to submit to fingerprinting."

Bill could feel his case coming together as he watched Al pace the office, obviously excited by the prospect. Al continued, "Don't serve them unless you have to. Start with an interview of Hersch. Maybe we can flip him like we did Knight. If he won't play, serve him."

Al stopped his pacing and looked intently at Bill. "Don't hit Hersch, though, until we give Knight a chance at Iannello. If Hersch doesn't play, he'll tell Iannello about the subpoenas, and Iannello won't deal with Knight."

Bill was eager to be away and start the wheels turning. "You got it, boss. This is what the guys have been waiting for."

Al thought for a moment, then called out to Bill as he headed out the doorway.

"You might as well get subpoenas for the other two banks that Knight dropped the bonds in, and pick those up too."

Bill paused to absorb what Al had said, replied simply, "Okay." Thinking some more, he backtracked toward the office. "Pam. Any way we can use her in this? As a listening post?"

Al had turned back to his desk, but his head came up as he heard the idea. "Good catch," he said enthusiastically. "Let's synchronize the approach to Hersch with Pam being with Strollo. Have her try to get Strollo to her place when we're pitching Hersch. If Hersch says no, he'll contact Iannello, who'll contact Strollo. Just documenting that succession of contacts will be probative. If we're lucky, Strollo will make an off-hand remark to Pam."

• C H A P T E R •
EIGHTEEN

When Iannello arrived at the Leisure Hotel, Strollo was in the first booth, on the phone to Amari. Iannello saw him, waved, and dropped into a lobby chair. Strollo nodded a greeting. The call was added to the FBI's growing file.

"Hello, boss, how's Miami?"

"Weather's perfect. After you handle our problem, come down. You earned it."

"I'm going to do that."

Out of habit, Strollo scanned what he could see of the hall and lobby through the glass of the closed telephone booth. "I talked to Tony. I'm meeting him here for something else, but he said he'd have final arrangements for you to pick up the stuff today.

"Let's look at day after tomorrow for the operation. If you tell me tomorrow that you're all set, I'll call them and tell them a lawyer will be delivering documents for them to draw against the money."

Strollo's eyes followed the progress of the desk clerk as he opened the street door, held it open, and looked out, apparently testing the outside temperature. Without taking his eyes off the clerk he continued, "Let's figure about six, at their place. I'll tell them they both gotta be there to sign some of these documents so they're joint on the accounts that's been set up. There's no way they know this guy you're using?"

"No, he's new, never met them."

Strollo noticed that Blue Eyes was being awfully curt, and he asked, "Does that sound all right?"

"Yeah, whatever it takes to get them both there."

This was said entirely without enthusiasm, and Strollo let some sternness enter his voice. "Okay, you call me when you're ready to go. Then I'll call them, and call you to let you know it's all set."

Strollo left the booth and walked over to Iannello. "Let's get a cup of coffee."

They walked into the adjoining restaurant and sat at a corner booth from which they could see both the hotel and the street entrance. They ordered coffee from a young waitress who obviously was a transplanted Texan. Strollo's gaze followed her every move, and he relaxed. "It's all right, Tony. Just guard a little what you say. There's nobody around."

"Well, boss, the scoop is, my guy is booked on an evening flight. I've got the stuff in my trunk. When we separate, I'll call Jersey and arrange for the drop, and then deliver it to my guy."

Iannello was leaning across the table, keeping the conversation low, just in case.

Iannello glanced about. "I need to talk to you about Knight and Hersch. You see, things have been coming at me. Knight called me yesterday, said he got a call from the bank that the stuff wasn't right. It came across as a tip from the VP who's in his pocket. Knight wanted to see me right away."

The waitress brought two coffees, and Iannello leaned back and waited until she left before continuing.

"It could have been a setup, but I needed to tell Knight the way it was, and to take his fall without finger-pointing. I cornered him at his office and stripped him down—he was clean. Then I told him to either pay off the loan or go to jail, it was his problem."

Strollo sipped his coffee and shrugged. "Sounds right. You're clean. Even if he points, there's no corroboration."

"Yeah, but then he calls me with what sounds like a proposition," Tony added, anxious to add some good news. "He wants some more bonds, but with a fifty-fifty split. I think the guy wants to float some loans at other banks, pay off the loans at the three banks we're in now, and get the bonds out of hock. We both know this just puts off his problem, but it makes us some money. Want to try a shot? Can you get more bonds?"

Strollo was not surprised at this ploy. The guy was a loser who wanted to double his bets.

"Yeah, there are more available. Talk to him, feel it out."

Iannello was watching him closely. So far this was rolling right off Strollo's back.

"Now my Hersch problem. The guy calls me, wants to meet right away. I make sure he's clean, and then he tells me he's wise to our bust-out, that his end is five percent of nothing."

Strollo couldn't hold back his laughter.

Iannello continued, "And that he wants a piece now, like we been getting, and a guarantee at the end. He says he knows how to handle the heat and ain't worried. I reminded him he's been getting two bills a week draw. This don't satisfy him."

Strollo did some mental arithmetic, and then said, "We're about three months away from substantially finishing, and being able to draw our last money from the banks. We need him for this period. If we fuck him at the end, can we keep him quiet or will he go to the cops?"

Iannello was reasonably sure he could control Hersch, but he wasn't about to give any guarantees. "He's got an awful lot to lose by going to the cops. He likes being a lawyer and CPA. He'd likely lose both of those if he talked." He hesitated a moment before adding, "If it looks like he's gonna make a deal with cops, there's always our friend in New Jersey."

Strollo snorted as if he'd just said the most obvious thing in the world. "The main thing is to keep him with the program. Tell him the money's out of the country, that none has been whacked up yet. We moved it all so it can't be found. There's no way anybody gets his piece until the thing is buried. We're only holding small amounts to operate with." As he spoke, new ideas were presenting themselves. "Let's give him some chump change too. Give him some shit about his great job, and increase his draw five hundred a week. Go to three thousand if you have to. If he won't sit still for that, we'll lean on him."

Iannello started sliding out of the booth. "Okay, that takes care of all my problems." He walked back to a phone booth in the lobby, from which he called Amari, and waited ten minutes for the call back. The FBI intercept picked up the following conversation:

"Jimmy? Tony."

"Yeah. Just talked to the boss."

"Yeah, he told me. We just finished our talk. You got a paper and pencil?"

"Yeah, go ahead."

"He's booked on the six o'clock American flight out of Lauderdale to Newark, flight 631, supposed to land at eight-twenty."

"I got it. You got a pencil?"

"Yeah."

"Tell him to go to the Continental departure area, where they sell tickets. There are some lockers between Continental and American. Put the package in one of the bottom lockers, put the key in an envelope, write the name Peter James on the envelope. Give it to a gal named Kathy at the Avis counter, on the lower level. Got that?"

"Bottom lockers between Continental and American, Peter James, Kathy in Avis. Yeah, okay."

"What's this guy look like and what will the pieces be in?"

"He's thirty, balding, five-eight, one seventy-five, wears glasses. The pieces are in a black Samsonite attaché case. He's got to check it as baggage. He can't walk through X-ray with it. So he'll pick it up in baggage claim and then go upstairs."

Amari decided to cinch the identification issue, making sure the delivery went right. "Just so nothing gets lost, have him go to the American lost-bag desk right by the baggage claim area, and ask to page Peter James to meet him at the lost-baggage desk. He should stay there for five minutes. That way I'll be sure to spot him and the case, and make sure what locker it goes in. I may even make a direct approach if it looks all right. Tell him to give the bag to anybody who says you sent him and says he's Sally. You got all that? Can this guy handle this?"

"Sure, don't worry. You'll have it tonight."

"Okay, I'll call the boss when I got it."

This call resulted in a hurriedly called conference at the FBI office. Instructions went out to the surveillance crew on Iannello to cover the person he delivered the attaché case to. The team was told specific instructions would follow.

Iannello left the phone booth and returned to Strollo. Neither paid any attention to the two camera-toting tourists having pie and coffee at the counter, from which they could observe the Strollo booth and, through the lobby door, the phone booths.

"We're all set," Iannello said. "I need to meet my guy, deliver the stuff, and tell him what to do."

Strollo replied gruffly, "Go do it."

Iannello drove west over the causeway to a prearranged meeting with his courier, Joe Balistrieri, a hanger-on bookmaker who wanted to be made. He was waiting in the Auto Show, a saloon on Biscayne near 123rd Street. It was a hangout for guys who played the role of being made, and girls who liked to think they were with real mobsters. Iannello hated the place, but it was convenient, and Balistrieri had selected it.

The bar smelled of stale beer and cigarette smoke. It took almost a good ten seconds for Iannello's eyes to adjust to the dark interior. He spotted Balistrieri, dressed in a dark suit and tie and trying to look like a hoodlum. With him, seated at the bar, was a girl who looked fifteen.

Iannello finally caught his eye and impatiently motioned him to the other side of the horseshoe-shaped bar. Balistrieri reluctantly left his honey and, drink in hand, walked over.

Iannello was not happy. "How long you been here?"

"Coupla hours, waiting for you. We on for tonight?"

"You been drinking all that time?"

"Naw, just had a couple. Had to be sociable with little Debbie. Ain't she something? Got a body won't quit. I can fix you up if you like her. She's friendly."

Balistrieri broke into laughter, but stopped abruptly as

Iannello grabbed his arm. "Look, you asshole," he growled, "this ain't no party we got going. If you want out, say so. If not, pay your fucking tab and follow me outside."

Balistrieri, subdued now, did as he was told.

Outside, Iannello angrily turned on him. "Your fucking brains've fallen into your balls. You shot your mouth off to that little cunt!"

The wannabe gangster threw up his palms. "Hey, no, boss. I know better than that."

"You're shit-faced! No way you can handle tonight."

"No, I'm fine. I'm ready to go."

"You fuck this up and you're meat."

"It'll get done. Just tell me what you want."

Iannello hesitated. He had no one else to send, especially at the last minute. All the arrangements were made. He certainly wasn't going himself.

"All right," he sighed. "Here's the round-trip tickets on American, flight 631 out of Lauderdale. Leaves at six, so you got to move."

Eager to please, Balistrieri started moving toward his car to make sure he caught the flight.

Iannello stopped him, his hand on his arm. "Where you going, asshole? You haven't got the case yet." Balistrieri stopped, and Iannello continued, "Now listen to this. This is the important part. Here's a pencil. Write it on the ticket envelope."

Balistrieri wrote as Iannello recounted the instructions Amari had given him. When he had finished, Iannello asked, "You got that?"

"Yeah, piece of cake."

Iannello exhaled slowly, shook his head, and walked over to his car. He opened the trunk, extracted a black Samsonite attaché case, and handed it to Balistrieri, who took the case without a word, a knowing grin on his face.

Iannello said, "Call a cab and go straight to the airport. No more Debbie. No more booze. Call me as soon as you make the delivery."

"Hey, no worry, boss, piece of cake."

Still unconvinced, Iannello got in his Jaguar and left as Balistrieri headed for the phone in the bar.

S-Two dropped Iannello and stayed with Balistrieri and the attaché case.

Balistrieri was observed calling a cab, which arrived within ten minutes. It was a Yellow Cab, radio-dispatched. Balistrieri opened the back door and got in. The attaché case was in one hand and his ticket envelope in his other. As he settled in, he started reading his scrawled notes on how to deliver the attaché case. Absently he gave directions to the driver. "Airport, American terminal. I'm a little late, so do it quick."

S-Two, aware of Balistrieri's destination from the telephone intercept, was already set up north, on I-95, to leapfrog the cab to the Fort Lauderdale airport.

Two cars were behind the cab as it headed for the I-95 entrance ramp. The cab did not take the north entrance to I-95, though, but headed south instead. The surveillance was in disarray as the cars north on I-95 sought to turn around, head south, and catch up. At Route 195 the cab headed west.

The supervisor of the S-Two surveillance broadcast his realization of what was happening:

"He's not going to the Fort Lauderdale airport. He's heading out of Miami."

Al and Bill were in Bill's office, trying to nail down a plan to cover the delivery of the guns. Bill had just got off the phone with the Newark office.

"Newark is on Amari now," he reported. "They've been on him all day. They'll go with him to the airport and perhaps ident his accomplice in the hits, then stay with him, or them, to wherever they intend to whack these people. It's the only way we'll be able to ident the victims."

Al got up from his chair. His thought processes worked better if he was on the move. After a few seconds he stopped pacing in Bill's small office and faced him. His voice was edged with finality.

"Relying on a surveillance to prevent two homicides is too risky. Surveillances can be lost. They may not be able to act before someone is killed. The guns can't leave Miami. We don't know enough about their plans yet to chance it."

Bill was somewhat disappointed: he wanted to know who the victims were. But he couldn't disagree with this cautious approach. Unsure how best to address the problem, he asked, "How do you want S-Two to handle it?"

Al's lawyer background served him in good stead on this issue. "The guns are contraband. They have silencers affixed. Contraband can be seized without a warrant. Tell S-Two to take the guns." A solid plan was evolving as he imagined the spit team at the airport terminal. "Try to do it in such a manner that the courier thinks they're lost. Use a ploy that will prevent them from knowing we're in the case. Remove the attaché case from the checked baggage if necessary. In other words, steal the goddam things."

Having arrived at this solution, Al sat down opposite Bill and explained his decision.

"I'm giving us the benefit of the doubt in my interpretation of the law. A court could disagree. The guns are not in plain view. We have to open the case to get at them. If I'm wrong, all we lose is the ability to use the guns as evidence against the courier. He's the only one with standing to object to our seizure. We can still use them against Iannello."

Bill accepted this, unsure if Al was right, but he was the boss. He nodded agreement.

"Bill, call S-Two. Tell them what we've decided, and add that they are to leave the courier alone. No arrest, no contact of any sort."

Bill was on the radio within minutes and relayed Al's instructions. In the meantime, S-Two had managed to regroup and now were covering the terminal for American Airlines.

Miami International Airport is a huge, sprawling complex of crowded humanity. As Balistrieri stood in line at the ticket counter to get his seat assignment and check his attaché case, two customers behind him was an agent. Balistrieri handed his ticket to the airline clerk and passed the case under the counter to the receptacle for checked baggage.

"One piece to check, headed for Newark tonight."

The clerk was apologetic. "I'm sorry, you've missed it. Our last flight to Newark left forty-five minutes ago."

Balistrieri objected, "No, flight 631 leaves at six." He pushed the ticket at her.

The clerk took the ticket, saying, "We have no flight 631." She opened the ticket, began reading, and looked up again. "I'm sorry, sir, but you're at the wrong airport. This flight leaves from Fort Lauderdale."

Balistrieri stood dumb in disbelief. He snatched back the ticket and read it for himself. The FBI agent behind him left the line to report to his crew.

Balistrieri picked up the attaché case, left the counter, and stood for several minutes, turning the problem over in his mind. There was no way he could make Fort Lauderdale in time. He had no choice. He had to call Iannello. He would have to go tomorrow.

There were banks of phones with short three-sided walls to hold in the sound off to his right. He walked over to one, set the attaché case down next to his leg, inserted his coin, and dialed Iannello's pager.

He was concentrating on entering the correct number when he felt a movement next to his leg. He glanced down. The case had disappeared. Panicking he looked up and saw a man with the case rushing for the exit. He dropped the phone and took off running after him. He saw the man threading his way through the crowd and approaching an exit door. Then he collided with a man and woman and was knocked down.

The man was most apologetic. "I'm sorry, sir."

A hand helped him up. "My wife and I were concentrating on the schedule on the board, and didn't see you. Are you all right?"

Balistrieri shook off the hand. "Get the fuck out of my way, you asshole."

By the time he got back on his feet, though, the man and his case were gone. He went out to the street but saw no sign of them. Reluctantly, feeling deadly sober, he returned to the phone bank.

The two agents who had blocked him left the building. The

agent who had stolen the attaché case was in his car, on the radio to inform Al they had the guns.

Groaning, Balistrieri redialed the pager and inserted his phone number. This was a call he would rather not be making.

Iannello returned the call in ten minutes from a public phone in the Paddock. These phones were not covered, and the FBI was not privy to the call.

Balistrieri answered the ring on his pay phone, "Tony?"

Iannello recognized the voice and was surprised. "Yeah. Why you calling me from a Miami number?"

"I went to Miami airport instead of Lauderdale. I just told the driver to go to the airport. I was reading the instructions in the cab, and he brought me here. I . . . I wasn't thinking."

Iannello erupted, "You stupid fucking asshole. You were shit-faced. I'll break your fucking legs for this." He was shouting in rage, and suddenly he realized people were looking at him.

In a low voice he growled, "Don't try to fly out of there. Their security's too tight. We'll do it tomorrow."

Balistrieri swallowed hard, wishing he had a double bourbon to knock back. "Ah, Tony, somebody stole the guns too."

The telephone in his ear exploded. "You're telling me what?"

"I was calling you and put the case down 'cause I needed both hands to hold the phone and to dial. And some guy grabbed it and ran. I chased him but couldn't catch him."

This was more than Iannello could grasp. He couldn't begin to assess the ramifications of what he had just heard. The news was so overpowering that he was reduced to sputtering. "Get your fucking ass to the Paddock. I want to see you—now!"

The phone slammed down.

Iannello stared at the swinging cord, fuming. How was he going to tell Strollo this? He gave the matter some serious consideration—this made him look like a two-bit turd—but there was no way around it. He had to tell him, and the sooner the better. Delay might make matters worse.

Rosa answered and gave the phone to Strollo.

Iannello pulled at his earlobe. "Boss, a serious problem. I got to talk to you. I'm up north. Can you call me?"

"Give me the number."

Iannello gave it to him.

"Call you in ten."

Iannello stayed at the phone, and within ten minutes, it rang. "Boss?"

"What's the fucking problem now?"

Iannello had carefully thought out how he was going to explain it, but it just tumbled out. "He lost the guns."

"Lost the fucking guns! How'd you lose the fucking guns?"

Iannello swallowed hard. There was no way this could sound good. "The, ah, guy carrying went to Miami instead of Fort Lauderdale. I know, I know, sounds stupid as shit. Obviously he missed the plane, so he called me. While he's on the fucking phone, some asshole rips the bag and runs."

Strollo was in a rage, his bass voice booming over the phone. "I can't fucking believe this. Who is this asshole you used? Is he screwing us?"

Iannello had no choice but to support his decision to use Balistrieri. "No, he's okay. Really, he's been with me for five years. You know that airport's full of fucking thieves. We got unlucky."

"Bullshit unlucky. Why'd you try to use Fort Lauderdale anyway?"

"They had the latest flight, and their passenger security is worthless. Checked as baggage, the guns would get through easy."

Strollo's anger was rising as he boomed, "How could he screw up the fucking airports? How could he go to the wrong one?"

"I don't know, boss . . ." Iannello said weakly.

Strollo, though, was already searching for another way of solving his problem. "Can you get some more guns?"

"I'll start on it right now."

"Good. I want them delivered tomorrow."

Tony grimaced into the phone. "I'll do my best, boss."

"No," Strollo barked. "You'll deliver them tomorrow. This is your fucking responsibility. One more screw-up by you and you're through."

Strollo slammed down the phone, furious. His follow-up call

to Amari was tense. The guns got lost, but a resupply would come tomorrow.

Amari was more concerned than ever. This kind of stupid screw-up was a bad beginning to a hit he didn't like.

• CHAPTER •
NINETEEN

Iannello was drinking more than usual, but it didn't seem to help in solving all the problems tangling him up. He needed to satisfy Hersch tonight, and he needed to see Knight before too long. Now overshadowing everything were Strollo's guns. He knew where there was one. He had no idea where he might find two, especially with only a day to work.

Strollo was really leaning on him, as though it was his fault some shithead had stolen the case. He hadn't liked this setup anyway. Now he was thinking that all he wanted was out. He yearned for the old days when all he had to worry about was odds and guys who owed his books.

Hersch finally arrived and ordered his usual Rob Roy. They moved to a table, and Iannello, preoccupied with the gun problem, absently relayed Strollo's deal.

Hersch shook his head unhappily. "No way. Another five hundred ain't going to begin to pay me for my grief. I need to be sure my piece is there when the shit hits the fan."

Coming to, Iannello snapped impatiently, "How much would it take to keep you happy until this straightens out?"

"Tony, you ain't listening. My piece. I want my piece up to date."

Iannello shook a meaty finger in the lawyer's face. "No,

Nate, you ain't listening. The money is put away. It can't be got until this is done. Nobody's got a piece yet."

Hersch was not going to let himself be intimidated. Leaning forward, he said, "Then change the rules. I want an offshore bank account in my name with my piece deposited. Tell your man I expect it in two weeks. In the meantime, and until this is over, I want to draw four thousand a week."

This determination was unlike Hersch, and for a moment Iannello sensed he was somehow losing control. One look at the lemon tie, the gold-and-white-print jacket, though, reminded him of where matters really stood.

He began in his low growl, "Nate, you're being unreasonable. I'll talk to the Man, but I can tell you right now he ain't gonna be happy." Menacingly he added, "You don't want to make an enemy of this guy. He can stop being friendly awful quick."

Hersch hesitated, not wanting to push too hard. He knew a threat when he heard one. He also knew these people were capable of carrying out their threats. He began to back down. "Tony, I ain't trying to rock the boat. I'm just being careful. What's the best he'll do on a draw?"

Iannello pretended to think about it a moment. "I can get you three a week."

"Okay, but I still want the offshore account."

Iannello waved his hand in dismissal. "Let me look at it."

Hersch left for his nightly crap game, and Iannello went back to his dark thoughts. He was mildly grateful that Hersch was off his back, at least for a few weeks.

There was no way to reach Russo about guns until the following morning, so he decided to try to get rid of the Knight problem now. Maybe tomorrow all he would have to worry about would be the guns.

Iannello went to the pay phone and called Knight's business. The answering machine came on, and Iannello hung up. He dialed Knight's pager and left the pay-phone number. Knight called back within a few minutes.

"Hello. I was paged from this number."

"Yeah. You want to see me?"

"Sure. Where? When?"

"Broadway Deli, now."

There was a slight catch in Knight's voice as he answered, "Okay."

Hanging up, Iannello glanced at his watch. If he split right away, he would beat Knight there by twenty minutes. He decided to leave now and park where he could see if anything happened when Knight arrived. He was not at all convinced that Knight was for real.

S-Two was again covering Iannello and was advised by the intercept agents that he had made arrangements to meet Knight at the Broadway Deli.

When he emerged from the Paddock, all but two cars had already gone. The two remaining surveilled him to the deli. One of the cars that had gone on ahead was equipped to receive and record the transmitter concealed in Knight's pager.

Knight was covered by only one car as he drove to the deli, just on the possibility he might be stopped en route. That car stayed back once Knight arrived.

Iannello saw nothing to indicate police presence, but he was wary all the same. His sixth sense was working, watching Knight get out of his car and walk toward the restaurant.

Iannello lightly touched his horn twice. Knight turned and saw him parked in front of one of the stores down from the deli. Knight hesitated, took a deep breath, and walked toward Iannello's car.

Iannello leaned over and opened the door. When Knight got in, Iannello went immediately on the offensive. "You called me. Said you wanted to see me."

"Yeah, we need—"

Iannello stopped him with a chopping stroke of his hand. "No, you listen. You don't talk. I'll tell you when to talk." He leaned across the seat, and Knight shrank from contact with him. "You called me. You got problems. I don't need your problems. I hear you're in trouble with the cops. Cops are always harassing me." He pinned Knight with a hostile stare. "You trying to set me up with some bullshit conversation?"

Knight started to answer, but Iannello interrupted, "Take your shirt off. You're wired to set me up, aren't you?"

Trembling, Knight removed his shirt. There was nothing to see, but Knight was rattled all the same. He felt Iannello somehow knew that he had made a deal with the FBI.

Iannello's hand shot out and grabbed him by the hair on the back of his head. Forcing his face close to his, he spat out, "Okay, asshole, do your best to set me up. What were you told to say?"

Knight was thoroughly cowed, convinced beyond doubt that Iannello knew he was cooperating with the FBI. His carefully rehearsed script melted into a blob of words that slid out:

"Get me some more counterfeit bonds. I'll get new bank accounts, and get loans like we did with the other three banks. That way I can pay off the first banks, and work on this and not have to go to jail."

Knight went into a fit of uncontrolled trembling as he tried to continue. "I want fifty percent this time, because—"

Iannello stopped him with a resounding slap across his face. Knight cowered in a corner of the car. The FBI heard the slap, and one car saw it. They were prepared to move if Iannello continued the attack.

Iannello growled, "You pathetic piece of shit. You're trying to save your ass by trying to frame me into something you did. I come here trying to help a guy, and this is what I get."

Iannello reached across, opened the car door, and shoved Knight out. "Go on, get!" Knight backed away from the car, relieved to be out, and Iannello started the engine and roared off.

Seeing Knight standing in the parking lot in his rearview, Iannello scowled. Maybe Knight had been all right. But he couldn't be sure. He had gotten all these bad vibes. Knight had been too nervous, too on edge. The way he blurted out all that stuff sounded too planned.

The postmortem at the FBI office was not upbeat. Nobody was pleased with Knight's performance. On the other hand, all grudgingly had to admire both the way Iannello had set him up and the way he had talked for the benefit of any recording. The conclusion was that Iannello was just too much for Knight to handle.

Al decided to use Nick's new relationship with Iannello. He told Bill he wanted to see him and Nick right away. When they were all assembled, Al outlined his plan:

"We are going to step into Hersch tomorrow about nine or nine-thirty, the time he usually leaves his condo for Towers. If he doesn't cooperate, let's pitch Iannello on everything but the homicide."

Nick was pleased with this assignment. It would be the first step in showing Iannello that he hadn't been conned.

Al, in shirt sleeves, his tie loose, was pacing animatedly, gesturing.

"Show him the phony audit, ask whether he's ever seen it before. He'll say no. That'll prevent him from later explaining how his prints got on it. Talk to him about Knight, Hersch, Strollo."

Al continued roving about the office, anticipating the action that was coming, feeling the climax of their work approaching.

"We can let Hersch know we're talking to Iannello. Then we'll let Iannello know we're talking to Hersch. All this, of course, if Hersch doesn't cooperate. We'll at least get the denial on the audit report from Iannello. What we probably will create is one hell of a lot of distrust, which could drive one or both to us. And create a lot of cover-up chatter on our taps."

Bill and Nick were jubilant. Both welcomed some action after lying back for so long.

"What about Strollo?" Bill asked. "Do you think we should talk to him?"

Al didn't hesitate. "No, not yet, but try to set up Pam with him, as you suggested before, to see if we get a reaction when Iannello contacts him."

The full impact of what she had agreed to do for the FBI had begun to build in Pam. It had been one thing to agree to get information from Strollo, but to have actually got him on tape admitting a hidden ownership in what was undoubtedly a criminal operation was something else entirely. Her voice was on that tape too. How would the FBI use it, she wondered, and what, she thought, shuddering, would happen to her if Strollo found out?

Pam wanted out, and when the FBI contacted her, she told them just that.

But Shirley and Jerry persuaded her to continue cooperating. The end was in sight. They just wanted one more shot.

Pam, against her instincts, consented to go along. "As long as it's just one more meeting."

She could not call Strollo at home, but she could page him, which she did. Strollo went to the room set aside for his office and returned her call. When he heard her hello, he said lightly, "Don't tell me you're hungry again."

She chuckled flirtatiously. "I can only paraphrase Shakespeare, 'You make hungry where most you satisfy.' "

Strollo snatched at the bait. "Tonight?"

"I can't. I've got late meetings, and I don't want to be all tired out for you. I was thinking of a nice leisurely early brunch tomorrow with double dessert."

Swallowing thickly, he said, "Okay, what's on the menu and what time?"

"Me at ten."

Knight was beside himself with worry. The agents tried to console him. They told him he had fulfilled his part of the deal.

Despite their assurances to the contrary, Knight felt he was in danger. If Iannello knew, he would try to kill him and his family. The FBI, though, declined protection as premature. Witness protection would be considered when there was some palpable danger.

Knight slowly found his way home. Connie was up, in the family room, dressed for bed, reading. Before he consciously thought out the consequences, the whole story of his troubles poured out. Connie sat, transfixed by this sordid tale. When he had finished, he dropped exhausted into a chair.

Connie, her book forgotten in her lap, stared in disbelief at what she had heard. "Harold, this is unbelievable. I knew about the women. I knew about the gambling, and the drinking. But jail! You're going to jail! You stole over a million dollars?"

Knight's chin was sunk on his chest. He couldn't raise his head to look at her. He just sat exhausted physically and mentally.

"What hold has this Iannello on you? How could he make you do this? What will happen to our children? Did you ever once think about the children?"

As soon as she said it she was sorry. She could see the unbearable strain he was under. The fact remained, though, that what he had done was unforgiveable. She and the children had done nothing, but they would suffer along with him. From what he said, they could even be in danger from this Iannello.

"Harold, the children and I are leaving tomorrow. Do you want to tell them what you told me, or are you going to make me tell them?"

Defeat in his eyes and voice, he raised his head slightly, still not meeting her eyes. "I'll tell them. But you stay here. I'll leave."

"No, I want to take them away from here. I'll go back to my folks in White Plains until I decide what to do."

Knight looked stricken. "Won't you stay with me? You gotta help me."

Connie was starting to cry. "Harold, I loved you. We have children. I remember the happy times we had. Those times are gone. What you did, you did alone. What you did has changed us. There's no love there anymore, only pity."

With difficulty Connie stood up, the forgotten book falling to the floor, and went to their bedroom.

Harold trailed after like a whipped dog. With tears coursing down her cheeks, she reluctantly turned and faced him.

"No, Harold, not even in the house tonight. Come for breakfast tomorrow. You can tell the children then."

In the depths of despair, Knight left the house and drove back to his office. On the way he stopped and bought a bottle of Jack Daniel's. He needed some company that night, even if it was only a bottle.

The night would disappear into the bottle.

When he looked at the clock on his desk, it was time for breakfast. Time to face his children and confess, as he had confessed to Connie. Connie had rejected him. The children would too. He pulled himself up and walked out to the waiting Lincoln.

Parked in a Bureau car a few feet from Hersch's Porsche in an underground garage that served the condo tenants, Brian and Ken were teamed to do the Hersch interview. His condominium in North Miami Beach occupied a generous portion of the tenth floor of the Dolphin Club and overlooked the intracoastal waterway.

The agents saw him exit the elevator and walk toward his car. As he punched a button on a tiny transmitter attached to his key ring, disarming the car alarm, confirmed by the squeak of the siren, they approached him.

Brian said, "Good morning, Mr. Hersch. I'm Brian Marion, and this is Ken Stacy. We're with the FBI." Both displayed their credential cases. "We'd like a few minutes of your time, please."

Hersch looked at the nondescript Brian Marion. Was this what feds looked like? Self-assured and cocky, he said, "Well, I'm on my way to work, a little late, in fact. What do you want?"

Brian, in his low-key way, answered, "We think you can help us with several matters we're working on, and would appreciate it if we could discuss some of them with you."

"Could we do this tonight? As I said, I'm late."

Brian eyed Hersch up and down: a dandified empty suit. Still calm, he persisted, "I'm afraid this evening might be too late. It's why we tried to catch you here, early, before you got to work."

Hersch looked at both agents, enjoying playing with them. "Now I'm concerned. Does this affect me?"

Brian said, "It could, yes, sir. We expect you'll be able to clear up any areas affecting you. That's one of the reasons we'd like to have this informal chat. We're really looking for your help."

Hersch had already decided to evade this talk, but he didn't want to seem uncooperative. He thought he'd give them a taste of his legal education.

"Before I talk to you, I'd like to know the areas you want to cover. What do you want from me? Who, or what, do you want to talk about?"

Brian saw the interview getting away from him. Hersch was dancing. He was doing the interviewing. Well, Brian thought, there was nothing to be lost by dropping a bomb. I'd do that if he refused, just to stir him up.

"We'd like to talk about Towers of Light. We'd also like to talk about Harold Knight, Tony Iannello, and Vincent Strollo."

Ken and Brian saw Hersch stiffen. He was no longer smiling. His arms crossed on his chest in a defensive posture. "I'm of course conversant with Towers of Light, it's where I work. I'm afraid, though, I have a policy of not talking blindly about my work or about people. My legal training, you know."

Brian quietly pushed him. "We felt that as an attorney, an officer of the court, you'd be receptive to assisting law enforcement."

Hersch countered, "Oh, I am. If you will address your inquiries in writing, so I have the opportunity to give fully researched answers, or if you desire me as a witness, subpoena me, I'll be happy to supply all the information I have."

Ken shook his head as though disappointed. "We were hoping to find you willing to assist without the necessity of coercive process, and the sometimes unpleasant notoriety that goes with it."

Hersch, regaining some of his composure, haughtily countered, "I think my position is both reasonable and correct."

Brian shrugged. "Very well, if you insist. Our partner Nick Lucania is talking to a much friendlier Tony Iannello."

Hersch went white. Were they bluffing? How much did they know?

Brian continued, "We're looking for information. At this point in time we're looking for someone to supply that information. We're willing to work out some accommodations. The first one in always gets all the prizes. As a lawyer, you certainly are aware of that."

Hersch wasn't standing as tall as he had been a moment ago. He wanted to climb into his Porsche, but was mesmerized by the things that these men were loading on him. His worst fears were being realized months earlier than he had expected. Could Iannello be contemplating cooperation?

Brian was speaking again. "Since you seem adamant in your decision not to cooperate with us, I do have those subpoenas you asked for."

He handed them to Hersch, who took them reflexively. The lawyer was now in a real quandary. This was no game. These agents had come prepared. He had asked for subpoenas as a bluff, and they handed them to him.

Brian added, almost apologetically, "You'll note one of those subpoenas calls for you to present yourself for fingerprinting. We could get that out of the way now."

Hersch swallowed hard and shook his head in refusal. He had trouble speaking. The word *fingerprinting* had hit him hard. They must have damning evidence of some criminal violation that might contain his fingerprints, and so could link him to that activity. His mind raced to recollect what that might be.

"I regret we can't do business today," Brian said, reaching inside his jacket. "Think about it, but not for too long. Here's my card and Ken's. Call us when you finally realize it's in your best interest to cooperate with us."

The agents left Hersch badly shaken. Climbing into his car, he mulled over the conversation. Suddenly he paused, struck by one odd thing. He didn't recognize the name Strollo. His first impulse was to call Iannello right away. Then he reconsidered. If Iannello was cooperating, he might incriminate himself in a conversation with him. He decided to call, but to feel Iannello out very carefully. Then he partially dismissed this. Iannello was made, he couldn't talk.

But other Mafia figures had, he kept thinking as he fought morning traffic. That *omertà* business wasn't all it was made out to be. Yes, it was time for another meet.

Iannello entered room 1242 in the Intercontinental Hotel and greeted Nick, who took his proffered hand.

"Tony, thanks for coming. Since I saw you last, we've been busy. It's time to bring each other up to date. What have you been able to do about the guy who wants the silencers?"

Iannello looked sleek and unruffled. "As far as I know, he's still looking."

"If he's looking, he's contacted others," Nick pointed out logically. "You ought to be clean if you give me the guy's name."

Iannello cursed himself for the careless way he had answered that question. "Nick, I can't yet. Let me work it a little more, find out where he's been. Then I can protect myself."

Nick shrugged. "Okay, but I'm disappointed. I thought you and me, we might have something going."

"Hey, Nick, we do. I came to you, I want to help."

That's enough of this crap, Nick thought. He had his big gun ready. "Well, there is another area you can fill me in on. Just general information."

"Sure, my friend."

Nick watched him closely as he said, "You know Nathan Hersch, right?"

Iannello flinched, just slightly. His hand went to his earlobe and tugged it. Exactly where was this going to go? "Yeah, I have a drink with him now and then."

Then Nick laid it out. "Tell me about Towers of Light."

Iannello paled. With rigid fingers he reached for his espresso to give him time to collect an answer.

"I just know Hersch works there. Got an interest, might even own it."

"Who are the investors?"

"Don't know."

"When will it be busted out?"

Iannello abruptly put down his cup, got up, and started walking out. When he reached the hotel room door, he stopped and turned. "What's this all about? I don't know why you're coming at me like this."

"No problem, Tony, just wanted to see if you knew anything about Towers. We're talking to Hersch about now, and I figure he'll tell us all we need to know."

Sensing doom, Iannello came back and perched on the edge of the bed. He wanted to find out what the FBI knew.

Nick walked toward him and stood over him. "If you can't help us with Hersch, maybe you can help us with Harold Knight."

Iannello's head snapped up.

Nick reached into his inside jacket pocket and drew out and unfolded a sheaf of papers. "Let me show you this. Ever see the original of this audit report before?"

Iannello accepted the copy of the report but hardly glanced at it. His answer was reflexive. "No, I don't know what this is all about."

"Come on, Tony, play straight with me. You've seen that report before now, haven't you?"

"I told you no. I think it's time to leave."

"We've talked to Harold."

"Hey, good for you. Why should I be interested in that?"

"You know Knight."

Iannello's composure began to return. He realized he had protected himself well with Knight and could improve that protection now. He once again spoke for the recording he knew was being made.

"Yeah, I know that weasel, and I'm surprised at you, Nick. He tried to entrap me last night in a phony conversation about something I can't even recall now. I threw him out of my car. So you set him on me."

Just then Iannello's pager went off. He looked at it and saw Hersch's number. It went off again as he was looking at it, and another number came on. Hersch was telling him to call at the second number.

Nick suspected the reason for the page and couldn't suppress a crooked smile. "Important call?"

"No, probably some insurance salesman."

The phone in the room rang.

"Hold just a minute, Tony, while I get this."

The caller relayed that Hersch had been approached and declined to cooperate. As Nick hung up, he decided to pitch Iannello now.

"Tony, you came to us offering to help with a homicide. I appreciate that, and we want to work with you. Since that meeting, though, we've picked up a lot of information about your, and Vincent Strollo's, involvement with Towers and with the counterfeit bonds Knight pledged. We can convict you now."

Iannello's cockiness was evaporating. This was exactly what he had been afraid of from the moment Strollo arrived in Miami. Now it was happening. His insurance on the homicides wasn't covering this. He needed to find an out.

Nick saw him wavering, indecisive. "Before it gets to that, I'm offering you the chance to come over on our side. You know the story as well as I do. You got something to trade, you'd better do it while there's a market. As I said before, we got everything Knight knows, and Hersch is talking to our agents."

Although Iannello wasn't surprised that they were talking to Hersch, he was worried and showed it.

Nick continued, "You're the guy with the most to sell. Tony, its time to look out for number one."

Iannello came somewhat unsteadily to his feet, marched to the door, and walked out of the room.

In the hotel lobby the surveilling agents saw him use a pay phone. He was returning Hersch's page. The guarded conversation, which the FBI was not privy to, consisted of nothing other than that the FBI had contacted each, mentioned some names, and given Hersch subpoenas.

The agents noted the time of that call and a second call that was to Strollo's pager using Iannello's home number followed by a call to Strollo's pager using the pay-phone number he was then at.

Strollo had arrived at Pam's ten minutes before. He was urging her toward the bedroom when his beeper went off. The microphone in the apartment recorded the time of the first page from Pam's remark:

"Did you just get paged?"

Strollo grunted, "Goddammit. Yeah. Forget it. It'll wait."

When the pager went off again, Pam said, "Back to back."

This time Strollo stopped and checked the messages. Irritated, in a hurry to get back to Pam, he picked up her phone and dialed the number of Iannello's pay phone.

The intercept picked up the call.

"Boss, I gotta see you right now."

Strollo's thoughts were of slowly undressing Pam, and he snapped, "Look, I'm busy. Can't this wait?"

"No, the FBI just talked to Hersch, gave him some subpoenas. They just got finished talking to me. They say they got Knight."

Pam evaporated from his thoughts. The FBI were on to them? He needed to find out how much they knew and where it was going. "Those bastards. Okay, your hotel as soon as you can make it."

Pam was talking for the benefit of the mike when she said innocently, "You look disturbed. Bad news?"

Absorbed in the gravity of what he had just heard, Strollo answered absently, "Yeah, some business problems that I've got to handle right away."

Pam, enjoying herself, adopted a sultry pose on the bed. "More important than our morning together?"

Strollo said irritably, "Yeah, this could be personal. We can play tomorrow."

Without another word he hurried out of the apartment. His major concern in all this was Magliocco. If the scam blew up in their faces, what would the boss do?

Al and Bill had listened to the tape of the Pam-Strollo conversation. The telephone call from Iannello and Pam's question, with Strollo's answer, was excellent. Al couldn't believe that the shock of the contacts had caused them to drop their guard to the extent it had. He believed the call, and remarks, would convict Strollo with just a little more development of the case.

Connie and the children were finishing breakfast. They had waited for Harold, but then had gone ahead. She was picking up the plates when the phone rang. The intercept recorded the call.

"Mrs. Knight?"

"Yes."

"This is Officer Thomas, Metro Dade Police. Is there someone with you now?"

Connie was perplexed. "Yes, my children. What is this about?"

"I've got some bad news for you. Your husband was in an accident."

"He's hurt?"

"Sorry, ma'am, his car struck a tree. He's dead."

• C H A P T E R •
TWENTY

The tall, very dark, mustachioed man who stood facing Jorge Ochoa exuded machismo. Ochoa was, in fact, a little afraid of him. One day, he thought, he would have to kill him, but for now the man served his purpose.

Ochoa was seated in a large, high-ceilinged room in a sprawling hacienda near Caceres. The walls boasted of Ochoa's beloved horses in displays of ribbons, trophies, and photographs. From a balcony off the room, the view to the east was of his stables, more ornate than many hotels. To the north was his helicopter pad. A private army ensured that the *patrón's* tranquillity would not be disturbed.

Ochoa, short, dark, and very heavy, bent over the mirrored glass of a small table and inhaled a line of cocaine through a gold straw. His companion looked on, disgust just visible in his hooded eyes. Nelson Borrego worked in the cocaine trade, but he had only disdain for those who used it. He served Ochoa because of the money and because, despite the cocaine use, Ochoa was the shrewdest of the *traficantes*.

Ochoa, now hyper from his snort, looked at Borrego, his eyes having difficulty focusing. "Go on, you have your orders. Kill them. And kill them slowly. When you return, tell me in detail, so I too may enjoy it."

Bórrego permitted himself a twisted smile. "I will send you their ears."

The contract killer left the hacienda and walked to the helicopter waiting to return him to Medellín. His next step would be a commercial flight to Caracas, and then Miami.

Strollo was seated in a corner booth of the coffee shop in the Leisure Hotel. When he saw Iannello enter, he was surprised at his appearance. He looked older and smaller. As he sat in the booth across from Strollo, he exhaled wearily. Strollo looked around.

"Let's take a walk."

Iannello agreed. "Let's find a bench, or a bar. I'm beat, and I need a drink."

"Okay to both. Let's hit the bar around the corner."

Paddy's was a typical Irish bar, with an abundance of green shamrocks. It was long and narrow, and they walked all the way to the rear. The tavern was empty, except for one old man drinking his breakfast at the bar.

The bartender, observing the pair moving to the rear of the tavern, shouted, "No table service."

Iannello, who had just seated himself in a booth, got up. "What do you want, boss?"

"Bloody Mary."

Iannello headed to the bar and ordered a Bloody Mary, plus a double bourbon with a bottle of Michelob.

When he was once again seated, Strollo leaned forward. "Now what the hell is all this?"

Iannello was about to relate his contact with Nick, then realized he needed to tailor the circumstances of that meeting somewhat. He was momentarily frightened. In the throes of his worrying he had almost made a fatal mistake.

"Ah, the FBI picked me up. They asked about Knight, said he spilled his guts. Asked about Hersch and Towers. Said they were talking to Hersch, and he was friendly. Yeah, that's the word they used, 'friendly.' They asked about you—"

Strollo interrupted harshly, "What did they say about me?"

Unnerved, Iannello slugged back some of the bourbon, followed by a long swallow of beer. "Nothing specific. Just asked me to tell them about you. All this was connected together, so it was you in connection with everything. They said they had enough to put me away in the bond thing and wanted me to co-operate."

He was now trying to be matter-of-fact, portraying himself as cool, in control. He regretted allowing Strollo to see his agitation. That could have been a serious mistake.

Strollo's brow knotted in concern. So the FBI had the big picture. Did they have the details yet? Could they somehow tie him to any of this? He decided that was possible only if Iannello talked. The question was, how well would Iannello take the heat?

Iannello warmed to his subject. "I told them to go fuck themselves, and walked out. They didn't stop me." He tried to gauge the effect of this on Strollo. But Strollo's face showed only concern.

"Hersch paged me, and I talked to him on the phone. There's no way of knowing whether he made a deal. I don't think so, though. He didn't say the things he'd want recorded, if he was with them. You know, stuff that would incriminate me if I agreed, or didn't say no. He didn't say nothing except he'd been contacted, and I told him I was contacted. He said he got subpoenaed."

Strollo smashed his hand down on the table, and he boomed angrily, "Those fucking white-shirted bastards. A bunch of goddam Boy Scouts. They've been on my ass before. They didn't touch me then, and they can't touch me now."

The bartender was looking their way with a quizzical expression. A second early drinker was now perched at the bar, more down toward their end, where the booths began.

Strollo lowered his voice, regaining control. "I'll handle Towers. I'm going to get with Blacky and Phil this morning. You get with Hersch. Be careful."

"I'll strip him down, like before."

Strollo ignored this entirely. "I want there to be a fire. A big fire. After tonight the fucking feds can subpoena ashes."

As Strollo gained his stride, his voice took on his old authority. "We'll take what we got out of Towers. Hersch can have it if he wants to go ahead. Encourage him—it might look good. Tell him Towers is his end, and we're out. Yeah, I like that. He can have what's left of Towers."

Iannello asked, "What about Knight?"

Strollo looked up from sipping on his Bloody Mary. "Fuck Knight. What's he gonna do? Point a finger? They got nothing but his statement. You never showed. You got no worry. If they got anything, let them show it."

Iannello was not convinced. His bourbon was gone and the beer almost empty. The alcohol was not helping.

He was thinking about the audit report Nick had showed him. He was trying to figure out why Nick had asked him about that and not about the bonds themselves. That report must have some importance to them, or they wouldn't have singled it out to ask him about it.

Could it be because Hersch had prepared it? That might be the answer. Hersch was in Towers up to his eyes, and in the bond scam only as far as the report. Iannello's thoughts were interrupted by Strollo.

"Hersch could be dangerous. You get any indication he's with them, and I think we call our friend in New Jersey."

That remark brought Iannello's thoughts back to his agenda for the day. "Oh, that's right, boss. That means we better forget about the problem up north that our friend was gonna solve, right?"

Strollo looked hard at Iannello, his mind working. That gold problem was really his Achilles' heel. If it got out he had made that score on his own, without cutting back to the family, he was in real trouble.

"Wrong! That problem's got to be solved, and quickly! The fucking feds don't know nothing about that. They talk to you about that?"

The bourbon and beer came up from Iannello's stomach, choking him. He couldn't tell Strollo he had talked about it. He managed to swallow it down.

Strollo looked at him. "You all right, Tony?"

"Yeah, boss. I guess I shouldn't drink in the morning. The beer ain't sitting too well."

The problem was, the FBI did know about the hit. He had told them. He had really told them almost nothing, but with all the information they had about everything else he was involved in, he had to believe they knew. How to convince Strollo of this without hurting himself was his dilemma.

"Boss, it's just too risky to consider whacking two people when the fucking FBI is all over us. We got to assume if they know about Towers and the bonds, they know about Blue Eyes."

Strollo knew that Iannello was right. Should he give the Siragusas some money to keep them quiet for a while? They were not going to be kept quiet with more promises. Then again, he reasoned, if I'm gonna kill them anyway, why throw away money that might not keep them quiet? Do it now. The feds'll know as much when I finally whack them as they do now. He had to chance it. He was more afraid of Magliocco than of the feds.

"Tony, it's just got to be done now. Do what I told you yesterday."

When the pair left, the second breakfast drinker followed shortly after, and prepared a memo for Bill of what he had seen, and what little he had heard.

The intercepted call to Connie was the first news of Knight's death to reach the FBI. Concerned it might be a Strollo hit, Bill sent an agent to inform the police of Knight's relationship to the FBI. As a result the police assigned the case to a Homicide team and allowed the FBI free access to the information they developed.

Within a few hours the agent was on the phone to Bill.

"Preliminary data looks like Knight had been drinking most of the night; empty bottle in his office, purchased last night. High alcohol concentration in the body, don't have a percentage yet. Wife says he told her everything. She threw him out. He went to his office after that.

"The road where the accident happened curves to the right.

The tree he hit is in that curve. It's a big old oak, didn't budge. Police estimate he was doing seventy. There are no skid marks. He never touched his brakes."

Bill felt he knew what was coming next. The agent continued, "He could have fallen asleep, but he hit that tree square, like he was aiming for it. Police think suicide."

Al called Karla and informed her of Knight's death. The bond case needed to be reevaluated, since their star witness was dead. Convicting Iannello without Knight would take some doing.

When Iannello left the bar he went back to the Leisure Hotel and called Hersch. This time he was on a phone the FBI was up on.

The secretary answered, "Towers of Light."

"Mr. Hersch, please. Tell him Tony's calling."

"Just a moment, please."

Hersch came on immediately. "Hello, Tony, you got more good news?"

"We need to get together. Same place as yesterday."

"When?"

"Now."

S-Two was advised of the call. They would have two couples in the bar, and would try to move wherever Iannello did.

Iannello arrived first and was having coffee when Hersch came in. Before he could speak, Iannello popped to his feet. "Look, Nate, we do what we did yesterday. I'll explain later."

Hersch didn't need an explanation. "I understand, Tony. I think it's a good idea."

Tony didn't know whether to be pleased or angry. Now Hersch didn't trust him either.

After a partial repeat of yesterday's ritual, they just stripped for each other, skipped the sauna, and went outside. They found their bench unoccupied and sat down.

The surveilling agents noted most of these activities and concluded the obvious: they were checking each other for wires. Part of the ploy was working. Seeds of distrust had been sown. One might flip if he felt threatened by the other.

Iannello could not escape this feeling of great weight on him as he sighed and began. "Nate, I'd be lying if I didn't tell you we got problems. I don't know how the feds picked up on Towers, but they don't have much or they'd've arrested somebody."

Hersch wasn't so sure of this. He knew that the FBI didn't rush into arrests but lay back and built their case, but he didn't interrupt.

"I had a long discussion with the Man. Towers has a lot of potential. It could be finished and make money. It's the association of Towers with me and the boss that's got the feds all worked up. We're gonna pull out."

Hersch's first reaction was one of surprise. Then he picked up on the word *boss*. Tony had never used that word before. He had always said "the Man." That name the FBI had mentioned—Strollo—could he be the boss? "Where does this leave me?"

Iannello, oblivious to Hersch's concerns, continued, "The boss said you've done great, and you got a piece coming. There's still a bunch of money in the construction loans. Keep the work going, draw on the loans. The boss is giving you the whole project. You can pick up the shells if you want, or go direct to the suppliers."

Hersch was astounded. He had expected them to walk away, force bankruptcy. He had been prepared, for the right price, to handle that. This was different.

His mind raced. If the FBI had him, they had him for what he had already done. If he played it straight from here on, he might salvage something for himself, make the project work, and screw up the FBI by not busting it out.

He got up and walked once around the tiny ornamental garden surrounding the small bench. When he sat back down, he wasn't as jumpy. "Possible, Tony. Got to think about it some."

"Sure, I understand. Now, the other thing. You're gonna have a fire tonight."

Hersch's head had been bowed in thought, but it snapped to attention.

Iannello didn't miss a beat. "The office is gonna burn. All the records are gonna be gone, ashes. Let the fuckers have ashes for their subpoena shit."

He did not mention that the shell companies would be torched as well.

"You want me to set this fire?"

"Who else?"

Hersch shook his head vigorously. "Tony, I'm no firebug. You want me to try to run Towers after you're gone. I don't want to know anything about this. You do what you have to. Count me out."

Iannello hadn't anticipated this. "What's the big deal about lighting a match?"

"That's contempt, obstruction, and half a dozen other things besides being arson. The FBI will be one pissed outfit. They'll come down hard. Tony, I didn't sign on for that."

Sometimes these civilians didn't make sense. "Nate, what's worse? They convict you with the records, or they try to prove you burned them?"

Hersch was genuinely frightened. This was a real crime— arson, not like what he had been doing in Towers. That was like . . . business.

"Tony, no argument. I'm out on this."

Iannello shrugged. Getting someone to light a fire was no big deal.

"Now I got a question for you, Tony. One of the subpoenas I got was for my fingerprints. Can you remember anything that would incriminate me, that my fingerprints would tie me to?"

Iannello couldn't care less about Hersch's problems. Without even thinking about it he answered, "No."

Hersch had given the matter a lot of thought, going over and over everything he had done with Iannello, looking for that fingerprint. "I can't either. I'll file a motion to quash, and then they'll have to tell me why they want them."

Iannello stood up. "I guess that's it. Let me know about how you stand on Towers. In any event, we're out."

Hersch nodded, and they left the garden.

Once on the road again, Iannello headed for Ray Russo and his remaining silenced .22. He had decided to pick up this gun and just tell Strollo he couldn't find any more. This was as far as he was going. He knew he had already gone too far.

Russo, somewhat perplexed by this sudden run on silenced .22s, sold him the gun and decided he didn't want an answer to his unasked question. S-Two reported the contact at the gun shop, and that Iannello had placed a package in his trunk. The agents knew they had more weapons to intercept.

Iannello called Strollo from a pay phone, and when Strollo got to the pay phones at the Leisure Hotel, they communicated, with the FBI listening.

Iannello informed him of the Hersch conversation, including the fact that Hersch adamantly refused to torch Towers, and that he had one gun and couldn't locate any more.

Strollo thought a moment, then said, "We can't afford any more fuckups. I'm talking to Blacky later. He'll call you. Give him the package, and I'll arrange for it to get to our friend."

Iannello was relieved not to have to try another move to New Jersey. But he didn't like what followed.

"We have to take care of the Towers office. I was going to have Blacky and Phil each take care of their own area, but Blacky'll be gone to New Jersey. When I talk to Phil, I'll tell him you two will take care of all three tonight. He'll be in touch with you to arrange it."

Iannello was not pleased. He wanted to distance himself from this, not get further involved in it, but he had no choice. There was no way he could refuse. "Whatever you say, boss."

After they disconnected, Iannello allowed a question to cross his mind. Under what conditions would I deal with the FBI? He realized that even considering that possibility spoke volumes.

The Strollo-Iannello call became the subject of considerable discussion. Bill knew Blacky and Phil had come down to south Florida, but so much manpower had had to be devoted to Strollo, Iannello, and the resulting cases that nothing much had been done on those two. The FBI had not been aware that they headed up the support for Towers of Light. Without open investigation or subpoena, little progress had been made on labor and material suppliers.

Bill was apologetic. "We should have put some emphasis on those two. Common sense should have told us they were working with Strollo."

Al was chagrined too. "Let's remedy that now. Put a surveillance crew together to take Plumeri when Iannello makes his delivery. You can cover Iannello light if you want. He's going to be with Milano. We should try to pick up Milano on surveillance before he meets Iannello."

Bill was taking notes and scheduling surveillances. He was determined to remedy the oversight.

Al continued, "Once those two are together I want saturation coverage. Use the airplane. They're taking care of three areas tonight. One of those is the Towers office." He regarded his supervisor with a knowing look. "This is what we expected and wanted. We're picking up their plans to cover themselves. If we handle this right, we'll have cover-up evidence that will convict them. Even though now we can't prove what they're covering up, that will come."

Iannello arranged to meet Plumeri at the Dadeland Mall. They pulled into the parking garage, went to the roof area, and parked their cars side by side. When no one was around, they opened their trunks, and Iannello transferred a black Samsonite attaché case. Plumeri drove off in his white Mercury Sable rental car.

The S-Two supervisor saw Plumeri exit the garage and queried his units. "Anybody eyeball them together?"

The airplane responded, "This is Eye. Two passed what appeared to be a black attaché case to the white Mercury. It went in the trunk."

The supervisor responded, "Steve and Rita on number two. Everybody else on the Mercury."

Strollo was paged from a pay phone within minutes of the delivery. Strollo called back from the Leisure Hotel.

Iannello was jubilant. "I just heard on the car radio: Knight drove into a tree last night; he's dead. We're clean. Without Knight they got shit."

Strollo was equally pleased. "See? I told you not to worry. We can forget about that shit. What about Blacky?"

"He's got it."

Strollo snapped his fingers. "Okay, now we do some tidying up tonight and everybody's fine."

He hung up and called Amari, who called back shortly. The FBI were listening intently.

"Jimmy?"

"Yeah, boss, what's up?"

"We only got one. Can you do it?"

Amari sighed. That meant the plan had to change again. "I guess I got to. I'll practice with it. I'll just have to go from one to the other real quick, and then go back again to each one to make sure." Thinking as he spoke, he went on, "I'll still take Sally with me, to make sure one doesn't run. Yeah, we'll try to get 'em in a room where there's only one door, or sitting at a table where I can get behind them. We'll have . . . Sally can sit like he's got something for them to read, then they'll sit down."

"That should do it. Okay, Blacky is bringing it up tonight. He doesn't know what it is. He'll be on the same flight as last night. Since you know each other, meet him in the Rest Inn Airporter. Be in the lobby. Go up on the elevator together. When you're alone on the elevator, he'll pass the bag."

"Okay. Call them tomorrow morning, and I'll do it in the afternoon. Tell them I'll be there at four-thirty or five."

"Remember, when you're through, head down here."

"See ya, boss."

The Newark FBI office, covering Amari, was advised, and a plan was worked out between the two offices. Both agreed that the murder plot had to be stopped. The FBI had been able to intercept the guns once and would do it again. It was decided to arrest Blacky Plumeri, Amari, his partner, and perhaps Strollo, in as incriminating a posture as possible, and try to get someone to talk.

When Plumeri boarded his flight an hour later, two agents, Roy Holt and Ron Little, boarded with him. When he landed in Newark, they pointed him out to the Newark team. When he claimed his attaché case, he was arrested.

After Plumeri was advised of his rights, Roy said, "Blacky, you got a problem. Let me play some tapes for you."

Roy played some of the Iannello and Strollo conversations with each other, and with Amari.

"You're the first arrest. You get the first chance."

Plumeri said the words that stopped the interview: "I want a lawyer."

Newark was on Amari, who was with Magaddino, the young punk he had recruited for the hit. They were in the lobby of the Rest Inn. A half hour after Blacky's scheduled arrival, Amari and Magaddino appeared nervous. Finally, using the airline phone, they called to see if the plane was in.

They waited another fifteen minutes before they left and drove over to the Ramada. They went into the lobby, looked around, and went to a phone.

The surveilling agents couldn't hear, but the conversation was very short, perhaps ten seconds.

This is what both offices had anticipated. Newark advised Miami. S-One, the Strollo surveillance, which this evening included Al and Bill, saw Strollo leave his house and head for the Leisure Hotel.

Strollo entered the hotel and placed the requested call to Amari at the Ramada pay phone. The intercept agents advised the Newark and S-One surveillance that Amari and Strollo were conversing.

"Hey, boss. Blacky didn't show. He made the flight?"

"Yeah, he made it. He's got to show. Where are you?"

"Ramada."

Strollo responded coldly, "Did I tell you Ramada?"

"No. I thought you said Rest Inn."

"That's what I did tell you."

"Boss, what'd you tell Blacky?"

"Shit, I'm sure . . . I think I said Rest Inn."

Al, Bill, and another agent walked into the Leisure Hotel as the S-One supervisor said on his radio, "Now." Miami told

Newark, "Now." And this was repeated to the Newark surveillance.

Al pushed open the phone-booth door and tore the handpiece from the hand of a startled Vincent Strollo. As Strollo started to reach to retrieve the phone, he was restrained by Bill, who grasped Strollo's wrist and put his credential card in Strollo's face.

The scene was repeated in Newark with Amari.

Al held the phone for a minute, then said, "Hello."

He heard Roy Holt's familiar voice. "Hello, boss. Blue Eyes isn't happy."

"Good work, Roy. Give my thanks to the Newark guys. Have a pleasant chat with Blue Eyes. Who's the other one?"

"Salvatore Magaddino. Small-timer—the Newark guys know him."

Hanging up, Al turned his attention to Strollo, who had been removed from the booth and was being held by Bill. "Vincent Strollo, I'm Al Lawrence, FBI. You're under arrest."

Strollo had recovered from his surprise, and he glared back defiantly. "What for?"

"The immediate charge is interstate travel in aid of racketeering. Before the night is over I guarantee at least six more."

Bill started putting handcuffs on Strollo, who recoiled in distaste. "This isn't necessary."

Al smiled and said, "Oh, indeed it is. We treat everyone the same, from *soldato* to *caporegime.*"

Bill read Strollo his rights, and Al followed up. "Blue Eyes and Blacky are both arrested. I'll play the tapes of all your conversations on the hit. We have the first two guns. Want to play let's make a deal?"

Strollo knew the words too:

"I want a lawyer."

Bill and Al relinquished Strollo to the other agents, and Al gave them instructions in Strollo's presence. "No calls. No communication until the rest of tonight's work is over." Then he turned to Strollo.

"You'll be glad to know you'll soon have more friends to keep you company."

• CHAPTER •
TWENTY-ONE

Ramon Odio was slender, light-complected, with a full head of black hair that was just beginning to gray. His well-pressed brown suit marked him as a businessman. He had come to the United States from Cuba in 1960, when he was seven, and in his pocket he had two sets of official identification: his FBI credentials and his diplomatic passport as legal attaché to the American embassy in Bogotá.

He glanced out the window as the wing of the plane dipped in a steep bank. Below were the mountains of the Cordillera Central, their peaks piercing the sky. In a valley they formed, five thousand feet high, was the sprawling city of Medellín.

The plane was a few miles from the runway when he first was able to see the toylike cars and ant people below. Medellín, formerly a sleepy village, was approaching two million people. Its thriving industries had been overshadowed by the most profitable export of all—cocaine.

As he prepared to deplane, his right elbow nudged the 9mm automatic on his right hip. The wide-open town he was entering had no love for American law enforcement. He was relieved when he saw the armored personnel carrier and the staff car of General Hector Suárez.

The general was the latest in a long line of commanders assigned to direct Colombia's antinarcotics efforts in the Antioquia department. His predecessors had either been assassinated or made wealthy when they looked the other way. Ramon thought this general was honest—most of the time.

Ramon came down the exit ramp, looked about apprehensively, but was somewhat reassured by the soldiers who were deploying around the plane, except for the two manning the .30-caliber air-cooled machine gun mounted on the carrier.

When he reached the tarmac he walked a few feet to the waiting car and slid into the backseat next to the general. "Hector, thank you for meeting me. As always it is good to see you, my friend."

"Think nothing of it. I am sorry to have to bring you from Bogotá, but this is news that really should be told in person."

Ramon glanced at the short, dark man of obvious mixed Spanish and Indian blood seated next to him. He knew the discussion would take place when the general thought the time and place was right.

At the general's office they shared some rich Colombian coffee from a neighboring plantation. Then the general suggested a stroll in the courtyard.

The general walked slowly with his head down and spoke in a low whisper. Ramon had to strain to hear.

"Do you recall the killings in Miami which involved the disappearance of Ochoa's man Zamorano along with many millions of dollars?" Ramon nodded. "Your people have told us that Ochoa was looking for Zamorano and his money. He believed Zamorano ripped him, but wasn't sure, so he was also trying to find out if anyone else was involved."

The short general stopped and faced the agent. "Yesterday our informant told us that Ochoa has sent El Loco, Nelson Borrego, to Miami. We do not know when he left or under what name he traveled. In the past he has gone from Colombia to Venezuela or Chile, then, using a passport from one of those countries, he travels to the United States."

Ramon knew of El Loco. He was Ochoa's principal assassin and had been in the United States dozens of times. They could only guess as to how many of Ochoa's enemies El Loco had killed.

"Do you know the purpose of his trip?"

"We think so. The informant tells us that Ochoa has developed information that two American officers were involved with Zamorano in the rip of the money. We do not know who they are or whether they are federal officers or local officers. El Loco is to find them, kill them, and, if possible, recover Ochoa's money."

Ramon decided to try for a flight back to Bogotá that evening. He had to get a coded cable off to Miami right away.

The SPIT crew assigned to find Milano was at first unsuccessful. Then at six-twenty they received a radio message from the S-Two group, now reunited on Iannello, that he had just met with Milano, and they were traveling in his light blue Ford Crown Victoria, a rental. The Milano SPIT surveillance merged with S-Two, affording them sufficient manpower to give in-depth coverage. Providing even more backup was the plane.

The first Milano-Iannello stop was a Publix supermarket in the mall at 168th Street. Two female agents from S-Two followed them in and observed them purchasing a dozen twelve-inch candles, three cartons of paper matchbooks, and six gallons of drinking water.

The puzzle of the water was solved when they were observed pouring it out in the parking lot and putting the empty plastic jugs into the trunk of the car. A stop at a self-service gas station refilled the plastic jugs.

The next stop was almost predictable, the Paddock. Two of the S-Two crew had memberships under assumed names, and each took three team members in.

Four couples were scattered about the bar area when Milano and Iannello began drinking and eating. The two mafiosi were bent on pleasure, not business. They started with Sapphire gin martinis and graduated to a cabernet sauvignon with prime rib. The dinner ended with Key lime pie, Rusty Nails, and coffee.

By nine-thirty, their leisurely dinner concluded, they headed toward Milano's car. The surveillance crew not in the Paddock had feasted on Big Macs and coffee. They had not been idle, however. The Milano Ford now had a magnetically attached tracking device on its undercarriage and a tiny ice-pick hole in its taillight. The tracking device, a transponder, sent out a coded radio signal that, received by specially equipped cars and the airplane, would pinpoint its location. What's more, the pinhole in the taillight would light up like a beacon at night, visually differentiating the car from all others for the airplane and ground surveillance.

The Ford drove to the Palmetto Expressway and headed west, then around the big curve and south. It turned west at the Turnpike–Don Shula Expressway exit and got off at 12th Street.

This was an area of office-warehouses in which myriad businesses were housed. At this time of night there was no traffic. The plane followed the car to its stop opposite a warehouse. With night-vision gyroscopic binoculars, both men were seen exiting the car and entering the building opposite. These binoculars, with low-light enhancement and a gyroscope that eliminated the movement of the airplane, allowed static viewing. They were the answer to the prayer of all aircraft surveillance people.

Once they were inside, the airplane transmitted: "Eye, they're inside a warehouse. Have one car come in, and we'll guide them."

With that, the S-Two supervisor dispatched a car into the area. Guided by the plane, they located the warehouse Milano and Iannello had entered.

The airplane also advised, "Subjects took jugs from trunk into building."

Milano and Iannello were in the warehouse about a half hour. From there they headed a few blocks east to an office complex and entered a large building. It was obvious the pair were creating timed fires. S-Two contacted the office.

"Subjects observed carrying jugs of gasoline into warehouse. Previous purchase of candles and intercepts indicate arson. Request search warrant."

Al was in his office seated at his desk with Bill sprawled on the sofa. They had left Strollo in an interview room. Both were listening to the surveillance radio traffic, and Al rose from his desk at the transmission concerning the arson and began walking to the radio room.

"They don't need a search warrant, and there wouldn't be time to get one."

Bill followed, worried about his people. "We don't know how they've timed the fires to start. Our guys could be walking into a fireball."

Both hurried down the corridor, and in the radio room Al took the microphone.

"S-Two, this is One. Search warrant not required. This is exigent circumstance. Make forcible entry. Make the premises safe. Do not search other than to locate and defuse the arson tools. Then secure the premises, keep someone there. We'll get a warrant for an evidentiary search later." Then he added, "Be damn careful. Get some firemen on the scene. Use your judgment in stopping them now."

"Ten-four."

S-Two issued Al's instructions to four of the agents. As they were breaking into the warehouse, S-Two recontacted Al. "One from S-Two."

"This is One."

"Another problem. Subjects in large office building. Unable to follow them in without being made. We think we have spotted office they entered."

Al groaned and sat down at the radio console. This was getting out of his control. There could be a fire at any moment.

S-Two continued, "From outside we saw lights go on in two windows after they entered. However, we can't be sure, since several offices are lit."

Al turned to Bill. "We need to go over there. This is getting sticky. Somebody could get hurt."

Then he broadcast to S-Two. "Get some people on the floor you think they're on, in a position to observe the suspect office. Try for cover, but if you're made, take them. If you spot the office, let them proceed to their next area. If not, take them as they exit the building. Search the office just like you're doing the warehouse."

"Ten-four."

S-Two dispatched four agents to the third floor. They used the stairwells as cover and were able to observe the suspect office.

"S-Two from One."

"S-Two, go."

"Four and I proceeding to your site."

There was relief in the voice that answered, "Ten-four."

The crew from the warehouse search came on. "One and S-Two, from twenty-three fourteen."

Al answered, "Go."

"Warehouse. Located four lit candles in two areas. In each area two candles placed three feet apart with paper balled up around and between them. Under the balled-up paper, at the base of each candle, were a dozen matchbooks with the flaps torn off, and the match heads against or around the candle base. Jugs of gasoline between the two candles, screw top removed, jug open. All file cabinets opened, contents spilled about. Gasoline splashed on the papers from the file cabinets."

"Ten-four."

Bill shook his head in dismay. "Not much left to chance with two of those set. That building would have exploded."

"They're desperate, Bill, or they don't care. That would be spotted as arson as soon as the fire department responded."

By the time the two had joined the surveillance, the office had been identified and searched. A similar fire initiator had been found but with only two candles and one gallon of gasoline.

Iannello and Milano were now headed north, apparently to the Towers of Light office.

After thinking the matter over, Al said, "I'd like to take them while they're in the office, but that's too dangerous. If they decide to run or fight, a spark or tipped candle could send us all up. We'll have to take them at the moment they close the door behind them."

S-Two watched a replay of the other two arson sites. Al

directed two agents to move in along the side of the building, hidden behind the corner of the wall. Three cars moved quietly to within thirty yards of the door, facing it. The cars were about ten feet apart.

Milano and Iannello had turned off the intrusion alarm and entered with a key. When inside, they turned on the lights and went to work. After twenty minutes, they emerged into the dark and began locking the door.

The three cars facing the door flipped on their high beams, flooding the area and blinding both of them. A car loudspeaker said, "FBI. You're under arrest. Face the wall."

The two agents came around the corner of the building while two more exited from the cars. Milano and Iannello were searched and cuffed in record time.

Al had accompanied the two agents from the cars and now spoke to the pair. "Would you like to come inside and watch us put out your candles? We've had practice at the other office and the warehouse."

Neither responded, and with a gesture from Al they were taken to separate cars. Separation was the norm. It produced conflicting stories and cooperation.

Al followed Iannello and had him placed in his car. He bent down as Iannello slid into the backseat.

"Tony, we've got you for obstruction of justice, interstate transportation in aid of racketeering, and half a dozen other charges."

The full impact of his arrest was beginning to weigh on him. He slumped in the seat, his handcuffed hands a rock in the small of his back.

Al continued, "Strollo was arrested tonight along with Jimmy Blue Eyes, Blacky, and Sally. We got all three guns you supplied. You're due for a long vacation."

Al read him his rights and walked away, leaving him alone in the backseat of the car. He was observed, at a distance, by an agent.

Iannello watched the agents make the building safe. After the operation was complete and agents had been posted to protect the premises until a search warrant could be secured and executed, Al returned to his car with Bill.

The lull had provided Iannello time to assess his predicament. He had been caught in the act of arson. They had seen him at the other two. It was obvious they knew about the homicides.

Bill slid into the driver's seat, glancing quickly at Iannello, wondering whether leaving him alone to think was working on him the way they expected. He started the car and drove toward the office.

Al turned on a tape recorder, and Iannello heard himself talking to Amari. His stomach started churning. Still, Al asked no questions. On the next tape, Iannello heard himself telling Nick about the possible homicide.

After a portion of that tape, Al turned off the recorder.

Iannello's thoughts raced in the ensuing silence. Strollo would kill him for that contact with the FBI. Plus, the FBI had him in so many cases there was no way he could beat them all. He had no place to go. He had been mentally preparing himself for this step. He knew it. It was why he had contacted Nick in the first place, to give himself an out. Now he had to take it.

"I want to talk to Nick."

From his position in the backseat Iannello could not see the smile on Al's face.

"We'll see if he's in the office when we get there."

At Al's instruction, Nick had been waiting in the office, anticipating Iannello might flip. When they arrived, Iannello was put in a small interview room alone. A concealed TV camera watched him.

After he had been left alone for fifteen minutes to let his anxiety grow, Nick opened the door, pausing for a moment as though waiting to be asked to come in.

"Tony, I'm sorry to see you like this. I hear you want to talk to me."

Iannello couldn't spill his guts just like that. He tried a weak bluff. "Nick, this is all wrong. You and me were working together. Tell these guys that. I'm trying to help."

Nick could hardly contain the smile of victory that struggled to surface. Coming inside, he approached the small desk in the center of the room. His shirt sleeves were rolled up, and the holster on his right hip was empty. He lowered his wiry frame into a chair, shaking his head.

"Tony, you weren't playing square with me. You had all the answers when you came to see me. You lied to me. You put me in a real bad spot with the boss. I could have got fired. You tried to use me as an excuse in case you got caught in the murder." Nick shook his head, a look of disgust on his face. "It didn't work, Tony, because we knew all about the murders before you came to me."

Iannello didn't respond but remained hunched in the chair. Nick leaned forward slightly, peering over the desk, concern on his face. "Tony, you still cuffed?"

"Yeah."

"Let me at least take those off. We may disagree, but we can at least show each other some courtesy."

Iannello smiled weakly, welcoming the friendly gesture. "Thanks, Nick."

Nick removed the handcuffs and slipped them over his belt in the small of his back. He seated himself and looked Iannello right in the eye. "So, you see, Tony, I know you were only screwing with me when you told me you wanted to help. Hey, I understand, it's all part of the game. I don't hold it against you, but I figure you owe me. You made me look bad with the boss."

Tony put on his best contrite face as he said, "Look, Nick, suppose I open up, give you everything, what can you do for me?"

Nick shrugged in apparent disinterest. "At this point I don't think there's much you can give us. I think we got the whole picture."

Tony was becoming desperate. "How about all the other shit that's down here? The other made guys, what they're up to?"

"Might be worth something. What terms are you looking for?"

"I'll give you cases on most of those guys, but I want to walk."

"No way, Tony. You're gonna do some time. The only question to be resolved is how much." Nick paused for a moment to let this sink in. "And there's no way I'm going to take a pig in a poke to the boss after the last con you tried to pull on me. I'll get you a break, and I'll work with you. If you want to buy in, I need, right now, from top to bottom, everything you can give us—an offer, a concrete detailed offer. With that I can talk to the boss, and then come back and tell you what we'll do for you."

Iannello knew he was boxed in. There was no place to go. He had already committed himself. In the next few hours the story all spilled out.

Hersch had early-morning company. This time they weren't waiting by his Porsche. They rang the bell on his condo door at six forty-five and woke him up.

He called through the intercom, half asleep, "What you want?"

Brian answered, "FBI, Hersch. We have a warrant for your arrest. Open the door . . . now!"

"I want to call a lawyer first."

Brian replied, "If this door isn't opening by the time this sentence is finished, I'm coming through it!"

Hersch screamed, "Wait!"

The door chain rattled, and the door swung open to reveal a now wide-awake, disheveled Nathan Hersch in silk pajama bottoms.

Ken pulled a card from his pocket. He couldn't resist the line he was about to lay on Hersch. "Although as a *lawyer* you know your rights, we'll read them to you anyway."

When he had finished, he asked, "Do you want to dress or go like this?"

Hersch was having trouble focusing. It was as though he were a bystander watching this happen to someone else. He heard himself answer them. "Dress."

Both agents took him back to his bedroom, made a quick check for weapons, and sat him on the bed. They took clothes from his closet and tossed them to him.

Ken, looking at the extensive wardrobe of expensive suits, emitted a low whistle. "You must have a big clothing bill. Just keeping all these suits pressed has to cost a lot. I guess we're doing you a favor. From here on Uncle Sam'll pick up the clothing tab. Won't be as flashy as these, though."

When Hersch was dressed, they handcuffed him behind his back.

Suddenly the full realization of what was happening to him came home. He was no longer the self-assured, dapper lawyer-accountant who believed he could handle any problem.

As they left the apartment, Ken set the door lock. "We're locking your apartment, but there'll be an agent outside to make sure no one enters, not even you, should you get out on bond. We're in the process of applying for a search warrant."

Hersch gasped slightly when he heard "search warrant." There had to be a way out of this for him. He was a lawyer. This couldn't happen to him.

Brian said, "We can tie you to the bonds. Your fingerprints will cinch it. You prepared the phony audit report. That's inter-state transportation of stolen property and Federal Reserve Act violations. Plus we've got fraud and obstruction. A few more will follow when the indictments come down on Towers of Light and the bonds."

The blood drained from Hersch's face, and he shivered. Ken held his upper arm tightly.

"If you want to talk to us, we'll listen. I doubt there's much you can tell us today that we don't know. You blew your chance yesterday."

Brian was gauging the effect they were having on Hersch. He thought he could see him beginning to crumble. They just needed to push the right button.

"Iannello's been arrested. They didn't succeed in burning anything. His boss, Vincent Strollo, a *caporegime* in the Magliocco family, and an assortment of other hoodlums are sit-ting with him. Your choice of company may earn you some ex-tra time."

As they walked slowly toward the Bureau car, Hersch began to tremble uncontrollably. Brian had him by his elbow but couldn't support him when he fell to his knees. He did stop him, though, from falling on his face.

The two agents lifted him up and opened their car door, laying him across the backseat. Ken voiced his concern to Brian.

"Should we call fire-rescue?"

Brian looked at Hersch, who seemed to be getting some color back. "No, let's wait a minute. I think he's coming out of it. Delayed shock."

Hersch brought himself up on an elbow. In a weak, high-pitched voice, he said, "Sorry. I don't know what happened."

Then he jerked rigidly upright into a sitting position. His breath came out in a rush. "Yes, I do, I'm scared. I can't go to jail! I can't! Whatever you want, I'll do it."

After they had taken Hersch's statement, Brian and Ken finished their long day with a visit to Connie Knight. Although they couldn't divulge everything they had learned about the bond scam, they were able to answer many of her questions. They felt they owed the family compassion, and what help they could give without compromising the investigation. Knight had done his best to help.

The children were in a terrible state of shock and grief. Connie blamed herself for Harold's death, for she had turned him away. His death had erased all the wrong and pain he had caused her. She could only feel love for him, and deep sorrow at the way their life together had ended.

On the way back to the office, Ken was deep in thought. He finally turned to Brian.

"I wish we could tell Knight's story to every potential sucker in the world. The way he was fed the swinging life and then hooked in debt was classic Mafia. He was captured, used, and thrown away. His family has been destroyed by those animals."

Rosa awoke that morning alone. Although her husband often stayed out to the early-morning hours, he was almost always home before she awoke. She wasn't so much worried as saddened. She assumed he was with a woman. She felt defeated.

She had not been able to interest him enough to change his habits.

She learned where he was when she heard a news summary on the radio.

Her attention fastened on the story about the intended double homicide in New Jersey. The radio didn't say who the intended victims were. Rosa willed the suspicion away.

There was no way Vincent could do that. But the suspicion kept growing. She became increasingly restive. She had to go to the jail and ask him.

• CHAPTER •
TWENTY-TWO

The bright Fort Lauderdale sun reflected off the glass top of the table in Carlo Magliocco's kitchen, making light patterns on the ceiling and wall. He had risen late and was just finishing a light breakfast of tomato juice, black coffee, and a prune danish. His wife had died years ago, and he lived alone in his seventh-floor condo, from which he could view both the ocean and the Intracoastal Waterway.

The nineteen-year-old girl who had ministered to him was being ushered out by Joey "Socks" Boccia, his bodyguard, and Magliocco was in a warm, expansive mood. He triggered his TV remote control in time to hear the local news highlights on *Good Morning America*. He heard the name James Amari, saw the face, and sat transfixed throughout the report.

The arrests had come too late for the morning papers, but the television news carried extensive coverage of the counterfeit bond scam, the attempt to destroy evidence in the Towers of Light case, the planned homicide of two people in New Jersey, and the fact that extensive wiretaps had been employed.

The identities and photographs of those arrested were played, and Strollo was identified as a *caporegime* in the Magliocco family. Magliocco was referred to as the "boss of all bosses."

The first clue Boccia had that anything was amiss was the old man's scream of rage, followed by a string of obscenities, half in English, half in Italian. When Boccia rushed into the room, he saw Magliocco standing in front of the television yelling, "He's dead! That cocksucker's gone! I want him on a meat hook. I want him hanging alive, with a meat hook up his ass. I'll spit on him while he dies."

It took several minutes to calm him to the point that he became coherent. At any moment Boccia expected him to have a stroke.

Magliocco, the veins in his neck bulging, roared in fury, "Carmine! I want Licata here! Now! Charter a plane! I want him now!"

He left Boccia, stormed to his bedroom, and slammed the door behind him. Boccia, forgetting about security, picked up the phone and called Licata at home.

"Carmine?"

"Yeah."

"Joey. The old man's screaming his head off, he wants you here now. He says charter a plane. I don't know what's wrong. I never seen him like this."

Licata knew the cause. "Listen to the radio, Joey. A lot of stuff's just happened." He paused, thinking, then said, "This ain't a good idea, but I'll come. Try to calm him down. He's got to deal with this as business."

Licata hung up. He'd fly down, but not on anything so obvious as a charter. He called the airlines and found he could be in Fort Lauderdale that evening.

For his next call he drove to a convenience mart, and from a pay phone he called a number he used infrequently.

The phone was answered, "Ardizonne Cheese."

"This is Mr. L. I'm calling at Mr. Carlo's request."

"Yes, sir."

"Is Mr. Ardizonne Senior available to make a call?"

"I believe I can reach him."

"Tell him I'll be at 347-1943 for the next ten minutes. It's very important I talk to him. If he can't be reached, tell me when I can get to him."

"We'll do our best."

Santo Ardizonne was the *consigliere*, the adviser, to the Magliocco family. He had achieved that distinction because of his level-headed approach to problems. At eighty, he had lived through several family wars, and was respected as much for his age as for his sagacity.

Just before the ten minutes was up, the phone at which Licata waited rang.

"Carmine?"

"Yes, Don Santo. Thank you for calling me back."

"I have heard the news."

"Good. I had a call from Socks. The Man wants me to come to him right away today. He is very angry. From what Socks says, in my opinion, there could be precipitate and perhaps ill-advised action caused by his fit of rage, even though you can't blame him." Licata paused, his cunning focused on finding an advantage for himself in this mess. "You have great influence. I am concerned that irreparable damage could befall the family. Are you in a position to come down too?"

"He has asked for me?"

"No, not as far as I know."

"I share your concern, but I hesitate to intrude when I have not been asked."

Licata persisted, "Would you call him, then, and evaluate the situation for yourself? After all, the fact this is in the news would justify a call."

Ardizonne agreed. "Yes, I was going to call him in any event."

Licata then switched to another area of concern. "If the accounts are to be believed, our friend has a heavy load of trouble. For his, and for our own, well-being, we should make sure he gets the right lawyer."

"I agree."

"With your permission, I'll call Madden and arrange it."

"Do so. I'll call you later in the day."

As soon as he hung up, Licata dialed Thomas Madden's number.

The phone was answered, "Madden Jones and Zwillman."

"This is a friend of Mr. Madden, Mr. Carmine. If he doesn't remember me, tell him this—write it down."

"Very well."

"A friend of ours is in trouble. Underline 'friend of ours.' Do you have it?"

"Yes, sir. Please hold."

Within a minute Madden was on the line. "Carmine, this is Tom Madden."

"Thanks for taking the call. Have you heard the news out of Miami?"

"Yes."

"We want you to personally handle Vincent, and anyone else you think appropriate, probably Jimmy. Arrange for the others who are friends of ours. As always, we need to protect the business. You will keep us advised of anyone who looks like they're developing a problem?"

"Of course. I can't go down immediately, but I'll call an associate I trust in Miami. He'll be able to handle it until I get there, probably within a day or two."

Madden and his firm were on retainer from several of the families, for their business was defending the Mafia. They would keep the defendants in line. With them as attorneys, the family could be sure no defendant would make a deal with the government. If any inkling of a deal came to their attention, the family would be advised.

Ardizonne called Licata at noon.

"I've talked to him. Stay here. We'll all meet tomorrow, here."

"He's coming up?"

"Yes. More can be done from here than there."

Al was reading over the growing flood of reports on the Towers of Light when his secretary came in quietly and handed him a cable from Bogotá. Al reluctantly put down a page of Iannello's statement and read the cable. What it contained brought him right out of his chair. Slapping his desk, he called out, "Dolores, get Steve Donnelly immediately."

A few minutes later, Donnelly poked his head in, wondering

what new development was threatening him. Al handed him the cable and was surprised at the ashen color that came to Donnelly's face.

Donnelly handed the cable back. "Have you told Juan yet?"

"No, I'm going to call him now, but that's not the most important question."

Donnelly looked puzzled. Al shook his head, sighed, and explained.

"We have to tell Morales and Fonseca this. We can't let them be sitting ducks for El Loco. But when we do, we will by implication be telling them that they are also our suspects."

Donnelly saw this as the end of him, unless—he couldn't believe he was thinking this—Ochoa killed them first. But perhaps there was another way. He had to get to them before Al did.

Al called Juan, and together they discussed how best to inform the officers of the Ochoa contract and whether, even though they would now be warned they were targets of the homicide investigation, it could be turned to advantage. They agreed on a course of action.

As soon as Donnelly was in his office cubicle, he paged Fonseca and Morales. They called him back immediately.

Donnelly's voice trembled, as he said, "I need to meet you both, now. Someplace quiet, where we won't be seen together."

Morales, who was on the phone, drew up his lip in a snarl. "Problem?"

"Yeah, the worst kind. But not on the phone."

Morales thought for a moment. "The old warehouse district off Miami Avenue at 40th Street. We'll be waiting."

Morales and Fonseca weren't sure what to think. Donnelly had never acted this way before. Had he somehow found them out?

Donnelly pulled into an alley strewn with discarded packing boxes behind dilapidated warehouses. Morales and Fonseca were waiting, and without a word Morales got into the front seat and Fonseca slipped into the back.

Morales forced a smile. "What's the terrible problem that brings you here, my friend?"

Donnelly swallowed hard and gripped the steering wheel

with both hands, his elbows locked, facing straight ahead. In his panic he had not thought through how to approach the pair. What he wanted was to ensure that whatever happened, they would help him cover up his false report and his sitting on Ruby's information.

He started where he should have ended. He yelled in desperation, "You killed them!" It just gushed out.

There was silence as he searched for what to say next.

Morales and Fonseca looked as if Donnelly had punched them. Morales reacted first. "That's crazy. Where'd that come from?"

The enormous stress Donnelly was experiencing robbed him of his normal judgment. "I first got it from an informant. And dammit, I sat on it, but I can't any longer. You guys have got to protect me."

Morales jumped on this news. "You haven't told anyone?"

"No."

"Who's this crazy informant?"

"She's good, always on the money. I told her to talk only to me about this, but she might tell Claude." Donnelly was talking as though he were in a trance.

Morales pushed. "Where can we talk to this crazy broad and straighten her out?"

Donnelly started to answer and then slowly turned to look at Morales. "You intend to kill her."

Morales grabbed Donnelly's hands, pinning them together in a vicelike grip. At the same time Fonseca looped an arm around his neck from the backseat in a stranglehold.

Fonseca slowly tightened the choke on Donnelly, who struggled to free his hands from Morales's powerful grip. His feet pounded the firewall as his body convulsed, trying to bring air into empty lungs. He was no match for the two weight lifters, though, and his face began to take on a purple hue as his body's oxygen was depleted.

Morales nodded to Fonseca.

"Let him have some air."

Fonseca loosened his hold, and Donnelly sucked air into his starving lungs.

"Now, Steve, we don't want this to go on, but you got to realize we need to talk to this broad."

Donnelly shook his head.

Morales's voice took on a threatening edge. "Steve, you know we'll find her even without you. You help us, we know you're on our side, you come in for a piece. You fuck us and we kill you."

Donnelly's eyes widened in terror. Twisting violently, he kicked at Morales but did not connect. Morales nodded, and Fonseca again applied pressure to Donnelly's windpipe.

Donnelly's body thrashed about even under the weight of the two cops.

At a signal from Morales, Fonseca let up again. Donnelly's mouth opened, gasping. Morales didn't have to ask.

Donnelly rasped out, "Ruby Gentry, don't have address, phone number in my book."

With his free hand Fonseca reached into Donnelly's inside jacket pocket and retrieved an address book. He flipped through it until he found Ruby Gentry.

Morales smiled and said, "Finish him off." Fonseca tightened the chokehold, really locking it, until Donnelly went limp. Morales looked at him for a moment and felt for a pulse. There was none.

"Let's put him in the trunk. We'll take him to the 'glades and feed him to Zamorano's friend."

As Morales pulled Donnelly's inert body across the driver's seat, preparing to drag him out of the car, they heard their call sign on the hand-held radio they had brought. Their pagers also beeped.

Startled, Fonseca asked, "Should we respond?"

Morales didn't hesitate. "Why not?" He eyed Donnelly's body, a crooked grin on his face. "Just a normal day's work, right?"

He responded to the radio, and the voice instructed them to report to their lieutenant at headquarters immediately.

Seeing Fonseca's look of panic, Morales shrugged it off. "Hey, man, don't sweat it. We see our fucking lieutenant, carry his bag for him, and come back tonight." He nodded toward

Donnelly's body. "We'll leave him in his trunk for now. Nobody ever comes by this place."

Fonseca was paralyzed by indecision. Every step along this road they had been piling up more bodies. And with every murder was the chance of a slip-up. "I think we're getting in too deep," he mumbled.

"Hey, snap out of it," Morales said. "This is a great break. If Donnelly is found, we got an alibi. We were working. And tonight we'll find that snitch broad and open her up." He punched Fonseca on the arm, much too hard to be friendly. "We got no worries. Just keep cool."

Al had moved on to Hersch's confession when he was interrupted by a call from Juan Marín. The Homicide chief got right to the point.

"We were reviewing Steve's memo on his contact with Zamorano when a problem came up. Morales and Fonseca's informant file on Zamorano does show a contact with him on that date, but there is no mention of Steve being there. I've also gone over our interview of the two of them, and while we never asked directly if Steve met Zamorano, their account of that meeting also did not mention Steve being there."

Al was perplexed. "What do you make of it, Juan?"

"I don't know. These are bad cops, Al. Bogotá says so, and the money screams it at us. Why they would not mention Steve in the reports and interviews is a mystery. There's no way his being there would hurt them. To the contrary, it makes them look good if they took him to Zamorano."

For Al, this was a troubling discovery. If Steve had lied about meeting Zamorano, that meant the FBI's entire involvement in the case had relied on the word of two cops who had turned bad. That would go a long way toward explaining all of Steve's strange lapses in this case.

"Juan, you know that meeting you're having with those narcotics officers? I want to be there."

When Morales and Fonseca arrived, they were directed to a conference room for a meeting with their lieutenant. He was waiting for them, along with Al, the captain and the two Metro detectives on the case.

The two looked like dopers right out of central casting, wearing jeans, silk shirts, Rolex watches, and pounds of gold and equipped with pagers and cellular phones. Al wasn't sure their disguise didn't actually make them as undercover cops.

After they had greeted one another, all took seats around the long table. Morales and Fonseca were uneasy, somewhat unsure they should have responded. They glanced from Al to the Homicide captain to their lieutenant. This much brass usually meant trouble.

By agreement, Al began, a disarming smile on his face, a concealed tape recorder catching every word. "Sorry for the short notice, but we have a couple of things we need to put out on the table, and I think you'll agree that we had no choice but to do this quickly. Before we get to the main topic, we have a couple of administrative-type details to clear up."

The Narcotics lieutenant as yet had no idea what this meeting was about. He had been instructed merely to get the detectives and sit in. For that reason he was only mildly interested. Fonseca and Morales, on the other hand, were gripping the table with their hands, their eyes darting from face to face.

Al continued, "We've been reviewing some of the reports on your excellent job of flipping Zamorano, and I noticed several statements in the contact reports that Zamorano was adamant in his refusal to meet with or deal with anyone but you. Those reports reflect contact only by you."

Morales tugged at his shirt sleeve, nervous, wondering where this was going. Fonseca was toying with his mustache, one question blasting in his mind: Did they know?

Al saw their nervousness but wasn't giving away anything. "We just wanted to double-check and see if you might have missed a memo or contact. Could someone else have been introduced to Zamorano or somehow contacted him?"

Morales's hand slid under the table to touch Fonseca's leg, signaling that he would handle this. He had no idea why the head of the Miami FBI office was asking this question, but whatever the reason they could answer it only one way. No one had met with Zamorano, not even them, until the night they killed him. Morales met Al's gaze as he said, "We tried to get him to meet someone else, but he refused. No, we were the only ones that ever contacted him."

Fonseca nodded in agreement.

Al hesitated but then decided to ask one more question. His legal training told him to quit when he got the answer he was looking for, but this was an agent's future he was dealing with. He needed to be sure.

"Was it possible that anyone"—here he purposely hesitated as though searching for a name—"Steve Donnelly, for example, could have met him?"

Morales's jaw clamped tight at the mention of Donnelly's name. Why these questions about meeting Zamorano? How did this impact on the homicides? He wished he could say that Donnelly or someone had met him. After all, Donnelly was dead. But the bastard would have done a memo. These Fee Bees wrote everything down. It was better to stay as close to the truth as possible.

"No. We would have known."

Al nodded in thanks and turned to Captain Marín to continue. They had decided to further protect the CI in Colombia by indicating the tip came from a Metro informant, and this was how Juan proceeded. "One of our informants has advised us that Nelson Borrego, known as El Loco, a hit man for Ochoa, is in town."

The two detectives began breathing easier. This was not aimed at them. They were receiving information, not being asked to supply it.

"We don't know yet what name he's traveling under or where he is, but we do know his assignment." He regarded Morales and Fonseca sourly. "He's here to kill the both of you."

Fonseca's mouth dropped open. Morales instinctively felt for his gun. The fear of the unknown gripped them both. After the first shock had been absorbed, though, Morales became suspicious. Could this be a ploy? Did this mean they were suspects in the homicides?

Juan continued blandly, letting the officers stew, "I'm sorry I don't have much more. As I said, we don't know anything about his movements. We do have an old passport picture of him."

He shoved copies over to the detectives. "The informant tells us"—both he and Al stared intently at the two—"that Ochoa ordered you killed because you stole his money."

Pandemonium followed. Morales and Fonseca shouted in protest, gesturing wildly. Their lieutenant bolted to attention, asking questions. Al smiled inwardly. The news had certainly had an effect.

After the furor had died down, Juan addressed himself to the lieutenant.

"I have told you all that we presently know. We evaluate the information as reliable. I'm sure you and your department will take appropriate security precautions. If we can get better information, you'll be advised immediately."

Then Juan decided to take the plunge he and Al had discussed. Eyeing the two suspected cops, he said sternly, "If either or both of you want to deal with us or the FBI, this is the time to do it. With us, you can use the law to help yourselves. With Ochoa there is no law. The time for any deals may be short. Not just because Ochoa may kill you but because the case is coming together and very soon you won't have anything to sell."

Morales shot to his feet; Fonseca followed his lead.

Morales shouted, "This is bullshit! You got crap! You're trying to set up two Miami cops to get you cocksuckers off the hook on homicides you can't solve." He leveled a finger at Juan and hissed, "Well, take your best shot, fuckhead!"

He stormed out, trailed by Fonseca.

Al accompanied the others to the office of the chief of police, and they briefed the Internal Affairs commander and the chief on the involved case.

Once back at his office, Al related the whole story in turn to Terry Washington, the ASAC who supervised Steve Donnelly. Al then told his secretary to have Donnelly report to him at once. She returned ten minutes later. "He's nowhere to be found, Mr. Lawrence. He didn't sign out of the office, but his car is gone."

• C H A P T E R •
TWENTY-THREE

She walked up to what looked like a bay window sticking out of the cement wall. There was a thick yellow glass partition behind which a man in uniform sat.

"I'm Mrs. Strollo. I'd like to see my husband, Vincent."

"You got ID? A driver's license?"

"Yes."

"Give it to me. I keep it till you come out."

Rosa had chosen a white linen suit to wear. She wanted to look proper at the jail and at the same time maybe brighten up her husband. She gave the guard her driver's license and was instructed to walk through a door, wait till it closed behind her, and then walk through the door in front of her.

Rosa had never been in a jail before. The green paint reminded her of someone's upset stomach. She imagined all the men living behind those bars, cramped together, and she shivered at the thought.

She sat on a hard bench watching guards and police and lawyers and prisoners who were trusties going in and out through the steel door. Finally her name and those of several others were called, and she walked through the steel door and a magnetometer.

As the door closed behind her, she was filled with a strange sense of claustrophobia. She peeked rather than looked at the people waiting in the large visiting room. Most were women, and she was repelled by their unkempt, dirty appearance.

After several minutes, Vincent came through a steel door at the far end of the room with several other men. When he saw her, he marched stiffly toward her. His expression was angry, and she couldn't understand why.

"What the hell are you doing here?"

She was surprised at this, but said, "I wanted to see you."

"Did the people in New York send you with a message?"

"No, I haven't heard from anyone."

Strollo seemed to lose interest in her presence.

Rosa summoned up all the courage she had and whispered, "Vinnie, you have to tell me, were you going to kill the Siragusas?"

She couldn't have had more effect on him had she picked up a bench and hit him with it. He stared at her for a second as though she were a stranger. "You stupid fucking broad, are you trying to kill me?" he roared. "Get the fuck out of here. Don't ever let me see you again."

A stupefied Rosa saw him turn his back abruptly and storm to the door by which he had entered. She broke into tears, wounded by the terrible things he had said to her.

But she knew. Her husband had intended to kill his cousins. She left the jail in a daze. Without knowing it she passed Sheldon Yale, the attorney Madden had contacted.

Frightened, Rosa returned home and did the only thing she could think of. She called the Siragusas.

Mildred answered the phone. "Hello."

"Millie, this is Rosa."

"Oh, Rosa. We were going to call you later. We heard the terrible news on the radio. Are you all right? What's going to happen to Vincent?"

"I'm okay, I guess. Oh, Millie, it's terrible. I went to see Vincent. The jail is horrible, and he said the most awful things to me. Millie, I just don't know what to do."

"Come stay with us for a while."

"No, Millie, I can't. There are things I've got to do here. I'm not sure what yet, but there will be things. . . ."

Her voice trailed off, and Mildred was quiet for a moment, sensing the other's confusion. Then Rosa said, starting to cry again, "Millie, the terrible things he said to me. It's like I don't know him, maybe never knew him. Not just what he said, but what he was going to do."

Again Mildred did not interrupt, and Rosa pulled her thoughts together.

"Millie, he . . . he was going to kill you and Petey so he could keep the money."

Mildred screamed and called for her husband. Rosa held the phone for a moment, about to hang up, then Peter came on.

"Rosa, what's happened? Millie screamed and handed me the phone."

"Pete, I didn't know until today. I went to see Vincent. Pete, he was going to kill you both for the money. You're the two people the news is talking about them planning to kill. Pete, I'm so confused. I'm going to have to leave him. What will the kids think?"

There was silence on the other end for several seconds as Peter tried to absorb what he had heard.

"Rosa, I'm sorry. I never suspected anything like this. I'm not sure what to do."

"Call the police, Pete. Tell them. If you don't, I will. They may still try."

"Yes, you're right. We will. God help you, Rosa."

The Siragusas, thoroughly frightened, called the police and related what Rosa had told them. Within a half hour two Newark FBI agents were getting the whole story of the two hundred pounds of gold.

Sheldon Yale, in a freshly pressed blue pinstripe suit, a white carnation in his buttonhole, took a moment to admire his reflection in a window. He smoothed his gray hair, thinking he looked pretty good at sixty, as a very shaken Strollo entered the attorney interview room.

Rosa's visit had caught him totally unprepared. His response to her question had been a reflex one, and bad. There was no telling what effect it had had on her, what she might do.

The lawyer extended his hand as Strollo entered. "Mr. Strollo, my name is Yale. Tom Madden called and asked me to see you. He hopes to be here tomorrow. I'll not ask you any questions—Tom will handle that. Your *friends* are concerned for you and arranged for your representation. Everything will be taken care of."

Strollo didn't like the popinjay oozing friendliness at him. Strollo released the weak hand and dropped into a chair, his baggy prison grays in contrast to the attorney's meticulous attire.

"I'll be asking for a bail hearing today, and we'll see if we can't get a bond set. From what I've been able to find out, Nathan Hersch gave a statement. Plus, there are extensive wiretaps. These are always vulnerable to attack, though. I'm sure Madden will file a motion to suppress them."

Strollo had a question that came out as a statement. "Frankie's in with me. Iannello ain't, and I'm worried about that."

"Yes, so am I. I've picked up some indication he's cutting a deal. Since you tell me he's not with you in here, that becomes more probable."

"Fucking little weasel. I'll kill him. So help—"

Yale interrupted with a raised hand. "Watch what you say, Mr. Strollo, I know you don't mean that literally. You're excited by the betrayal of a friend. But others may misinterpret your remarks should they hear them."

An obscene comment about what Yale could do was forming, but Strollo held back. He folded his arms on his chest, almost eager to be rid of this lawyer.

"Be patient, Mr. Strollo. Your friends will see you through this."

Yale left, and Strollo had the unpleasant duty of informing Milano that Iannello had made a deal. They both recognized that the government had a winning hand if Iannello testified.

The bond hearing that afternoon resulted in $100,000 cash or surety bond for Milano. Karla had fought for higher bond, while Yale contended he should be released on his own recognizance. Milano had not been charged as yet in the Towers scam. When the additional charges were made the bond could be increased.

Fidelity Bonding wrote his bond immediately, and he was released. Fidelity wasn't worried about collecting its 10 percent fee or his jumping bail. The Mafia was trustworthy where bonds were concerned.

Strollo was a tougher nut for Yale. The government had evidence of a contemplated homicide and argued he was a danger to the community. The judge finally set a cash or surety bond of a million dollars. It took three bondsmen to write that amount, splitting the $100,000 fee. Strollo was out that night. The judge also required Strollo to contact the U.S. Marshals Service twice a day, by phone, from Dade County, where he was to remain. The times were set at ten in the morning and four in the afternoon.

When Strollo got home he found a note on the kitchen table.

"Vincent, I'm with the children. Don't call me. I'll let you know what I decide. Rosa."

Strollo grunted, balled it up, and threw it in a corner.

Amari, represented by Madden, was released on a $500,000 bond, with his travel restricted to New Jersey and Dade County, where the charges had been laid. Madden waived removal hearing.

After his release, Amari met with Madden, as per the lawyer's whispered instructions during the bond hearing. He was waiting in his car at the exit from the jail. Amari walked up to the car, and Madden rolled down the window.

"Jimmy, I got a message for you. You're to go to the Cheese Factory on Route 27. Ask for the Carmine party. Be there by seven."

Madden rolled up his window, started his car, and drove off.

The Cheese Factory was a large, well-known restaurant just outside New Brunswick. Amari arrived by six-thirty, wanting to scope out the place. As he entered he saw a long bar with cocktail tables and overstuffed chairs on the right. Straight ahead was the main dining room, broken up by decorative dividers into areas accommodating four tables each. To the left were four private dining rooms of varying size.

Amari asked for the Carmine party and was escorted to one of the private dining rooms containing four round tables, each seating six people. One table was set for two, and wine was waiting on the table. The maître d' poured Amari a glass before leaving. Amari pulled out a chair facing the entrance door and sat, sipping his wine and nibbling on some provolone, bread, and pepperoni.

Ever since he had been informed of this meeting, he had been thinking over the reason behind it. Two possibilities occurred to him. One was why he faced the door. The other, though, was more likely and weighed heavily on him as he waited.

At five minutes after seven, having satisfied himself there was no police surveillance, Carmine Licata entered the room. Amari rose to greet him, but Licata waved him back to his chair.

"It's good to see you, Jimmy. First we eat, then we talk."

Amari was more at ease now, at least concerning his personal safety. But that left the other possibility.

A waiter carrying a tray followed Licata in, and was soon arranging dishes in front of both men.

"Jimmy, I took the liberty of ordering veal. This is one of the few places that know how to cook it."

Amari nodded in acquiescence, and they commenced eating. There was no conversation.

A bottle of spumante appeared for dessert. The waiter disappeared, not to return, and Licata leaned back in his chair and lit a cigar. "First we need some music."

From his pocket came a portable radio, which was soon at full volume on a rock-and-roll station. Then he moved his chair close to Amari, and with his mouth to Amari's ear he delivered his message.

"My friend, Don Carlo is most concerned about you. He personally arranged for Madden and will stand behind you. He ordered me to see you tonight and to talk to you about these troubles."

It was about what Amari had expected. He could not fault

the language Licata used, but he kept his ears pricked for any threat to him. He inclined his head in a token of appreciation, and Licata continued.

"He has asked to be informed whether you were going to do a piece of work on two people as the newspapers say. If so, who are they, and who authorized this action?"

Amari had expected this to come up. He felt he had no choice but to respond truthfully to the question. With his mouth at Licata's ear, he said, "I was ordered to pop a husband and wife. Their name is Siragusa." He paused, struggling with himself, not wanting to say what he knew he must. "The order came from Strollo. He said he authorized it."

"Didn't you ask for other authorization?"

"No. I didn't like it, but I told him I'd do it."

"Who are these people? Why were they going to be whacked?"

Amari had hoped this question wouldn't be asked but knew it had to come. He had searched for some way to evade it. Strollo was his closest friend, and they had been through a lot together. Their families were close. But he saw no way out. In a low voice, his discomfort evident, he replied, "They are cousins of Strollo. They turned over a great quantity of gold to Vincent, perhaps two hundred pounds. He sold it through Littman. I expect they wanted their money."

"Is Don Carlo aware of this?"

Amari permitted himself a lie. "I don't know."

"Are you telling me Strollo may have been stealing this gold from the family? Keeping it for himself?"

He lied again. "I don't know."

Licata reared away from Amari and contemplated how best to proceed. After a long pause he leaned forward again. "Go home. Be there at ten tomorrow morning."

Amari was tired. It had been a long day, but he was nonetheless careful. "What can I expect? What will happen tomorrow?"

Licata's expression was completely opaque. "Nothing for you to be concerned about. I must discuss what you have told me with Don Carlo. I repeat, you are not to worry, but decisions will be made."

Licata stubbed out his cigar and left the room. Amari followed in about five minutes.

Licata traveled to Brooklyn, where he found Magliocco, the *consigliere* Ardizonne, and the seldom seen or mentioned *sotto capo* Thomas Ferrigno awaiting his arrival at Caesar Augustus, a favored restaurant. Magliocco had taken an afternoon flight, having decided that this situation required top-level consultations.

Licata recounted his meeting with Amari. When he had finished, Magliocco said nothing. He merely ground out his half-smoked cigar.

Ferrigno stepped into the pause. "You were right in your evaluation, Don Carlo, but it is even worse." He slapped the table resoundingly, emphasizing his point. "He was stealing from the family."

Magliocco addressed Licata. "You will contact Littman and retrieve the family's property."

Licata nodded his assent.

Ardizonne looked at the *capo* and shook his head. "He must go. Not just for his theft, but because he poses a threat. In his position he could be tempted to talk."

Magliocco swiftly pronounced his sentence. "Kill him."

Not unhappy to hear that one of his chief rivals was being removed, Licata moved to implement the sentence. "Don Carlo, if you want Jimmy to handle this, it will be necessary, I think, for you to talk to him. He is very close to Strollo."

Ardizonne raised a bony, almost transparent hand. "He's right. We must impress on Amari that this is authorized family business. It will put him at ease."

There was silence for a moment, then Licata raised another subject.

"Iannello apparently has betrayed his oath. The lawyers tell us he is talking to the FBI."

Magliocco responded, "Kill him. Kill him."

Ardizonne nodded in agreement and again added his thoughts. "He will be in the protection plan. He cannot seriously hurt the family. He can hurt Strollo, though, which is a reason Strollo must go. He may also be able to hurt some of the soldiers of other families who are in Miami. I suggest we inform the other families of his treachery, and cooperate toward eliminating him. But he will first have to be found."

He looked up, his thin purple-veined face and watery eyes reflecting all the violence he had survived.

"I suggest, though, that his elimination is not as urgent as Strollo's. We can get at Strollo now, so we must move quickly." As all nodded in agreement, the old adviser bowed his head. His next statement might not be as welcome. "I further suggest that we consider Amari's fate. He has been an excellent soldier, but he has been involved in many delicate matters, and now with this Strollo problem he may pose a threat himself. He should have reported this gold to you as soon as he learned of it."

For the first time Magliocco seemed pained. "Let's take one thing at a time. But, yes, look for someone who can put Amari away."

• C H A P T E R •
TWENTY-FOUR

Stirred by the persistent ring of the telephone, Blue Eyes swept the blanket aside with one arm, swung his feet over the edge of the bed, and sat hunched over for a moment, trying to focus on what had disturbed his deep sleep. His wife moved beside him, muttering for him to answer the phone. He finally lifted the handpiece from its cradle on the nightstand. Groggily he glanced at the clock, which registered five-ten.

He finally responded, "Hello."

Licata's voice said, "Do you know who this is?"

In one chilling rush Amari became fully awake. "Yes."

"Be at the phones in front of the 7-Eleven on Highland Boulevard in ten minutes."

Amari dressed in moments and hurried the four blocks to the phones. There were three of them in a bank to the right of the door. The store was closed, the parking lot empty. Only an occasional car on the boulevard passed by.

At precisely five twenty-one the center phone rang, and Amari picked it up. "Hello."

Magliocco was on the other end. For this call he spoke English. "Jimmy, my friend, do you know who this is?"

Even with no one present, talking into a telephone, Amari nevertheless gave a shallow bow. "Yes, of course."

"Once more we have need of your considerable talents. I have authorized our very dear friend with whom you had dinner yesterday to take measures against two people who threaten the family. You will follow his instructions as though they come from me, for indeed they do. May I once again rely on your service?"

Amari hesitated. He knew the order would be to kill Strollo. He had been with Strollo for thirty years. They were as close as two men could be. The thought of rejecting this order flashed into his mind for a second and then was gone.

Strollo had been wrong. He knew the rules. Amari, by all rights, should have refused the request in the first place.

Amari answered, "Yes."

The hesitation was not lost on Magliocco. There was no question that Amari would have to be killed after the hits on Strollo and Iannello.

"Thank you, Jimmy. Please stay at the phones a few more minutes. You will receive another call."

Within five minutes, the phone on the right rang, and Amari picked it up.

Licata began without preamble. "Strollo has stolen from the family and ordered you to perform an unauthorized action. All things considered, he is a very serious problem that you will solve just as soon as possible." Amari's hand tightened on the receiver, wishing he did not have to listen. "Iannello has spilled his guts to the cops. He also must go."

Iannello was of little concern to Amari. That pop would not disturb him at all.

"Socks will meet with you. Whatever you need he will provide."

Amari was taken aback at this. Socks was Magliocco's bodyguard and constant companion. He and Magliocco had made bones together. Socks had been the principal enforcer before Amari and was no longer involved in doing a piece of work.

Licata continued, "You have a legitimate reason to go to Florida. Madden is representing you both. He can arrange for Strollo to be vulnerable. He has been instructed to arrange a meeting between you for that purpose. Do you have any questions?"

"No."

Amari hung up the phone and drove back to his house, profoundly disturbed by what he had been ordered to do.

Bill appeared at Al's door at seven-thirty that morning, and Al waved him in.

Bill gestured toward Al's teletype pile. "New York CI says the bonds are from the Cleveland family. He also says Magliocco is pissed and has ordered Iannello hit. No word on Strollo."

"Great!" Al replied. "Get something off to Cleveland right away. Send them good photos of the numbers on the bonds."

Bill was puzzled. "What good will that do?"

Al grinned at this next stage of his plan. "Those bonds and their coupons had serial numbers on the face, about fifty individual impressions of the same number. Those numbers come from a numbering wheel, really a series of wheels connected together. It's a complex and very expensive instrument, not used with great regularity."

Al almost chuckled at the way the counterfeiters had trapped themselves. "The number wheels, the many used here, would most certainly have been rented. The wheels are indexed to the press so that they make fifty, or whatever, impressions of the same number on precise spots on the bond, all at the same time. They then reset themselves to the next consecutive number and print on exactly the same spot on the next bond, and so through the whole printing process of the hundreds of individual bonds."

Bill was making notes for the teletype.

Al concluded, "Tell Cleveland to identify printing supply houses in their area that have numbering wheels for rent. Each rented wheel will have microscopic imperfections—all such machinery does—and those imperfections are in our photographs. Find the wheels and you'll find the people who rented them."

Bill was infected by Al's enthusiasm. They were doing damage all over the place. He looked up, a knowing smile on his face. "Got it. It'll be off this morning. By the way, we're beginning our trace of the money from the banks and from Towers. I'm sure we'll end up in offshore banks."

At that moment, Ken passed the office and stuck his head in. "Got a moment, Al?"

"Sure. We were just discussing your case."

"Got a problem for you, I'm afraid." He entered the office and sat down next to Bill. "After our meeting yesterday, Karla took me aside. It seems our United States attorney, Neil Miller, is mighty upset with the way this case has developed."

Al and Bill looked at each other uncomprehendingly. What more could a prosecutor ask for?

"We made a bunch of arrests," Ken went on. "Biggest impact on organized crime in the Southeast in fifty years. National media attention, FBI all over the place. But"—he raised a finger in sarcasm—"nobody said boo to Miller. This was the chance to make his career, and he's pissed."

Al shook his head in total disbelief that this could be happening.

"He told Karla no more arrests on probable cause or complaints. All future charges will be based on sealed indictments. So we'll be getting arrest warrants based on sealed indictments from now on."

Bill was livid. "That sorry sonofabitch. We had to cram those T-3s down his throat. He fought us every step of the way, and now he's pissed because we succeeded."

Al started laughing, the irony tickling his sense of humor. "He's a piece of work, all right. You know what this means, don't you? By returning sealed indictments he precludes us from making any press releases. We go out and arrest, and then he unseals and announces the contents of the indictments to the world, so the media think this Mr. USA is doing it all."

Ken was incredulous at this sleight of hand. "Can he get away with that?"

"I'm afraid so," Al answered. "You know, when I was an ASAC, I had another politically ambitious USA in another office try that on me. We buried him at the press conference, because he didn't know what he was talking about. But the problem was, we had an enemy for life. It's probably not worth it."

Al was about to move on to another topic when he saw the disagreement on Ken's face, so he added, "It's nice to have the world know you're doing the job, but it's more important that you know it. This isn't worth a confrontation that might affect nailing these guys. Let me handle it."

Terry Washington stuck his head in the door. "Got a minute?" His expression was as grave as Al had ever seen.

All levity drained from Al's face, and he motioned for Bill and Ken to leave.

"Donnelly?"

Terry nodded and eased onto the sofa. Al dropped into a chair opposite him.

"He didn't come home last night. We can't find his car. I've turned out his whole squad to look for him. Should we do a missing person APB for him? This isn't like Steve."

"Not yet, Terry. Advise the Bureau he's missing and that we were in the midst of an administrative inquiry."

"Al, you don't suppose he found out and went off the deep end?"

The intercom came to life with a buzz, and Al answered his secretary's call.

"Metro on the line, a Lieutenant Godfrey. They found one of our cars, and I think you might want to talk to him."

Al acknowledged and greeted the lieutenant, who hesitated for a second when he found himself talking to the SAC.

"I'm in auto theft, Mr. Lawrence. We got a tip this morning from an anonymous caller. He and his girl were parked about one A.M. near a canal in southwest Dade and a car drives up. The driver gets out and apparently releases the brake and lets the car drive into the canal. A cop picks up the driver. We put divers down this morning and found it and are in the process of bringing it up now. The car's one of yours, license CZY 105."

Al knew whose car it was but checked his list to confirm it. "Anything"—Al almost said "anyone"—"in the car?"

"No, but we can't pop the trunk until we get it out of the canal."

"Give me the location and I'll have some men there in a few minutes."

The lieutenant furnished the location, and Al quickly filled in Terry and had him dispatch two cars to the scene.

"Terry, I don't like this. I intend to fire Steve if he can't explain the false report. But even if he knows that, I can't believe that's the reason for his disappearance." Without his being aware of it, his fingers were tapping on the desk blotter. "Two men involved bothers me. Ignoring the administrative inquiry, was anything else gnawing at Steve?"

"Nothing that I'm aware of."

Al rose abruptly and walked over to a small closet. Taking out his suit coat, he began putting it on.

"Terry, stay here and cover this end. I'm going out to the canal scene, and then I want to visit with his family. I talked to his wife by phone late last night, she's distraught. I don't want her to hear about the car from a news account. I want you to go over all his cases, interview anyone, like his secretary and clerk, who was close to him, find out what was troubling him. Let's see if we can't put a motive to his disappearance. Whatever problems we may have with him, he's still one of us."

He avoided mentioning the Miami cops, but he couldn't shake the idea of those two men. Could they be capable of killing an FBI agent? He shook his head as though trying to rid himself of the thought.

Al was driving out of the ground-floor garage when the radio called him. "Station, One."

He picked up the mike and depressed the transmit button. "One, go."

"ASAC requests you return for a call from Metro Homicide."

Al's blood ran cold as he backed into the garage. He took the stairs to the elevator landing two at a time and was in his office in seconds. Terry Washington was on the phone, and he passed it to Al. "Juan from Metro. I figured you'd want to talk to him."

"Juan, Al. What's up?"

"Uniform got a disturbance call last night. By the time they got there it was a homicide. In doing a crime scene on the apartment we found a Who's Who of Miami dopers plus a nonpub number that comes back to your office. The way it's set up, phony name and all, we figured it was a hello phone for informants."

Al's head sank onto his hand. That's all he needed today, a dead CI. "What's his name?"

"It isn't a him. Her name's Ruby Gentry. And whoever did her was looking for something. They tore her and the place apart."

Joey "Socks" Boccia met with Amari in the Bergen Mall, just across the river from Manhattan. Boccia was an old "mustache" and had been Amari's teacher. About sixty-five and heavy, he could still move fairly well but had not made any bones in years.

They walked around each other for fifteen minutes until satisfied there was no surveillance. Even then they walked through the mall as they talked.

"Joey, I'm open to suggestions," Amari began. "Strollo's been down this road. How do I take out a guy like that by surprise? Too friendly a move and he's going to know it's the kiss of death."

Socks nodded. "I agree, so maybe try the opposite."

"How?"

Boccia shrugged. "Fight him. Accuse him, but not too strong, of causing this problem. Ask for a meeting."

Amari shook his head. "No, he and I have done that before too. The 'make peace' move."

The old teacher offered another suggestion. "Can you put him in a position where he won't know you're there?"

"That's possible. A bomb?" Amari said doubtfully.

Boccia scoffed, "Naw, they're too unreliable. We can't afford not to get him on the first try."

"You're right. The only dependable way is a face-to-face whack."

Boccia tossed a glance at a lingerie-shop display before he offered a possible solution. "The lawyer'll get the two of you together."

Amari reflected, "The boss always said to use the lawyers, but don't involve them direct."

Boccia didn't disagree. "So don't involve them. Whack him after the meeting. It'd be natural to go somewhere. After all, you ain't setting up the meeting."

Amari fastened on this idea. "Yeah, or before. His car. He's got to drive to the lawyer's. We'll know time and place. He's got noplace to go in a car. He's trapped inside. That's when I'll do it. Now I just have to decide with what."

Boccia stopped in front of a luggage store, pretending to admire a line of suitcases. "Shotgun would be the surest."

"Yeah, but how do I carry it in Miami? No overcoats there."

"Briefcase?" Boccia said, indicating one in the window.

"Socks, me and a briefcase is fucking out of character. The best thing would be to have nothing in my hands when I walk up to the car."

They started strolling again, and Boccia threw out, "If you're willing to be loud, the next best after a shotgun is a .45. Eight slugs from that would put anybody away."

Amari looked over in interest. When Strollo had been looking for a piece on the Siragusa hit, he had mentioned .45 machine guns. "Yeah, MAC-10s with silencers, they're all over Florida. All the dopers use them. They're quiet as hell and hold twenty rounds." Grinning, he snapped out a finger and pulled the trigger. His technical problems had been solved.

"That's what I'll use. I can wear a light jacket and sling it under my arm. They ain't much bigger than a .45 pistol but with a pipe on the end."

Amari turned to his old teacher with a smile of satisfaction. "Joey, get me one, but two silencers. I want a fresh silencer for the day I whack him. They wear out, you know. Four clips, about five hundred rounds of hollow-point ammo. I need to practice with it."

"The boss said you get what you want. I'll try to have it tomorrow."

Pam called Shirley as soon as the news of the arrests broke, and the agent agreed to come by with Jerry that afternoon.

When the agents arrived at her apartment, they found her alternating between a martini and a glass of ice water. She was wearing a rumpled housecoat, and she obviously hadn't looked into a mirror yet that morning.

"Murder! He was going to kill two people!" she exclaimed. "What about me? Does he know about me?"

Shirley tried to calm her. "No, he doesn't. Even if he did, doing anything to you would gain him nothing but another charge. The evidence is all on tape. We don't need you as a witness."

Pam was having none of this. She pulled at her robe as though covering herself with its protection. "At some time he'll know about me, won't he?"

Shirley sighed. "It's possible, but perhaps not. If it looks like the prosecutor is going to make your tapes available, we'd tell you beforehand. Until that happens, don't borrow trouble. Act normal."

"There may never be a trial," Jerry offered. "He may plea-bargain. It's much too early to tell."

Pam reached for the half-empty cocktail shaker on the coffee table and refilled the martini glass. "What should I do if he calls or comes by? He's out, you know."

Shirley nodded at the glass in Pam's hand. "For one thing, go easy on those. You'll need your wits about you." Pam looked blearily at her glass, not wanting to comprehend the implication of Shirley's statement.

"If I were you," the agent said, "I'd tell him you don't want to see him again. The reason is obvious."

Jerry interjected, "Or you could continue seeing him if you want. If you choose that option, we'll have to have a long talk."

Pam surfaced through her gin fog to ask, "What do you mean, long talk?"

"He's represented by counsel," Jerry said. "We can't talk to him without his lawyer being present unless he initiates the conversation. Since you've been cooperating with us and working under our direction, the courts look at you as an extension of us."

Pam began to relax a bit, whether from the martini or the

288 • Arthur F. Nehrbass

conversation the agents were not sure. "My decision is not to see him or talk to him."

Jerry agreed easily. "Sure, that's the wise decision. Try not to worry. We'll stay with you in this. If you have any questions, call the office right away."

The day after his release, Strollo woke early to an empty house. He would have to make his own breakfast or go out. Scowling, he decided on toast and coffee. After yesterday, he wasn't even sure if it was safe to go out.

He burned the toast, and the coffee turned out weak. Rosa knew how he liked it. These were only minor concerns, though, in a far deeper gloom he was feeling this morning. "I shouldn't have snapped at her like that," he muttered to the airy, sun-filled kitchen.

As he ate, he reached for the Yellow Pages. He had to get busy. The directory was of no help. Frustrated, he called the company that controlled his car and home security alarm systems.

"Good morning, Personal Protection."

"This is Mr. Strollo. You have my car and home alarm. I need to talk to someone about a modification."

"Just a moment."

Within seconds a voice came on. "This is Samson, Mr. Strollo. How can I help you?"

"I want a remote starting device installed on my car today."

"You want to be able to start your car from a distance by radio?"

"That's it."

"Certainly. Bring it in."

"No, you come here and do it today."

"We'll have to charge extra for that."

"Just do it," Strollo snapped.

"We'll be there before noon, if that's satisfactory."

"Fine. If I'm not here, the car will be in the driveway. You have the keys and code. Just leave the switch in the patio area."

Rising from the table, Strollo felt very alone. For the first time in his life he had no one. The family had always been there before. Now he wasn't sure. Rosa had always been there, and now she had left him. There was Pam. He dismissed her: she was just a lay. Rosa was the one who knew him, inside out. She had always been there for him—until she pulled that dumb-ass stunt at the jail.

He had to get her back. He knew exactly where she would have gone. He called her at his son Tommy's house on Long Island.

Rosa answered on the third ring. "Hello?"

"Rosa, I need you."

She sounded as if she had been expecting him to call. "Vinnie, you said terrible things to me. You were going to do terrible things to our cousins. Vinnie, I can't come back."

"Rosa, I'm sorry for the way I talked to you. The strain of the arrest, being in jail, I wasn't myself."

Strollo couldn't believe he was doing this. He had never begged for anything, certainly not from a woman, especially not from Rosa.

"Look, this whole thing is a misunderstanding. My lawyers are straightening it out now. But I need you home."

Rosa wasn't sure what to make of all this. He had never pleaded with her like this before. He had demanded and she had complied. Now he was asking for her, and she could refuse.

Her husband needed her. Was this the new beginning she had been hoping for?

"All right, Vinnie, I'll fly out this morning and be home this afternoon. I'll call when I get reservations."

"Good. I'll pick you up."

The conversation terminated, and Rosa paused, wondering if she had done the right thing. He had not thanked her. He had not even said he loved her. But then he had never really said that in their whole marriage. Rosa wished he would. Just once. When she got home she'd ask him.

• CHAPTER •
TWENTY-FIVE

Al's trip to the canal produced nothing. Steve's trunk contained only the usual Bureau equipment.

His trip to Ruby's apartment served to remove any thought of lunch. The woman had been brutally beaten and tortured and her throat sliced with a knife. He had to assume the motive was related to her work as a CI. He ordered her file thoroughly reviewed and everything given to Juan. Two agents were assigned to work the case with Metro.

Later that day, he met again with Bill. They were shortly joined by Ken Stacy, Terry Washington, and Brian Marion, arriving one by one. They all squeezed into Bill's small office, and the meeting just kind of happened. Al had been addressing a problem with Bill that had been presented in a phone call from New York.

"One of the New York CIs just called in to report that Joey Boccia is trying to locate a MAC-10 with suppressor."

Terry's face registered surprise. "There's little doubt what they need that for."

Al agreed. "Right. But who?"

He had drawn up a list of candidates. Plumeri, Milano, Magaddino, Amari, but his eye kept returning to the last name:

Strollo. Could Magliocco consider hitting one of his *caporegimi*, his biggest moneymaker?

Al continued, "The next question is, how do we warn Strollo and the others involved about a potential hit on them?"

Bill shifted in his chair. "It does present a problem. Strictly speaking, we can't talk to Strollo. He's represented by counsel. Since his lawyer works for Magliocco, if we talk to him, we talk to Magliocco. Anything we tell him would go right back to the family."

Brian disagreed. "Do we have to tell him anything? There's no hint they're targeting him."

Al thought for a moment. "I think we have to assume that the hit is intended for Strollo. Amari's in New Jersey. There's nothing we can do there. Newark can handle that if they see fit. Iannello and Hersch are in protection, and the other three aren't significant."

The meeting broke up, and Al took Terry Washington by the arm, turning him toward his office.

"If you agree, I'd like you to drive out to Strollo's with me. I'll give him an abbreviated version of the teletype information, and maybe we can plant a seed of distrust."

Al made this request because he realized this move could be second-guessed by everyone from Bureau headquarters to the U.S. attorney and the judge. It wouldn't be fair to lay it on a street agent.

They drove over to Strollo's house in Al's car and pulled into the circular driveway in the early afternoon. Al rang the bell.

Strollo looked through the peephole in the door and recognized Al. "I got nothing to say to you. Go see my lawyer."

"We don't want you to say anything. We came by to tell you something that just came into the office. Can we talk?"

"No. You got something to say, say it from there."

Al knew what he was thinking. If anybody saw him with an FBI agent . . .

"Okay. Magliocco has ordered a hit down here. We don't know who they're going to whack or who's been ordered to do it. The reason I'm telling you this is that we don't let people get killed, not even a *caporegime*."

Standing to one side, Terry coughed uneasily, not sure what Strollo might do.

Al concluded, "That's all we know right now. You certainly can tell your lawyer about this, but you obviously know he works for Magliocco."

Al waited a second for a response, and when none was forthcoming, he motioned to Terry, and they left.

Strollo stood at the door for several minutes. He was almost certain that he was the target. Magliocco had found out about the gold. The hits in New Jersey had been unauthorized. His plans down here had blown up.

Could he change Magliocco's mind? There had to be a way out. Until he found it, he would look out for himself. Already a .380 Walther rested in his jacket pocket.

Perhaps he should call Magliocco. He certainly had nothing to lose. He made money for the family. Money was what the family was all about. Yes, if Magliocco had ordered him whacked, he could reverse it.

He knew why the FBI had showed up. They wanted him to come over, would offer him protection. But he was no small-time bum like Iannello. People respected him. He would lose that respect if he talked.

Late that night, Amari had his MAC-10, and early the next morning he was in a remote area of Lebanon State Forest, adjoining Fort Dix, practicing with it. Soon he was confident he would be able to operate it smoothly and accurately when the time came.

Morales and Fonseca had declined protection from their department, telling their superiors they didn't believe what they had been told and in any event could take care of themselves. In reality, though, they had a lot of things to clean up and couldn't do it if they were being protected. Steve Donnelly had to be deposited in the Everglades, his car had to be hidden, and Ruby's knowledge of the rip had to be determined. By two-thirty in the morning, the last detail had been taken care of, and they were on their way back to headquarters to drop the unmarked police car they had used for added protection.

After parking in the police garage, they walked over to the lot where their own cars were parked. The night was dark, and only a sliver of a moon, low on the horizon, pierced the overcast sky. The streetlamps were mostly out, the victims of vandals and muggers, the former enjoying the thrill of destruction, the latter creating a safe work environment.

Fonseca was shaking his head. "You think we got all we could out of the broad?"

"Hey, man, she opened up to us after that first shot to the gut," Morales said cheerfully. He was starting to get a taste for killing people. "All the rest was to make sure she couldn't add nothing. Why should she hold out? Would you have held out anything with our treatment?"

"You're right, I guess. There's nothing more there than what we got from that captain, what's-his-name."

"But we got a lot."

Morales opened the double chain-link gate through a fence topped with razor wire. A glance showed their cars to be intact.

"They're looking at us because Ochoa's looking at us. It won't take much for them to find we got too much bread."

Fonseca frowned at this, edgy again. "We should have waited longer, like we agreed, before we started buying shit."

Morales looked up from deactivating his car alarm. "Hey, six months, the whole thing was almost forgotten. Nobody expected a cokehead in Colombia to come up with anything. We had a right to start enjoying."

"So what do we do if they do investigate our finances?"

Morales drummed his fingers on the roof of his car, and finally came to a decision. "Maybe it's time we were gone. Tomorrow we go to headquarters, dump all our shit on the lieutenant's desk, tell him to shove the job, that we don't work where we ain't trusted. Then we disappear for a long vacation. Let's start with Argentina or maybe Spain. We still got almost all the money in cash. We each got a few hundred thou in the house, and we'll leave the rest buried until later. Outside the country we make a connection to move it all, come back, dig it up, and ship it to wherever."

Fonseca looked relieved. "Yeah, I like that. What time you want to meet?"

"Oh, maybe about ten. Come over to my place. We'll make travel arrangements so we can leave right after we dump our shit."

Fonseca nodded his agreement and started getting into his car. "What about the girls? They go along?"

Morales considered this. "No, let's tell them we got to go on business and have to leave them here for a while in case we need someone on this end. We tell 'em nothing, not even where we are. They can be our listening post here. We can call and find out whether there's any heat. They can also run errands for us. They don't know nothin', so they're no threat."

Fonseca smiled. He liked that. He was getting bored with Monica anyway.

Almost as an afterthought, Morales added, "Also, we need to buy a lawyer. We need to get with a guy like Flowers. He's the best, got connections in the state attorney's office and with some of the judges. If he can't fix a case, he can find out what's coming down. He can also help us move the rest of the money when we want to. Tomorrow we lay fifty or a hundred big ones on him."

They waved a final greeting, and each headed to his own house.

Morales's house was in Kendall, a booming, largely Latin yuppie enclave of upscale developments west of Miami. As he approached the house, set on almost an acre of land, he activated a small transmitter that opened a security gate in the cinder-block wall around his property. He drove up his driveway as the gate closed behind him. The house was a large pink stucco ranch with attached garage. It was lighted with floods on the outside, but the interior was dark except for the kitchen and the master bedroom, where a night light was on. Another button on the transmitter opened the garage door, and the Porsche purred into the three-car garage next to a white Mercedes. The other car in the garage was a white BMW Morales had recently

bought for his live-in girlfriend, Kori, a tiny nineteen-year-old blonde he had met bar-hopping.

Morales tucked his soft leather handbag under his left arm and entered through the unlocked kitchen door. He walked through the kitchen and around a corner to the bedroom, where he tossed his bag on the dresser and began to kick off his loafers. It was then he heard a muffled sob. His left hand went to the bag, which contained a Glock 9mm, as he turned toward the sound. It had come from the bathroom. Then he saw that Kori was not in bed.

By the time his hand had reached the gun, he spotted the unmistakable ugly snout of a silencer at the edge of the bathroom doorframe.

A voice called out in Spanish, "Drop it! Don't move!"

Morales ignored the somewhat contradictory commands as he reflexively drew and began to level the automatic.

The voice cried in desperation, "Don't!"

Morales began firing as the machine gun spit a burst of five rounds that caught him in the stomach. He dropped the Glock and clutched his stomach, wrapping both arms about him as if to hold in the blood and gore spilling out.

The five rounds were .45-caliber silvertip hollow-points that expand almost double upon impact. One severed his spinal column. His weight and solid body mass kept him upright for a split second. Then, in what seemed a slow-motion turn, he collapsed to his right and crashed to the plush light blue carpet, which was turning bright red with the blood gushing from his wounds.

The shooter swore in Spanish. Behind him were muffled screams of terror from the bound and gagged Kori. The shooter stepped into the doorway through which Morales's hasty shots had harmlessly passed. He was a tall man, balding, dressed in a dark blue business suit. He walked over to the groaning Morales and kicked away his gun. Another man dragged Kori into the room. Her eyes bulged in terror.

The shooter went down on one knee next to Morales, avoiding the spreading pool of blood. In a low voice he said, "My friend, I'm sorry this happened. We did not want to hurt

you, but you gave me no choice. We want only what belongs to us. Return to us the money you took and we will get a doctor for you, and the girl will come to no harm."

Morales opened his mouth to speak, but only blood trickled out. He choked, gave a small cough, followed by a rattling sound.

The shooter put his fingers to Morales's carotid artery and shook his head. He drew a switchblade from his pocket, made two cuts, and then rose from the floor. Without a word he walked over to where Kori lay in a fetal position and put a burst of three rounds into her head.

The pair had already searched the house and had found a floor safe in a corner of the master bedroom's closet. Kori had shown them where Morales had written the combination on the bottom of a dresser drawer. The $215,000 from the safe had gone into a plastic shopping bag.

They realized Morales's shots had probably wakened the neighbors and police would be called. They quickly searched him, found nothing, and hurriedly left by the front door. Beyond the electric gate a waiting car appeared in response to their summons, sent via a hand-held radio.

Fonseca lived in an older home in Coral Gables. He had just activated his automatic garage door opener when he saw what appeared to be a flicker of light from the bedroom. It was too late for Monica to be up. The moment of concern quickly evaporated, though. She had probably just gotten up to use the toilet.

He yawned and stretched as he entered the house. He was tired but still hyper from the day's events, so he decided on a drink. The bar was in the family room, and he headed toward it, dropping his leather handbag and the 9mm Glock it contained onto the kitchen counter.

At the bar he poured a generous amount of Dewar's scotch into a tall glass. He opened the small ice maker under the bar and dropped a handful of ice into the drink. After a few swirls he began to drink. After the first swallow he sat the glass on the bar, feeling the relaxing warmth spread through him.

That's when he detected a movement out of the corner of his eye. Turning questioningly, he expected to see Monica. Instead he saw a tall, smiling, mustachioed man dressed in a blue guayabera and light tan slacks. Hanging loosely at his side was a MAC-10 with a long black silencer attached.

Momentarily stunned, Fonseca quickly regained his senses. He twisted sharply and dropped a hand to lift his left trouser leg. He heard the man laugh, and the machine gun gave a sharp metallic cough. The bones in his right hand shattered and his left shin was broken. The backup Walther PPK in the ankle holster was driven into his leg.

Nelson Borrego, El Loco, was still laughing as Fonseca fell onto his back. The short burst of four rounds had been well aimed. He had crippled Fonseca but had not killed him.

Borrego strode rapidly over to retrieve the Walther and tossed it away. He wiped the blood from his hand on Fonseca's shirt. Then, smiling, he said in Spanish, "You look uncomfortable. Would you like to get up and sit in a chair?"

Without waiting for an answer, Borrego nodded to someone Fonseca had not yet seen. The second man was almost as tall as Borrego and much heavier. A strong hand grasped a handful of his hair and another his right arm. Grimacing in agony, Fonseca was flung into a chair.

At Borrego's head motion toward the bedroom, the big man disappeared.

"We're bringing out Monica. We might save ourselves some time and you some pain if you see we mean to get the answers to our questions." The assassin was no longer smiling. "Where have you hidden the money?"

Fonseca's mind was racing. These had to be Ochoa's men. That captain hadn't been lying after all.

His face was distorted by the unbearable pain in his leg and hand. He clenched his teeth and forced out a response. "In the floor safe."

Borrego flashed a smile of pure sadistic pleasure, and Fonseca shivered. He knew what was coming.

Then he saw Monica. Or what had been Monica. Her once beautiful face was a bloody, bruised mass of flesh. Her now

298 • Arthur F. Nehrbass

mostly toothless, bleeding mouth was open, sucking in breath, and her nose was no longer discernible. One of her arms hung at a strange angle, broken.

"We no longer need her—we have you."

Borrego nodded, and the other man loosed his hold on her. She crumpled to the floor, settling into a disheveled heap. Borrego shot her in the head.

He turned to Fonseca. "Don't play games with me. We got the money from the floor safe. I ask you again where is the money? If you do not tell me now, you will soon beg me to listen."

Fonseca knew that once they had the money they would kill him. He had to stall for time. Perhaps someone would come, something would happen.

"Morales. My partner, he has it."

The machine gun came up, leveled at his stomach. "I hope you are telling me the truth. He has some friends of mine with him now."

Borrego paused and thought for a minute. "No, I think you're lying, but I need to confirm it. Tie him up."

The other man gagged and bound the unresisting Fonseca, and they dragged and carried him to his car in the garage. He was stuffed into the Mercedes's tiny trunk, and the two drove to a farm in a remote section of the Redlands.

When they arrived, Fonseca was dragged from the trunk and carried to an old barn. He screamed in pain as a rope was tied to the wrist of his shattered hand. His other wrist was looped as well, and he was hoisted up until only his toes touched the ground.

The car from Morales's house pulled in, and Borrego learned of Morales's death. He cursed the shooter for his stupidity, and then they turned their attention to Fonseca.

Within two minutes, the hard-driving Narcotics officer had divulged the location of four large metal chests buried at an old fish camp in Collier County. As insurance, Fonseca would live until the chests were recovered. Then he would be alligator meat.

Al had just hung up the phone after being briefed by Juan on the homicides of Morales and the two girls and on the missing Fonseca. Terry Washington and Bill Baskin were in the armchairs waiting to discuss the Strollo case. Al slowly looked up from the phone, his face reflecting the turmoil in his mind.

Speaking absently, almost thinking out loud, he repeated what Juan had told him.

Afterward, Terry voiced the question on everyone's mind:

"Where does Steve fit in all this? Could El Loco have hit him? Was he dirty with the two cops?"

"I don't think so," Al said slowly. "We were on Steve's case because he lied about having met with Zamorano. Had he and the cops been working together they would have agreed on this important fact."

Bill shook his head in bewilderment. "So what's happened to him?"

Al was racked with a wave of sadness. "We can't be sure. The car in the canal tells me he's dead. Who killed him? I don't know. Was he tortured for information? Was that the reason for taking him?"

Terry was silent for a moment before he put in, "I should have mentioned this earlier, but when we interviewed Steve's secretary, she told us that he had received a long call from Ruby a few days before this all went down."

All three chewed on this information for a while. All the pieces finally were coming together. As in almost every investigation there was an unanswered question, but they thought they knew why Steve had told Ruby's killers who she was.

Two days later Borrego sat with Ochoa on the wide veranda of one of his haciendas about ten miles south of Bucaramanga. They looked out over countless hectacres of trees laden with the rich Colombian coffee bean. The green of the foliage was strong and oily. They were sampling some of the farm's product as *café con leche*.

A small box was on the floor at Ochoa's feet. In it were four brown leathery objects. Two pairs of ears.

Ochoa was smiling as he looked down at the ears.

"They suffered long and hard?"

Borrego sighed. For the third time he assured Ochoa that the death of the two detectives had been painful.

"Fonseca was made to understand that his lingering, painful death was because he had stolen from you. The other was gut shot, in great pain, but he died quicker than we would have liked."

Ochoa nodded. "Good. Good."

"They had spent just over nine hundred thousand on houses, cars and women, but we recovered the rest. It was given to our group there and should be here within the week."

Ochoa thought, Borrego has succeeded again. He was getting a reputation. Ochoa would have to talk to his brother. It was time Borrego was removed. They could always raise another Borrego. There were plenty of hungry men.

• C H A P T E R •
TWENTY-SIX

Standing just inside his front door, Strollo pressed the first button on the small transmitter in his hand. The intrusion alarm on the car beeped and was disarmed. He pressed the second button, and the engine of his car started. Strollo waited a minute, then walked toward the car and got in.

He drove west on the causeway toward the airport. Before picking up Rosa, he had decided, he would call Licata and try to get through to Magliocco. He parked in garage number two and walked across the roadway to the terminal and upstairs to a bank of phones.

On the second ring the phone was picked up and he heard, "Hello, Funny Valentine."

"Dominic there?"

"Who's calling?"

"Mr. Vincent, from Miami."

Strollo heard a sharp intake of breath. After several seconds a voice came on.

"Mr. Vincent, Dominic here. How can we help you today?"

"I need to talk to Carmine, now. Have him call me at 259-2772. I'll be here for fifteen minutes."

Strollo hung up without waiting for a reply. Ten minutes later the phone rang and he answered, "Hello?"

"Vincent, how are you, old friend? We were distressed to hear about your problems. As you know, we sent help right away. If there's anything you need, you have only to ask."

Strollo listened restively to this pointless chatter. He'd been down this road himself. He didn't even bother to reply. "Carmine, I need to talk to Don Carlo."

Licata was surprised, but then he thought he should have expected this. After all, they were dealing with Vincent Strollo. Cautiously he said, "I don't know if that can be arranged. I'm sure if you were here he'd meet with you, but I doubt if he'd be able to talk to you by telephone."

Licata himself did not like the idea of talking to Strollo on the phone. What if this call was being recorded for the feds? Yet on further reflection, he saw that talking to Magliocco might be a good idea. It was important to allay Strollo's fears, for there could be no other reason for the call.

"On second thought, perhaps I can arrange it. You must understand, with all the people listening to things down there, one has to be cautious."

"I understand," Strollo said coldly. "This is a random pay phone."

"Vincent, leave it in my hands. Go home, and I'll be in touch."

Strollo walked downstairs to the baggage claim area, where he saw Rosa standing by a luggage conveyor. She was wearing a pink silk dress that gave her a warm, feminine appeal, accented by a white sweater around her shoulders. Her black hair framed her ivory complexion.

He was genuinely glad to see her. Not just for the help she might be to him but because he knew she loved him and was loyal to him.

He walked toward her, and she ran to him, put her arms around his neck, and asked, "Do you love me?"

Strollo was surprised, first by the public embrace, and second by the question. Fortunately his response was reasonably prompt. "Of course. That's why I called and asked you to come back."

Rosa was satisfied, for the moment.

He picked up her garment bag and small overnight bag and began walking toward the car. Rosa hindered him by holding on to his arm, but he didn't want to shake her off. Actually, it felt good to have her near him, touching him.

On the drive to the house, Rosa was chatty and happier than she had been in a long time. Yes, he thought, he was glad to have her home.

The lasagna she prepared for him was excellent. Strollo was on his second glass of wine and another helping when the doorbell rang.

He absently patted his pants pocket, assuring himself of the Walther's presence. "I'll get it, Rosa." He walked to the door and through the peephole saw Thomas Madden. Lawyers didn't pose a threat.

As soon as he opened the door, Madden said, "The party you wanted to talk to is on the line now. Let's go talk to him."

With that, he put his hand on Strollo's elbow and guided him toward his car. Strollo's hand strayed to his pocket and the Walther.

"Where are we going?"

"To a pay phone."

"With who? Who'll be there?"

"Nobody, just us."

Strollo thought for a moment and decided to risk it. He turned, called to Rosa, "I'll be right back," and closed the door.

Perplexed, Rosa ran to the front of the house, calling after him. But the car was already leaving, and he did not hear her.

She had not had a chance to talk to him about what she had decided at their son's house. The only way they could have a future together was if Vincent cooperated with the FBI. He had to get out of the Mafia. If he became a witness, they could go into protection. She had read about this. They could start a new life. Tomorrow she would go to the FBI and see what she could work out for them.

Madden drove off the island to a small shopping center on the beach and parked the car. He walked to a phone and punched up a number. When it rang, he handed the phone to Strollo.

Strollo rudely took Madden by the arm and positioned him as a shield between him and the street. "And stay there, Tom," he growled.

Strollo recognized the Sicilian accent instantly. "Vincenzo, I'm so glad we could have this talk. I fear there is misunderstanding between us. Two old friends should not allow that to happen."

Strollo observed the pleasantries. "It is I who am in your debt for agreeing to talk to me this way when I know we both would prefer to meet face to face."

"Well, Vincenzo, I shall allow you to start. Tell me what has happened that brings you to this unfortunate situation."

Strollo knew where his value lay. He had made millions for the family, and more was to come if he ducked the charges against him. "First, let me assure you that all of the profits from Towers and the bond situation were moved by me before this happened, and should be all right."

Strollo had to assume he knew about the gold, and this issue had to be addressed straight out. "There is one area that I have not yet been able to satisfactorily adjust. I was able to obtain about eight hundred and seventy-five thousand dollars in gold, which Littman handled. That money was transferred, but has not as yet been distributed to the family. I can arrange for that with Madden, if you like, or forward the information to Licata. Since I have these problems, I should not do it myself."

Magliocco's voice remained even, giving no hint of whether he knew about the gold. "I agree. Give the information to Madden. He will handle the transfer."

Then Strollo's voice became harsh. "I assume, Don Carlo, that arrangements have been made to meet the threat of Iannello."

"That is being handled."

"Perhaps," Strollo said, getting to what he was really after, "I can assist whoever has been assigned that duty."

Magliocco knew what Strollo was fishing for—the identity of the hit man—and decided to try to mislead him. "No, you have yourself to look out for. Let us handle this. Ordinarily it would fall to Jimmy, but he, like you, must be allowed to work on his own problems. It is what the family is for, to help at a time like this. So I have arranged with other parties to handle this."

Strollo did not like this evasiveness. "Don Carlo, do you see any problems down here besides Iannello?"

"No, we have looked at it carefully. Everyone else is handling himself properly, with respect."

Strollo gripped the phone tightly, wanting to believe this was true. "For myself, words fail me in expressing my regret at the problems this venture has caused the family. It is true that we have realized almost eight million from these activities, but they should not have come to this."

Magliocco's voice was smooth, almost oily, filled with concern. "Do not distress yourself. We'll talk of this when you have found your way out of these difficulties. I am satisfied that you exercised every reasonable precaution." Knowing that he needed to make this believable, he added, "There are some areas you should not have ventured into without my permission. This we may talk about, and handle, when your present problems are concluded."

That was as far as Strollo could reasonably expect Magliocco to go. Magliocco's voice, his inflection, his manner, had not been threatening. Perhaps he could relax a little.

"Don Carlo, thank you for permitting this conversation. You may rely on me. When this is finished, I swear to you I shall enrich the family beyond anything that has ever gone before."

"Vincenzo, I know that. My best to Rosa."

As Madden drove him back to his house, Strollo was more relaxed that he had been at any time since the arrest. He looked out the car window at the placid bay on one side of the causeway. The breeze was light, and a Windsurfer was having trouble catching it. Farther out, a water skier was smoothly jumping her boat's wake in a crisscross pattern. He thought when this was over he might buy a boat. He had the dock behind the house.

As they turned onto Star Island, Madden said, "Indictments will be returned, I don't know when. Amari waived a removal hearing in Jersey and is coming down for his appearance, prob-

ably tomorrow. It would be good if the three of us could get together. I obviously need to know where we're going with this,
and there are some options available. We might, if it looks bad,
want to talk about a plea agreement."

They arrived at Strollo's house and pulled into the circular
drive. Madden concluded, "I'll let you know when we should
get together. We can do it here, or at my hotel. Don't worry
about bugs when you talk to me. The government can't do that.
Attorney-client and all that happy horseshit."

Strollo nodded almost absently. "Okay, whenever you're
ready. Oh, Don Carlo said to give you something. Come on in."

Madden came in and was introduced to Rosa in passing.
Then went to Strollo's office, and Strollo opened a floor safe
and handed Madden an envelope.

"Give this to Licata or Don Carlo. They'll know how to
handle it. Don Carlo says he wants you to retrieve it. It's money
in an offshore account. Everything you'll need is in there."

Madden departed, and Strollo was left with his thoughts.

A few minutes later, Rosa appeared at the door. He felt her
there rather than saw her and didn't look up. She was dressed
in a sheer white nightgown with a lacy, plunging neckline. She
stood for a moment, trying to gauge his mood. Then, gathering
up all her courage, she advanced on him. He finally looked up,
and his face went blank with surprise. It was early in the evening, too early for bed.

Her expression was one of determination. His surprise became astonishment when she cupped his face in her hands and
turned it up toward her. He did not resist. He was excited by
this aggressiveness, something she had never before displayed.
She bent over him and kissed him.

He could smell her freshness and felt the hunger in her kiss.
Coming up out of his desk chair, he took her in his arms, holding her tight.

Rosa relaxed. Her daring had succeeded. She pressed her
body into his and could feel his reaction to her. She was happy;
she had her husband back. She took him by the hand and led
him to their bedroom.

Afterward, Strollo lay on his back, on the edge of sleep.

Rosa's coming back had been good. He had been a fool to ignore her. He'd had no idea she loved him so much. And he felt
good with her. He had to admit he had enjoyed her more this
time than any of his girlfriends. Once he had licked his problem
with the FBI, as he had before, they would go away for a long
vacation.

Rosa reached over and stroked his shoulder. She began
speaking in a low voice that came through Strollo's half-sleep.

"Vinnie, we're changing. I feel for the first time you need
me. I've always needed you. I want us always to be together like
this. Like good, regular married people."

Strangely, Strollo found himself in his lethargic state agreeing with her.

Rosa continued, "I don't want you to go to jail. Seeing you there was horrible. It did terrible things to you. I think
you should quit this"—she hesitated, finding it difficult to use
the word—"Mafia thing. Go to the FBI. Let's go into protection. You could turn a new leaf, away from these terrible
people."

Strollo was awake now, but he didn't move. He sighed. Respect, he had respect. That and money had been his life. He
couldn't give up either. Selling himself to the cops, he'd lose
both. Let Rosa dream, though; he liked this new Rosa.

He turned on his side, facing her, and gently touched her
cheek with his hand. "Rosa, your idea might be a good one, but
we've got to think about it some before we act on it. We'll talk
about it tomorrow."

Al was wrapping up the day, ready to go home. Bill looked in
the open door and Al, grinning, waved him off. "No problems!
I'm leaving."

"Just a thought." Bill persisted. "Newark hasn't been
surveilling Amari, and we haven't been on Strollo. Both are arrested, so the case ought to be over, but this one isn't."

Al nodded in agreement. "You're right, of course. I dropped
the ball. Should have thought of that."

"Come on, Al, nobody came up with it. Maybe we better
cure that, though. Amari should be in town tomorrow."

"Okay, have SPIT get on them. They could be the targets Magliocco is aiming at, so make sure the guys are prepared. We don't want anyone getting hurt. If it looks at all like a problem could develop, I want both of us out there with SPIT."

• C H A P T E R •
TWENTY-SEVEN

The MAC-10 was shipped same-day express to Waste Handlers in Fort Lauderdale, a firm specializing in industrial waste removal. From there the package was carried to Thomas Madden, who had it in the trunk of his car, unopened, when he picked Amari up at the airport.

When they arrived at the hotel, Amari took it out of the trunk as he removed his suitcase. As he was tucking it under his arm, Madden, overcoming his normal fear of the killer, stepped in front of him.

"I don't know what's in that package, and I don't want to know. I'm only a messenger boy. I've been told to set up a meeting between you and Strollo for tomorrow. I don't know why, and I don't want to know why. But whatever the purpose, I insist that I not be involved in it. What's between you and Strollo is your business. Take care of it when I'm not there. Do I make myself clear?"

A smile spread across Amari's face, and he peered deep into Madden's eyes. The lawyer took a step back. A chill went through his body, and he could feel his flesh crawl as goose bumps formed on his skin. He had the feeling he had just seen the face of death, his death.

Amari said quietly, "Don't be concerned, Counselor. Nothing will happen that involves you."

He turned and walked into the hotel lobby, leaving Madden more frightened than he had ever been in his life.

Upstairs, after dropping his bag on the bed, Amari's first concern was checking the MAC-10, its new suppressor, and the four full clips. Satisfied, he then rented a car and drove to Madden's hotel to survey the parking lot as a possible place to take out Strollo.

SPIT had been on him since Madden had picked him up.

Amari decided he'd have to be there well before Strollo. He drove around the lot several times, stopping occasionally, observing.

He leaned over the steering wheel, his hairy forearms resting on each side of it. If Strollo was slow enough in parking, and he could get to Strollo's car before he got out, he'd whack him before the meeting.

He sank back against the seat, thinking of alternatives. If he couldn't get to Strollo before he was out of the car, but the location of his car was favorable, he would call Madden and say he couldn't make the meeting, and take Strollo when he came back to his car. But he'd need a hiding place for that.

His heavy brows rose slightly as his thought process continued. If neither of those was feasible, he'd park near Strollo and go to the meeting. He'd walk back to their cars with Strollo and hit him there.

This alternative was the least desirable, since he wasn't sure he could conceal the MAC-10 under his light coat during the entire meeting. Strollo might even wonder why he didn't remove his jacket.

A beefy hand was turning the key in the ignition when another alternative came to him. Madden had a suite. He might be able to conceal the gun in Madden's bedroom and retrieve it before he went down to the car. If Strollo moved to embrace him while he had the gun, he'd have to take him out right there.

Whatever happened, the meeting would be where Strollo

met his end, even if he had to do it in Madden's hotel room with Madden there. Screw it. Lawyers were cheap.

Amari returned to his hotel and telephoned Strollo.

Rosa was in the kitchen and answered, "Hello."

"Hello, Rosa, this is Jimmy. How's the prettiest girl in Bensonhurst?"

"Jimmy!" He was one of Rosa's favorite people. She had known him since childhood and was godmother to his son. He was unfailingly polite and considerate of her. "That Bensonhurst was a long time ago, you know."

Amari laughed. He liked Rosa. She did not try to avoid him, as some of the wives did, because of his job in the family. He had always felt welcome in her house.

"I'm okay. I just got in. Madden picked me up. They didn't think it would look good with Vincent and me together if somebody's watching. Myself, I think that's crazy. Everybody knows we're good friends. Speaking of which, is Vincent around? Just want to say hello."

"Sure, just a minute." She motioned to Strollo, who had come into the kitchen to see who was on the phone. "It's Jimmy."

He took the phone from her, unconcealed pleasure in his voice. "Jimmy! I heard you were coming in for your appearance tomorrow. How you holding up?"

Amari heard the warmth in Strollo's voice and was himself pleased to be talking with him. In spite of his mission, he was genuinely eager to see Strollo and visit.

"Ah, it's okay. I been down this road before. It'll all come out right. You all right?"

Strollo answered, "Yeah. Really looking forward to seeing you."

"Well, let's see. My hearing's in the morning, at ten. I expect the meeting'll be soon after I get out. And screw Madden. After the meeting let's you and me have a long lunch, someplace special. You pick it. We can't let these bastards get to us."

Strollo was smiling, nodding his head slightly. Just like old times. But it would be wise to be cautious about going out until he could be absolutely sure of Magliocco.

"We'll see, Jimmy. I'm glad you're in town. We got a lot to talk about."

Al was in early the next day, as usual, reading his teletypes. Bill came in through the always open door.

"There's another teletype from New York. Doesn't add much. New York still doesn't know who the shooter is or who they intend to whack."

The ever present coffee was in Al's hand as he gave his full attention to Bill. "Amari arrived last night for his court appearance this morning. SPIT is on him. He checked into the Omni downtown, rented a car, and drove over to Madden's hotel. Madden's at the airport Hilton."

He scratched his head for a moment, trying to figure something out. "The odd thing is, Amari didn't go into the hotel. Just drove around the parking lot for about ten minutes, stopping occasionally. From there he went back to the Omni, made a call from a pay phone. From what we could overhear, with an occasional walk-by, he was talking to Strollo."

Al was deep in thought. "That drive around the parking lot is interesting. When's he due back?"

"He's got return reservations to Newark for tonight. I think like five or six."

Al got up and walked over to the corner windows. He noticed vaguely the gentle swaying of the trees as he puzzled the matter through. Finally he turned to Bill.

"With Amari in town for today only, we have to believe today is the day somebody's going to act. Keep me advised of every detail SPIT turns up. Make sure they stay on their toes. There's no telling what might happen."

If Strollo was anything, he was careful. It was how he had survived so long. He had no reason to expect any motive in the Madden-Amari meeting other than what the lawyer had told him. Yet it was a meeting. People would be able to predict his movements. It was how he and Amari had taken out . . . nine, he thought.

He picked up the phone in his office to call Madden's hotel. When Madden came on, Strollo began:

"Tom, your hotel sounds good for the meeting, but there's no way of knowing what time, since it'll have to be after Jimmy's hearing. You and Jimmy call me at home when you're finished, and we'll settle on a definite time. That way I won't be sitting around just waiting."

Madden was eating breakfast in his room. He was a large man and his ample stomach hung over the cord of his pajama bottoms. "All right, sounds good to me. I expect we'll be finished about eleven or eleven-thirty. We can have lunch sent up to the room, and eat while we talk."

"Fine. I'll wait for your call."

Madden had waived a removal hearing in New Jersey on orders from Licata, for the sole purpose of getting Amari to Florida for a plausible purpose as soon as possible. The appearance was over by ten forty-five, and Amari's bond continued. The hearing was in the new courthouse, and there were phones in the area just outside the courtrooms. Amari and Madden proceeded to one, and Madden called Strollo.

"Vincent, we're finished. We can meet at the hotel in half an hour."

"Tom, Rosa talked to Jimmy last night, but hasn't seen him. She cooked up some clam sauce, we got pasta, and she's talking chicken. Why don't you and Jimmy come to the house? We'll visit a bit and discuss our problem."

The sudden change made no difference to Madden. "Sounds good. We'll be there in fifteen or twenty minutes, if that's all right."

"Sure. See you then."

Madden hung up and relayed the news to Amari. The color drained from Jimmy's heavy face. Madden had never seen him so shocked and confused.

"I need a minute to think about this, Madden. Why did you agree to this change of meeting?"

"Why not? His place or mine, what's the difference?"

"Rosa's going to be there?"

Madden's alarm bell went off at this question. "I expect so.

He said she wants to cook and see you." He paused, gulping slightly. He had a premonition of disaster. "Say, I don't like this. I told you before not to involve me in anything. You go to this meeting. I'm out."

Amari had recovered from his original shock, and he advanced on Madden, backing him up against the marble wall. His face inches away, he said, "You're fucking out of this when I say you're out. You do exactly what you're told. You understand me?"

Madden couldn't focus on Amari's face, but he could feel his breath and smell his morning coffee. Madden broke out in a sweat. With a great effort he brought a fit of trembling under control. He had to keep this on an intellectual plane. It was the only defense he could muster.

"Sure, Jimmy, sure. I'm just trying to be your lawyer. Lawyers can't function right when they're involved. I'll do what you want, but you'd be smart not to get me in anything where I can't defend you."

Amari backed off, having heard not a word. "Good. Let's walk down to the cars. We'll take separate cars to Strollo's."

As they walked out into the bright sunlight and headed for the parking lot, he took Madden by the arm and halted him. He could feel Madden's urge to shake off his grasp.

Amari smiled, attempting to allay Madden's fears. It wouldn't do for Strollo to pick up on it.

"I need to stop in that drugstore for a minute. I hurt my arm in the arrest, and it's been bothering me. I'm going to have to rest it. Wait here. I want us to arrive at Vincent's together."

They went down to Al's car in the garage. He opened the trunk, took out a cased shotgun, and placed it on the backseat. As Bill drove the car out of the garage, Al picked up the mike and announced they were in service.

SPIT heard them come on the air and updated them. Amari had gone into a drugstore and was now sitting in his car, apparently struggling with some object they couldn't see. Madden was in his car, just waiting.

Al was heading south toward the courthouse area when one

of the SPIT units announced: "Both packages moving. Mouth following Snake."

Bill smiled and said, "If you haven't guessed it, 'Mouth' is Madden and 'Snake' is Amari."

Within minutes another SPIT agent said, "Both heading east."

Then followed with, "North on Biscayne."

Bill slowed. They might intercept the path of the surveillance, which was now moving in a direction opposite to theirs.

One of the SPIT agents announced, "East, looks like MacArthur Causeway, could be going to Cap's."

As Bill maneuvered for that exit, Al remarked, "I take it 'Cap' is short for *caporegime*—Strollo?"

Bill nodded as they continued down I-95, approaching the area of the surveillance.

Minutes later there was another SPIT transmission. "Turning onto the bridge into Star Island. Shit, this is tough."

Strollo's house was on a small residential island. The bridge was the only way in or out. There was one elliptical road, off which all the homes were built.

The airplane with the gyroscopic binoculars would be the best platform to observe the house. Traffic on the island was sparse, usually just residents. Two vehicles would try to position themselves. One of the units was a bogus Florida Power and Light truck, the other a pickup with tools in the back.

The airplane advised, "Pulled into Cap yard. Mouth exited car. Snake out, left arm in sling. Don't recall that before. At front door."

Strollo answered the bell. He saw Madden, with Amari behind him. When he opened the door, Madden looked pale, but Strollo took the extended hand. Amari came next. His left arm was in a sling, and he was touching it gingerly with his right hand.

With a broad smile he said, "Nothing serious, Vince. The FBI got a little playful and popped it out of joint when they cuffed me."

He moved his right hand from the area of the sling and offered it to Strollo, who took it and affectionately grabbed Amari's thick upper right arm with his left hand.

"I won't aggravate it with a bear hug."

A SPIT voice said, "They're in the house."

The SPIT supervisor came on. "Anybody see an arm sling before?"

There was silence, then a SPIT agent came on. "I saw him when he got in his car after leaving the drugstore: no sling."

Al frowned and remarked to Bill, "I don't like the smell of this."

• C H A P T E R •
TWENTY-EIGHT

Strollo led the way through the house. As the three men passed through the large living room, Rosa saw them from the kitchen and ran out to greet Amari. Before he could stop her, she threw her arms around his neck and kissed him on the cheek. He pressed his upper arm to his side to conceal the bulk of the MAC-10, grasped her waist as best he could to keep her at a distance, and kissed her back. She held on to him, though he gently moved her away.

"Oh, Jimmy, it's so good to see you again. I'm so happy you got time to have lunch with us. You hurt your arm?"

Amari smiled weakly as they released each other. "It's nothing, Rosa, just a sprain. These doctors got to make a big deal so they can charge a big fee. It's good to see you. We'll talk as soon as these two tell me business is finished."

Rosa smiled and said, "Good, but not too long. I've got clam sauce that spoils if it stands. It's my mother's recipe, the one she used to make special for you."

She saw a hint of pain in Amari's face, but ascribed it to his arm.

"I remember, Rosa," he said. "She was like a mother to all of us, a wonderful woman. That was a long time ago." Again he winced, hating what must happen.

Rosa, concerned, said, "You look like you're hurting."

"It's nothing, just comes and goes."

"Jimmy, come on," Strollo said. He led them into the room he had turned into an office. "This room was swept for bugs last week, but in case there's some here, we can tell them this is a lawyer-client conversation and they can't listen. Right, Counselor?"

"That's correct, Vincent. It would be a violation of your constitutional rights for law enforcement to listen to this conversation."

Strollo began laughing, and was joined by Madden. Amari, lagging in the doorway, did not laugh. A familiar rush of adrenaline was building in his system, making his blood pound at his temples.

Strollo settled into the chair behind his desk and Madden into a chair to the left. Amari, the last one in, turned his back to the room as he closed the door. As his hand left the knob, it went up under his jacket, felt the hard metal. He hesitated for just a moment before drawing the MAC-10 from under his slung arm.

When he turned around, the MAC-10 was in his right hand, his left arm was out of the sling, his left hand wrapped around the fat, cloth-wrapped black suppressor which protruded from the square muzzle of the weapon.

Strollo had been watching Madden open his briefcase and pull out papers. In his peripheral vision he saw Amari turn from the door. Sensing a flash of metal, he immediately focused on the weapon in his hands.

Utter disbelief showed on his face as he began to lift himself from his chair. As if on its own, his right hand sought his pocketed Walther.

Madden, looking in his briefcase, saw Strollo rise out of the corner of his eye and heard a series of sharp metallic coughs so close together they were almost as one.

Eight hollow-point bullets hit their target in an overwhelming avalanche of force. Strollo's hands came up reflexively as he fell back, as much in a futile effort to escape the bullets as from the impact. Smacking against the chair, he tumbled over the back of it, the chair falling under him.

Tom Madden looked to his left and saw Amari with the machine gun now pointed at him. He screamed, "Noooo!"

He felt a very hard punch in his chest and toppled over in his chair. Groggily he looked up and saw Amari approaching Strollo. He heard that metallic sound and whoosh again.

Strollo lay on the floor, his chair next to him. And then Amari was standing over him, looking down at him. He could see partway down the barrel of the silencer. That was the last thing he saw.

Amari extracted the clip from the butt of the gun and inserted another. He saw there were still three rounds in the old clip.

He had hit Strollo eight times, scattered from lower stomach to just below his collarbone. His lungs and heart had been destroyed instantly. Amari had made sure with two rounds to the head.

Madden had been hit five times. Two had gone through his left arm and into his upper chest. Three had entered his upper left chest and coursed downward. The heavy, large-caliber hollow-points had exploded his heart and lungs. He too received two rounds to the head.

Amari stood still, listening. He saw the large pools of blood spreading from the dead men.

He knew he would have to kill Rosa. For the first time he squarely faced it. He had avoided thinking about such a terrible idea, letting himself believe that he could somehow spare her.

Strollo had broken the rules, but Rosa was a different case entirely. She was a good wife. She had taken no part in what Vincent had done. Even worse, Rosa had been like a little sister to him as they grew up. She and Vincent were godparents to his son. She occupied a very special place in his affections. His restless fingers combed through his wirelike hair as he tried to remove these images and recover his cold impersonality.

He knew that to leave Rosa alive would be the height of stupidity. The odds were overwhelming she would tell what she had seen.

He shook himself and blanked his mind entirely. He had to concentrate only on the job. Steeling his nerve, he dropped his hand to his side. He used his body to partly conceal the gun as he opened the door.

Rosa was busy in the kitchen, tuned to a classical music station. She had heard nothing, she did not even hear his approach. He knew she would see him as soon as he came around the corner into the kitchen area. He hugged the wall to keep out of sight as long as possible.

If she was still in the kitchen, depending on where she was, she could be as much as thirty feet away. He decided that if he was going to kill her, he wanted it to be quick.

He paused; his mind churned. If? There could be no if. It had to be done. Volpe's wife at the chicken farm had been no different. Just another piece of meat.

He cautiously peered around the corner. She was at the sink, her right side toward him. She appeared to be rinsing some salad makings. There were two pots on the stove, cooking. He would have to shoot left-handed if he wanted maximum concealment.

His back was flat against the wall. He could hear her humming an Italian tune of his childhood. He had never hesitated before. What was wrong with him? This was business.

Irritated with himself, he abandoned the silent approach and flung himself off the wall, not caring whether he was seen. He came around the corner, facing her square, gun up.

Sensing movement, she turned toward him. Jimmy was crouched, pointing a black thing at her. She opened her mouth wide in shock.

He touched the trigger, aiming for her head. He wanted it to be quick. Five rounds whooshed out of the suppressor. One caught her in the throat just below her chin, another just above her right eye. Three missed and buried themselves in the cupboard on the wall behind her.

Amari clamped his eyes closed and grimaced for several seconds. Slowly he willed them open. He had to leave. He forced himself to walk over to the bloody thing on the kitchen floor. The back of her head was mostly gone.

He knelt on one knee, beside her, and tenderly touched her cheek.

"Rosa, I'm sorry. This wasn't supposed to happen."

Then he took off the cotton arm sling and walked over to the office door. He used it to wipe the doorknob clean of his fingerprints. He did the same with the front door. The MAC-10 went under his left arm, suspended by a cord around his shoulder, which slipped through and around the butt.

Leaving the house, he walked over to his car and got in. He wriggled out of his jacket, then laid the MAC-10 on the seat next to him. He covered it with his jacket. He took the clip with three remaining rounds out from the small of his back and placed it under the jacket. Then he reached into the glove compartment, where there were two more full clips, and placed them under the jacket as well.

The car started on the first turn of the key, and he headed back toward the city. His reservations called for him to fly out of Fort Lauderdale at four to Chicago, under the name Peter Anthony. The reservations and ticket for James Amari, returning to Newark, would never be used.

There was no way he could do Iannello this trip.

The SPIT Florida Power and Light truck had been able to position itself by a neighboring house to observe the Strollo yard. The airplane was also on the house, doing slow, lazy, silent circles. It was right in the flight path of incoming and outgoing commercial traffic, and was driving the air controllers crazy. The plane was about to drop off this surveillance area to give the controllers a break when Amari exited the house.

SPIT in the truck broadcast: "Snake exiting alone. No arm sling."

Al looked at his watch. "He was in that house about three minutes."

He also knew that Bill and he were still at least five minutes from the house.

Bill searched for an explanation. "Maybe he forgot something, or he's going out to the store for something."

SPIT continued, "He's moving around in his car. Taking off his jacket, I think. He's started the car. He's leaving."

Al picked up the mike, chafing because he was still too far away to be of use. "SPIT, One."

"One, go."

"Have your electrician pretext the house, see who's home."

SPIT's Florida Power and Light truck answered, "Ten-four."

The truck left its observation spot and drove into the Strollo yard. One of the agents walked up to the door as another SPIT unit transmitted: "Snake on the bridge, signaling right turn, back toward the city."

The agent at the Strollo door rang the bell, waited, and rang again. He broadcast: "One, no answer at Cap. Tried the door— it's locked."

Al said, "Damn. We should have left earlier."

Bill said, being practical, "Our being there wouldn't have changed a thing."

Al knew he was right, but was angry at himself for not being at the scene.

"SPIT, this is One. Back out, electrician. Put a car with loud-speaker in there. Call the house. If no response, put a stone through a window. If no response, break in. Advise Metro by radio. Be careful. Subjects inside could mistake you for bad guys. Wear vests and raid jackets."

The SPIT supervisor came on the radio. "He'll likely either go north on Biscayne back to his hotel or straight west on the expressway, to the airport. Need two units north on Biscayne and two west on the expressway, ahead of him."

Four units responded that they were in position.

The airplane reported: "He passed the Biscayne exit. He's west on 395, heading toward the airport."

The next transmission was from the SPIT unit behind Amari. "Negative on airport. He's signaling right. He's going north on 95."

Al and Bill were south on 95, just approaching 395, the southern route west to the airport, which Bill had intended to take. He took that exit, got off at 12th Avenue, looped back east, and exited north on 95.

The airplane broadcast Amari's location as he passed 62nd Street. Bill speeded up and was soon behind the SPIT car on Amari's tail. There was another SPIT car ahead of him. The other SPIT vehicles were moving to catch up.

As they passed the Miami Gardens Drive exit, the agent at Strollo's house keyed his mike. "All units, Strollo, Madden, and female shot numerous times. Looks like he used .45 machine gun. Am advising Metro, will stay on scene."

Bill asked, "Take him when he stops?"

Al shook his head negatively.

"We don't know where that'll be. He's got a machine gun. There could be a lot of bystanders where he stops. I hate to do a moving takedown at turnpike speed, but it may be safer for the public. Out here there's nothing but traffic."

As he was talking, he lifted the shotgun from the backseat, cranked a round into the chamber, engaged the safety, and placed it muzzle-down between him and Bill.

Al drew his .357 Combat Magnum, emptied the hollow-point rounds into his right hand, and placed them in his jacket pocket. He drew a flat plastic shell carrier holding eighteen rounds from the glove compartment. The carrier contained both hollow-point and metal-piercing ammunition. He loaded with six .357 158-grain metal-piercing rounds. These were angular, sharp-pointed, steel-jacketed bullets that would not ricochet off angled metal.

Al continued, "The great risk here is a multicar pile-up if he runs. He's going to run. We've got to keep him from running in the car."

Amari was driving at fifty-two miles per hour, three miles under the speed limit. The general speed on I-95 was sixty, and often sixty-five or seventy. So Amari was in the right lane.

Al wondered out loud, "Would he stop if he was involved in an accident?"

Bill provided an answer. "If I had just whacked three people, I sure as hell wouldn't."

"You're probably right about us, Bill, but this guy's a stone killer. It's like he's driving home from a luncheon."

Al continued, "If we try to stop him with a pretext accident and he doesn't stop, we've lost our element of surprise. He'll be ready for us, and somebody could really get hurt."

Al reached his decision.

"No, we stop him without warning. My first inclination is to just drive up next to him and shoot him. We can't do that, so we'll do the next-best thing: shoot his car."

Bill was not sure this was a good idea.

"Do you think you can stop his car? And if you do, he'll still come up shooting."

"I don't have a perfect solution to this problem. Whatever we do involves risk, but we've got to do something—now."

Al keyed his mike.

"All units, I'm going to pull alongside him and fire into his engine. Jerry, you be on his tail. When you see me leveling my gun on him, broadcast our identity on your loudspeaker and hit your light. As soon as I fire, we're going to slow until we're nose to his tail. We'll stay in the passing lane.

"When he stops, one car rear, one forward, we're center, let him run east. We'll do it when we hit the sound barriers along the road and where there are six lanes. He can't scale them, and they'll stop any stray bullets."

The cars responded, "Ten-four."

Bill asked, "What do we do if we don't stop him?" Then he saw the tall wooden sound barriers coming up. Time for discussion was over. He began to accelerate slowly.

Al rolled down his window and edged toward the center of the seat, his right leg angled under him. When the open window was about even with Amari's hood, he came up to a semi-kneeling position, hunched over, and in a two-hand combat stance, extended his hands and gun out the window. He aimed for where the engine block should be and let off all six rounds rapid-fire.

At the first shot, Jerry's loudspeaker came on.

"FBI, stop! FBI, stop!" The blue light on Jerry's dash was whirling.

Amari saw the gun and almost simultaneously heard the shots and felt the impact of the slugs crashing through the hood and into the aluminum block of his engine.

He reached for the MAC-10 with his right hand as he stepped down on the accelerator. The engine sputtered, caught, and sputtered again.

By the time Amari had the MAC-10 up, the shooter's car had dropped back. Amari pumped the accelerator as he brought his right arm across his chest. Pointing the gun over his left shoulder, he fired a short burst.

He continued to pump the accelerator out of desperation, even after the engine died. He tried to steer right, but without the engine he had no power steering, and his one-handed effort moved the car very little. He found his power brakes had also failed. Finally, he just stood on the brake pedal.

With one continuous movement, Al opened the cylinder of the combat Magnum, dumped the empty cartridges, and loaded six hollow-points from his speed loader.

Bill saw the muzzle of the MAC-10. He hit the brakes. The unaimed five-round burst was wide and high.

Al and Bill saw Amari brake. The driver behind Jerry had his blue bubble on his roof and was trying to keep oncoming traffic from colliding with Al's car, which had come to a stop in the second lane, slightly behind Amari.

Amari, the three loose clips bunched in his left hand, the MAC-10 in his right, slid over to the passenger door. He dropped the gun on his lap to free a hand to open the door.

Al was out and on the road before Amari. Bill, with the shotgun, exited behind Al, also on the passenger side.

Amari came out running. He slowed as he saw the huge sound barrier facing him. He turned.

Al took cover behind the left rear tire of Amari's car, leveling his pistol across the trunk.

Five voices yelled, "Freeze!"

The machine gun came up as Amari began to drop to a prone position.

Al fired six rounds as Amari was dropping. Bill fired three rounds from the shotgun, and Jerry fired several from his 9mm.

Amari emptied his clip, but the unaimed machine gun had fired its remaining ten rounds well over the heads of the agents, and he did not move to reload.

326 • Arthur F. Nehrbass

There was silence except for the passing cars, which were slowing to see what was going on.

Al dropped behind the car, dumped his empties, and reloaded with the six he had put in his pocket. Coming to a two-handed stance, he and Bill edged forward cautiously.

When they were over Amari, Bill kicked the MAC-10 out of reach. Al holstered and felt Amari's carotid artery. The man was dead.

Amari had taken nineteen of the thirty-six shotgun pellets in his chest, legs, back, and head. Al and Jerry had hit him ten more times.

Al turned to Bill. "Call the Broward sheriff's office. We'll need their shooting team."

Jerry voiced all their sentiments: "That couldn't have turned out better. This guy was crazy."

"You all did a great job," Al said. "For an unrehearsed arrest, it went down just right. Unfortunately, Magliocco wins."

Jerry looked puzzled.

Al explained, "Strollo's dead. So's Amari. No cooperation from them. We're not losers, but Magliocco takes the last trick."

While Al and the others involved in the Amari shooting were giving statements to the Broward County sheriff and to the FBI shooting team that had arrived the next day to investigate, a conversation was taking place in a New York restaurant.

Tommy Ferrigno, *sotto capo*, John Ardizonne, *consigliere*, and Carmine Licata *caporegime*, were discussing the deaths of Strollo and Amari. Licata decided to venture into a sensitive area. "Pure luck saved us this time."

Ardizonne said, "You are absolutely right. But this should never have happened. Don Carlo was not exercising his authority. Strollo should have been controlled. Don Carlo let him run wild."

Ferrigno agreed. "He is either getting too old or too disinterested to run the family properly. He did not consult with us before making crucial decisions. His reaction to the Miami arrests was emotional. Only our intervention saved us from total disaster."

Licata hesitated, trying to read their faces. He had to say this right. If he was wrong in his judgment of them and spoke too strongly, he might be finished. "I have been thinking for some time that a change is necessary."

"Yes," replied Ardizonne. Licata breathed more freely, and Ardizonne continued, "It is unfortunate, but he is no longer a friend of ours."

Licata looked at Ferrigno. "We need someone to give us leadership. I hope, Don Thomas, you will consent to do that."

This was exactly what Ferrigno wanted to hear, but he was cautious. "That is a very heavy responsibility that I would undertake only if you, Carmine, were *sotto capo.*"

Ardizonne finalized the deal. "That arrangement would benefit the family."

Ferrigno hesitated. He could feel the power that would come to him as *capo* of the largest of the Cosa Nostra families and chairman of the Commission. But it was the Commission that gave him pause. What would they do? Could he claim the chair over the body of Magliocco, whacked without their permission? Yet there was no way he could go to the Commission for authority to hit its chairman.

"What of the Commission? We have no authority for this."

Old Ardizonne gently placed a skeletal hand on Ferrigno's forearm.

"All of the Commission have been hurt by this. Iannello is talking. All of their business will suffer irreparably. They would look to Magliocco to take responsibility for their losses. We have merely anticipated their wishes."

Ferrigno was satisfied. He wanted the rank, and Ardizonne's explanation fit. He moved to the next problem.

"How do you suggest we 'retire' Magliocco?"

Licata was prepared, and a smile of victory came over his face. *Sotto capo* now, tomorrow—*capo.*

"He will be lunching at Pappagallo on Thursday. Joey Socks will leave for a moment. I have two young men who will handle the rest."